SHERRYL WOODS

The Inn at Eagle Point

MIRA®

MIRA®

ISBN-13: 978-0-7783-2626-7
ISBN-10:   0-7783-2626-8

THE INN AT EAGLE POINT

Recycling programs
for this product may
not exist in your area.

www.MIRABooks.com

Printed in U.S.A.

For Morgan and Taylor... Welcome to the world, little girls! You're definitely going to keep your moms and dads and big brothers on their toes!

Dear Reader,

Launching a new series is one of my very favorite things. I get to enter a whole new setting, meet fascinating, complex new characters and, hopefully, create situations and conflicts that will resonate with all of you. When I was deciding the details of this latest series, I kept coming back to the Chesapeake Bay, an area near and dear to my heart. Though I don't actually live on the bay, my summer home is on the Potomac River just above where it enters the bay. There are few places on earth more beautiful and serene.

Setting, however, isn't the only thing that matters. Even more important are the characters who will fill these pages, and for this I wanted a huge, complicated, dysfunctional family. Thus, the O'Briens. You'll meet four generations of them over time, many of them with major issues with each other. There will be stories of betrayal, reconciliation and, of course, love. There will be meddling and matchmaking and tough choices. And along the way, there will be lots of laughs and a few tears.

The Inn at Eagle Point is Abby's story, but it is also a story about sisters and how they stand up for each other without question. It's a story of a powerful love, first lost, then found again. And of two proud men who struggle to believe in second chances.

So welcome to Chesapeake Shores. I hope you'll come to love the O'Briens and their world.

All best,

Sheryl Woods

Prologue

The arguing had gone on most of the night. In her room just three doors down the hall from her parents' master suite, Abby had been able to hear the sound of raised voices, but not the words. It wasn't the first time they'd fought recently, yet this time something felt different. The noisy exchange itself and fretting about it kept her awake most of the night.

Until she walked downstairs just after dawn and saw suitcases in the front hallway, Abby hoped she'd only imagined the difference, that the knot of dread that had formed in her stomach was no more than her overactive imagination making something out of nothing. Now she knew better. Someone was leaving this time—quite possibly forever, judging from the pile of luggage by the door.

She tried to quiet her panic, reminding herself that her dad, Mick O'Brien, left all the time. An internationally acclaimed architect, he was always going someplace for a new job, a new adventure. Again, though, this felt different. He'd only been home a couple of days from his last trip. He rarely turned right around and left again.

"Abby!" Her mother sounded startled and just a little edgy. "What are you doing up so early?"

Abby wasn't surprised that her mother was caught off

guard. Most teenagers, including Abby and her brothers, hated getting up early on the weekends. Most Saturdays it was close to noon when she finally made her way downstairs.

Abby met her mother's gaze, saw the dismay in her eyes and knew instinctively that Megan had hoped to be gone before anyone got up, before anyone could confront her with uncomfortable questions.

"You're leaving, aren't you?" Abby said flatly, trying not to cry. She was seventeen, and if she was right about what was going on, she was the one who was going to have to be strong for her younger brothers and sisters.

Megan's eyes filled with tears. She opened her mouth to speak, but no words came out. Finally, she nodded.

"Why, Mom?" Abby began, a torrent of questions following. "Where are you going? What about us? Me, Bree, Jess, Connor and Kevin? Are you walking out on us, too?"

"Oh, sweetie, I could never do that," Megan said, reaching for her. "You're my babies. As soon as I'm settled, I'll be back for you. I promise."

Though her declaration was strong, Abby saw through it to the fear underlying her words. Wherever Megan was going, she was scared and filled with uncertainty. How could she not be? She and Mick O'Brien had been married for nearly twenty years. They'd had five children together, and a life they'd built right here in Chesapeake Shores, the town that Mick himself had designed and constructed with his brothers. And now Megan was going off all alone, starting over— How could she not be terrified?

"Mom, is this really what you want?" Abby asked, trying to make sense of such a drastic decision. She knew plenty of kids whose parents were divorced, but their moms hadn't just packed up and left. If anyone had gone, it had been the dads. This seemed a thousand times worse.

"Of course it's not what I want," Megan said fiercely. "But things can't go on as they have been." She started to say more, than waved it off. "That's between your father and me. I just know I have to make a change. I need a fresh start."

In a way, Abby was relieved that Megan hadn't said more. Abby didn't want the burden of knowing what had driven her mother to go. She loved and respected both of her parents, and she wasn't sure how she would have handled careless, heated words capable of destroying that love she felt for either one of them.

"But where will you go?" she asked again. Surely it wouldn't be far. Surely her mother wouldn't leave her all alone to cope with the fallout. Mick was helpless with emotions. He could handle all the rest—providing for them, loving them, even going to the occasional ball game or science fair—but when it came to everyday bumps and bruises and hurt feelings, it was Megan they all relied on.

Then again, why wouldn't Megan assume Abby could handle all the rest? Everyone in the family knew that Abby took her responsibility as the oldest seriously. She'd always known that her parents counted on her as backup. Bree, who'd just turned twelve-going-on-thirty, and her brothers would be okay. With Megan gone, Bree might retreat into herself at first, but, mature and self-contained, she would find her own way of coping. Kevin and Connor were teenage guys. They were pretty much oblivious to everything except sports and girls. More often than not, they found their exuberant, affectionate mother to be an embarrassment.

That left Jess. She was only a baby. Okay, she'd just turned seven last week, Abby reminded herself, but that was still way too young not to have her mom around. Abby had no idea how to fill that role, even temporarily.

"I won't be that far away," Megan assured her. "As soon

as I've found a job and a place for all of us, I'll come back for you. It won't take long." Then, almost to herself, she added, "I won't *let* it take long."

Abby wanted to scream at her that any amount of time would be too long, any distance too far. How could her mother not see that? But she looked so sad. Lost and alone, really. Her cheeks were damp with tears, too. How could Abby yell at her and make her feel even worse? Abby knew she would simply have to find a way to cope, a way to make the others understand.

Then she was struck by another, more terrifying thought. "What about when Dad goes away on business? Who'll look out for us then?"

Megan's expression faltered for just an instant, probably at the very real fear she must have heard in Abby's voice. "Your grandmother will move in. Mick's already spoken to her. She'll be here later today."

At the realization that this was real, that if they'd made arrangements for Gram to move in, then this separation was permanent and not some temporary separation that would end as soon as her parents came to their senses, Abby began to shake. "No," she whispered. "This is so wrong, Mom."

Megan seemed taken aback by her vehemence. "But you all love Gram! It'll be wonderful for you having her right here with you."

"That's not the point," Abby said. "She's not *you!* You can't do this to us."

Megan pulled Abby into her arms, but Abby yanked herself free. She refused to be comforted when her mother was about to walk out the door and tear their lives apart.

"I'm not doing this *to* you," Megan said, her expression pleading for understanding. "I'm doing it *for* me. Try to understand. In the long run it's going to be best for all of us."

She touched Abby's tearstained cheek. "You'll love New York, Abby. You especially. We'll go to the theater, the ballet, the art galleries."

Abby stared at her with renewed shock. "You're moving to New York?" Forgetting for a moment her own dream of someday working there, making a name for herself in the financial world, all she could think about now was that it was hours away from their home in Chesapeake Shores, Maryland. A tiny part of her had apparently hoped that her mother would be going no farther away than across town, or maybe to Baltimore or Annapolis. Wasn't that far enough to escape her problems with Mick without abandoning her children?

"What are we supposed to do if we need you?" she demanded.

"You'll call me, of course," Megan said.

"And then wait hours for you to get here? Mom, that's crazy."

"Sweetie, it won't be for long, a few weeks at most, and then you'll be with me. I'm going to find a wonderful place for us. I'll find the best private schools. Mick and I have agreed to that."

Abby desperately wanted to believe it would all work out. At the same time she wanted to keep her right here answering questions until she forgot all about this crazy plan, but just then a taxi pulled up outside. Abby stared from the taxi to her mother in horror. "You're leaving right this minute, without even saying goodbye?" She'd guessed as much earlier, but now it seemed too cruel.

Tears streamed down Megan's cheeks. "Believe me, it's better this way. It'll be easier. I've left notes for everyone under their bedroom doors, and I'll call tonight. We'll be together again before you know it."

As Abby stood there, frozen with shock, Megan picked up the first two bags and carried them across the porch and down the front steps to the waiting cab. The driver came back for the rest, followed by Megan.

Standing in the empty foyer, she tucked a finger under Abby's chin. "I love you, sweetheart. And I know how strong you are. You'll be here for your brothers and sisters. It's the only thing that makes this separation okay."

"It is *not* okay!" Abby replied vehemently, her voice starting to climb. Until now, she'd mostly kept it together, but the realization that her mom wasn't even sticking around to handle the initial fallout from this made her want to scream. She wasn't an adult. This wasn't her mess to solve.

"I hate you!" she shouted as Megan walked down the steps, her spine straight. She shouted it again just to make sure her mother heard the anger in her voice, but Megan never looked back.

Abby would have gone on shouting until the taxi was out of sight, but just then she caught a movement out of the corner of her eye and turned to see Jess, her eyes wide with confusion and dismay.

"Mommy," Jess whispered, her chin wobbling as she stared through the open doorway at the disappearing taxi. Her strawberry-blond hair was tangled, her feet bare, the imprint of her old-fashioned chenille bedspread on her cheek. "Where's Mommy going?"

Calling on that inner strength everyone believed she had, Abby steeled herself against her own fear, tamped down all the anger and forced a smile for her little sister. "Mommy's going on a trip."

Tears welled in Jess's eyes. "When's she coming back?"

Abby gathered her sister in her arms. "I'm not sure," she said, then added with a confidence she was far from feeling, "She promised it won't be long."

But, of course, that turned out to be a lie.

1

15 years later

Being an overachiever sucked, Abby O'Brien Winters concluded as she crawled into bed after midnight, mentally and physically exhausted after a roller-coaster day on Wall Street. She'd managed about twenty minutes of quality time with her twin daughters before they'd fallen asleep barely into the opening paragraph of *The Velveteen Rabbit*. She'd eaten warmed-over Chinese takeout for the third straight night, then pulled out a half-dozen voluminous market analysts' reports she needed to absorb before the stock exchange opened in the morning. Her bedtime reading was a lot more challenging than what Caitlyn and Carrie chose.

She was good at her job as a portfolio manager for a major brokerage company, but so far it had cost her a marriage to a great guy, who'd tired of playing second fiddle to her career, and more sleep than she could possibly calculate. Though she shared custody of the twins with Wes, she often felt as if she was barely acquainted with her five-year-old daughters. It sometimes seemed as if they spent more time with the nanny—and even her ex-husband—than they did with her. She'd long since lost sight of exactly what she was trying to prove and to whom.

When the phone rang, Abby glanced at the clock and groaned. At this hour, it could only be an emergency. Heart thudding, she reached for the receiver.

"Abby, it's me," her sister Jessica announced. Jess was the youngest of the five O'Brien siblings and the real night owl among them. Abby stayed up late because it was the only way to cram enough work into a twenty-four-hour day. Jess did it because she was just starting to hit her stride when the moon and stars came out. "I called earlier, but the nanny said you weren't home yet. Then I got distracted with a project I'm working on. I hope it's not too late. I know you're usually up till all hours."

"It's fine," Abby assured her. "Is everything okay? You sound stressed. Is something going on with Gram? Or Dad?"

"Gram's amazing. She'll outlive us all. And Dad is off someplace building something. I can't keep track of him."

"He was in California last week," Abby recalled.

"Then I guess he's still there. You know he has to oversee every single detail when one of his projects is being built. Of course, then he loses interest, just the way he did with Chesapeake Shores."

There was an unsurprising note of bitterness in Jess's voice. As the youngest of five, she, more than the rest of them, had missed spending time with their dad. Mick O'Brien had already been making a name for himself as an architect and urban planner when he'd designed and built Chesapeake Shores, a now-famous seaside community on the Chesapeake Bay. He'd done it in partnership with his brothers—one a builder, the other an environmentalist. The town had been built around land that had been farmed by Colin O'Brien, a great-great uncle and the first of the O'Briens to arrive from Ireland in the late 1800s. It was to be the crown jewel in Mick's body of work and the idyllic place his family would call home. It hadn't turned out that way.

Mick and his brothers had fought over the construction, battled over environmental issues and even over the preservation of the few falling-down historic buildings on some of the property. Eventually they'd dissolved the partnership. Now, even though they all coexisted in or near Chesapeake Shores, they seldom spoke except on holidays, when Gram insisted on a pretense of family harmony.

Abby's mother, Megan, had lived in New York since she and Mick had divorced fifteen years ago. Though the plan had been for all of the children to move to New York with her, for reasons Abby had never understood, that hadn't happened. They'd stayed in Chesapeake Shores with their mostly absent dad and Gram. In recent years, one by one they had drifted away, except for Jess, who seemed to have a love-hate relationship with the town and with Mick.

Since moving to New York herself after college, Abby had reestablished a strong bond with her mother, but none of the others had done the same. And not just Jess, but all five of them had an uneasy relationship with their father. It was Gram—who'd been only a girl when her family had followed their O'Brien predecessors to Maryland—with her fading red hair, twinkling blue eyes, ready smile and the lingering lilt of Ireland in her voice, who held them together and made them a family.

"Did you call to complain about Dad, or is something else on your mind?" Abby asked her sister.

"Oh, I can always find something to complain about with Dad," Jess admitted, "but actually I called because I need your help."

"Anything," Abby said at once. "Just tell me what you

need." She was close to all her siblings, but Jess held a special place in her heart, perhaps because of the big difference in their ages and her awareness of how their mother's departure and their father's frequent absences had affected her. Abby had been stepping in to fill that gap in Jess's life since the day Megan had left.

"Could you come home?" Jess pleaded. "It's a little too complicated to get into on the phone."

"Oh, sweetie, I don't know," Abby began, hesitating. "Work is crazy."

"Work is always crazy, which is exactly why you need to come home. It's been ages. Before the girls came along, you used work as an excuse. Then it was the twins. Now it's work *and* the twins."

Abby winced. It was true. She had been making excuses for years now. She'd eased her conscience with the fact that every member of her family loved visiting New York and came up frequently. As long as she saw them all often, it didn't seem to matter that it was almost always on her turf rather than Chesapeake Shores. She'd never stopped to analyze why it had been so easy to stay away. Maybe it was because it really hadn't felt like home after her mother had left.

Before she could reply, Jess added, "Come on, Abby. When was the last time you took a real vacation? Your honeymoon, I'll bet. You know you could use a break, and the girls would love being here. They should spend some quality time in the town their grandfather built and where you grew up. Gram could spoil them rotten for a couple of weeks. Please. I wouldn't ask if it weren't important."

"Life-or-death important?" Abby asked. It was an old exchange, used to rank whether any crisis was truly monumental or only a temporary blip in their lives.

"It could be," Jess said seriously. "At least in the sense that my whole future's at stake. I think you're the only one who can fix this, or at least the only one I'm willing to ask for help."

Struck by the somber tone in her voice, Abby said, "Maybe you'd better tell me right now."

"You need to be here to understand. If you can't stay for a couple of weeks, then at least come for a few days. Please."

There was something in her sister's voice that Abby had never heard before, an urgency that suggested she wasn't exaggerating her claim that her future was at stake. Since Jess was the only one of the five siblings who'd been floundering for a focus since reaching adulthood, Abby knew she couldn't turn her back on her. And admittedly a break would do Abby herself a world of good. Hadn't she just been bemoaning her workaholic tendencies earlier tonight?

She smiled, thinking about how wonderful it would be to breathe the salty Chesapeake Bay air again. Even better, she would have uninterrupted time with her girls in a place where they could swing on the playground her father had designed for the town park, build sand castles on the beach and run barefoot through the chilly waters of the bay.

"I'll work something out tomorrow and be down there by the weekend," she promised, giving in. She glanced at her jam-packed schedule and grimaced. "I can only make it for a couple of days, okay?"

"A week," Jess pleaded. "I don't think this can be fixed in a day or two."

Abby sighed. "I'll see what I can work out."

"Whatever you can arrange," Jess said at once, seizing the compromise. "Let me know when your flight's getting in and I'll pick you up."

"I'll rent a car," Abby said.

"After all these years in New York, do you actually remember how to drive?" Jess teased. "Or even how to get home?"

"My memory's not that bad," Abby responded. "See you soon, sweetie."

"I'll call Gram and let her know you're coming."

"Tell her not to go to any trouble, okay?" Abby said, knowing it would be a waste of breath. "We'll go out to eat. I've been dying for some Maryland crabs."

"No way," her sister countered. "It's a little early in the season, but if you want steamed crabs, I'll find 'em somewhere and pick them up for Friday-night dinner. We can eat on the porch, but I'm not about to stop Gram from cooking up a storm. I say let the baking begin."

Abby laughed at her enthusiasm. Gram's baking—pies, tarts, cookies, scones, cakes—was pretty amazing. There'd been a time in her life when Abby had wanted to learn all those traditional family recipes and open a bakery, but that was before she'd discovered an interest in and aptitude for the financial world. That had been her ticket out of Chesapeake Shores.

Now, after more than ten hectic years away—years spent climbing a treacherous corporate ladder, marrying, giving birth to twins and divorcing—she was going home for a real visit, something longer than a rushed weekend with barely time to relax before it was time to fly back to New York. She couldn't help wondering, based on the dire tone in Jess's voice, if that was a good thing or not.

"Couldn't you at least put on a tie?" Lawrence Riley grumbled, scowling at his son. "If you're going to take over this bank, you need to set a good example for the employees. You can't come in here looking as if you just climbed off the back of a Harley."

Trace regarded his father with amusement. "That's exactly what I did. My bike's in the parking lot."

His father's frown deepened. "I thought I told you to drive your mother's car. You have an image to uphold now."

"What was Mother supposed to do?" Trace asked reasonably. "I couldn't see her riding my Harley to her garden club meeting."

"She has a dozen different friends who would have been happy to pick her up," his father countered.

"And apparently not a one of them had any desire to run all her errands with her after the meeting," Trace responded.

"You have an answer for everything, don't you?" his father grumbled. "This situation is never going to work if you don't take me or this job seriously."

"I always take you seriously," Trace said. "As for the job, I don't want to take it at all. I have a perfectly good career in New York. Just because I don't have to wear a suit or use a calculator doesn't mean it's not respectable." In fact, his career as a freelance design artist not only paid well, enabling him to live and work in a large loft in SoHo, it didn't require him to answer to his father. That was quite a perk in his book.

His father's scowl deepened. "So, what? I should let this community bank get gobbled up by one of the big banking conglomerates?"

"Maybe so," Trace said, knowing his response would only push his father's hot button. "That's the way the banking world is going."

"Well, *this* bank won't, not as long as I have any say about it," his father said stubbornly. "Chesapeake Shores Community Bank serves the people in this town in a way that one of those faceless, impersonal behemoths never could."

Trace couldn't argue the point. He just didn't want any part of running the place, family heritage or not. "Why not put Laila in charge?" he asked, referring to his younger sister. He warmed to the topic. If he could convince his father to put Laila in the job she'd always wanted, he could be on the road back to New York by morning. All he had to do was sell his father on the idea. "Think about it, Dad. She has a head for numbers. Her SAT math scores were through the roof. She aced all of her college business courses. She has a master's degree from the Wharton School of Business. She'd be a natural."

"I thought of that," his father admitted. "I even spoke to her about it, but your sister told me to take a hike."

That was unexpected, Trace thought. "Why?"

His father shrugged. "She said she wasn't going to be anybody's second choice, even mine."

Trace regarded him with bewilderment. "But you asked her first."

"When has your sister ever paid any attention to logic? She's convinced I only asked her because I knew you wouldn't want the job."

"I don't suppose you tried to convince her she was wrong," Trace said.

"How could I when she was right?"

"Do you think you two will ever learn to communicate?" Trace grumbled. He and his dad might be at loggerheads ninety percent of the time, but Lawrence Riley and Laila were rarely on the same page about anything, from a choice as inane as breakfast cereal to a decision as critical as who ought to run the bank. It had been that way from the moment she learned to talk.

"You mean communicate the way you and I do?" his father retorted wryly.

"Yeah, at least that well," Trace responded. "Look, I'll talk to her. I'll smooth things over between the two of you. Her pride's been hurt because you've made it plain over the years that you want me back here, but she'll come around."

His father hit his fist on the desk. "Dammit, you're the one who needs to come around, Trace. What ever happened to family loyalty? A man works his whole life to build up something good for his son, and you toss it aside without a second thought."

"I've had a lifetime to think about it. You've never made a secret about what you expected. I've given it a second thought and a third, for that matter, ever since you called. Dad, come on, you know the whole nine-to-five drill would never work for me. I like a job that's creative, a word that tends to make bankers nervous as hell."

The faint hint of a smile finally touched his father's lips. "True enough," he admitted. "How about this? We give it six months. If you still hate it, you can take off again with my blessing. That's fair, isn't it?"

As a respected and in-demand artist working freelance for several of New York's top ad agencies, Trace had the flexibility to do as his father asked. He could even keep up with a few accounts to keep himself from going totally stir-crazy in Chesapeake Shores. If it would buy him his freedom permanently, surely he could survive six months in a suit. He owed his father that much respect. And in the long run that short-term display of loyalty would be wiser than causing a family rift.

Moreover, he could spend the time trying to convince his sister to forget about her stupid pride and being second choice. She'd wanted this job since she'd learned to count. She ought to grab it, rather than wasting her talent by keeping the books for a few local businesses. Unfortunately she'd inherited their father's stubbornness. It would probably take Trace every single day of the allotted six months to make peace between the two of them.

"Okay, six months," Trace agreed. "Not one day longer."

His father beamed at him. "We'll see. You might discover you have an aptitude for banking, after all."

"Or you'll realize I'm incompetent when it comes to math."

"I have your college test scores and grades that say otherwise." He stood up and held out his hand. "Welcome aboard, son."

Trace shook his hand, then studied his father intently. There was a glint in his eyes that suggested there was more to the negotiations than Trace had realized. "What are you up to?" he asked warily.

"Up to?" Lawrence Riley had a lousy poker face. Half of his pals at the country club would testify to that. For the past thirty years, they'd lined their pockets with his losses.

"Don't even try to play innocent, Dad. You're up to something, and it has nothing to do with me becoming your protégé around here."

"We've made a business deal, that's all," his father insisted. "Now let me show you your office. It's fairly Spartan now, but if you decide to stick around you can decorate it however you want. Meantime, I'll have Raymond go through some loan folders with you. We have a meeting of the loan committee first thing Tuesday morning. You'll need to have your recommendations ready then."

Trace held up a hand. "Hold on a second. I don't know enough to make recommendations on whether loan applications should be approved."

"Raymond will show you the ropes. He's been my right hand for years. And they're not all loan applications. There's a possible foreclosure in there, too."

Trace's stomach knotted. "You want me to decide whether or not someone's home should be taken away and put up for auction?"

"It's a business, not a home. And you won't be deciding

on your own, of course. The board will have the final say, but we'd likely act on your recommendation."

"No way," Trace said. Who was he to rip someone's dreams to shreds? Businesses in Chesapeake Shores were small, family-owned operations. It would be like taking the food right off someone's table, someone he knew, more than likely. He wasn't sure he had the stomach to do that.

"You can't be softhearted, son. It's strictly business, a matter of dollars and cents. You'll see once you've taken a look at the paperwork." His father patted him on the back. "You start looking over those files and I'll send Raymond in."

Trace scowled at his father's departing back, then turned to the stack of folders sitting neatly in the middle of the huge mahogany desk that took up most of the corner office. Right on top sat one with a large, ominous red sticker pasted on the front.

He sat down in the leather chair behind the desk, his wary gaze on that folder. Curiosity finally got the better of him, and he flipped open the file and stared at the first page.

"Oh, hell," he murmured as he read it: *Possible notice of foreclosure—The Inn at Eagle Point. Owner: Jessica O'Brien.*

He knew Jess O'Brien, but it wasn't her image that immediately came to mind. It was that of her older sister, Abigail, the woman who'd stolen his heart years ago on a steamy summer night, then disappeared without even a goodbye. Over the years he'd told himself it was ludicrous to cling to such an elusive memory. He'd tried to chase it away with other relationships, most of them casual, but even a couple that had promised a deeper intimacy. In the end, he hadn't been able to shake his desire for someone with auburn hair, laughing eyes and a daredevil spirit that matched his own.

Now he was supposed to decide the fate of her sister's inn? One thing he knew about the O'Briens, they stuck together. If he took on Jess, he'd be taking on the rest of them, Abby included. Was that what had put the gleam in his father's eye earlier?

He shook off the possibility. His father couldn't know that he'd been carrying a torch for her all these years. No one did.

Except Laila, he realized. His sister had been Abby's best friend. She'd even covered for the two of them that amazing night they'd spent together in a secluded cove on the beach. Could she and his father be conspiring?

Damn straight, he thought with a shudder. Maybe he was finally about to get his wish and see Abby again. Or maybe he was about to land in a whole mess of trouble. He wondered if, with Abby involved, he'd actually be able to tell the difference.

An hour later with the inn's dismal financial figures still in his head, Trace climbed on his bike and took a drive to see the property. He was hoping he'd find something—*anything*—to convince him to let the loan stand. He needed arguments he could take to the board and his father with total confidence.

Winding along the coastal road, he breathed in the salty air and relaxed as the sun beat down on his shoulders. It was late spring, but there was still the scent of lilacs on the breeze as he rounded the curve by the Finch property. Widow Marjorie Finch, who'd been bent and wizened when he was a boy, loved her lilacs. They'd been allowed to grow and spread until they formed a hedge all along the road. When honeysuckle had grown up in the bushes, she'd attacked it as if it were an alien invader. Her loving attention had paid off. The bushes were heavy with fragrant, delicate blossoms.

To his right, along the narrow strip of land that ran along the beach, ospreys were building their nests back in the same bare branches where they'd built them for years. To his amusement, one intrepid osprey was constructing an elaborate configuration of branches, bits of string and even a strand of yellow police tape on a post at the end of someone's dock. The owner was going to be ticked as hell to discover that his dock would be off-limits for the rest of summer while the birds of prey took up residence.

Eventually he reached the turnoff to the inn, converted from what had once been a sprawling Victorian home on a pinnacle of land overlooking the bay. The last time he'd been here, the place had been badly in need of paint, its boards weathered by the sea air and harsh winter winds. The Adirondack chairs and rockers on the porch had been in an equally sad state of disrepair. The once perfectly manicured lawn had gone mostly to crabgrass, the gardens to weeds. The Pattersons hadn't put a dime into the place for years, and the neglect had shown.

Now, though, there was plenty of evidence that Jess had been hard at work remodeling the inn. The exterior was a soft white that seemed to reflect a hint of blue from the nearby water. Shutters were a bold red. The grass wasn't as lush as it had once been, but it was green and well-trimmed. The azaleas and lilacs were in bloom, and one overgrown purple rhododendron spilled its huge blooms over a porch railing at the back of the house. The inn's sign had been freshly painted and hung from brass hooks on a new pole at the edge of the driveway. It looked to him as if the place was ready to make a comeback.

Jess's payment record, however, told a different story. Since taking out the loan a year earlier, she already had a history of late payments, had missed several altogether. She'd spent every penny of her small-business loan, and no opening date for the inn had been set. Her cash flow was nonexistent. She'd already had a couple of formal warnings from the bank. Ever since the credit disaster in the mortgage industry, banks were getting jittery about loans that looked as if they were going bad. On paper, it appeared the bank had no choice except to issue a foreclosure notice. Trace cringed at the prospect.

Even as he sat on his bike in the driveway, the door opened and Jess stepped outside. She caught sight of him and frowned.

"What are you doing here, Trace?" she asked.

Scowl in place, she crossed the lawn, hands on hips, her feet shoved into a pair of rubberized, all-weather clogs from one of the big outdoor apparel companies. Her jeans and T-shirt were splattered with paint—white, plus something close to Williamsburg blue, if he remembered his color palette correctly.

When she was standing practically toe-to-toe with him, her defiant gaze locked with his, she reminded him of another O'Brien with a fiery Irish temper.

"Well?" she challenged.

"Just looking things over."

"For your father, no doubt."

"For the bank," Trace corrected.

"I thought you'd left town years ago, that you wanted no part of the bank."

"I don't. I'm just filling in for a few months."

"Long enough to make my life hell?"

He grinned at that. "Maybe longer." He made a sweeping gesture toward the house and grounds. "You've been busy."

"It's taken a lot of work. I've done most of it myself to save money," she said, her chin lifted with pride and a hint of belligerence.

"Might have made more sense to hire people and get it done sooner, so you could open."

"I didn't see it that way."

"Obviously not."

"Do you want to take a look around inside?" she asked, her expression hopeful, her tone filled with enthusiasm. "Maybe once you've seen how great it looks, you'll be able to go back and tell your father to be patient."

"It's not that simple, Jess. I know he's warned you that you're getting too far behind. The bank looks at the bottom line, not at whether or not you're doing a good job with a paintbrush."

"When did you turn into a hard-ass, by-the-numbers guy like your dad? You weren't that way when you were seeing my sister." She gave him a considering look. "Or were you? Is that why the two of you split up?"

Trace stiffened. "You really don't want to go there," he warned. "Abby has nothing to do with this."

"Doesn't she? For all I know, you're absolutely thrilled by the prospect of payback for whatever she did to you. She was the one who broke it off, wasn't she?"

The comment was not only intrusive, it was insulting. "Dammit, Jess, you don't know a thing about what happened back then and you sure as hell don't know anything about me if you think I'd use you to get even with your sister."

"Really?" she said, her expression innocent. "She's coming back, you know. She'll be here tomorrow."

Trace tried not to let his immediate and unsteady reaction to the news show. "Tell her I said hey," he said mildly. He started his bike. "See you around, Jess."

Her show of defiance faltered. "What are you going to tell your father, Trace?"

"I have no idea," he said candidly. He looked into her eyes. "But I will promise you this, it won't have anything at all to do with Abby."

She nodded slowly. "I'll take you at your word about that."

As he rode off toward town, though, he couldn't help wondering if she should. When it came to his conflicted feelings for Abby O'Brien, his word might not be entirely trustworthy.

2

"Where are we going, Mommy? Tell us again," Caitlyn commanded.

"When are we gonna get there?" Carrie whined. "We've been driving and driving forever. I wanna go home."

"It's barely been a half hour since we left the airport," Abby told Carrie, her patience already frayed by the long security line at the airport in New York and the even more tedious wait at the car-rental counter in Baltimore. The flight itself, less than an hour from LaGuardia to BWI in Baltimore, had gone smoothly. The girls had been excited to be on a plane, but now they were tired and cranky and completely uninterested in the scenery as they drove south toward Chesapeake Shores. They might have been pacified by a stop for ice cream or some other treat, but Abby was determined not to reward them for bad behavior just to get a few minutes of peace.

"Why don't you try to take a little nap?" she pleaded, glancing in the rearview mirror for a glimpse of them in their car seats. "When you wake up, you'll be at Gram's, and I know she's going to have sugar cookies and milk for you. Remember how much you loved those when she baked them for you last time she visited us in New York?"

"I like chocolate chip better," Carrie grumbled, clearly determined to be displeased about everything.

"Well, I *love* sugar cookies," Caitlyn countered. "So I'll eat them all."

"No, you won't!" Carrie screamed. "Mommy, tell her she can't have all the cookies. Some are mine."

Abby bit back a groan. "I'm sure there will be plenty of cookies for both of you. Now close your eyes. If you're this impossible when we get there, you can forget about getting any treats. You'll be going straight to bed."

The girls fell silent, but another glance in the mirror revealed them making faces at each other. Abby let it pass. She needed to focus all of her attention on the traffic, which had increased at least tenfold since the last time she'd driven home. She could hardly wait to turn onto some of Maryland's less-traveled roads.

Unfortunately, the traffic never completely let up. It seemed everyone had the same idea about heading to one of Maryland's many seaside communities on a Friday night. Once, the only traffic nightmare had been getting to Ocean City or the other beaches along the Atlantic coast, but now it seemed people had discovered the smaller towns on the western shores of the bay, as well.

She pulled out her cell phone and hit Jess's number on speed dial.

"The traffic is awful," she said when her sister answered. "At this rate, it's going to be another hour before we get there."

"I'll let Gram know," Jess said. "I'm on my way over there now. Take a deep breath. I'm picking up crabs and I'll have wine waiting."

"Thank you, thank you," Abby said. "See you soon."

It turned out to be an hour and ten minutes before she could make the turn into the community of Chesapeake

Shores. At last, though, the traffic had eased. She debated going straight to the house, but since the girls were finally asleep, she wound through downtown, getting reacquainted with the Main Street businesses that lined a four-block stretch from the waterfront up to the town square.

There was one visible vacancy, but all the other shop windows were filled with colorful displays. Barb's Baby Boutique was next to Ethel's Emporium, which carried everything from souvenirs and penny candy to fancy hostess gifts and locally produced jams and jellies. The Kitchen Store, which sold every gourmet gadget imaginable, was next to Seaside Gifts, where all the items had a nautical theme. There was a designer clothing store, which carried resort wear. And all of the stores had pots overflowing with colorful pansies and trailing vines by the doors and crisp blue-and-white awnings shading the windows. The pansies would be exchanged for bright red geraniums once spring turned to summer.

With her car window open, she drew in a deep breath of the familiar salt air, then heard the soft refrains of an outdoor concert drifting up from the banks of the bay. She'd forgotten about the tradition of free Friday-night performances in the band shell during the late spring, summer and early fall months when the weather drew crowds to the town. It was jazz tonight, a little heavy on the sax, it seemed to her.

She smiled, thinking of the debates she'd once had with her father about the appropriate mix of music for the early concerts. If it had been up to Mick and Gram, every week would have featured Irish singers and dancers.

"Mommy, I hear music," Carrie murmured sleepily. "Are we going to a party?"

"Nope, but we're almost home," Abby told her. "Five minutes and we'll be there."

She turned away from downtown and took the shore road to the very end where it began a winding climb up a gentle hill. At the top she made a left into the long driveway that ended in back of a classic beachfront home with a wraparound porch, lots of glass to take in the spectacular bay views and lights shining from every window. Two figures, one spry, the other a bit more stooped, emerged from the shadows on the porch as she pulled to a stop.

"Gram!" Caitlyn shouted, already struggling to free herself from the car seat.

"And Aunt Jessie!" Carrie boomed, trying to get the door on her side open. Abby released the child safety locks and Carrie sprang free, racing across the lawn to fling herself at her favorite aunt.

Jess stumbled back, then caught her niece up in a massive hug, even as Caitlyn reached up to her great-grandmother for a more demure embrace, as if she knew instinctively to take more care with the older woman.

Abby took in the scene with a smile. Why hadn't she done this more often? Was she truly so busy? Or had she been making excuses because of her mixed feelings about home and the way she'd forced herself to walk away without looking back? Until now she hadn't realized how much she missed being right here, with the sea breeze rustling through the trees, the sound of waves lapping against the shore and the promise of a whole pile of Maryland crabs and cold wine waiting on the porch, along with whatever Gram had baked that day.

Her grandmother caught her eye and gave her a knowing smile. "It's good to be home, is it not?"

"It's better than I expected," Abby admitted. "How are you, Gram? You look good." She certainly didn't look her age, which was somewhere near eighty by Abby's calculations, though her grandmother wouldn't admit to it. Whenever any one of them had tried to pin her down, even for the sake of genealogical research, the date of her birth shifted to suit her.

"I'm better with the three of you here for a bit," Gram said. "Shall we feed the girls first, then have our own meal when it's quieter?"

"That sounds perfect," Abby said.

"Why don't I take them inside and show them their room, then? I've put them in Connor's since he has the twin beds in there. I can't get your brother to take away a single one of his sports trophies and ribbons, though. It looks as it did when he was still sleeping there himself."

Abby grinned. "Cluttered and messy, then," she said. "They'll love it."

After the three of them had gone inside, she turned to her sister and gave her a fierce hug. "Now then, are you ready to tell me why I'm here?"

Jess gave her a wry look. "Always eager to cut to the chase, aren't you? Can't you even take five minutes to relax?"

"Not if you expect me to solve this problem, whatever it is, in a few days."

"I think it can wait a little longer. I don't want to get into it until after Gram's gone to bed. I don't want her worrying."

Abby frowned. "It's that serious?"

"I told you life or death, in a manner of speaking," Jess said impatiently. "Come on. I need a glass of wine—maybe two—before we get into all this."

Judging from her sister's mood, Abby had a feeling she might need a few glasses of wine herself.

Jess wasn't entirely sure how she'd made such a mess of things. All she knew for certain was that she dreaded admitting any of it to her confident, successful big sister. Still, when her plans had gone south and she'd realized just how deep a hole she'd dug for herself, calling Abby—the family's certified financial whiz—had seemed like the only sensible thing to do.

She didn't want to lose the inn. Even as a little girl, when she'd first seen the sprawling structure less than a mile away from their own house, Jess had imagined herself owning it. Just over a year and a half ago, right before Christmas, in fact, she'd spotted the For Sale sign in front of the inn as she was driving home. Bored silly by her job at Ethel's Emporium, her heart had immediately done a stutter step. For the first time since she'd come home after college, she could feel a sense of anticipation and excitement building deep inside. This was it, her chance to grab the brass ring, to give herself a sense of purpose, to build the kind of future her family would approve.

Initially, she'd told no one in her family of her plans. She wasn't entirely sure why. Probably because she'd feared their ridicule or their lack of faith that she could possibly succeed. She was, after all, the baby and the wild child. She'd never stuck with anything for long. Unlike her sisters or her brothers, she'd never displayed a real passion for work, never found her niche. She'd been drifting, and everyone in the family had known it. Worse, they'd expected nothing more of her.

"Oh, you know Jess. She never sticks with anything for long." How many times had she heard some family member say that, especially her father? When it came from Abby or her brothers, she took it in stride. When Mick said it, it cut Jess to the quick. She'd grown up believing she would never measure up to the high standards he set for all of his children. The inn was her chance to prove him—to prove all of them—wrong.

Fortunately Jess, like her siblings, had a modest trust fund that had come due when she'd turned twenty-one. It had been invested wisely, the amount growing, especially since Abby had taken over managing the account. It was enough, she'd hoped, for a down payment.

Impulsively, she'd made an appointment the next morning with the Realtor. Naively and because she was caught up in the dream, she hadn't asked to see the books or any other proof that the inn could be operated in the black. She'd done a cursory inspection and found it to be in good shape. After all, one thing she knew about her father and Uncle Jeff, they designed and built things to last. She'd made a conservative bid, which had been accepted at once. The Pattersons were anxious to leave. All that remained was to get the financing in place.

That's when she should have called Abby, she realized now. Or her father. Even her brothers could have offered sound advice, but, stubbornly independent to the end, she'd handled it all herself. To keep the payments within reason, she'd accepted an interest-only loan for the short term, then planned to refinance once the inn was open and operating at a profit.

Best-laid plans, she thought now, sipping her wine as she waited for Abby to come back from tucking the kids into bed. Nothing had gone as she'd anticipated. The Pattersons had never installed any kind of up-to-date reservation system. The heating and air-conditioning systems were barely functioning and needed to be replaced with something more energy-efficient. While the building itself was sound, the rooms were shabby, the curtains faded, the linens unacceptable. The exterior looked dilapidated, which had been easy enough to fix, but even a coat of paint cost money.

The down payment had depleted her funds, so she'd

applied for a business loan, using the inn as collateral. She'd been approved easily.

Filled with excitement, Jess had finally revealed her purchase to the rest of the family. Predictably, Gram and her siblings had been delighted for her. Mick had asked a thousand and one perfectly reasonable questions for which she didn't have adequate answers. That was when she'd gotten the first nagging sense that she was in over her head.

Then, a few months ago, while she was still trying to complete the necessary redecorating, she'd gotten a letter from the bank pointing out that she was behind on her payments for the mortgage and for the business loan. She'd scrambled to come up with the cash, embarrassed that in her zeal to spruce up the place, she'd overlooked the due dates for those payments. It had happened again a couple of months later. With her funds depleted, she'd missed two payments in a row after that.

That's when she'd received the warning notice that she was in violation of the terms of both agreements, her mortgage and her small-business loan.

"Meaning what?" she asked Lawrence Riley when she'd called the bank in a panic.

"Meaning with your very spotty payment history, we could start foreclosure procedures. I've been keeping an eye on things at the inn. You have no cash flow."

"I'm renovating. The grand opening is scheduled for July first. I'd hoped to make it by Memorial Day, but it just wasn't feasible."

"How do you expect to make these next payments or the ones the month after?"

"I'll find the money," she assured him, even though she had no idea where.

"Maybe you should speak to your father," he suggested. "I'm sure he'd be willing—"

Jess cut him off. "This is my project. My father's not involved."

Her comment silenced him, which she thought was a good thing. But then he said, "If I thought your father was backing you, I could look the other way for the short term...."

"Well, he's not," Jess repeated. "You'll get your payments, Mr. Riley. You know what potential the inn has. You know it's going to be a success."

"With the right management, yes," he said. "I'm no longer convinced you're the person who can accomplish that."

His condescension and lack of faith infuriated her. She would have told him off, but even Jess was wise enough to recognize her already precarious standing with the banker.

"Please, be patient," she said instead. "These are good loans, Mr. Riley. You know me. You know my family."

"As I said, if you want to bring your father in, we can discuss—"

"No," she'd replied fiercely.

"It's your decision, of course. I'll expect the payments on my desk on time," he said. "Good day, Jessica."

That conversation had taken place on Tuesday. She'd called Abby on Wednesday, the minute she'd realized there was no way she'd have the money in time. She knew Abby was going to flip out when she heard the kind of deals Jess had made without consulting her, but in the end she'd help her fix things, because that was what Abby did. She made things right. Even when her marriage was falling apart, she'd found a way to keep her equilibrium, stay on track at work and give the twins the kind of attention they needed to get through the turmoil. If she'd handled all that, this would be a piece of cake, Jess thought confidently.

Of course, that was before she'd realized that Trace was part of the equation. She had no idea exactly what had happened between him and Abby all those years ago, but it hadn't been good. There was a history there, and despite Trace's assurance that he wouldn't let it interfere with the bank's decision, Jess wasn't a hundred percent sure she could believe him. Nor was she certain how Abby would feel once she knew she'd be dealing with her old flame. It might be better not to mention that at the outset.

When Abby finally joined her on the porch, Jess asked about work, how the girls were doing in kindergarten, whether there were any new men in Abby's life. Abby finally regarded her with impatience. "You're stalling," she accused.

Jess flushed. "Maybe a little, but I did want to catch up. We never get to have a real heart-to-heart anymore. I miss that."

Abby's expression softened. "Me, too. But a life-or-death problem tops catching up. Talk to me."

An hour later, after Jess had spilled her guts and seen the dismay in Abby's eyes, she wasn't so sure this was going to be as easy to fix as she'd hoped.

"We can straighten this out, can't we?" she asked her sister, unable to keep a plaintive note out of her voice. "I know I've made a mess of things so far, but when you see the inn again, you'll understand why I had to do it exactly this way. It's going to be amazing."

"It will only be amazing if you can keep the bank from foreclosing," Abby said direly. "Why didn't you call me sooner? I would have loaned you the money."

"I don't need your money," Jess insisted. "I can do this on my own. I just need to buy a little more time. A couple of months, max."

"You have reservations coming in?"

"We're booked solid the rest of the summer, and we're starting to get reservations for the fall," Jess said proudly. "Plus, once word of mouth kicks in about how cozy the place is and how fabulous the food is, that should take care of the rest of the year, at least on weekends. I'm going to offer some holiday specials, too, to try to boost bookings in November, December and even the long weekends in January and February. I really do have a great marketing plan, Abby."

"In writing?"

"No, but I can put it on paper, if that will help."

Abby nodded, her expression thoughtful. "Do that. Maybe it's the bargaining chip you need. First thing tomorrow I'll meet you over there and we'll go over all your financials. We can put together some realistic budget projections, then I'll go with you to the bank on Monday."

Which meant, Jess knew, that she'd come face-to-face with Trace. Maybe that wasn't such a good idea. "I know how busy you are. Once we put everything together, if you need to go back to New York, I can take the paperwork to the bank."

"It'll be okay. Let's face it, I speak their language and you don't. This is your dream, and you tend to get sidetracked by all your plans. I can talk hard, cold facts and numbers."

Jess gave in, because she knew Abby was right. She'd get emotional, while her sister could keep her cool. "If you're really sure it won't be too big an imposition, then thank you. I'll never be able to repay you for doing this for me, Abby. I have to keep the inn. I just have to. It's the first thing that's really mattered to me, ever. It's my chance to prove I'm as good as the rest of the O'Briens."

Abby stared at her with a shocked expression. "What are you talking about, Jess? Of course you're as good as the rest of us."

"Come on. I've always been the screwup, the hyper one with no ability to focus. You probably expected me to mess this up from the beginning." The belated diagnosis that she had attention deficit disorder had come when she was ten and struggling in school. From then on, it had been her curse and, all too often, an easy excuse for her failure to follow through on things.

"That is not true," Abby said, though her expression said otherwise. "Sweetie, you have ADD. We all understand that. Despite that, look at all you've accomplished. You graduated from high school near the top of your class. You got your college degree. Those are huge accomplishments for someone with ADD. You'll figure out how to manage everything at the inn, too."

"I barely got through college because I kept changing my major. And I've drifted through half a dozen dead-end jobs since then," Jess reminded her, determined to keep it real. "I'm twenty-two and I've never even had a relationship that's lasted more than a few months."

"Because you haven't found the one thing or the one person you were passionate about," Abby argued. "Now you have the inn. I remember how you used to talk about it when you were little. You loved going over there. I was so excited for you when you told me you'd finally bought it." Her expression turned determined. "Stop worrying. I intend to do everything in my power to see that you keep the inn."

"Short of bailing me out with money," Jess reiterated. "I won't let you do that."

"Let's just see how it goes, okay? I have the money to invest in a sure thing and I have faith in you."

Tears welled up in Jess's eyes. "I love you, sis."

"Love you more. Now let's get some sleep, so we can get started on all this first thing in the morning. What time should I meet you at the inn?"

"Nine?" Jess suggested. She owed her sister one lazy morning at least.

"Make it eight."

Despite her emotions being all over the place, Jess grinned. "Not bad. You must be relaxing. I was figuring you'd say seven."

"Watch it, kid. I could change my mind."

Jess was on her feet at once. "See you at eight," she said hurriedly, then started down the steps. At the bottom, she turned back. "I'm glad you're home, Abby, but I'm sorry I dumped all this on you."

"That's what family's for," Abby said. "Don't ever forget that."

Despite her sister's words, Jess wondered if she'd ever truly believe that, at least where her disapproving father was concerned. Once Mick heard about this, there'd be plenty of I-told-you-so's to go around.

And once Abby realized that she was going to be dealing with Trace Riley and that Jess had kept that fact from her, Jess was very much afraid she might walk away and leave Jess to fend for herself.

Abby walked into the kitchen shortly after dawn, awakened by the sound of the robins, bluebirds and wrens outside her open bedroom windows. She'd forgotten how noisy nature could be, especially in the spring. As early as it was, she wasn't surprised to find her grandmother there ahead of her.

"You're up early," Gram said, her tone chiding. "I thought you'd sleep in for a bit on your first morning home."

"I have a lot to do today," Abby said, pouring herself a cup of the strong tea Gram had brewed. She laced it with milk, then sighed with pleasure after the first sip. "It never tastes like this when I make it."

"That's because you use tea bags and brew it in the microwave, I'll bet."

Abby grinned. "Could be."

"A good pot of tea takes time to steep. If you put a little time and love into it, it shows."

"I have enough trouble finding time to love my girls without worrying about how my tea feels," Abby replied.

"Which means you're working too hard. You never have learned how to relax. Why don't you grab a book and take it outside to the hammock this morning. I'll keep an eye on the girls. I'll take them into town and show them off."

"If you wouldn't mind watching the girls, I'll take you up on that," Abby told her. "But the hammock will have to wait. I promised Jess I'd meet her at the inn in an hour."

Gram's expression immediately sobered. She sat down across from Abby and stirred her tea, then lifted her gaze to Abby's. "She's in trouble with that, isn't she?"

Abby didn't want to betray her sister's confidence, but she'd always been a lousy liar. She settled for asking, "What makes you think that?"

"For one thing, this is Chesapeake Shores, where gossip is everybody's favorite hobby. For another, Violet Harding's sister works at the bank. She told Violet that she'd seen something about foreclosure on a file with Jess's name on it. Of course that old gossip couldn't wait to spread the word. The Hardings are still furious that Mick bought up all their family's land to develop this town. Never mind that it was their good-for-nothing father who sold it to him because he needed cash, somehow it's Mick's fault that they don't own all that acreage anymore." She waved off the topic. "None of that matters. Is Jess going to lose the inn the way Violet said?"

"Not if I have anything to say about it," Abby told her firmly. "And please don't tell her you know. She's so afraid of letting all of us down."

Gram shook her head. "Does she honestly believe we care more about that inn and whether she succeeds or fails than we do about her?"

Abby nodded. "I think she does. She wants desperately to prove herself, especially to Dad."

"Now that I understand," Gram said, her mouth set in a grim line. "Why those two can't communicate without starting a fight is beyond me."

"It's because they're exactly alike," Abby said. "They both have more pride than sense and a mile-wide stubborn streak. And neither one of them can stand to be wrong about anything. Even though I wasn't around when Jess bought the inn, I'm sure Dad was the first to suggest she was making a mistake and will be the first to say I told you so if she fails."

"That's it in a nutshell," Gram agreed. "I don't remember him being that ornery with the rest of you."

"Trust me, he was," Abby said. "But with the rest of us, we could let it roll off our backs. We knew we had you and Mom in our corners, no matter what. With Mom gone, Jess has always taken everything Dad said to heart, even offhand comments he's forgotten about as soon as he's made them."

"You're right. I've talked to him about that myself, but he doesn't see the problem. Your father's always believed that blunt honesty is a virtue, even when it hurts. He thinks mollycoddling is a waste of time. He believes you children should know without a doubt that he loves you, no matter how harsh his criticism might be."

"That worked fine with the rest of us, but not with Jess. She's had too many obstacles to overcome."

Gram regarded her worriedly. "Are you going to be able to help her to straighten this out?"

"I'm going to try," Abby said. "Don't worry, Gram. I

know how important this is. The bank won't take that inn away from her without a fight from me."

Gram's expression turned thoughtful. "Maybe it would be better if she had to save it for herself, instead of letting you rush to the rescue."

"It probably would be," Abby admitted. "But based on what she told me last night, I don't think that's going to be an option. She's waited too long, and now there's not enough time for her to pull everything together."

"Does she want to borrow money?"

Abby shook her head. "She's adamantly opposed to that. All she's asked for is my business expertise."

"Is that going to be enough?" Gram asked.

"I won't know until I see her books," Abby said honestly.

"Well, Jess made the right decision when she called you," Gram said. "She's been counting on you since she was a little bitty thing, and you've never once let her down."

"Pile on the pressure, why don't you?" Abby replied as she stood up. She leaned down and pressed a kiss to her grandmother's cheek. "Thanks, Gram. I love you."

"I love you, too. And Jess. It's going to be okay. When O'Briens stick together, there's nothing we can't do."

"That's what you've always taught us," Abby agreed.

Unfortunately, she was very much afraid it was going to take a lot more than family spirit and loyalty to save Jess's inn.

3

Mick hadn't been home for a month, not that Chesapeake Shores felt much like home anymore. He'd spent most of that time in a frustrating battle of wits with officials over building permits for his latest planned community north of San Francisco. Given the number of hurdles, he was beginning to question the wisdom of going through with the development. Then again, he'd put his reputation on the line for this one, and what would it say if he folded up and went away without a fight?

He'd just finished a meeting with his associates from O'Brien & Company, his contractors and the subcontractors about the latest delay when his cell phone rang. Glancing at caller ID, he saw that it was his mother, who rarely ever called him these days. In the past she'd only called in an emergency, and there'd been plenty of those with five kids in the house.

"Hey, Ma, how are you?" he said, walking away from the other men so he could have the conversation in private.

"Fit as a fiddle," she said. "Wish I could say the same for your daughter."

Mick felt his pulse speed up. "Is something wrong with Abby? Or Bree?" he asked. Then added almost as an afterthought, "Or is it Jess?"

"Interesting that your concern for Jess came last," she said, her tone accusing. "That's always been the problem between you two. Sometimes I think you forget you have three daughters. It's little wonder the girl works so hard to try to get your attention."

"I hope you didn't call just to give me another lecture on how I've shortchanged Jessica. We've had that conversation too many times to count."

"Then it amazes me that it has yet to sink in," she retorted. "And actually that's exactly why I called. When was the last time you spoke to her?"

"A few days ago, I suppose," he said, searching his memory, but unable to come up with anything more precise. That gave some credence to his mother's accusations, but he wasn't planning to admit that anytime soon. He hadn't spoken to Abby or Bree, either.

"More like a month, I imagine," she said. "If I had to guess, I'd say it was when she drove you to the airport. I doubt you've given her a second thought since then."

He winced as the barb hit its mark. "Okay, that's probably right. What's your point? She's a grown woman. She doesn't need her dad checking up on her."

"Checking up on her, no," his mother agreed with undisguised impatience. "But how about checking in just to see how she's doing, maybe asking how the inn is coming along, inquiring if she could use any help in getting it ready to open? Would those things be too much to expect from a loving parent, especially one with an entire construction company at his disposal?"

Mick bristled at the suggestion that he wasn't interested in his own daughter's life or that he'd been unwilling to help her out. "Jess made it plain she didn't want my interference. You sat right there at the kitchen table when I offered to send one of my guys around to look things over and she turned me down flat."

"Mick, for a bright man, you can be denser than dirt," she

chided. "Maybe she didn't want one of your men over there. Maybe what she needed was *you.*"

Mick might be past fifty, but he still hated being called on the carpet by his own mother. He'd rather face down a hundred bureaucrats than be made to feel that somehow he'd let down his family. It wasn't as if he didn't know he'd failed them by making life so miserable for Megan that she'd left him. He hadn't been able to fix that, and it was likely that whatever was going on right now with Jess wasn't something he could fix, either. What kind of man was he? He'd built an international reputation as an architect and urban planner, but he couldn't keep his own damn family together.

"Ma, why don't you just say whatever's on your mind? Is Jess in some kind of trouble? Does she need money? One of my crews? What? You know I'll do whatever I can to help. All she needs to do is ask."

His mother sighed heavily. "Mick, you know she'll never do that."

"Why, for God's sake?" he asked, frustrated. "Who else should she ask? I'm her father."

"Exactly. And she's been trying to prove herself to you since the day her mother left. She thinks that was her fault because she was too much trouble, because she wasn't smart enough."

"Jess is smart as a whip," he protested, exactly as he always did.

"Well, of course she is, but learning came hard for her. She thinks that was what sent her mother running. Kids as young as Jess was back then always think a divorce is their fault."

"You've been watching Dr. Phil again," he accused. "Don't try to psychoanalyze my relationship with Jess."

"Well, somebody has to fix it. It's way past time. How soon can you get back here?"

"A few weeks, maybe. Longer unless you tell me what

the hell is going on in plain English that my poor denser-than-dirt male brain can comprehend."

"Don't smart-mouth me. I'm still your mother."

Mick nearly groaned. "Ma, please."

"I think it's possible she's going to lose the inn before she even gets the doors open. If that happens, it will break not only her heart, but her spirit."

The news caught him completely off guard. Even he recognized how that could affect his daughter, assuming it was true and not just the product of the local gossip mill. "What makes you think she's going to lose the inn?"

"I've heard rumors the bank is considering foreclosure. And before you dismiss that as nothing more than speculation, I'll tell you my source was reliable."

Mick's frustration mounted. "Dammit, I knew she was getting in over her head, but she signed all the paperwork and plunged into this without talking any of it over with me."

"Because she needed to prove to you that she could do this all on her own."

"Well, exactly what will she have proved, if the bank forecloses?"

"Michael Devlin O'Brien, don't you dare come back here if all you're going to do is throw her mistakes in her face. She needs her father, not a judgmental businessman."

Now it was Mick's turn to sigh heavily. If what his mother was saying was true, it put him between a rock and a hard place. "Ma, we both know I could fix whatever's going on with one call to Lawrence Riley, but you know as well as I do that Jess won't thank me for it."

"True enough," she admitted. "But we have to do something, Mick. Jess needs to make a success of this."

"Do you really think she could lose the inn? Maybe it's not that bad."

"Jess called her sister, that's how bad it is. Abby's here now trying to help, but from the grim expression on her face this morning, it could take more than some sort of financial wizardry on her part to fix this. Come home, Mick. Whether she admits it or not, Jess needs your support right now. And of course, if you flew home tonight, you'd be able to spend some time with Abby and your granddaughters."

"Tonight?" he asked, trying to work out the all-but-impossible logistics in his head. "I doubt I could get on a flight on short notice."

"Spend some of that fortune you make on something important for once. Hire a private jet, if you have to."

He thought of having one daughter and his only grandchildren under his roof again, of being there when another daughter might actually admit she needed him, and made a decision. His mother was right. If ever there was a time he belonged at home with his family, this was it.

"I'll see what I can arrange," he said at last.

"That's good," his mother said. "And let's just pretend, you and I, that we never had this conversation."

Mick laughed for the first time since the uncomfortable conversation had begun. "You're still a sly one, aren't you, Ma?"

"I pride myself on it, in fact."

Abby spent all day Saturday buried in paperwork at the inn. As her sister had assured her, the projections were positive, but Jess clearly had little sense of money management. If she'd wanted fancy, top-of-the-line shower curtains or thick, luxurious towels, she'd bought them, even if it broke the budget.

Not that she'd ever put a budget on paper in the first place or even the sort of business plan that Abby would have expected the bank to require. Obviously she'd been flying by the seat of her pants, and the bank had let her get away with it because she was an O'Brien in a town where that meant something. Any national bank would have adhered to much stricter guidelines than the Chesapeake Shores Community Bank apparently had followed.

Abby sat Jess down at the kitchen table on Saturday night and laid it all out for her while Gram was upstairs reading the girls their bedtime story. "You have little to no operating capital. How were you planning on buying supplies for the restaurant? Or soaps and toiletries for the rooms, for that matter?"

"Credit?" Jess said weakly, looking as if she were about to cry. "I haven't maxed out my credit cards yet."

Abby bit back a groan. "You'll dig a hole so deep doing that, you'll never get out. Like it or not, I'm going to give you an infusion of cash and a strict budget. Assuming, that is, that we can get the bank to go along with this. I'm just praying that they haven't officially started foreclosure proceedings. I'm going to be on the doorstep over there at nine sharp Monday morning and we'll see where we stand."

"I'll come with you," Jess said. "This is my project."

Abby agreed reluctantly. "Okay, but let me do the talking, unless they ask for information I don't have."

"Fine," Jess said, not meeting her gaze.

Abby studied her sister. Jess's cheeks were faintly flushed. Maybe it was just embarrassment that she'd let her finances get so messed up, but Abby thought it was something else. She looked guilty.

"What aren't you telling me?" Abby asked her. "Has the foreclosure process gone further than you've admitted? Are there more bills you haven't wanted me to see?"

Jess hesitated, then declared, "No. You've seen every single piece of paper, every bill I owe."

"Then why do you look guilty?"

"Guilty?" She widened her eyes in an attempt to look innocent.

Abby didn't buy it. "Don't even try that act with me. I've known you too long and too well. That's the look you used to get when you'd snuck out the bedroom window at night to meet Matt Richardson and Gram called you on it."

Jess's flush deepened. "Okay, maybe there is one other thing you should know before Monday."

"Tell me," Abby ordered, the knot of dread forming yet again in her stomach. "Don't you dare let me walk into that meeting and get blindsided."

Before Jess could reply, the door burst open and their father strode into the kitchen. Jess looked from him to Abby and back again.

"I see the cavalry's arrived," Jess said sourly. She scowled at Abby. "Did you call him?"

"Of course not," Abby said, trying to soften Jess's reaction by standing up to give her father a warm hug. She beamed up at him. "Why didn't you let us know you were coming home?"

"It was a spur-of-the-moment decision," he said, casting a wary look toward Jess. "Something going on you didn't want me to know about?"

"Nothing," she said firmly, shooting a warning look at Abby that pretty much tied her hands. With obvious reluctance, Jess stood and gave Mick an obligatory kiss on the cheek. "Hi, Dad. Welcome home. I'd love to stay and catch up, but I need to get home."

"Last time I checked, this was your home," he said.

"I'm staying at the inn now," she said, as she gathered up all the papers on the kitchen table and shoved them into a briefcase. Clearly she didn't intend to take a chance that Mick would lay eyes on them.

She was already heading for the door when she said, "I'll talk to you tomorrow, Abby."

Abby wanted to argue that they still had things to discuss right here and now, but clearly Jess didn't want anything revealed in front of their father. She'd just have to wait until Sunday to find out what Jess had been keeping from her.

As soon as her sister was out of earshot, Abby turned to her father. He looked tired, but otherwise robust. There were threads of gray in his curly, reddish-blond hair, but his broad shoulders and trim waistline testified that he was still maintaining his fitness regimen even with all the traveling and dining out he did. His complexion was ruddy from working outdoors and there were a few more lines around his blue eyes, which were filled with concern as he stared after Jess.

"Gram called you, didn't she?" Abby asked him.

He hesitated for a split second, then nodded. "She wanted me to know you and the girls were here. I caught the first flight I could get, so I could spend a little time with you. It's been a long time since you've graced us with your presence down here."

"Too long," she admitted. "Was that all she told you?"

Mick went to the counter and poured himself a cup of tea, then sat down without replying. He stirred sugar into the strong brew and took a sip, then met Abby's gaze. "Sure. Is there something else going on?"

"Don't play games with me, Dad. You're really back because she told you Jess is in trouble."

His lips twitched at that. "Did she really? Are you a mind reader now? Or did you eavesdrop on a private conversation?"

"Of course not."

"Then take what I'm telling you at face value," he ordered. "It's better that way. Now tell me where my darling girls are."

"Asleep, I hope," she said. "And we're not going to wake them up at this hour. I'll never get them back to sleep if we do. They'll be too excited if they see you. You can spend all day tomorrow with them." She gave him a stern look. "And no spoiling them rotten, either. I think you bought all the toys in FAO Schwarz the last time you were in New York."

"It's a grandfather's privilege to do a little spoiling," he argued. "That's what we're meant to do."

Abby rolled her eyes. A few days of all that extra attention from Gram and now Mick, and the twins would be little terrors by the time she got them back to New York.

She realized that Mick was studying her over the rim of his cup. "You look worn-out, Abby. You're working too hard."

"That's the nature of what I do."

"Does it leave you enough time for those sweet girls?"

"Not really," she admitted, then added pointedly, "but you should know better than anyone what it's like to make hard choices, to do what's best for your family." In some ways they were two of a kind, which she supposed made at least some of her criticism sound hypocritical.

"I do know about hard choices," he said, not taking offense. "And you should know as well as anyone what the cost was. I lost a woman I loved. And not a one of you could wait to leave this place. So what good did all this money and success do for me in the end?"

"Jess is still here."

"And not a day goes by that I don't wonder why."

"I think I know the answer to that," Abby said. "She loves it here, more than the rest of us ever did. And she's still trying to prove herself to you, here, in a place that once meant everything to you. I think she believes it will create a bridge between you eventually."

"There's nothing she has to prove. My love for you, Jess, Bree and your brothers is unconditional."

Abby saw that he honestly believed it was that simple and

that obvious. She decided to be candid for once, rather than skirting around the real issues this family had. "Dad, when Mom left, you might as well have. From that moment on, you passed through our lives when you could spare a few days, but you didn't know anything about us. For Connor, Kevin, me and even Bree, it was hard, but we were almost grown by then. Jess was still a little girl."

He frowned at that. "What are you talking about? I knew everything there was to know about all of you. I knew when you were sick. I knew when one of you won an award at school or scored a touchdown. I was there for graduation. I paid the bills for college and saw the report cards."

Abby's temper stirred. "And you thought those things were all that mattered? A private investigator could have told you any of that stuff, though of course in your case it was Gram who filled you in. We needed our father here, cheering for us, drying our tears, calling us on it when we made mistakes."

His cheeks flushed and his tone turned defensive when he reminded her, "You always had your grandmother for that."

"And she was wonderful. She did all of those things, but she wasn't you or Mom." Abby shook her head, resigned to the fact that he would never understand. "What's the point of fighting about this now? It's all water under the bridge. We survived. Not every kid has an idyllic family, and our lives were certainly better than most."

"I did the best I could," Mick protested.

She gave him a pitying look. "Perhaps you did, but you know what? Maybe it's because I'm the oldest, but I remember a time when you were better than that."

She stood up then, rinsed out her own cup and put it in the dishwasher. "Good night, Dad. The girls are going to be thrilled to see you in the morning."

She wished she could say the same. Though she knew

with everything in her that he'd come home to try in some way to help with Jess's predicament, she had this awful feeling that his presence was only going to make things worse.

Sunday morning Trace was sitting on the family's dock, his feet dangling in the water, when Laila appeared. In her short shorts, halter top and with her long blond hair caught up in a careless ponytail, she looked about sixteen, not twenty-nine.

She handed him an icy can of soda. "How's the prodigal son?" she inquired, kicking off her flip-flops and dropping down beside him on the smooth wood that had been warmed by the sun. Overhead, an eagle swooped through the air, then settled high in an old oak tree to watch over the scene from his lofty perch.

"Chomping at the bit to get back to New York," he responded. "Which I could do if you weren't so obstinate."

She nudged him with her elbow. "Come on, admit it. You like being here."

"For a visit," he insisted. "I've never wanted any part of the bank. That was your dream, not mine."

"Unfortunately, Daddy doesn't see it that way. In his male-dominated world, the family estate must go to the eldest son. Daughters get whatever's left over."

He frowned at her. "Not the way I heard it. Dad said he offered you a position at the bank."

"Did he happen to mention what that position was?"

"The same one I'm in, I assume."

"Well, you assume wrong. He expected me to work as Raymond's assistant, which, in case you haven't figured out the pecking order there yet, amounts to a clerical job that any high school kid could do."

Trace winced. "That was not the impression he gave me."

"Ask him, if you don't believe me."

Unfortunately, Trace believed her. It would be just like his father to dangle a job in front of Laila, knowing that it was beneath her and that she'd turn it down. Then he could claim—as he had to Trace—that he'd given her a chance.

"I'm sorry," he said.

She shrugged, pretending it didn't matter, but Trace knew better.

"Don't be sorry," she claimed anyway. "It was just Dad being his usual sexist self. I'm used to it by now."

"I don't know if it helps, but I've told him you're the one he should be grooming to take over."

"Oddly enough, it does help."

They sat in silence for a few minutes, before she glanced his way. "Abby's in town. Did you know that?"

"I'd heard she might be coming for a visit," he replied neutrally.

"Have you seen her?"

He shook his head. "But I imagine we'll cross paths before she leaves."

"How do you feel about that?"

"We're adults," he said with a touch of impatience. "It's been a long time. I'm sure we'll manage to be civil, Laila."

"I didn't ask how you expected to behave. I asked how you feel about seeing her again. We both know she was the love of your life and you've never gotten over her."

He regarded her wryly. "Oh, we both know that, do we?"

"Well, *I* know it," she said, giving him a crooked smile. "You, however, may be too stupid and stubborn to admit it. You are a guy, after all."

"I'm not discussing Abby with you."

Laila wasn't easy to deter once she'd gotten her teeth into a subject. "Come on, Trace. Admit it. It just about killed you when she left town. I was here. I saw what it did to you."

"Then why would you want to remind me of all that now?"

"Because this could be your chance to find out what happened."

"I know what happened. Abby made a decision to cut me out of her life. End of story."

"That's not the end of the story," his sister contradicted. "It's only the part of the story you know. Find out the rest. Maybe it will put an end to that whole episode once and for all, so you can move on."

"I moved on years ago," he claimed.

"Baloney!"

He stared at her, his lips twitching. "What are we, five?"

"I'm not, but that seems to be your maturity level when it comes to this one thing. Adults face each other and deal with their issues."

"I'm not the one who left. Have you had this conversation with Abby?"

"I did ten years ago," Laila admitted.

Trace flinched. "Really? And what did Abby reveal to you that she didn't bother telling me?"

"She told me to butt out, as a matter of fact."

He laughed, but there was little humor in the sound. "Seems like good advice to me."

He was struck by the same nagging thought that had come to him at the bank on his first day there. "You haven't shared any of this with Dad, have you?"

"About you and Abby? No, why?"

He studied her face, trying to decide if he could trust what she was saying. "It just seems awfully convenient that Dad decides to push this whole idea of getting me to work at the bank right when there's going to be a battle with the O'Briens that was bound to bring Abby back to town."

"You mean that possible foreclosure at the inn?" she asked innocently. "Do you think that's why Abby's here?"

"Don't you?"

"I suppose that makes sense," she conceded. "Abby's always been smart about business, and she's always been the first one Jess turns to."

"And none of that crossed your mind when you heard about the bank foreclosing on Jess's property? Or when you heard that Dad was dragging me back here?"

"Believe it or not, I don't spend a lot of my spare time coming up with conspiracies with Dad. And if it had been up to me, you'd still be in New York, and I'd be in that big corner office at the bank dealing with Jess."

"Okay, then," Trace said, deciding he might as well take her at her word. He was probably imagining a conspiracy where none existed. After all, Abby was here and he was just about one hundred percent certain to see her. How that inevitable confrontation had been set into motion hardly mattered. He just had to brace himself for it, so he didn't make a complete fool of himself when they crossed paths. Throwing her across his desk and kissing her was probably a bad idea. And actually he hoped he wouldn't want to.

Gram fixed a Sunday dinner that could have fed an army and insisted that all of them sit down at the table together, including Caitlyn and Carrie, whose table manners left a lot to be desired. Still, Abby thought they provided an excellent buffer between her sister and her father. Jess was shooting distrustful glances at Mick, to which he seemed to be oblivious. He kept asking questions about the inn that were supposedly innocent. Under the circumstances, though, they were as highly charged as an entire crate of explosives.

"No business at the table," Gram finally said when Jess

looked as if she was about to throw down her napkin and bolt. "I'm sure we can think of other things to talk about. After all, when was the last time we had a chance to be together under this roof? Let's make this meal as special as the occasion calls for."

"How are Uncle Jeff and Uncle Tom?" Abby asked, seizing on the first thing that came to mind.

"How would I know?" Mick responded bitterly. The implication in his tone was that he didn't much care, either. Obviously neither time nor Gram had mellowed his mood when it came to his brothers.

The breakup of the business partnership had taken a personal toll. It had exposed all of the philosophical and environmental differences of the brothers. Since like all O'Briens, none of them were willing to back down from a stance, working together had been a really bad idea from the beginning. That they'd actually completed Chesapeake Shores at all had been a miracle.

Gram scowled at Mick, then turned to Abby. "They're fine. Tom's working on legislation to protect the bay and trying to get funding to clean up the waters of both the bay and its tributaries. Jeff's running the management company that handles the leases on the shops downtown. His daughter, Susie, is working for him."

"Gosh, I haven't seen Susie in ages," Abby said. "She was still a kid when I left for New York."

"She graduated from college last year," Jess said. "Magna cum laude, right, Gram?"

Gram ignored the hint of sarcasm in Jess's voice and said evenly, "I believe that's right. Jeff was real proud of her."

"How's your mother, Abby?" Mick suddenly blurted. "You see her, don't you?"

Abby saw the deep hurt in his eyes and felt the same pity

she always did when her mother plied her with questions about the rest of the family. "We get together for lunch every couple of weeks and she spends time with the girls on Saturdays when she can. She's doing well. She loves living in the city."

"I'm sure she does," Mick said with undisguised bitterness, clamping his mouth shut when Abby pointedly nodded toward the girls to remind him that they didn't need to hear so much as a whisper spoken against their grandmother.

"Grandma Megan's beautiful," Caitlyn said, then looked at Mick with confusion. "Do you know her?"

Abby realized that since her kids had never seen Mick and Megan together, they couldn't possibly understand the complexities of the relationship.

The shadows in Mick's eyes deepened as he responded to his granddaughter. "I used to," he said softly.

"Grandma Megan used to be married to Grandpa Mick," Abby explained.

That stirred a spark of interest in Carrie's eyes. "Did you get a 'vorce like Mommy and Daddy?"

Mick nodded. "We did."

"Did you still love your kids?" Caitlyn asked worriedly. "Mommy and Daddy say they'll love us forever and ever, even if they don't love each other anymore."

"Moms and dads never stop loving their children," Mick assured her. His solemn gaze flicked to Jess when he said it, as if trying to communicate that message to her. She resolutely turned away, focusing her attention on cutting the meat on her plate into tiny pieces which she then shoved aside and left uneaten.

Sensing that this topic was no safer than business, Abby stood up. "Girls, why don't I get you some ice cream and we can eat it outside? You'll excuse us, won't you?" She was already rising when she asked and didn't wait for a reply.

Carrie and Caitlyn scrambled down from their chairs with a shout and raced for the kitchen, Abby on their heels. It wasn't until she was safely away from the tension in the dining room that she sighed with relief. Okay, she'd just thrown Jess to the wolves in there, but right this second it felt like every woman needed to fend for herself.

"What kind of ice cream can we have, Mommy?" Carrie asked, tugging on her slacks.

"Let's see what Gram has in the freezer," she said, though she knew the answer. There had never been a time when the freezer wasn't stocked with strawberry, Gram's favorite, and with chocolate, which had always been Mick's, hers and her brothers' first choice. Jess's had always been vanilla fudge ripple, so that was bound to be there, too.

She gave the girls their choices—they agreed on strawberry, for once—then dished up a scoop for each one. "Outside," she said as she handed them the plastic bowls and spoons. "I'll be right behind you."

She gave herself a double scoop of chocolate, then covered it with hot fudge sauce for good measure. The way this day was going she was going to need every bit of chocolate decadence she could find to get through it.

4

Abby was glad she'd flown home still dressed in the black power suit she'd worn to work on Friday morning. She pressed it before putting it on Monday morning, then drove over to pick up Jess. When Abby arrived, Jess was still wearing paint-splattered shorts and a faded T-shirt. Abby barely held in a sigh. It looked as if Jess had gotten distracted by one of her decorating projects.

"Sorry," Jess said, her expression flustered. "I lost track of the time. I couldn't sleep, so I started painting at the crack of dawn, then someone called in a reservation—"

Abby cut her off. "Jess, we don't have time for this. You can't go to the bank like that," she said, trying not to lose patience. Jess was obviously tense enough without Abby yelling at her. "You know how important this meeting is. It's critical that we handle it as professionally as possible. Change, and do it fast, please."

"Five minutes, I promise. You go on ahead. I'll meet you there."

Abby nodded and drove off, relieved in some ways that she was going in alone. She could say things then that she wouldn't want to say in front of her sister, admit to Jess's failings but stress that her sister had backup now and that things would be on track from here on out.

When they opened the door at Chesapeake Shores Community Bank, she walked in as if she owned the place and headed straight for Lawrence Riley's office. She beamed at Mariah Walsh, who'd been working there as far back as she could recall.

"Abby, what on earth are you doing back in town?" Mariah asked.

"Visiting family," she said. "How've you been?"

"Same as always. Just a few more years on me."

Abby nodded toward Mr. Riley's office. "Is he in?" she asked. "I need to speak to him."

"What's it about?" Mariah asked, already picking up the phone.

"Jess's loans on the inn."

Mariah frowned and hung up. "Then you'll need to speak to Trace."

Abby felt her heart lurch at the mention of Trace Riley. It had been years since they'd seen each other, and it was ridiculous that hearing his name was enough to make her falter. But in that instant, she realized exactly what Jess had been keeping from her. Jess had known that Trace was involved in this situation and that Abby would have to deal with him and not his father.

Trying to recover her equilibrium before Mariah could see how thrown she'd been, she said, "Trace is working here? I'm surprised." He'd always sworn that hell would freeze over before he'd work in a bank, much less for his father.

Mariah grinned. "Hell's sure enough frozen over, huh? He just started last week and he says it's just temporary. His father's hoping that'll change. In the meantime, though, he's in charge of the loan department."

Damn, Abby thought. Maybe that could work in her favor, but she doubted it. The last time they'd seen each other, she'd slept with him, told him she was in love with him and then she'd taken off for New York without another word.

Over the months and years that followed, she'd convinced herself that she'd had no choice, that Trace was a distraction she couldn't afford. In fact, she'd had a whole litany of reasons that had made perfect sense to her at the time. She'd even told herself she was cutting things off for him as much as for herself.

Of course, she should have had the guts to tell him that in person, though. Instead, she'd taken the coward's way out, because he tempted her in ways she'd found all but impossible to resist. Had she seen him one more time there was no telling what might have happened to her resolve to go to New York and start a career on Wall Street. She might even have been persuaded to stay with him right here. He'd obviously caved in to parental pressure, just as she'd always feared he might. That fear had made it impossible to trust all the pretty words he'd said, all the promises he'd made about their future.

Mariah gave her a knowing look. "His office is down the hall on the left. Want me to call and tell him you're on your way in?"

"I think I'd better surprise him," Abby replied, then stiffened her spine and headed for his office. She'd had enough uncomfortable meetings to steel her resolve for this one. She tapped on the door, then walked in without waiting for a reply.

Trace was on the phone, his gaze directed out the window. Distractedly, he waved her toward a seat without even turning around. She breathed a sigh of relief at the reprieve. It gave her time to study him.

He looked good. Really good. The sleeves of his shirt were rolled up, revealing tanned forearms. The laugh lines that fanned out from his eyes were carved a little deeper now. His hair, thick and dark brown with golden highlights from the sun, was a little long and windblown. She grinned. She'd bet anything he'd ridden to work on his Harley. That bike had been his first major rebellion way back in high school, and the possibility that he'd never given it up gave her an unexpected sense of hope. That was the Trace she remembered, not a man who'd turned into a by-the-book banker like his dad. She could deal with that man, challenge him to bend the rules.

When he finished the call, he swiveled around and caught sight of her for the first time. Something dark and dangerous flashed in his eyes, but he kept his expression neutral. "Well, look who the cat dragged in."

"Hello, Trace."

"I'll bet you didn't expect to find me here," he said.

"It was a pleasant surprise, all right."

"Pleasant?" he inquired doubtfully.

"For me, yes. We were friends, Trace. Why wouldn't I be glad to see you again?" she asked, though she knew the answer. She'd just hoped to finesse her way past the awkwardness. The simmering anger in his eyes suggested that wasn't likely.

"Friends?" he echoed with a lift of one brow. "That's not exactly the way I remember it. Maybe my memory's faulty, but I thought we were more than that."

Heat stained Abby's cheeks. "It was a long time ago, Trace. A lifetime, in fact."

He hesitated for what seemed like an eternity, his gaze level, then finally he looked away and reached for a folder with an ominous red sticker on the front. "I imagine you're here about this," he said, his tone suddenly abrupt and very businesslike. "Jess has gotten herself into quite a mess."

Taking her cue from him, Abby opened her briefcase. "We're aware of that, and we're prepared to give the bank every reassurance that things will change from here on out."

"You'll have to do quite a bit of tap-dancing to pull that off," he said. "She doesn't have any management skills. I think that's plain. I have no idea why the bank approved these loans in the first place. I imagine they did it as a courtesy to your father."

Just then the door to his office opened again, and Jess stepped in. She frowned at his words. "You couldn't be more wrong, Trace. They did it because it was a sound investment. That's exactly what your father said when he called me to tell me the mortgage and the loan had been approved." She regarded Trace unflinchingly and added, "It still is."

"Not according to these papers I have in front of me," Trace countered. "It's time to cut our losses, and that's exactly what I intend to recommend to the board tomorrow."

"No," Abby said fiercely. "Not until you've heard us out."

She tried not to notice the alarm on Jess's face or the brick-red color that flamed in Trace's cheeks. Instead, she plunged on, throwing diplomacy to the wind. "If you have even an ounce of business savvy in that rock-hard head of yours, you'll see that this plan makes sense."

"Why should I believe anything you tell me?" he asked.

Abby swallowed hard. This was all going to blow up just because she and Trace had a history. Why hadn't Jess warned her? If she had, Abby would have stayed far, far away from the bank. But since she was in the thick of it now, she refused to let him goad her into backing down.

"Don't make this about us, Trace," she said quietly. "It doesn't reflect well on you or the bank."

Trace scowled at her. "Well, aren't you full of yourself? Trust me, you had nothing to do with my decision. It's all right here in black and white. People might lie, but numbers don't."

Abby knew he was right about that, but she wasn't giving up without a fight. She'd seen the flicker of guilt in his eyes when she'd accused him of letting his feelings for her get into the equation. She intended to use that to force his hand and make him reconsider.

She tempered her tone. "Will you at least hear me out? You owe us that much."

"Really?" he said quizzically. "How do you figure that?"

"You want to prove that you're making a totally unbiased decision, don't you? Then you have to consider all the facts. Otherwise I'll have to insist on meeting the board myself, and you'll wind up with egg on your face after barely a week on the job."

Again, he gestured toward the file. "The facts are in here."

"Not all of them," she insisted. She handed him a set of the papers she'd spent all Sunday afternoon preparing, partly because she'd wanted them to be strong enough to make her case and partly as a way to steer clear of Mick. "Take a look. As you'll see, there's a new investment partner. Jess has more than enough cash now to make good on the loan payments and to capitalize the running of the inn for the first six months, longer if she's careful. There's a solid business plan on pages two and three. And on page four there's a plan for refinancing that egregious interest-only mortgage that should never have been offered in the first place. I think we could make a case that the bank was hoping she'd get herself into financial trouble just so they could foreclose and lay claim to the inn once she'd poured a lot of money into renovations."

Trace stared at her incredulously. "You can't be serious. You think this was the bank's fault?"

She smiled. "I do."

"You're crazy!"

"Want to test my theory in court? I think people are furious over the kind of lending practices that turned the whole industry upside down. I think we could make Jess into a very sympathetic victim."

Trace regarded her with a glimmer of new respect. "Not bad. You almost had me going there for a minute."

"I wasn't joking," Abby assured him. "My next stop will be a lawyer's office unless I can make you see reason."

He looked taken aback. "I'll have to take this proposal of yours to the board," he said eventually.

"Of course. They meet tomorrow?"

"At ten o'clock," he told her.

"Then you should have an answer by noon?"

He nodded. "I'll meet you at the yacht club at twelve-fifteen and fill you in over lunch."

Abby hesitated. She could stay, had planned to stay, in fact, but with Trace involved it was too complicated. "Jess will be there, but I can't be. I have to get back to New York tonight."

His gaze clashed with hers. "You'll be there if you expect this to be approved."

"Why? This is Jess's business, not mine."

"You'll be there because I intend to recommend that the board approve this on one condition only."

Jess sat up a little straighter. "What condition?" she asked suspiciously.

Trace looked at her as if he'd forgotten she was even in the room. "That your sister take over as manager of the project."

"No!" Abby and Jess said at once.

"It's my inn," Jess protested. "You have no right to dictate who manages it."

"I do when this bank's money is involved and you have a history of failing to make your payments," he said, his gaze unrelenting. "Abby stays or it's a deal-breaker."

"But the plan," Abby began.

"Isn't worth the paper it's written on unless you remain

involved," he said. "There's no assurance it won't be frittered away on who knows what before the next payment's due."

"Come on, Trace, be reasonable," Abby pleaded. "I need to get back to New York. I have a job. Jess knows what has to be done. I trust her."

"You're her sister. I'm her banker," he said. "Unless you agree to my terms, we'll proceed with the foreclosure."

He looked from Abby to Jess, then back again. "Well, what's it going to be? Will I see you tomorrow?"

Abby bit back the sharp retort on the tip of her tongue and nodded slowly, afraid of what she might say if she spoke. She held her breath, praying that Jess would be as diplomatic. When she glanced at her sister, she discovered Jess looked furious, but at least she remained silent.

For the moment, he had them both over a barrel and they all knew it. Once the board went along with this insane plan of his, though, Abby was convinced he'd be satisfied with the victory. After that, she could make him see reason. She was sure of it.

Then again, she'd learned a long time ago that a man whose pride had been damaged could turn into a fierce and stubborn adversary. For now, anyway, Trace Riley held all the cards, so she and Jess were going to have to play the game his way...at least until she could come up with a new set of rules, and then make him believe that he'd come up with them all on his own.

Outside the bank, Jess stood on the sidewalk, trembling. She whirled on her sister.

"What the hell just happened in there? I thought you were on my side."

"Of course I'm on your side," Abby said, looking genuinely bewildered by Jess's attack. "This was all about keeping you from losing the inn."

"I might as well have lost it," Jess snapped. "He's put you in charge. Way to go, sis!"

Abby frowned. "Jess, calm down. Let's go to Sally's for a cup of coffee and talk about this. We need to plan our strategy."

"Strategy for what? Getting your name on the deed?"

"Jess!"

There was a flash of hurt in Abby's eyes, but Jess didn't feel like relenting. She was spitting mad and she needed someone to take it out on. Her sister was the most obvious choice, since Jess couldn't go back inside the bank and start pummeling Trace. Even in her fury, she knew that would be counterproductive.

"I should have let Mick handle it," she said. "He'd have made a couple of calls and the bank would have backed down. I might have had to listen to his I-told-you-so's from here to eternity, but that would have been better than being stabbed in the back by you."

Temper flared in Abby's eyes, and Jess knew at once she'd gone too far.

"That's it," Abby said, her tone icy. "I came down here because you asked me to. I didn't create this mess, but I found a way out of it. I convinced Trace to go along with it, so you could keep the inn." Her scowl deepened. "And now you want to blame me because Trace put a condition on his terms for not foreclosing? Did you hear me ask for this? Didn't you hear me tell him no? Do you honestly think I want to be tied to Chesapeake Shores for who knows how long, when my life is in New York?" She shook her head. "It really is true—no good deed goes unpunished."

With that, she turned and walked away. Guilt flooded through Jess. Abby was right. She hadn't asked for this outcome. And maybe, just maybe, if Jess hadn't kept the fact that she was going to be dealing with Trace from her, Abby would have expected something like this and could have come up with a different strategy. As it was, she'd been blindsided, exactly as she'd warned Jess she didn't want to be. And Trace had clearly gone back on his promise not to let his personal feelings interfere with the bank's decision. No way had this been about anything except getting even, forcing Abby to remain in contact with him, just so he could... What? Humiliate her? Date her? She hadn't figured that part out yet.

Jess drew in a deep breath, then ran after her sister. "Abby, wait!"

Abby didn't even slow down. In fact, she was in such a fit of temper that she'd just stormed right past her rental car. Jess finally caught up with her in the next block.

"I'm sorry," she said. "It wasn't your fault. I know that. He just made me so furious."

"Join the club," Abby said dryly. "Why didn't you tell me Trace was working at the bank and that he was involved in this? You knew, didn't you?"

"Not when I called you," Jess swore to her. "He hasn't lived here in years. Right before you got here, he came by the inn to look things over. That's the first I knew about him being back in town, much less working at the bank. I was afraid if you knew, you'd bail on me."

Abby lifted a brow. "Don't you know me better than that?"

"I had no idea how deep the bad blood ran between the two of you. You never said why you broke up with him. Everyone in town knew you broke his heart. What no one seemed to know was why, or if maybe he'd broken yours, too. You never wanted to talk about it. Remember, I asked about a million times until you told me if I mentioned him one more time you were going to stop calling home?"

"You really were a pest," Abby said, but her lips quirked

at the reminder. "Okay, I suppose I understand why you didn't want to tell me I'd be dealing with a man I'd dumped."

"Let's not forget that I did try to tell you," Jess reminded her. "Dad arrived home, remember?"

Abby nodded. "I remember."

Jess extended an olive branch. "Want to go have that coffee, after all? I'll treat."

"With what?" Abby retorted. "Every penny you possess has to go into the inn. I'll treat."

Jess grinned. "Fine by me, but just so you know I'm ordering two eggs, bacon and waffles, too. My stomach was too queasy for me to eat breakfast before the meeting. Now the whole infuriating discussion has left me famished. How about you?"

"If Sally served liquor, I'd have a double shot of something, but since she doesn't, waffles sound good," Abby replied.

They were silent until they got to the café in the next block. When Abby reached out to open the door, Jess put her hand on top of her sister's, then waited until Abby met her gaze. "I really am sorry for what I said."

Abby sighed. "I know."

Jess studied her sister, then grinned. "Bet I know something you *don't* know."

"What's that?"

"Trace Riley still has the hots for you."

"You're crazy."

Jess shook her head. "Know something else? I'm almost a hundred percent certain it works both ways."

Abby drew herself up until her back was ramrod-straight, her expression regal and dismissive. "You could not be more wrong."

Jess wasn't impressed by her sister's performance. "We'll see."

In fact, watching the two of them trying to deny what was obvious to any observer, might be just about the only amusing part of this entire messed-up situation.

Abby was in no mood for the interrogation that awaited her at home. Gram and Mick were going to insist on hearing every detail about the meeting, and she wasn't sure she had the stomach for filling them in. Of course, it had occurred to her more than once that one sure way of extricating herself from the situation would be to let her father step in. Even Jess had mentioned that possibility, though she'd looked thoroughly defeated when she'd said it. Abby had known right then that she couldn't do it.

When she got to the house, she found Mick on the porch looking more frazzled than she could ever recall seeing him. There were unidentifiable stains on his shirt, his complexion was pale and he was leaning over the railing drawing in deep breaths.

"Dad?" she asked, alarmed. "Are you okay?"

Color flooded his cheeks.

"Dad, talk to me. What's wrong?"

"With me? Nothing. It's the girls. Both of them started complaining of headaches and looked glassy-eyed right after you left here this morning. I figured they didn't get enough sleep last night, but your grandmother seems to think they both have the measles. She said you didn't get them vaccinated."

"That's right—at the time the thinking was that the MMR vaccine might overwhelm an immature immune system, and there was even a theory it caused autism. I didn't want to take the risk. How are they now?"

"They're asleep, so I came out here for a couple of minutes."

"You probably ought to shower and change your clothes," she said, astounded by the obvious signs that he'd pitched in and helped. "I'll go up and take over from Gram. I'm sure she could use a break, too. I wish you'd called me."

"We agreed that the meeting at the bank was too important to be interrupted. Besides, we've both had plenty of experience with sick kids before. They weren't in any danger," he said defensively.

"I know that. Thanks for taking care of them."

"Part of the job," he said with a shrug. "You want to tell me how the meeting went?"

"I really want to check on the girls first."

He nodded. "Of course you do. You need anything, holler."

Inside, she was on her way upstairs when she met her grandmother coming down. "I'm so sorry you had to deal with all this. If I'd had any idea they'd even been exposed to measles, I wouldn't have brought them down here to visit."

"Pretty hard to keep children from getting sick when they're around other kids. Tricky with two of them, especially. It's a good thing your father was here. Did you see him?"

"He's on the porch. I think seeing them sick rattled him more than he wants to let on."

"No one wants to see someone they love in pain," Gram said. "Your father's no tougher than the rest of us on that score."

"Well, as soon as I've looked in on the girls, I'll come down and make you both some lunch or some tea, whatever you want."

Upstairs, she changed quickly into shorts and a blouse, then slipped into Connor's old room and noted the pile of dirty sheets beside the door. She'd take those downstairs with her and get them into the washer. Kneeling between the twin beds, she was able to put a hand on each girl's forehead. They were feverish, but not burning up. For the moment, they seemed to be resting comfortably, oblivious to the itching that was bound to set in soon given the spreading rash on their skin.

"Love you, babies," she whispered, then rose and picked

up the sheets and took them down to the laundry room off the kitchen. Gram was sitting at the kitchen table with a cup of tea, Mick across from her with a beer.

"They okay?" her father asked, his gaze filled with real concern.

"Sound asleep," she said. "How about lunch? Have either of you eaten?"

"I could eat a sandwich," Mick replied. "Ma, what about you?"

"Maybe some of that potato soup I made yesterday," she said. She started to stand up.

"Sit," Abby ordered. "I can fix a sandwich and warm up some soup. Dad, you want soup, too?"

"Sounds good. What about you?"

"Jess and I ate a late breakfast at Sally's after our meeting at the bank," she said, deliberately keeping her back to them as she prepared the meal. She was hoping that would discourage more questions, but of course, it didn't.

Once she'd served them, she sat at the table with her own cup of tea. "Okay, here's where things stand," she said, summarizing what had happened at the meeting.

Mick looked increasingly agitated. When she finished, he was on his feet and reaching for the phone. "I'll put an end to this right now."

Abby grabbed the phone from him. "No, Dad, leave it alone. Trace will get the bank to back off. They won't foreclose."

"And you're willing to stick around here the way he wants you to?" he demanded.

"I'll call my boss and work something out. A lot of what I do can be handled online and by phone or fax. Once Trace has had time to think about it, he'll see how absurd he's being."

"Not if it's his way of keeping you underfoot," Gram said, her expression knowing.

"What are you talking about?" Mick asked.

"Oh, for goodness' sakes, Mick, Trace always did have a soft spot for Abby. Surely you remember the way he was always hanging around here? It wasn't just to play catch with Kevin and Connor, I can tell you that." Her gaze met Abby's. "Maybe his feelings for you ran deeper than you ever said, am I right? I always had the feeling something happened between the two of you before you took off for New York."

Mick looked confused. "So what then? He's blackmailing her into staying here?"

"Don't make it sound ugly, Mick," Gram chastised. "Men in love will do a lot of crazy things to get their way."

"Trace is not in love with me," Abby protested. "Come on, Gram, we're focusing on the wrong thing here. All that matters is helping Jess keep the inn."

Now it was Mick's turn to give her a considering look. "If that's the only thing that matters, then why not let me call Lawrence Riley? Is it because you're happy with this turn of events?"

Abby frowned. "Of course I'm not happy with it, but I can handle it. I can handle Trace."

"Doesn't look that way from where I'm sitting," Gram said, though she seemed surprisingly pleased about it. "If you handled that man all that well, he wouldn't still be carrying a torch for you ten years later."

"Will you stop it?" Abby pleaded. "I'm going upstairs to check on the girls. Then I'm going to call the office and tell them I'll need to work from here for a few more days until I can get all this sorted out."

She hadn't gone far when she heard her father say, "Abby and Trace Riley? Why didn't I know about that?"

"Because you weren't around," Gram replied. "And you never listened to half of what I told you, especially if it concerned your daughters' love lives. If it had been up to you, none of them would have gone on a date before they hit thirty."

"You say that as if it would have been a bad thing," he grumbled.

Abby sighed. At least her father wasn't trying to interfere in Jess's business for the moment. Apparently he'd suddenly discovered that her life was a lot more fascinating. Unfortunately, who knew where that could lead? To nothing good, that's for sure. The only thing worse than having a disengaged father was having one who meddled.

5

Mick stood up from the kitchen table, his mind made up. He couldn't sit on the sidelines and let Trace Riley manipulate things in a way that was bound to cause problems between his daughters. He didn't care what Abby said about it.

"Where are you going?" his mother asked suspiciously.

"Thought I'd take a drive," he said evasively.

"Into town?"

"Possibly. Is that a crime?"

"It is if you're thinking of stopping at the bank. You heard Abby. She'll work this out."

He regarded her with frustration. "Ma, how can I let Trace Riley get away with this? You know how it's going to end. Jess will wind up resenting Abby the same way she'd resent me for interfering. I'm used to it. I can live with Jess's anger and with Abby's, for that matter, but I don't want anything to come between those girls. Abby's always looked after Jess, and Jess has always turned to her big sister. The bond those two share shouldn't be risked over a couple of loans I could guarantee with the stroke of a pen."

"Leave it alone, Mick. They'll figure things out for themselves," his mother said confidently. "You said it yourself, those two have always stuck together. There's no point in making things worse between you and Jess, which is exactly what would happen if you step in and try to fix things at the bank. Abby probably wouldn't be happy about it, either."

"You're asking me to sit back and do nothing," he grumbled. "That's not my nature."

She gave him a chiding look. "Did I ask you to do nothing? Seems to me that a man who's feeling restless could use a walk," she said, her expression sly. "The inn's only about a mile away. It wouldn't hurt to ask your daughter to give you a tour, show you all the improvements she's made."

Mick considered the idea. He had to admit he was curious about the work Jess was doing. Finally, though, he shook his head. "She'll just think I'm over there spying on her."

"Or maybe she'll think you're taking an interest in something that really matters to her. Just keep your opinions to yourself unless she asks for them." When he was about to reply, she held up a hand. "I know that goes against your nature, too, but for once just listen to me and follow my advice. I didn't spend twenty-five years married to the world's most stubborn man and raise three impossible boys without learning a thing or two about biding my time."

"Take a walk. Tour the inn. Keep my mouth shut," he mimicked. "Do I have that right?"

She gave him a satisfied smile. "I think that sums it up. I'm going up to take a nap. I hate to admit it, but taking care of those girls this morning just about wore me out."

Mick regarded her with concern. "Are you okay? Should I call your doctor?"

"Heavens, no. I'm just a little tired. Spend the afternoon with Jess. That's where you're needed."

"Okay, then," he said, bending down to press a kiss to her brow. "If you need anything, or the girls do, I'll have my cell phone with me."

"We'll be fine. Just focus on mending fences with Jess."

There was a breeze blowing in off the bay as he set out on his walk. It kept the air cool, despite the warmth of the sun. Since it was a weekday there were only a handful of pleasure boats bobbing on the water. He spotted a couple of watermen checking their crab pots for needed repairs, but most of them had returned to dock by this time of the day, especially this early in the season. In another few weeks, they'd be out before dawn, chugging along, trying to make a living from the dwindling supply of crabs, croakers and rockfish in these beautiful but increasingly polluted waters.

It made him sick the way people took the bay for granted. Thank God for people like his brother Thomas. They might have mixed like oil and water when they'd tried to work together, but Mick admired the way Tom fought for the environment, trying to protect the bay's natural resources. Mick had tried to build Chesapeake Shores responsibly, but even with all of his best efforts, he hadn't been able to meet his brother's high standards. And neither of them had been much good at compromise, though eventually they'd hammered out a plan they could both live with.

He'd left more open spaces than he'd initially planned, steered well away from the wetlands and tried not to remove any trees that didn't absolutely have to go. He'd landscaped with plants from a very specific list his brother had compiled for him. If Tom had had his way, not a single tree would have been felled and the dilapidated general store once owned by some O'Brien ancestor or another would have become the centerpiece of downtown. Mick had agreed to renovate the family's original farmhouse and to save an old structure that had doubled as a school and church, but that's where he'd drawn the line.

He was still thinking of the lively shouting matches

they'd had over all that when he rounded the final curve in the road and saw the inn for the first time since Jess had bought it. He was taken aback by how good it looked. She'd brought back its inviting facade, almost as if she remembered how welcoming it had originally looked when he and Jeff had first built it. But Jess had only been a baby back then. How had she remembered it so clearly? The Pattersons certainly hadn't kept it looking like that in years. The yard was shaded by ancient oaks, and there were even a few weeping willows far enough from the house that they wouldn't mess with the water pipes. The inn had gotten its name from a lone eagle that his brother had spotted during construction. Since then, there were more in the region, including a pair that took up residence in the highest branches overlooking the bay and the inn.

"Dad!"

He heard the surprise in Jess's voice, then spotted her sitting on the porch with a glass of iced tea, her bare feet propped up on the railing. "Hey, Jess," he greeted her, trying to keep his tone casual. "I was out for a walk after lunch and found myself heading in this direction."

"Why?" she asked, radiating suspicion.

"I just wanted to see what you've done with the place," he admitted, sitting down next to her. He glanced sideways, saw the tension in her shoulders and inquired, "Any more of that tea?"

She hesitated, looking as if she weren't all that happy about the prospect of spending time with him. Then she stood, ingrained hospitality winning out over her reservations. "Sure. I'll be right back with some."

Mick sighed after she'd gone. She wasn't going to make this easy for him, he concluded. Then, again, why should she? Ma was right about one thing. He'd always criticized her.

Early on, he'd excused it, thinking he'd been as tough on all his kids. But then, when they'd found out that Jess had a relatively mild case of ADD, he hadn't been able to stop himself from continuing with the same pattern, as if he'd thought she could change her behavior if she wanted to badly enough, even without the medication that doctors thought she probably didn't need. Mick sighed, wondering if they shouldn't have revisited that. Maybe she *had* needed it.

Because he'd recognized that his attitude wasn't helping, he'd always assumed she was probably happier when he was away, but maybe that hadn't been true. Maybe she'd felt abandoned, just as his mother had suggested. He vowed to try a different approach.

When Jess returned with his glass of tea, he lifted it in a toast. "Congratulations, Jess! You've done a fine job here. It hasn't looked this good since the day Jeff and I sold it to the Pattersons."

"They really did let it fall apart," she said. "But thanks to you, it had good bones. Most of what I've had to do is cosmetic."

"I'd like to see what you've done inside, if you have time to show me around."

She looked surprised by that. "Really?"

"Why not? I'm here. Unless you don't have time."

"No, come on," she said, though she seemed to be struggling to balance her eagerness to show off what she'd accomplished with her fear of his reaction. "I can at least take time for the fifty-cent tour."

Mick followed her inside, reminding himself to keep all of his comments positive and superficial, no matter how badly he wanted to give advice. By the time they'd reached the third floor, though, he realized that his mental warning had been unnecessary. She was doing a great job without any input from him. She had her uncle Jeff's intuitive sense of style. Mick could design a structure that would last, a development that could become a community, but it was Jeff who'd given each home its individual character.

"I'm impressed," he said when they'd toured all of the rooms, including the kitchen where every stainless-steel surface gleamed. The old appliances looked a little time-worn by contrast. "You really do have a knack for this, Jess."

To his surprise, she blinked back tears. "Thanks," she murmured, then turned away, busying herself by pouring more tea.

He rested a hand on her shoulder. "I'm really proud of you."

She turned slowly, her eyes welling up with tears. "You've never, ever said that to me before."

"Of course—"

Her jaw set stubbornly. "No, Dad, you haven't."

"Then I'm sorry. This is certainly not the first time it's been true."

The smile that broke slowly across her face made his heart ache. How had he not seen how much she needed a simple thing like him voicing his approval? He vowed to be more generous with his praise. Right now, though, he had another issue that needed to be dealt with, and he was wise enough to know he had to tread cautiously, even if that wasn't his usual blunt style. Still, he hesitated about bringing up the meeting at the bank and ruining this moment of hard-earned peace with his youngest child.

In the end, because the outcome of that meeting still stuck in his craw, he couldn't stop himself. "Jess, how do you feel about what happened at the bank?"

She frowned and backed away, ending their rapport and literally putting distance back between them. "I'm not happy about it, but I guess I see Trace's point. Abby's better at finances than I am, and it's not like she's going to take the inn away from me. She'll just stay involved until I'm on a solid financial footing." She met his gaze, worry in her eyes. "Why? Did she say something? She's not going to back out, is she?"

"No, she's determined to see this through. I just wanted to be sure it wasn't going to cause problems between you, because I could call Lawrence Riley and put an end to Trace's plan."

"How?"

"I'll cosign your notes."

"Absolutely not," she said at once. "I don't want you to bail me out."

"It wouldn't be a bailout. It would just make me your backup, so your sister could get back to her life. It's my signature on a few papers. That's it."

She gave him a wry look. "That wouldn't be it, Dad, and you know it. You'd think your signature entitled you to make a few suggestions and the next thing you know you'd be running things."

"I won't even be around," he protested. "I'll be heading back to California in a few more days. Come on, Jess. Let me do this for you."

"Why are you pushing so hard for this?"

"Because you're my daughter. I want to help out with something that matters to you. You've finally found the one thing you really seem to care about. I don't want that taken away from you."

"Abby will see to that, Dad. She's always been there for me. And having her here again, that'll be great for both of us. Maybe she'll actually learn how to relax. And it's going to be wonderful for Caitlyn and Carrie, too. This will be a win-win, Dad. I'm sure of it."

He sighed. "I hope so."

"Look, I appreciate the offer. I really do, but it's better this way. Abby won't boss me around."

Mick gave her a disbelieving look. "Have you met your sister? She grew up bossing people around."

Jess laughed. "True, but she doesn't scare me."

"And I do?"

"More than you know," she admitted.

That was another thing he'd have to live with and figure out how to change.

"Okay, then, I'll back off," he said, brushing a strand of hair back from her cheek. "But if things get tense between you two, remember that the offer's on the table. I don't want anything to come between you and Abby, okay? Promise me you'll call me if you think that could happen."

"I will," she said. "I'm glad you came by."

"Me, too. Is there anything else I can do for you? I'm still halfway decent with a paintbrush. I could help with the last of those rooms upstairs."

He saw her struggling with herself. She was too bloody stubborn to admit she could use any help at all, even from him. Maybe *especially* from him. He leaned down and kissed her cheek. "Never mind. I know you want to do every single thing yourself. But that offer's on the table, too, if you change your mind."

"Thanks for understanding, Dad." To his surprise, she stood on tiptoe and kissed him. "Love you."

"Right back at you," he said. "You coming over for dinner tonight?"

"I might."

"I should warn you that Caitlyn and Carrie have the measles."

"Oh, my gosh, Abby must be beside herself."

"She has Gram and me for backup."

"Then you all have more than enough to do. I'll skip dinner, but call me if any of you need anything."

"Right," he said. He was halfway down the walk when he called back, "By the way, I noticed that rhododendron in back of the porch could use trimming."

To his surprise, Jess laughed. "I knew it. I knew you couldn't get away from here without finding at least one thing to criticize."

He silently cursed himself for speaking up. He tried to brush off the comment. "Hey, it's only a bush. No big deal."

Jess shook her head, her lips still twitching with amusement. "If you want to, bring your clippers over tomorrow and trim it yourself."

It was part invitation, part challenge, but Mick felt as if his daughter had just opened the door a tiny crack to a real relationship. Now he just had to wiggle through without causing a ruckus that would send them back to square one.

Trace was feeling very pleased with himself over his strategy to keep Abby around where he could get to know her again. He had no idea what was going on in her life these days, but he'd noted the lack of a ring on her left hand about two seconds after he'd realized she was the woman in his office. Years ago he'd seen her with another man, seen an engagement ring on her finger, in fact, but that ring had been nowhere in sight yesterday. He had no idea why this mattered so much to him, but it did. Maybe he just wanted a chance to even the score, to get her all tied up in knots so he could abandon her the way she'd walked out on him. The prospect of payback did have a certain sweetness to it.

Then again, if he'd learned nothing else in that meeting, he'd discovered that she was a woman who could hold her own. She'd come in there prepared for battle and she'd handed over a sound financial proposal to back up her position. He wondered if Jess had any idea how lucky she was to have someone with that much business savvy in her corner.

Convincing the board to hold off on the foreclosure and to give the new management a chance to get the inn on solid ground had been relatively easy. Not that he intended to let Abby know that. He wanted her to be grateful that he'd fought the good fight on her sister's behalf.

He walked into the Chesapeake Shores Yacht Club promptly at twelve-fifteen, expecting to find Abby waiting for him. He'd deliberately chosen the yacht club where they'd be seen by the town's movers and shakers. Abby had always hated its pretentious atmosphere, which meant he'd have the upper hand.

A scan of the dining room showed she was nowhere in sight. Had she bailed on him, after all? The possibility rankled.

"Hey, Liz," he greeted the hostess, who'd been in his high school class. "Any sign of Abby O'Brien?"

"It's Abby Winters now," she corrected him. "She called and said she was running late. Something about the twins getting sick. She'll be here as soon as she can get here. She said to call her if you don't feel like waiting."

Trace winced at the mention of a married name and nearly groaned at the mention of twins. Maybe he'd gotten it all wrong after all. Maybe Abby wasn't available. Maybe that was why she was so anxious to get back to New York. If so, he'd just gone out on a limb for nothing. Well, not for nothing. The inn did deserve a chance to make it, but he couldn't deny that he'd had his own agenda.

He took the slip of paper that Liz held out with Abby's number written on it. After dialing, he jotted down a takeout order for Liz as he waited for Abby to pick up. "Ask the kitchen to put a rush on this, would you?" he asked Liz, just as Abby finally answered. She sounded completely frazzled.

"Good, you're still there," he said, then announced, "I've ordered takeout. I'm on my way over."

"Bad idea, Trace," she protested. "I can be there in twenty minutes."

"Which means I can just as easily be *there* in twenty minutes," he reminded her.

"But it's a little chaotic over here."

"Then you need to stay put," he said. "I've ordered the food. It'll be ready in a few minutes and I'll head on over. Tell your grandmother not to fix lunch. There's plenty for her, too."

"Why are you being so nice?"

"Because I'm a nice guy."

"A nice guy wouldn't be blackmailing me into staying in Chesapeake Shores."

"I prefer to see it as protecting the bank's investment," he countered. "See you soon."

Actually he was delighted by this turn of events. Ever since he'd seen Abby again, he'd wanted to check out the lay of the land, so to speak. What better way than to survey it for himself?

The last person Trace expected to find waiting for him when he reached Abby's was her father. Mick was sitting on the top step, his expression forbidding, his seemingly deliberate positioning on that step pretty much blocking Trace's path.

"Heard you were coming over," Mick said, his tone not the least bit welcoming.

Trace held up the takeout bags. "I have a meeting with Abby. I brought lunch."

Mick patted the step beside him. "Maybe you should sit down so you and I can have a talk before you get together with Abby."

Just as Mick uttered the words, the screen door banged

open. "Trace, you're here!" Abby said with forced gaiety. "Come on inside."

Mick scowled. "Trace and I were about to have a chat."

Abby scowled at her father. "It can wait," she said firmly.

Trace watched with interest, wondering how the test of wills would play out. To his amusement, it was Mick who finally backed down. He stood up and moved out of the way.

"Guess I'll go over to the inn and deal with that overgrown rhododendron," he muttered, picking up a pair of hedge clippers.

Abby faltered. "Does Jess know you're coming?"

"It was her idea," Mick assured her.

"Then it sounds like a great idea," Abby enthused.

After watching Mick amble away, Trace turned to Abby. "Why do I have the feeling that you just saved me?"

"Because I did. He's not happy about this little scheme of yours."

"It's not a scheme. It makes perfect financial sense," he reiterated.

"Blah-blah-blah," she said. "We both know otherwise."

Trace met her gaze and held it. "Do you really think I'd use Jess's loan as a way to, what, get even with you? I thought we'd settled that the other day."

"Not to my satisfaction," she told him. "From what I hear, you're trapped here for at least six months. Why not make my life miserable by trapping me here, too?"

"I'm not trapped. I made a deal with my father. This is a six-month trial run. Of course, I know the outcome will mean I leave and Laila will get the job she should have had all along, but my father's optimistic things will work out differently."

"Would you be here working at the bank if your dad hadn't forced you into it?"

"He didn't force me into it," Trace said. "I agreed mostly to prove a point."

"What point?"

"That my sister should be the one working there."

She smiled. "By doing what? Failing miserably?"

"Not miserably," he said. "Just look at the deal I struck with you. I'd say I proved myself with that."

"We're not going to agree on what's going on here, are we?"

He shrugged. "Probably not."

"Then let's have lunch. Gram's set the dining room table. She seems to think this meeting requires more formality, being strictly business and all."

Trace chuckled. "Is she as ticked at me as your dad is?"

"Pretty much."

"Then this should be fun," Trace said, holding the door, then following her inside.

To Abby's regret, Gram was nowhere in sight when they reached the dining room, and the table had only been set for two. Trace grinned when he saw it.

"Now, isn't this an interesting turn of events?" he murmured. "Could it be that your grandmother's matchmaking?"

"Absolutely not!" Abby said fiercely.

"Because you're married? At least I assume with kids, there must be a husband in the picture."

"There was," she admitted, regretting the divorce for a fleeting moment, if only because she sensed the existence of a husband would get that wicked gleam out of Trace's eyes.

"Separated? Divorced?" he asked, as he removed containers of chopped salad from the bags he'd brought. Without asking, he went about dishing the salad onto the formal, gold-trimmed china Gram had put on the table.

"Divorced," she said, gritting her teeth against the personal turn the conversation was taking. "Look, we're here to discuss the inn, not my life."

"Just catching up," he said, as he reached into a second bag and removed a container of what appeared to be the yacht club's decadent chocolate mousse, one of Abby's all-time favorite desserts. Sometimes that mousse had been the only way Trace or her family could lure her into that stuffy atmosphere. They'd even ladled an extra dollop of whipped cream onto the top, just the way she liked it.

She frowned as he set it in front of her place. How had he remembered that? And why had he bothered? Was this just another way to get to her, to throw her off-kilter right before he hit her with some other blow she wasn't expecting?

She waited warily until he sat down, then asked, "What's going on here, Trace?"

He regarded her innocently. "We were supposed to meet over lunch. I brought lunch. I don't see anything sinister in that. In fact, I thought I was being downright considerate given that your kids are sick. Twins, right? I think that's what Liz said."

"Carrie and Caitlyn," she said tightly, still not entirely trusting all this thoughtfulness. "They came down with the measles yesterday. In fact, they should be waking up soon from their naps, so we need to get our business out of the way. Did the board meet?"

"They did."

"Don't make me drag this out of you. Just tell me what they decided."

"Everything remains in place, as long as you're on board."

Abby wasn't sure why she'd been hoping for a reprieve. Maybe she'd thought that collectively the board might see through Trace's scheme and overrule him. Obviously she hadn't taken into account his persuasiveness or his determination.

Swallowing her desire to start another argument she

wouldn't win, she leveled a look at him. "How do you see this working? I do have a career, Trace, and it's in New York. I can easily oversee all the expenditures from there, stay on top of payments and so on."

He shook his head. "Not good enough. Come on, Abby, you know Jess. The second your back is turned, she'll go right back to her impulsive spending, and you'll be scrambling to cover for her."

She regarded him earnestly. "I'll make sure that doesn't happen. You have my word on it."

"Not good enough."

She bristled at that. "Excuse me?"

"I've had some experience with how unreliable your word is, remember?"

"That's ridiculous. It's another situation entirely. And besides, I never gave you my word about anything ten years ago."

"You told me you loved me. I took you seriously."

"I did love you," she said, frustrated by his determination to use old news to manipulate the present.

"And yet you vanished without so much as a goodbye, much less an explanation. I'm not taking any chances on that happening again, not until the bank feels comfortable that these loans are protected."

"You mean until *you* feel comfortable," she said. "It has nothing to do with what anyone at the bank needs. There's plenty of cash in the inn's account to cover expenses, and you know it. This is payback, pure and simple, Trace, and I resent it. You're taking out our drama, if you want to call it that, on my sister. You know perfectly well she'll pay back every penny of those loans. So does the bank. This is about you and me."

"Is it really?" he said, his expression innocent.

"I had no idea you could be so vindictive and hateful."

"Which just goes to prove that we never really knew each

other at all, because I didn't have any idea you were capable of being cruel and a coward."

His words cut right through her. She knew she deserved them, because that was exactly what she had been, cruel and cowardly. That didn't make it any easier to hear them or to have them coming back to haunt her all these years later.

She regarded him with bewilderment. "If you think so little of me, why on earth do you want me around here now?"

"Because you were always the most intriguing, infuriating person in Chesapeake Shores," he said. "I figure your presence will keep the next few months from being boring."

"So, what—I'm the mouse and you're the big bad cat who gets to toy with me just for entertainment?"

"Something like that."

She stood up, shaking with indignation. "You're despicable," she said, grabbing the crystal pitcher filled with ice water.

His gaze narrowed. "You really don't want to do that," he warned.

"Oh, but I do," she countered, dumping the contents over his head. She gave him a considering look as he sat there drenched, his expression startled. Then she smiled in satisfaction. "Yep, that was exactly what I wanted to do."

Then she whirled around and went upstairs to check on the girls. Pleased with her little demonstration of temper, she was taken aback when she heard his laughter echoing after her.

She met Gram in the hallway.

"What's going on?" her grandmother asked.

"I just dumped a pitcher of water over Trace's head."

Her grandmother's eyes twinkled, but she fought to contain a grin. "Was that wise?"

Abby sighed. "Probably not, but it felt darn good."

Thinking of how she—and perhaps even Jess—were likely to pay for it, though, made her just the tiniest bit nervous.

6

Making himself at home, Trace wandered into the kitchen, found a dishtowel to mop up his face and sop some of the water from his shirt, then took another towel into the dining room to clean up the mess there. He regarded the dish of chocolate mousse with regret. It hadn't exactly turned out to be the peace offering he'd intended it to be.

"Chocolate mousse? Abby's favorite," Nell O'Brien noted as she walked into the dining room and spotted it in his hand. "Nice touch, though I imagine suggesting the yacht club for your meeting was your idea of a power play. You know perfectly well she hates that place."

He winced at the accuracy of her comment. "None of it worked out quite the way I'd planned," he commented wryly.

"I don't suppose she poured that pitcher of water over your head because you brought her dessert," she said.

"No, I believe it had more to do with a few unflattering things I said to her."

She shook her head. "You two act like you're six and still on the playground. Go in the kitchen and take off your shirt. I'll throw it into the dryer, and then maybe I'll give you a few tips on handling my granddaughter."

Trace frowned at her, not entirely trusting the seemingly

magnanimous offer. Nell hadn't been one of his biggest fans ten years ago. He couldn't imagine why that would suddenly change.

"Why would you do that?" he asked.

"Because it's obvious to me that the two of you will manage to mess it up for a second time, if you're left to your own devices," she said with more than a touch of impatience. "And I'd like to see my granddaughter happy."

"What is it you think we're going to mess up?" Trace asked, though he knew she wasn't talking about their new and mostly awkward business relationship.

She merely rolled her eyes, as if she found the question ridiculous, the answer obvious. "Go," she ordered.

Trace left, stripping off his shirt as he went. Nell carried in a tray filled with the remains of their aborted lunch and set it on the counter, then took the shirt from him and tossed it into the dryer.

"Shall we have a cup of tea while we wait?" she asked, not waiting for his reply as she put cups on the table and started pouring.

Trace was smart enough not to object to the ritual. He'd learned years ago that Abby's grandmother marched to her own drummer and it was best to go along. Those who didn't want to do that at least had the good sense to stay out of her way.

"That should warm you up," she said, as if it weren't nearly eighty degrees outside and even warmer in the kitchen, despite the overhead fan circulating the air. When she'd stirred a tiny bit of sugar into her own tea, she leveled a look at him. "What do you want from Abby?"

"I want her to keep the renovations at the inn moving along on schedule and to keep her sister on budget," he said without hesitation.

"Nonsense," she said. "That's your excuse. What you

want is another chance with her. At least be honest with yourself about that much."

Trace frowned at her assessment. He didn't want Abby back. He wanted to retaliate for the way she'd treated him, wanted to make her suffer the way he'd suffered, wanted to turn her life inside out, the way his had been when she'd walked off without a word of explanation.

"You're wrong," he said flatly. She had to be. Otherwise, it would mean he was a glutton for punishment.

"Am I?" she responded. "Then this is about revenge for something that happened ten years ago? You certainly do know how to hold a grudge, don't you?"

He didn't like hearing the truth, not from a woman who'd always been kind to him, if not entirely approving of his relationship with Abby. "I wouldn't put it exactly that way."

"Then how would you put it?" she inquired, her tone mild. "You say it's not about wanting her and it's not about revenge. I say it has nothing to do with securing the bank's loan on the inn. What does that leave?"

Trace wanted to squirm exactly the way he had years ago when she'd asked him what his intentions were toward her granddaughter. He'd been honest then. He'd admitted he wanted to marry Abby. He simply hadn't been willing to set a timetable for it. He'd seen the disappointment in her eyes, but he hadn't been willing to commit to something that life-altering, not when his goals for himself kept shifting as he tried to find solid footing for fighting his father and going after his own career.

To Nell O'Brien's credit she hadn't kicked him out or banished him from Abby's life. She'd left the two of them to figure things out on their own, but he'd sensed her displeasure every single time they'd crossed paths after that. He'd always wondered if that unspoken disapproval from the woman she respected most in the world had anything to do with Abby's abrupt departure.

"You used to have an answer for everything right on the tip of your tongue," she said to him when he remained silent.

"I've learned that answers aren't always simple and that the first ones that come to mind may not be the right ones," he told her.

"You're not being tested. There's not a right or wrong answer, just the truth."

He gave her a wry look. "Maybe that's why I'm having so much trouble with it. I'm not sure I know the truth."

She nodded, looking surprisingly satisfied. "Now we're getting somewhere. It takes a certain amount of maturity to realize that things aren't always black and white. Want to know what I think?"

He sat back and grinned, happy to be off the hot seat, if nothing else. "By all means."

"I think you're still crazy in love with Abby, just the way you were all through high school and college. I also think you're still angry and hurt about the way she left. What I don't understand, what I never understood, was why you didn't fight harder for her back then."

Trace thought back to those first humiliating days and weeks after she'd left town. He'd just turned twenty-two. He was still operating more on hormones than sense. He was battling with his father over his future, determined to strike out on his own with his design work. Abby's abandonment when he'd needed her support the most had been a crushing blow. Somehow he'd lumped that in with his father's attitude and concluded she had no more faith in his artistic talent than Lawrence Riley did.

Later, when the pain was still eating at him, he'd discovered the blow had truly been to his heart, not just his ego.

That's when he'd realized that pride didn't matter in the end. All that mattered was finding her and getting her back.

"I went after her," he said eventually. It was something only his sister knew. He'd figured the fewer people who knew about it, the less embarrassment he'd suffer if Abby ditched him for a second time. It wasn't surprising then that Nell looked shocked.

"I never knew about that," she said. "Abby never mentioned it."

"She didn't know about it, either," he admitted. "My timing was lousy. I waited too long. Laila told me where she was. She thought of Abby as a big sister. They stayed in touch. I followed Abby to New York. Instead of going straight to her, I spent months finding work to be a hundred percent sure I could support her. Then I went down to Wall Street one day, determined to set things right or at least to take a stab at picking up where we'd left off."

"And what happened?"

"Abby walked out of this fancy skyscraper, arm in arm with a guy in an Armani suit, a diamond the size of a rock on her left hand. I'd gotten my life together, gotten my career off the ground, but I couldn't compete with that."

"You were scared off by a fancy suit and a piece of jewelry?" she asked, regarding him with disappointment for the second time in all the years he'd known her.

He shook his head. "No, what sent me away was the expression of total happiness on Abby's face, the love I saw shining in her eyes when she looked at him. I knew that look. I knew what it meant. I couldn't delude myself anymore that I could fix things. Abby had moved on."

She regarded him with sympathy. "I'm sorry."

"It was my own fault, because you're a hundred percent right about one thing. I should have fought harder, and I should have done it a whole lot sooner."

"If you know that, why are you taking it out on Abby because things didn't work out?"

"I'm not taking it out on her," he swore. "In my stupid, most likely misguided way, I'm fighting for a second chance."

"By telling her she was cruel and cowardly?" she asked incredulously. "I was on my way downstairs and I heard what you said to her."

He regarded her with a chagrined expression. "That may have been a mistake."

"Really? Do you think so?"

Her sarcasm made him wince. "You have to admit it got her attention," he said defensively.

"So it did," she acknowledged. "Call me crazy, but wouldn't you rather have her kissing you than dumping water over your head?"

Before Trace could reply, Abby walked into the kitchen and stared at her grandmother with an indignant expression. "Are you giving him advice about me?"

"Somebody certainly needs to," her grandmother retorted without batting an eye. "If you'll excuse me, though, I think I'll go outside and work a bit in the garden. My tomato plants can use the attention."

"Gram," Abby said in a tone that had her grandmother hesitating in midstride. "From here on out let me deal with Trace, okay?"

"Suits me," she said, an unrepentant twinkle in her eyes. "From now on, though, just try doing it in a way that doesn't require one of you to wind up stripping off clothes in order to avoid pneumonia."

If Abby didn't adore her grandmother, it would have been incredibly tempting to throw something at her after she'd made that glib remark, then sashayed off to leave Abby alone with Trace and his rock-hard abs and bare shoulders. She marched into the laundry room, snatched his still-damp shirt from the dryer and tossed it at him.

"Put this on and go," she ordered.

"Not just yet," he said, sitting right where he was, though he did put the shirt back on.

Worn to a frazzle by trying to straighten out her sister's financial mess and by the twins, who were starting to feel just well enough to be demanding and impossible, Abby didn't think she could cope with Trace, too. "Go," she repeated. "I really don't have time for this."

Just then Carrie and Caitlyn slipped into the kitchen, their feet bare, their strawberry-blond hair a tangled mess, and enough spots on their sweet faces to make them look pitiful.

"Mommy, can we have ice cream?" Caitlyn pleaded, before catching sight of Trace. "Who're you?"

"This is Mr. Riley," Abby said tightly. "My daughters, Caitlyn and Carrie." She gestured to them in turn, though it was likely a wasted effort. No one meeting them at first could tell them apart.

If she expected the sight of them to send him fleeing, he proved her wrong. Instead, he grinned and cupped Caitlyn's chin, turning her head this way and that as if in admiration. "Quite a display you've got going on there," he said, then turned to Carrie. "You, too. Have you counted to see which one has the most spots?"

Carrie looked vaguely intrigued by the idea. "Why? Would the winner get a prize?"

"Absolutely," Trace said. "All the ice cream you can eat at Sally's once you're well."

Both girls regarded him with wide eyes. "Really?"

He nodded. "That's what I got when I had more spots than my sister when I was about your age and we both got chicken pox at the same time."

Caitlyn's expression turned serious. "I don't think Mommy would let us eat as much ice cream as we want."

Trace looked up at Abby with an appealing smile. "Come on, Mom. There should be some reward after you've been sick."

"Are you suggesting that being well again isn't reward enough?" Abby found herself asking, feigning a stern demeanor.

Trace looked at the twins. "I say no. What about you girls? Don't you think there should be a prize?"

"Yes," they shouted in unison.

Abby couldn't help laughing at their enthusiasm. "Okay, ice cream for the winner when you're well. For now, though, you get juice. After you've finished that, I want you to go back upstairs, count those spots and then take a nap."

"But we've been sleeping and sleeping," Carrie argued. "We're not tired anymore. And we itch too much."

Caitlyn nodded. "We really, really itch."

Abby had foreseen this problem. "Okay, I'll be right up and you can get into the tub. I have something that will soothe the itching."

Caitlyn turned to Trace. "Can you come, too?"

Abby stepped in before he could reply. "Mr. Riley doesn't have time to help you two take a bath. Besides, that's not something you ask strangers to do."

"But he's not a stranger," Caitlyn replied, looking puzzled. "He's your friend."

"That's exactly right," Trace said, giving Abby a pointed look. "Your mom and I are very old friends. But she is right about one thing, I do need to go back to work."

"But when we're well, you'll come with us to have ice cream, won't you?" Caitlyn asked.

Carrie nodded. "To make sure we get all we can eat."

"That's a date," he said, his gaze locked with Abby's in a way that made her toes curl. "It was very nice to meet you,

Caitlyn." His gaze went straight to the right girl. He then turned to her sister. "You, too, Carrie. I hope to see you both again soon."

How had he been able to immediately tell them apart? Abby wondered in amazement. He'd accomplished it despite the matching nightgowns, identical mussed hairstyles and spotty faces. How had he picked up so quickly on the personality differences—Caitlyn's somber reflectiveness and Carrie's feistiness—that set them apart? Obviously he'd given them his full attention, something few adults bothered to do.

"See you soon, girls," he said as he headed for the back door.

Abby was about to release a sigh of relief, when he paused beside her and dropped a deliberate kiss on her forehead. "Bye, Mom."

The twins giggled appreciatively, but Abby was left speechless. Trace knew he'd gotten to her, too. His expression was smug as he left, then waved jauntily from the back steps.

"Can we have ice cream at Sally's tomorrow?" Caitlyn pleaded. "We'll be all better by then."

"Yeah," Carrie echoed. "And we want to see Mr. Riley again. He's nice."

Abby wanted to tell them not to trust all that sweetness and charm, but how could she? He had been nice to the twins. And if she didn't trust anything else about Trace, she knew with absolute certainty that he would never intentionally hurt her daughters.

When Trace got back to the bank, Mariah called out to him as he was en route to his office. "Your father wants to see you."

Reluctantly, Trace turned in that direction. He paused at Mariah's desk and leaned down. "What kind of mood is he in?" he asked in an exaggerated whisper. "Warpath? Or peacekeeping?"

She laughed. "I think you're safe enough. Go on in."

When he entered, his father looked up from the financial paper he was reading, then beamed at him. "There you are. Where have you been?"

"I had a business meeting."

"With Abby O'Brien?"

"Abby Winters," Trace corrected. "But yes. I was meeting with her."

His father seemed to take a closer look at him. "Are you sure this was about business? And why is your shirt wet? She didn't shove you in the bay, did she?"

Trace didn't intend to discuss the whole incident with the pitcher of water with his father. "What did you want to talk to me about?"

"I wanted to make sure she agreed to run things for Jessica. These loans could go bad very quickly if we don't stay on top of this."

"I assure you I intend to keep a very close eye on the situation," Trace said.

His father gave a nod of satisfaction. "I thought you might." He waved him off. "That's all. You can get back to work now. I believe Raymond has some paperwork he wants you to take a look at."

"I'll check with him," Trace promised. "Then I have an appointment I need to get to."

"Bank business?"

"No, I'm looking at a couple of places to rent."

He almost laughed at his father's reaction. He looked as if he couldn't quite decide whether to be irritated that Trace might be moving out of the house or overjoyed that he might be planning to stay around Chesapeake Shores after all.

"Why rent?" he asked eventually. "Buying makes more sense."

"Not for six months," Trace said firmly.

"You won't find a short-term lease anywhere in town," his father protested. "You might as well stay put with your mother and me."

"Actually I already have a few possibilities. And it'll be better if I'm on my own. Sometimes I work on my design projects until late at night—"

"What design projects?" his father demanded. "You're working for the bank now and it's going to require your full attention."

"It won't require twenty-four hours a day," Trace said evenly, determined to stick to his point and not get drawn into a fight with his father over his freelance work. "And when I work, I have things strewn all over the place. It would make Mother crazy, to say nothing of how I'd react if the maid came through and tried to tidy things up for me."

"I see your point," his father said. "Okay then, suit yourself."

Trace intended to do exactly that. With luck, he'd be in his own place by the weekend. He'd have his studio set up in no time and be back at work on the two assignments he'd just accepted by the first of next week. Between those jobs and his plans for frequent contact with Abby, the next six months should fly by.

Abby had finally gotten the twins down for another nap, checked on all her e-mails from work and responded to them and was now on the porch with a glass of iced tea, when Jess's car came flying up the driveway and screeched to a halt, kicking up dust. As soon as Jess emerged, it was evident she was in a really lousy mood.

"Are you behind this?" she demanded, tossing a handful of credit card pieces at Abby.

Abby regarded her blankly even as she gathered up the bits of plastic. Whoever had cut it up had been thorough.

"What happened?" she asked, keeping her voice calm if only to counter Jess's near-hysteria.

"What does it look like?" Jess said, pacing back and forth in front of her. Steam was practically rising all around her. "My credit card was rejected when I went to buy more paint. Not only was it turned down, but it was cut up right in front of my eyes with a whole line of people watching. I've never been more humiliated in my entire life. I swear if you're behind this, I'm never speaking to you again."

"Don't look at me," Abby told her. "I've had zero contact with any of your credit card companies."

"You swear it?"

"Of course I swear it," Abby said, bristling. "When have I ever lied to you?"

Jess's expression turned apologetic. "Sorry. It was just so awful and I couldn't imagine how else it could have happened. And of course, the store won't tell you anything."

"Have you called your credit card company?"

"Not yet."

"So rather than going to the people who could actually tell you what's going on, you came right over here to yell at me?" Abby asked, exasperated.

Jess winced. "Something like that. I'll call them as soon as I get back to the inn."

"Did you get your paint?"

"No, I left it there. I was too embarrassed to try a different credit card. I was afraid they'd all been cut off."

"You told me the other day you hadn't maxed any of them out," Abby reminded her.

"I haven't," Jess assured her.

"And you've been paying the bills on time?"

"Sure," Jess said at once, then frowned. "At least I think so. You know how busy I've been."

Abby groaned. She also knew how easily distracted Jess could be when it came to things she wasn't interested in doing, like paying bills. This was the ADD effect. Though Jess's case had improved some with age, her ability to focus was still unpredictable at best. Since she mostly functioned at an acceptable level, her doctors had never recommended that she take medication, at least not as far as Abby knew. It would be just like Jess, though, to refuse to take pills of any kind.

"I'll drive over later and we'll go through all the papers that have piled up on your desk, see if maybe some bills got overlooked," Abby told her. "I'm sure we can straighten this out."

Jess sighed and sank down onto the chair beside her. "I just keep messing up. How can you stand to keep bailing me out?"

The truth was that Abby didn't know if she could do it for the long haul, not without losing her patience entirely. What she needed to focus on were her sister's skills, not her flaws, then figure out a way to compensate for the things Jess was least likely to remember on her own. Hiring a bookkeeper was the most obvious solution, but there was no room in the budget for that, at least not yet. The bookkeeping job was evidently going to fall to her.

"What have you been doing today?" Jess asked, grabbing Abby's glass of tea and finishing it off.

"Trying to keep the twins from going stir-crazy and taking Gram and me with them, having lunch and then a fight with Trace."

"That's quite a day," Jess said, regarding her with concern. "You okay?"

"Let's just say I'd rather match wits with the bears and bulls on Wall Street. It's less stressful."

"But everything's okay with the loan, right?" Jess asked worriedly, her concern over Abby quickly taking a backseat to her own issues. "The bank agreed to your plan?"

Abby nodded. "As long as I'm in charge."

"I'm really sorry I dragged you into this," Jess said. "If it helps, you'll have my undying devotion."

"I don't need your undying devotion," Abby told her. "What I need is for you to make a real effort to help me get things back on track. Will you do that?"

"I will. I promise," Jess said. "You tell me what to do and it's done."

Though Jess's response was heartfelt and convincing, Abby couldn't help wondering how long her commitment would last when she bumped up against financial reality for the first time. Her reaction to having her credit card destroyed did not bode well.

7

It was just after four when Trace left the bank to meet Susie O'Brien, Abby's cousin. A year younger than Jess, Susie worked for O'Brien Management, which handled leases for some of the small apartments that had been built above the businesses along Main Street.

When Mick and his brothers had been designing Chesapeake Shores, they'd thought these residences would add to the charm and liveliness of downtown. A few business owners had bought the upstairs units for themselves. The rest were rented, mostly to singles and young couples who wanted to be at the beach but either couldn't afford the larger properties in town or liked the urban feel of living in the heart of even such a small downtown where they could easily walk to restaurants, shops and the beach.

Susie had the obvious O'Brien genes, though she wasn't the beauty that Abby and her sisters were. Her hair was bright red, her cheeks slightly freckled, but she had the family's trademark blue eyes, long legs and winning smile. She also tended to exaggerate her Southern roots, affecting a drawl that few natives of the area possessed.

"Trace Riley, you surely are a sight for sore eyes," she told him enthusiastically, giving him a kiss on the cheek. "I could hardly believe it when our receptionist told me you'd called. It's about time you decided to move home."

"I'm not moving here permanently," he told her. "I'm just looking for a short-term rental."

"That's what Pat said, but I figured you just wanted something to tide you over until you could build a house or until something else opened up."

"No, this is it. I'm here for six months, then I'll be going back to New York."

"Well, that's just a downright shame," she said. "But I do have a few things I can show you. Shall we start right here? There's a two-bedroom above Ethel's Emporium. It's probably the largest and because it's way down at the end of the street it has a view of the water, if that matters to you."

"Let's take a look," Trace said, already striding in that direction, eager to get this settled. He cared a lot less about size and location than he did lighting. He needed plenty of windows for the kind of work he did.

Susie had no difficulty keeping up with his pace. He recalled that she'd run track in high school and had obviously kept up with her running. A block before Main ended, she turned right and went to the alleyway that ran behind the building. "You know the entrances are back here, right? And there's space for one car to park. I'm afraid visitors will have to find parking on the street or along the waterfront, which can be tricky on weekends."

"No problem," he told her. "I'm not expecting a lot of company."

"Well, then, let's go up and take a look." She bounded up the enclosed staircase and unlocked the door, then stood aside to let him enter. "You just take your time looking around," she said. "I'll wait on a bench by the water, if that's okay. I've been racing around since early this morning. I can use the break, and most people like to get the feel of a place on their own without me babbling on about the obvious."

"Fine with me," he said, already focusing on the apartment.

The rooms weren't large and the furnishings were comfortable, but uninteresting, a mix of styles that offended his artist's eye, but would certainly do for the length of time he planned to be in town. The master bedroom was at the back and had lousy lighting, but he didn't much care about that, either. It was the second bedroom, the one he'd likely use as his studio, that mattered.

When he walked into that spacious room, a slow smile spread across his face. Sure, with the wide expanse of windows open there would be noise from the street, which was obviously why it hadn't been chosen to be the master bedroom, but light flooded through the windows along two walls. There was a spectacular view of the bay to the east and an overview of the town square to the north. It would be ideal for his design work. In fact, the whole apartment was perfect for his needs, and it was easy walking distance to the bank.

Sold at once, he locked up and went in search of Susie. "Draw up the lease," he said when he found her feeding bread to a flock of eager seagulls.

"You like it," she said, sounding surprised. "I thought you'd be put off by the decor. It's only a slight step up from early thrift shop, but Mrs. Finch refuses to upgrade anything. She said the things from her attic would do for people just passing through."

Trace grinned. He could hear the elderly widow saying exactly that. "I'm surprised she doesn't have vases of silk lilacs all over the place, given the way she loves them. I suppose I should be grateful for that."

"You didn't notice that the air in there smells of lilacs?"

Susie asked. "Whenever it's vacant, she comes over herself once a week to dust. She never leaves without spraying a lilac scent around every room."

"As long as she doesn't do it again until I've moved out, I'll be fine," he said, shuddering at the thought of the widow spritzing his apartment with her favorite fragrance.

"Oh no, she would never intrude on a tenant," Susie assured him. "So, this is it? You're sure? You don't want to see the other places?"

"This is it," he told her.

"Okay then, I'll have the papers ready for you to sign in the morning. Just stop by the management office. Maybe you'll run into my dad. I know he'd love to see you."

Trace knew there was little love lost between Jeff O'Brien and Mick, but he'd always found Jeff to be more approachable. And after his encounter with Mick earlier, it might be nice to see a friendly O'Brien male. "I'll look forward to it," he told Susie.

Now he just had to go home and tell his mother he was moving out. He had a feeling she was going to be a whole lot less understanding about it than his father had been.

Mick wandered into his den and found Abby behind his desk, her laptop set up, her cell phone at her ear and CNBC with its stock market ticker running silently on the big-screen TV across the room. It was a side of her he'd never seen in action. To him, she was still his firstborn, the little girl who'd run to welcome him home every single night dragging a battered Raggedy Ann doll that Gram had made for her.

"Yes, yes. Got it," she murmured, while tapping at the computer keys. "No problem, Jack, I'll handle it right away. I agree we're overloaded with financials. Let me take a look at which ones we should dump and I'll find a few recommendations in the tech sector for you to consider. I'll get back to you within the hour."

When she'd disconnected the call, Mick grinned at her. "I should have guessed way back when you were eight and insisted on buying a Certificate of Deposit, instead of opening a savings account, that you'd grow up to become some sort of financial tycoon."

"I'm hardly a tycoon," she protested, but she was smiling as she said it, clearly at least a little pleased by his assessment.

"How much money were you talking about just now?" Mick persisted.

"Half a million, give or take, if we do this trade, but it's not my money. When it comes to my own bank balance, I'm not in the tycoon category."

"But you do okay for yourself, that's obvious."

"I suppose I do. What matters to me is that I love it. There's a huge amount of pressure knowing that I'm dealing with other people's money, their life savings, their retirement accounts, but on a good day, it feels great to know that I'm actually helping some people amass a personal fortune." She shrugged ruefully. "Of course, on a bad day, let's just say I should buy stock in antacids."

"You've been at it a while now, so you're obviously good at it."

"My bosses seem to think so," she said modestly.

Mick studied her thoughtfully. "I have some investments that aren't performing so well. Want to take over?"

"I don't think so," she said at once.

He frowned at the quick response. "Why not?"

"Because the first time anything took a dip, you'd blame me. I think it's better if we keep *your* money out of our relationship."

"But what's the good of having an investment guru in the family if you can't turn your money over to her?"

She seemed startled, but once again his comment appeared to have struck a positive chord with her. "You'd really trust me with your investments?"

Mick was surprised by the hint of vulnerability he heard in her voice. Had he been so lousy at communicating that even his confident Abby didn't realize how proud he was of her?

"Of course I trust you," he said emphatically.

Still, she hesitated, still looking vaguely uneasy. "How about this? Why don't you leave your statements with me. I'll take a look and then we can discuss some ideas, but you'll make the final decisions."

"If I'm going to be paying for your advice, then I ought to take it, right? I don't need to sign off on every transaction."

"I'd rather you would," she countered. "At least at first. Then we'll see how it goes."

"Okay," he said. "That'll work. I'll dig out the most recent statements this afternoon, and we can go over them before I take off."

She regarded him with obvious dismay. "You're leaving?"

"I've already stayed longer than I'd planned to," he said, unable to keep a defensive note out of his voice. "I need to be back in San Francisco for a meeting tomorrow afternoon."

"Does Jess know?"

So that was it, he thought. She was worried about her sister's reaction, rather than being disappointed for herself. Had she always put other people's needs and feelings ahead of her own? Or was that something she'd taken on after Megan left? Granted, she'd been seventeen when her mother moved out, almost an adult, but she shouldn't have had to take on adult responsibilities for all her siblings. Mick suddenly felt incredibly guilty for his own role in costing her the last carefree days of high school.

Rather than getting into that, though, he merely responded to her question. "I haven't mentioned it to Jess yet. Why? She'll probably be glad to have me out of her hair."

Abby shook her head. "You are so clueless about her, Dad. Haven't you seen how pleased she's been to have you hanging around over at the inn?"

"The only thing she's let me do was to trim that rhododendron."

"That's the point. It was just about getting to spend time with you. Jess doesn't need you doing anything or telling her what to do. When was the last time the two of you just hung out together?"

Mick thought about that. "Never," he said, vaguely embarrassed by the admission.

"I rest my case," Abby said. "You used to go fishing with Connor and Kevin. Bree always liked to help when you were landscaping the new houses. And when I was little, you used to ride me around on your shoulders while you supervised the construction sites. I even had my own little hard hat, remember? Mom found it somewhere. It was bright pink, which looked awful with my red hair, but I loved it."

Mick smiled at the memory. "I'd forgotten all about that. You were treated like quite the little princess. Half the crew carried around candy for you."

She laughed. "Why did you think I begged to go?"

"So in your own diplomatic way, you're telling me that Jess got shortchanged because I was gone so much."

"That's exactly what I'm telling you. And I know Gram's told you the same thing, so don't act as if it's a surprise. Having you here these past couple of days has meant so much to Jess. Just the fact that you came all the way from California because there was a crisis really proved something to her. It showed her you do care."

"Well, of course I care. I'd do the same for any of you," Mick said.

"I think the rest of us have probably always known that. Jess hasn't."

He bit back a sigh at just how complicated it was figuring out what to do with kids once they were grown, especially daughters, who seemed to be more sensitive to every nuance. His relationships with Kevin and Connor certainly weren't this complicated.

"She's not going to think I've abandoned her again because I have to go back, is she?" he asked worriedly.

"Why don't you ask her that?" Abby suggested. "Just talk to her, okay? Will you do that?"

Mick stood up. "On my way," he said, then glanced back. "You and me, we're okay?"

"Sure," she said.

Mick thought her smile looked a little forced, but he chose to take her at her word. Dealing with Jess was tricky enough. He'd have to work harder to figure things out with Abby the next time he saw her. He'd thought the whole investment thing he'd suggested earlier would create a bond, but the truth was until they sat down and talked about where her mother fit into both their lives, things between them would never be easy.

After her visit with her father and dealing with the portfolio realignment with her boss, Abby needed to get out of the house for a while. She craved fresh air and a change of scenery.

"Gram, do you mind if I run into town for a bit? The girls are down for their naps."

"Not for long, I imagine," Gram said. "But we'll be fine. I'm teaching them to play checkers. They're beating the socks off me already."

"Remember, they're not to have any snacks except juice. No cookies."

Gram gave her an innocent look. "Are you telling me how to feed a sick child? Didn't I do okay with you and your brothers and sisters? Every one of you made it to adulthood."

Abby laughed. "Okay, there will be cookies but I'll pretend not to notice." She gathered up her purse and keys. "I'll be back in an hour."

"Take your time," Gram said. "Shop a little, why don't you? Bring the girls back a surprise. They deserve it. They've been awfully good."

"I'll do that," Abby said.

In town she found a parking spot on Main Street right in front of Ethel's Emporium. The awning-shaded window was filled with a colorful display of beach towels, sand pails, beach balls and Chesapeake Shores T-shirts and swimsuits worn by exceptionally well-endowed mannequins.

Though she'd intended to go to Sally's to have a late lunch, maybe even a slice of old-fashioned apple pie if Sally had any, she decided to take Gram's advice and look for trinkets for the girls. They would probably love a couple of beach toys or maybe a souvenir T-shirt.

She was just stepping out of the car when Trace rounded the corner from behind the building. Dressed in a suit and tie, his hair gleaming, he would have fit right in among the men she worked with every day on Wall Street. There wasn't so much as a hint of the rebel he'd once been or the one she still glimpsed in the occasional twinkle in his eyes. In some ways that saddened her, but she had no idea why. Trace's choices and his future had nothing to do with her.

She gave him a halfhearted wave, which she hoped would discourage him from stopping to chat, but of course he headed her way.

"I'm surprised to see you here in town at this time of day," he said, falling into step beside her as she walked straight toward Ethel's.

"Why is that?" she asked.

"I figured you'd be at the inn."

"Doing what?"

"Managing things."

She turned to face him down. They needed to get a few things straight and now was as good a time as any. "Look, you may have been able to manipulate things to keep me in Chesapeake Shores for the time being, but you don't get to control how I spend my time. Even the lowliest peon gets a lunch break. For instance, you're out here on the street, instead of sitting behind your desk in the middle of a workday. Should I report you to your father?"

His lips twitched. "Okay, point taken. How are the girls?"

"Feeling better," she said. "I'm going to see if Ethel has any little treats I can take home to surprise them."

"I'll come with you," he said at once. "Then maybe I can talk you into having lunch with me."

She frowned at him. "Why?"

"Why what? I'll shop with you because it sounds like fun. I'd like to have lunch with you for the same reason."

Abby didn't entirely trust his motives on either count, but it seemed pointlessly rude to tell him to disappear. And she could hardly tell him that spending time with him made her nervous. Heck, she didn't even want to admit that to herself. She'd spent a lot of years making certain she never left herself vulnerable. Whatever insecurities she'd felt had been buried deep so she could cope, first with being there for her siblings after Megan had gone, and later with her professional life and her kids after her marriage had fallen apart.

"Suit yourself," she said finally, stepping inside the Emporium and immediately being carried back to childhood when the sight of all those gaudy tourist trinkets had enchanted her. So had the display case of old-fashioned colorful penny candy, the same kind that members of her father's construction crews had kept on hand for her. The price was higher now, but the assortment was still tempting, if only for nostalgia's sake.

Trace grinned at her and headed straight for the candy. "Jawbreakers or red hots?" he asked.

"Cherry Twizzlers," she countered without hesitation.

"Hey, Ethel," Trace called out. "How about an assortment of candy?"

Ethel came across the store, beaming at him. "Trace Riley, I've been wondering when you were going to come in here," she said, barely sparing a glance for Abby. "I hear you're moving in upstairs."

Ignoring Ethel's cool, though not unexpected, reaction to her, Abby turned to Trace with surprise. "Really? You've rented your own place? I thought you were going to stay with your folks." She wasn't sure why that disconcerted her, but it did. Had something changed? Was he more committed to staying right here in Chesapeake Shores than he'd led her to believe? And why did that even matter?

His gaze locked with hers. "I thought there might come a time when I'd want some privacy," he said meaningfully.

Abby's pulse promptly skipped a beat or two, so she turned away, but not before she caught the satisfied grin on his face. "Pig," she muttered under her breath.

Trace laughed. "I heard that."

"So did I," Ethel said, chuckling. "You two always were fussing with each other." Her attitude toward Abby warming slightly, she added, "I suppose if Trace is around, that means I'll be seeing a lot of you, as well, Abby."

Abby realized then what a mistake she'd made by coming

in here with Trace and what a mistake it would be to be seen having lunch with him at Sally's. There was little that the year-round residents of Chesapeake Shores liked more than local gossip. And a couple of old flames being seen around town together would give them plenty to talk about.

"I doubt you'll see much of me," she told Ethel. "I'm helping Jess get the inn ready to open. After that, I'll be going back to New York," she added, giving Trace a defiant look that dared him to contradict her.

Ethel looked as if she wanted to pursue Abby's statement, but Trace pointed to the candy in the display case. "We'll take three bags. Make sure you add a variety to each one."

"Three bags?" Abby asked.

"You have to take one apiece home to the twins. I'll bet they don't get candy like this in New York."

"They don't, which is probably why they haven't had any cavities yet," Abby said.

Trace shrugged off the comment. "They'll just brush their teeth longer tonight. And if you don't agree to take the candy home to them, I'll bring it by myself later."

Abby could see she wasn't going to win. "Whatever," she mumbled and went to look at the selection of T-shirts. She found two adorable ones—in turquoise for Caitlyn, lime-green for Carrie—and took them up to the counter.

"Bet they'll like my treat best," Trace murmured in her ear just as Ethel handed her the bag with the T-shirts inside.

She was so startled by his unexpected closeness and the provocative whisper of his breath across her skin, she dropped her package. To her annoyance, he grinned knowingly as he picked it up and handed it back to her.

"Is everything a game to you?" she grumbled as she headed out the door.

"Not until lately. You must bring out my competitive spirit."

"Well, get over it," she said. "And I am not having lunch with you."

"Why not? Does the prospect of sharing a booth at Sally's with me scare you that badly?"

"Of course it doesn't scare me," she said indignantly, tossing her package and the bags of candy he insisted on handing her into the car.

"Then come with me," he coaxed. "We haven't really had a chance to catch up, Abby. We'll have a couple of burgers. You'll steal some fries from my plate, and then we can share a slice of Sally's apple pie the way we used to."

It struck Abby as a very bad idea to do anything the way they used to do it. That had only led to trouble and heartache. Still, she couldn't seem to make herself turn down the invitation that he'd deliberately turned into a challenge.

"Okay, fine," she said eventually, slamming the car door, then marching right past him.

When they reached the entrance to the café, she stopped and looked directly into his eyes. "When we get inside, you are not to hint in any way that we are together. If Sally asks, we're discussing business, nothing else. This is not personal. It is not a date."

"That's going to make it hard to catch up," he suggested.

"Those are my terms."

He regarded her with a determinedly serious expression that was belied by the amusement in his eyes. "Yes, ma'am," he said. "Anything you say."

"I'm not kidding," she warned.

"I get that."

"I don't want half the town whispering behind my back about the two of us."

"Then we probably ought to sit in separate booths," he said, then paused thoughtfully. "Then again, that would stir up its own kind of gossip, wouldn't it? It's so hard to know what to do in a situation like this."

The mocking note in his voice was exasperating, but she let it pass. "Believe me, I'm willing to go the separate booth route to find out," she said.

"Well, I'm not. Besides, you don't want me thinking you're a coward, do you?" He feigned a dismayed expression. "Oh, whoops, I already know that about you, don't I?"

Abby had never once in her entire life had a greater desire to haul off and kick someone soundly in the shins than she had right this second. "Have you forgotten that pitcher of water already?"

"Fortunately for my suit, Sally only serves water by the glassful," he commented as he opened the door and stood aside to let her enter. His solemn gaze met hers. "Truce, okay? Just for the next hour."

Abby looked into those once-familiar eyes and felt herself drowning. Suddenly a hundred different memories swirled in her head, all of them enticing. She swallowed hard and looked away. This wasn't good. It wasn't good at all. She ought to be running for her life.

Instead, though, she lifted her gaze, met Trace's and managed to keep her voice steady as she replied, "Truce."

It was an hour, after all. How hard could it be? Amazingly, though, right now it promised to feel like an eternity.

8

Trace noted the speculative glances when he and Abby walked to a booth by the window in Sally's. He wondered if she remembered that it was the same booth they'd always chosen if it was available. He could recall a hundred different conversations right here, dozens of lingering glances and even a few stolen kisses when he'd squeezed in beside her, rather than sitting across from her. Even though he wanted to do that right now, he opted not to rile her and slid in on the opposite side of the booth.

Abby promptly hid her face behind the menu, which was quite a trick since Sally's specials were listed on a blackboard and the menu itself was a single laminated sheet of paper. People who came here regularly for breakfast and lunch knew their choices without consulting either one. Weekdays the breakfast special, for example, was always two eggs scrambled with grits, toast and bacon or sausage. On Saturdays it was pancakes and on Sundays French toast. The lunch specials rotated among burgers, tuna melts, Reubens, a crab-cake sandwich and grilled cheese, all accompanied by potato salad or fries.

The desserts and pastries, however, were subject to Sally's whims. Trace had noted on the blackboard by the door that today's was apple pie, something he'd been hoping for since he knew it was Abby's favorite—or at least a close second behind the yacht club's chocolate mousse.

"Do you know what you want?" he asked, after studying her, rather than the menu, for several minutes.

"Just a small house salad," she said with a sigh.

"Come on now," he coaxed. "When was the last time you had a big, juicy burger? With the twins starting to feel better, you'll work it off in no time," he said, then quickly amended, "Not that you have anything to worry about in the first place. You look as good as you did ten years ago. Better, in fact. Though you were beautiful then."

"Are you through trying to dig yourself out of that hole?" she inquired, her eyes dancing with amusement.

He grimaced. "Pretty much."

"Thank goodness. I will have that cheeseburger, though."

"Fries?"

She considered the suggestion thoughtfully, then shook her head.

"Which means you'll be stealing mine," he lamented. "I'll have Sally double the order."

"I am not going to touch your fries," she insisted, then grinned. "I'm saving the calories for pie."

Just then Sally approached. Unlike Ethel, she didn't seem the least bit startled to see them or to find them together. Obviously her link to the grapevine was in fine working order. "Two cheeseburgers, fries and apple pie," she said, already writing it down before either of them could speak.

"No fries for me," Abby told her firmly.

"I'll just add a few more to Trace's plate, then," Sally said.

Trace chuckled at Abby's indignant expression. "Your reputation is pretty much stuck in a rut in here," he told her after Sally had headed for the kitchen. "It's one of the delights and annoyances of growing up in a small town. Everyone thinks they can predict what you'll do, what you'll order and who you'll be with."

"Which is one reason I'm so grateful to be living in New York," Abby said. "I like the anonymity."

"Do you really?" Trace asked. "Over the years, I've found myself missing this."

"Where are you living? I don't think you've said. Or rather where were you before you came back here?"

"SoHo," he said, watching her expression closely. "I still have my loft there."

Abby blinked, clearly startled. "SoHo? In New York?"

He nodded. "You sound surprised."

"I am. I thought you were probably living…" Her voice trailed off. She shrugged. "I don't know, I guess I thought you were living closer to here, maybe Baltimore or Washington."

"Nope. I've been in New York close to ten years now, practically as long as you have. I figured you would have heard."

"I don't keep in touch with that many people from here," she said. "Besides family, anyway."

"Not even Laila? You used to be close with my sister."

"We talk from time to time," she said. "But believe it or not, your name doesn't come up. Sorry if that offends your ego."

"My ego can weather a few hits," he replied, though he wasn't actually sure how many, and especially from her.

"What were you doing in New York? Will you have to find a new job if you go back?"

"No. I pretty much take my work wherever I go. I do freelance design work for several different ad agencies and some of my own clients."

For the first time since they'd encountered each other in his office at the bank, she actually looked intrigued, maybe even a little impressed. That wall she'd erected around herself when she was with him tumbled down. She leaned forward slightly, clearly curious. "Would I recognize any of the work you've done?"

"That depends on how much attention you pay to the ads you see in magazines," he said. "I have some major-league clients." He named several and enjoyed watching her eyes widen.

"Wow, I had no idea. I guess I never really thought you were serious about any of that."

He gave her an amused look. "Even though I studied graphic design and art in college?"

"I thought you did that primarily to annoy your father," she admitted. "After all, you also got the business degree he expected."

"Because I figured knowing how to manage a business would never be wasted and it was easier than fighting him," he said. He frowned at her. "I told you all this back then."

"I guess I wasn't convinced you really meant it."

Trace was oddly hurt by her lack of faith in him. Hadn't she known him better than anyone? How often had he confided his hopes and dreams to her?

"Why not?" he asked, suddenly edgy.

She hesitated. "Do you want the truth?"

"Of course."

"Even though you made it sound as if you were simply taking a pragmatic view, I saw it as a sign that you'd never stand up to your father. Even though I knew what you really wanted, I couldn't imagine you ever leaving Chesapeake Shores or walking away from the bank."

Trace was stunned by her low opinion of his resolve back then. "Sweetheart, I may come across like an easygoing guy, but I do have a backbone. How could you, of all people, have misjudged me like that? I thought you were the one person who really understood me."

She looked away, her expression sad. "Apparently I didn't."

"Is that why it was so easy for you to walk away? Did you think I didn't mean a single word I said about us building a future together?"

She shook her head. "I thought you meant it at the time," she admitted. "But I couldn't take a chance that you'd change your mind. I knew exactly what I wanted and where I needed to be to get it. If…" Her voice trailed off.

"If you'd trusted me and I'd caved in to my father's wishes, you would have lost your dream, is that it?"

She nodded. "Pretty much."

Sally returned just then with their meals, but Abby pushed hers away. "I'm not hungry anymore."

"Eat," Trace ordered brusquely. "I don't want to be accused of ruining your appetite, too."

She seemed startled by his tone. "Why are you angry?"

"Because if we had just talked about all this ten years ago, things might have turned out differently. Instead, you just ran off. Look at all the time we wasted."

"You're wrong," she corrected quietly. "Don't you see, Trace, it wouldn't have changed anything. I was too scared to take anything you could have told me at face value. I think I had to be free to go after what I wanted. It's true that I didn't entirely trust what you said, but I didn't trust myself, either. I was afraid of how I felt about you and what I might do because of it. If you'd asked me to stay here and wait until you could straighten things out with your father, I might have done just that. We'd have fallen into some comfortable rhythm and never moved on."

Trace didn't buy it. They'd both been stronger and more determined than that, even if Abby didn't recognize it. "Oh, please," he scoffed. "Just admit it, Abby, you never really loved me at all," he said flatly, pushing aside his own meal.

"Yes, I did," she insisted. "I loved you." Her expression turned sad. "It just wasn't enough."

The weight of those words settled in Trace's stomach like lead. "I need to get to work," he claimed, tossing a few bills on the table. "That should take care of lunch."

He'd just started away from the table when Abby said softly, "I'm sorry. I really am."

"Yeah. Me, too." She had no idea how sorry. Because for the first time he realized he'd never really understood her at all, either. All these years he'd been carrying a torch for an illusion.

When Mick arrived at the inn to tell Jess he was leaving, he found her upstairs in the attic digging through an old trunk filled with nothing but junk, as near as he could tell. Given the time crunch she was under to get the place ready to open, it didn't seem to him to be the best use of her time.

"Hey, kiddo, what are you up to?" he asked, working hard to keep his tone light, rather than voicing the criticism that was on the tip of his tongue. He didn't want to ruin their recent rapport with a few careless words.

"I came up here to see if there was any way to turn this into another couple of rooms and found this." She held up a dusty volume of what appeared to be poetry. "Look at this. I think it might be a first edition of Emily Dickinson poems. It's signed, too."

"That's great," he said, trying to feign enthusiasm.

Jess regarded him curiously. "Why do you have that edge in your voice?"

"What edge?"

"The one that says you don't give a hoot about a book of poems and that I shouldn't, either."

Mick regarded her incredulously. "You got all that from what I said?"

"I've had a lifetime to learn to interpret what you really mean. If you're annoyed with me for some reason, just spit it out."

Mick hesitated. He really didn't want to end this visit to Chesapeake Shores on a bad note with Jess. Anything he was likely to say, though, was going to do just that. Still, how could he let her waste time and what amounted to Abby's money dawdling over some dusty old book, no matter how rare it might be?

"I guess I'm just surprised to find you up here, when there are still two or three rooms that need to be finished before you open," he said, trying to choose his words with care, something he rarely bothered to do.

"I took a break, for heaven's sake. Is that a crime?"

Mick backed off. "Of course not. I just thought that with a deadline staring you in the face—"

Jess cut him off. "I'm perfectly aware of our timetable and what needs to be done," she snapped. "I don't need you over here supervising to make sure I do my job. I suppose Abby sent you. Did the two of you sit around and decide whose turn it was to keep tabs on me?"

"No one's keeping tabs on you," he said, his temper fraying. "All anyone is trying to do is help you achieve your dream. *Yours,* Jess. Not Abby's and not mine. I'd think you'd be a little more grateful and maybe work a little harder to be sure what Abby's doing for you doesn't go to waste."

To his dismay, tears welled in her eyes. "I really thought you were starting to believe in me," she whispered, her chin wobbling. "My bad. Instead, you've just been hanging around waiting for me to screw up. Well, Dad, that's just what I do. I screw up, so you might as well go on back to California knowing that I'm right on schedule for doing it again."

His annoyance drained away. "Ah, Jess, come on now. I never said you were screwing up. Haven't I said how proud I am of what you've accomplished here?"

She sniffed. "Yes, but that doesn't mean you believe I can actually pull this off."

"Of course I do," he insisted. "But you do have to stay focused."

"By never leaving here? By never taking five minutes to do something else?"

He hunkered down in front of her and clasped one of her hands in his. Hers was ice-cold and rough from all the work she'd been doing to fix up the inn.

"Tell me this, then," he said quietly. "How long have you been up here in the attic?"

"I don't know. A few minutes or so."

"What time was it when you came up here?" he persisted.

"I don't know. Nine-thirty, maybe ten o'clock. Not that long ago."

"It's after noon now."

She regarded him with dismay. "I had no idea."

"That's exactly what I mean. Once this place is open, you'll have plenty of time for poking around in the attic or anything else you want to do, but losing a couple of hours now, when there's painting to be finished…" He shook his head. "You can't afford that, Jess. That's all I'm trying to tell you."

She sighed heavily, her expression contrite. "I'm sorry I overreacted. You're right." She stood up and brushed the dust from her hands. "I'll get back to work right now."

"I could help for an hour or two," he offered. "Then I have to leave to catch my flight."

She stopped in her tracks. "You're going back to California?"

Mick nodded.

"I thought you'd be here, at least till the opening."

"I'll come back for that," he promised. "There's no way I'd miss it. And if you need anything in the meantime…" He saw the resigned expression settle on her face and bit back a sigh. "Just call me if there's anything you need, okay? I can send a crew over here to help you finish up if you need it. All you have to do is say the word."

"No," she said stiffly. "I can handle it."

Mick studied her with regret. It seemed they were destined to end this on a sour note, no matter what he said now. Whatever progress they'd made in the past few days had died. He'd killed it with a few pointed comments meant to help, comments she'd taken to heart and viewed only through the prism of their past relationship. It seemed unlikely there was anything he could say now to fix that.

Again, he offered to help with the painting, and again, she turned him down.

"I'll see you in a few weeks, then," he said. When he tried to hug her, she held herself stiff. "I love you, Jess." He forced her chin up, so she had to meet his gaze. "I love you," he repeated.

"I know," she whispered.

The flat, sad look in her eyes told Mick she didn't believe him. Not entirely. And as far as he could see, there wasn't a damn thing he could do to convince her.

Jess was so furious with herself for letting her father catch her goofing off that she doubled her efforts as soon as he'd gone.

She worked nonstop in what she was now referring to as the yellow room with its sunny walls, white trim and deep blue carpet. The furniture in here was white—an old-fashioned iron bed, an antique dresser with a beveled mirror and a washstand, also painted white. She'd found the perfect drapes with tiny white, yellow and blue stripes. The comforter and cushions for the chairs had similar stripes, but there were sprigs of yellow and blue flowers scattered over the background of the fabric. It was going to look amazing.

She'd just finished painting the last of the woodwork when Abby found her.

"Oh, I like it," her sister enthused. "It looks so cheerful."

"Wait till you see the drapes and comforter," Jess said, basking in Abby's praise. "If you want a peek, I've stored them next door until I get the paint scent out of here. I'll leave the window open overnight and it should be okay by morning."

"Show me," Abby said eagerly.

Jess led the way into the room next door and pointed to the packages piled next to the bed. "All the comforters, drapes and pillows for the last three rooms are in there. The blue and yellow ones will go next door. There's turquoise for the room at the end of the hall and dark green for the last room on this floor."

Abby admired all the things Jess had spent so much time choosing. "You really do have good taste. Every room will have its own personality."

"That's what I'm hoping," Jess said. She hesitated, then said, "Dad was here earlier. He's going back to California."

Abby nodded. "I know. He told me before I went into town."

"It figures he'd take off just when there are a million things to do," Jess said.

Her sister frowned at the accusatory note in her voice. "Hold on, Jess. How many times did he offer to help out and how many times did you turn him down flat?"

Jess sighed. "Okay, I know you're right, but this is the way it always is. He always has one foot out the door."

"That's the nature of his business," Abby pointed out impatiently. "Why are you on his case again? Did something happen when he was over here?"

Jess was sorry she'd brought it up, but now she admitted, "He called me on the carpet, as usual. He accused me of wasting time and money."

"Why would he say that?" Abby asked, looking bewildered. "He knows how hard you've been working."

"He caught me looking through an old trunk I found in the attic, instead of working down here. I'd just gone up there to see what it would take to add a couple more rooms and baths up there. I saw the trunk and found all this cool stuff in there. So, I was up there a little longer than I should have been. So what?"

"You realize you're on a very tight deadline here, don't you?" Abby said.

"Dammit, not you, too," Jess said, her temper flaring. "I'm sick to death of everyone thinking they need to remind me of what's at stake here. Don't you think I know?"

"It's just that sometimes you…"

"I what? Take ten minutes for myself? Sit down and have a glass of tea or look through an old trunk? I am not going to defend myself to you or Dad or anyone else," she shouted. "You may think you're in charge of the inn because Trace said so, but you're not in charge of me."

She whirled around and left the room with Abby staring after her. Thundering downstairs, she grabbed her purse and keys from the table in the foyer and took off. She had no idea where she was going, but she had to get away from here, away from all the voices judging her.

Usually when she was in this kind of a mood, she would go to Gram for some quiet sympathy and wise advice, but she could hardly go there when Abby was likely to turn up right behind her. When it came to a fight between her and her sister, there was no way Gram would take sides, no matter which of them she thought was in the right. In fact, she'd be so darn impartial and reasonable, Jess would wind up grinding her teeth to keep from yelling at her, too.

As Jess drove along the shore road, her temper slowly cooled until she started thinking about Trace Riley and his role in all this. It was his fault that Abby was in her face, his doing that her father was on her case about wasting Abby's money.

The next thing she knew, she was parked outside the bank. Without giving herself time to reconsider, she stormed inside, marched right past an obviously startled Mariah Walsh and threw open the door to Trace's office.

"This has to stop," she told him, when he regarded her with wariness.

"Why don't you sit down and take a deep breath?" he suggested.

His calm tone only inflamed her more. "Don't you dare patronize me. I've had more than enough of that for one day."

He nodded. "Okay, fair enough. Then tell me what's on your mind."

"I want Abby gone."

He reacted with obvious shock. "Excuse me?"

She waved off the comment. "Not forever, for goodness' sakes. I just want you to tell her she can go back to New York. If I wind up losing the inn, then it's all on me. I don't want my big sister involved in this anymore."

Trace's face set stubbornly. "It's too late for that, Jess. You know the terms we agreed to, so that the bank wouldn't foreclose immediately."

"I never agreed to anything. You and the board decided what you wanted, you dragged Abby into it and I just had to go along with it."

"That pretty much sums it up," he agreed. "As far as I can tell, nothing's changed."

Jess stared into his unrelenting gaze and sighed. She sat

down, feeling more defeated than she ever had in her entire life. "You won't even consider letting someone else oversee the business affairs at the inn?" An idea struck her, and she brightened. "Laila! Put your sister in charge. You trust her, don't you? And the bank certainly couldn't find fault with that choice." She warmed to the idea. "Come on, Trace. It's the perfect solution."

"No," he said flatly.

"Why not?"

"Abby stays."

"You're just being stubborn," she accused, and then understanding dawned. "It's because you want her here, isn't it? You want another chance with her."

"This is strictly business," he replied stiffly.

The fact that he couldn't meet her gaze when he said it spoke volumes. "Hogwash!" Jess declared. "This is all about buying you time so that you can hook up with her again. I wonder what your father would think if he knew about that."

Trace gave her a rueful look. "He'd probably be pleased as punch. I'm about ninety percent certain that he and my sister conspired to get me back here at this particular time just so I could deal with this one piece of bank business. They knew it would throw me together with Abby."

Jess stared at him incredulously. "You're kidding. They would do that?"

"Of course they would. My father wants me settled down with a wife and kids, and Laila knows that I've always loved Abby. Opportunity knocks and here we are."

"Wow, your family is even more devious and mixed-up than mine. Does Abby know?"

"I think your sister is blissfully ignorant of the undercurrents and the scheming—theirs, anyway. I think she suspects my motives, but she doesn't have conclusive proof of anything."

Jess leaned forward, distracted for the moment from her own problems. "So, do you have a plan?"

"Since the last time I saw your sister, I left her sitting in Sally's and took off in a huff, my current plan is to steer clear of her till I cool down."

"What did you fight about?"

"Misunderstandings, lack of trust, love's inability to conquer all, the usual relationship stuff," he said dryly.

"Must have been quite a conversation," Jess said, trying to imagine it. "And you were in Sally's?"

Trace nodded.

"Then the whole town knows by now," she concluded. "That won't help."

"Believe me, I'm aware of that."

"You really do need a plan," she told him.

"Not from you," he said at once. "I think you and Abby have enough issues of your own to resolve without you trying to team up with me. She would not appreciate having you switch allegiance from her to me."

"I'm not taking sides. This is all about fixing things between you two. That's all good. You're happy. She's happy. In fact, with any luck, she'll be so happy, she'll stay out of my hair at the inn." She beamed at him. "If we do this right, this will definitely be a win-win all the way around."

She bounced up and headed for the door. "I'll be in touch when I've formulated a plan."

Trace groaned. "Heaven help me."

"Heaven's not the least bit interested in your love life," she told him, then grinned. "But, lucky for you, I am."

9

When Abby arrived home after her back-to-back confrontations with Trace and Jess, she found Carrie, the more intrepid of the twins, trying to scramble up onto the porch railing in an apparent attempt to walk it like a tightrope. Gram and Caitlyn were nowhere in sight.

Watching Carrie wobble precariously made Abby's blood run cold. She slammed on the brakes, cut the engine and bolted across the lawn just in time to grab her daughter before Carrie could release her grip on a post and stand upright on the narrow railing.

"What do you think you're doing?" Abby demanded, setting Carrie on her feet on the porch floor, then hunkering down until their gazes were level. "You know better than to climb up on things, especially with no one around watching you. Where is Gram?"

"She's inside. Caitlyn got sick again, but I'm all well," Carrie said proudly. She seemed clueless about how much trouble she was in.

"You may feel better, but you're not a hundred percent well." Abby gave her a stern look. "And if I catch you trying to balance on this railing again, you'll spend one whole day confined to your room."

Carrie regarded her with alarm. "But there's nothing to do in that room. Everything in there is for boys. And there's not even a TV."

Abby wasn't about to relent on this one. Carrie and Caitlyn had a fairly firm grasp of big-city dangers—traffic, strangers, getting little fingers caught in elevator doors—but the dangers here were newer and obviously alluring. Cupping Carrie's chin and looking at her directly, she said, "That is why the room is the perfect place for a little girl who's being punished for breaking the rules. Do you understand me?"

Storm clouds brewed in Carrie's eyes. "I wanna go home! I like *my* room! I don't wanna be here anymore!"

Abby could relate. She wouldn't mind being back in her own room, her own apartment, her own *life,* but for the moment that seemed to be out of the question. And the fact that Jess wasn't even appreciative of the sacrifice she was making really exasperated her. The whole scene at the inn had been uncalled for. It wasn't as if she'd created this situation. She'd merely rushed to her sister's aid.

On some level, she knew that Jess's explosion had little to do with her. It was a reaction to her earlier battle with Mick. Add in Abby's untimely criticism and the two incidents had combined to set her off.

Suddenly she felt a tentative pat on her cheek.

"Mommy, are you sad?" Carrie asked worriedly. "I didn't mean to make you sad."

"It's nothing you did, sweet pea. Mommy's just had a very long day."

Carrie looked puzzled. "Longer than mine?"

Abby laughed. "Just the same as yours. I've just had a lot more things going on."

"Do you think me and Caitlyn will be well enough to go for ice cream tomorrow?" she asked hopefully.

"More likely the next day," Abby told her.

"But I'm all well now," Carrie protested. "It's only Caitlyn who's still sick. You can stay with her and I can go with Mr. Riley. I won, anyway. I had the most spots."

"When we go, we'll all go together," Abby said. "You'll just have to be patient."

As for her, she would have to have nerves of steel, because the more time she spent around Trace, the more she learned about the mistakes and bad assumptions they'd both made, then the more tempted she was to put the past behind her and take another look at what the future might hold. And that, she knew with everything in her, was very dangerous thinking.

Trace had been up all night. He'd gotten a call on his cell phone around four yesterday afternoon from one of his regular clients. There'd been an unexpected opening for an ad in a trade publication and they needed something designed within twenty-four hours in order to take advantage of it. He'd agreed to tackle the job.

He'd worked nonstop through the night, using art he'd created for a previous consumer-oriented campaign, then blending that with the new slogan and copy that had been created for this particular professional audience.

For whatever reason, it hadn't come together the way he'd wanted it to. Maybe it was exhaustion. Maybe it had to do with the words of his argument with Abby playing over and over in his head as if they'd been recorded on some mental tape deck. Or maybe it was because he'd been away from his design work for a couple of weeks. Sometimes a break that long was enough to ruin his concentration and his rhythm.

He stopped trying to figure out the problem around 9:00 a.m. and made himself another pot of coffee. His brain might not be functioning on all cylinders, but at least he was wide-awake. Since the only food in his refrigerator was a carton of eggs, a package of cheese and some margarine, he scrambled the eggs, threw in a slice of cheese and then ate while standing at the counter in the kitchen, his gaze fixed on the artwork propped up on the sofa across the room. Something was still off, but he couldn't pinpoint it. It was driving him crazy.

Maybe it was the combination of colors, he concluded, running water over his plate and then heading back to his computer. He made a few adjustments, studied the results, then tweaked it again. It did look better, but it still didn't jump off the page the way he knew it needed to. He could e-mail it to the client for a second opinion, but he hated to show him something that he wasn't happy with himself.

Sighing, he decided to take a shower. Maybe that would finish off the job started by the coffee and would give him a fresh perspective.

Eventually, the hot water pounding down on his shoulders eased the tension in his muscles and a final burst of icy-cold water on his face revived him. He was back in his office in fresh jeans and a clean shirt, when someone pounded on the door.

"Trace, are you in there?" his father demanded impatiently. "Answer the door or I'll have someone come and break it down."

Alarmed, Trace yanked the door open and regarded his father with bewilderment. "What on earth are you so worked up about?"

"It's midmorning on a workday. You didn't come in. You didn't call. For all I knew, you'd been murdered in your bed."

Trace stared at him incredulously. "Have there been a lot of murders in Chesapeake Shores?"

His father scowled at his attempt at humor. "There's a first time for everything. You scared your mother to death."

"How? She wasn't expecting me at work, was she?"

"No, but I called her when you didn't show up. I thought maybe you'd stopped by the house."

"So, naturally, now she's all worked up, too," Trace concluded, realizing it was going to take some adjustments to get used to having to account for his time after years of answering to no one except himself. "Dad, I'm sorry I didn't check in. A last-minute job came in yesterday afternoon, and I was up all night working on it. It's due in a couple of hours." Before his father could respond, Trace held up his hand. "No excuse. I should have called Mariah."

"Yes, you should have," his father grumbled, but he was calmer. "I'd best call your mother and let her know." He took out his cell phone, made the call, then handed the phone to Trace. "She wants to hear your voice for herself."

"Hello, Mother."

"You really must be more considerate," she scolded. "Your father was in an absolute frenzy."

"I know. It won't happen again."

"You really are okay? He's not making that up for my benefit?"

"I'm perfectly fine."

"Then I'll expect to see you for dinner one night this weekend, so I can look you over and see for myself that you're doing okay."

"Sure. I'll call you later to set it up. Bye, Mother." He cut off the call and turned to hand the phone to his father, but he was nowhere in sight. Trace found him in his studio, staring at the computer screen.

"You did this?" he asked.

"I did," Trace acknowledged, waiting for the inevitable criticism.

"It's a good ad," his father admitted, his tone grudging.

"Thanks."

His father studied the ad more intently, then said, "It could use a little more contrast, though."

Trace was startled by the observation. He leaned over his father's shoulder. "What do you mean?"

"Right here, this gray blends right into the background. It doesn't pop enough, at least that's how it seems to me. You're the expert, though."

Trace studied the part of the design his father had indicated and realized he was exactly right. The words, in a muted shade of gray, simply didn't pop enough against the sky-blue background. They should have been black, or maybe even navy-blue. Red would be even more bold.

"You've got a good eye, Dad," he said. "I've been staring at this thing for two hours, and I couldn't figure out why it wasn't quite right."

"You were probably overanalyzing it," his father suggested. "Well, now that I know you're okay, I'll get back to the bank. One of us needs to work today."

"I'll come in later," Trace promised. "As soon as this gets the client's okay."

"Take the rest of the day off," his father said. "If you want to do something, run by the inn and check on things, see how Abby's coming along on getting all the bills in order."

"You're as transparent as glass," Trace accused. The innocent look on his father's face was a nice effort, but Trace wasn't buying it.

"I have no idea what you mean," his father claimed. "Following up with Abby is just part of your job. You want to turn it into something else, that's up to you."

Trace grinned. "I'll remind you of that next time you start trying to push us together." He walked his father to the door. "Thanks for coming by, Dad, and I don't mean just for checking on me. You really were a help just now."

Even as he spoke, he saw the spark of real pleasure that lit his father's eyes and realized that Lawrence Riley, for all of his stuffy affinity for numbers and business success, needed the occasional pat on the back just like everyone else.

Abby approached the inn with trepidation. She had no idea what kind of mood she'd find Jess in this afternoon and she wasn't in any frame of mind herself for another fight. Fortunately Jess's car was nowhere in sight. While that was a relief, Abby did find herself wondering why her sister wasn't inside, hard at work.

Using her key, she went in, poured herself a cup of coffee from the pot in the kitchen that Jess had apparently made earlier, then went into the office. An inch-thick pile of bills were stacked on the desk, unopened. Sighing, she went to work sorting through them, grimacing when she saw the bills for all those beautiful drapes and linens Jess had bought for the remaining rooms. Clearly her good taste came at a high price, and none of the conversations they had about cutting costs had sunk in. Abby knew she'd have to try again to get Jess to economize.

She was in the middle of writing checks when her cell phone rang. Glancing at the caller ID, she recognized her ex-husband's number and grimaced. She'd known this call was coming. Wes had been away when she'd first come down to Chesapeake Shores. She'd left several messages for him, so he'd know where the girls were, but he wasn't going to be happy when he found out they wouldn't be back in New York by the weekend.

"Hey, Wes, how are you?" she said, injecting a note of enthusiasm into her voice. "How was your trip?"

"Long," he said. "I'm glad to be home."

"You got my messages?"

"I did, but you weren't making a lot of sense. I got the part about going to Chesapeake Shores for a visit, but why are you still there?"

"It's a long story, just some family business I have to deal with." She really didn't want to get into it with her ex. He'd never had much patience with Jess. He thought Abby was entirely too understanding of her mistakes. Like Mick, he'd believed tough love was the answer for something that Abby knew needed compassion instead.

"But you'll be back by Friday, right? I've missed the girls. I'm anxious to spend time with them."

"I'm afraid not," she said. "I really can't leave here." She drew in a deep breath and offered an alternative. "You're more than welcome to come down here, though. There's plenty of room at the house."

"Come on, Abby. You know that's a lousy idea. Your whole family blames me for the divorce."

"They do not," she protested. "I've always told them that it was my fault, that I was the one who didn't devote enough time and attention to our marriage."

"Which none of them believed for a minute," he countered. "Mick certainly didn't. I got an earful from him when he found out. I'd just as soon not be on the receiving end of another one of his lectures."

"Mick's in California, and you know Gram would never say a bad word to you or about you. She adores you. And the girls would be over the moon to have you here. I'll even make myself scarce, so it won't be awkward for you. You'll have the twins all to yourself. It'll be like taking them on vacation. In fact, if you wanted to, you could drive up to Ocean City for the day."

She waited as he weighed the decision, but she knew what it would be. In the end, Wes was a terrific father who adored his daughters. He wasn't going to let his annoyance with her or the situation interfere with seeing them.

"I'll be there first thing Saturday morning," he said finally. "But I'd rather not stay at the house. What about that inn? I could stay there."

"Actually it's not open at the moment. It's being renovated, so it's the house or you'll have to find a hotel in one of the nearby towns. I could make some calls for you."

He sighed heavily. "No, that doesn't make sense. I'll stay with you and the girls. You will be back in New York before my next scheduled visit, though, won't you?"

Abby winced. "I don't think so. I'm going to be here at least for a few more weeks."

Silence fell and lasted for what seemed like an eternity as Abby waited for his reaction.

"Then the girls will come back to New York with me," he said with finality. "I'll have the nanny come here during the week and I'll handle evenings and weekends until you get back up here."

"Absolutely not," Abby said at once. She didn't intend to be denied time with the girls, either, and they were enjoying themselves here.

"Well, I certainly can't keep running down to Maryland every other weekend," he said impatiently. "And you can't send them up here alone on a plane."

"Of course not."

"Then you tell me how we should handle this," he said. "So far, you and I have been able to keep the whole custody thing totally civil, but I'm not going to give up my time with my daughters."

"Wes, that's not what this is about," she argued. "I'm dealing with something here. I just need you to cooperate for a few more weeks, not an eternity. Can't you do that much?"

He was quiet for so long, she thought he might not answer, but eventually he said, "We'll discuss this when I see you. I don't want to be unreasonable."

Abby breathed a sigh of relief. That was the thing about Wes, he never wanted to be unreasonable. That's why they'd finally divorced. She'd seen how miserable her long hours at work were making him, but he'd never demanded that things change. One day he'd simply hit a wall and asked for a divorce. The only surprise to her had been that he'd waited so long.

"Thanks, Wes."

"I'll plan to take an early flight, but I'll call you if I get held up. Otherwise, expect me around ten."

"Okay, I'll see you then. Have a safe trip."

She'd barely cut off the phone when she realized she wasn't alone. She looked up and discovered Trace standing in the doorway. Rather than the suit and tie she'd grown accustomed to him wearing, he was dressed in faded jeans and a navy-blue T-shirt that emphasized his broad chest and well-muscled arms. His windblown hair suggested he'd ridden over on his Harley. This was the sexy, rebellious man she'd fallen for all those years ago, the one who made her good sense go flying out the window.

"How long have you been standing there?" she inquired testily.

"Long enough to figure out that your ex-husband isn't happy about you having the girls down here."

"He'll deal with it," she said tightly.

He looked vaguely guilty. "I'm sorry, Abby. I never stopped to consider what it might mean to have your kids separated from their dad while you're here."

"There are a lot of things you haven't considered when it comes to me," she retorted. "Look, I'm in no mood for another heart-to-heart with you. Are you here for any particular reason?"

"Routine follow-up," he claimed. "Just making sure all your creditors are happy."

"You'll have to ask them how they're feeling. If what you're really asking is whether they're being paid, the answer is yes." She plucked the mortgage and business loan payments out of the stack and handed them to him. "Here, you can save me the cost of two stamps."

His lips twitched. "How very frugal of you."

"Just following your instructions to keep a tight rein on expenses."

"Where's Jess?" he asked.

The question was entirely predictable and reasonable, but Abby wasn't overjoyed by the response she had to give him. "No idea. Why? Did you need to speak to her about something?"

"I just assumed she'd be hard at work," he said with a shrug.

This time it was Abby's lips that curved into a grin. "I suggest you not mention that to her. I got an earful the last time I did. Apparently she has her own way of juggling her responsibilities, and she doesn't appreciate my interference."

He turned the chair beside the desk around backward and straddled it. "That discussion wouldn't have taken place about this time yesterday, would it?"

"As a matter of fact, it did. Why?"

"Because about fifteen minutes later she barreled into my office and told me off. She also said fairly emphatically that she wanted you gone."

Abby knew Jess had been mad, but she hadn't expected her to go that far. She was curious, though, about how Trace had responded. "I assume you refused."

"Of course."

Abby shook her head. "So, between us, we've got my sister in an uproar. Because of you, I have my ex-husband in a dither. Are you happy yet?"

"Not really." He grinned. "I could be if you'd go for a walk on the beach with me."

"And step away from my desk in the middle of a workday?" she queried with feigned shock. "What if the boss catches me?"

"It's his idea. In fact, it will earn you lots and lots of brownie points with the boss."

She leaned back and studied him. "You're in an odd mood today. What's going on?"

"*My* boss gave me permission to play hooky. In fact, he encouraged it. He all but handpicked my playmate, too, in case you were wondering."

Abby bit back a laugh. "Your father sent you over here to go for a walk on the beach with me?"

"He didn't spell out the details. The walk was my idea." He met her gaze, then held it until the air in the room seemed to crackle with electricity. "Interested?"

Oh, God, yes, a little voice in her head murmured fervently. Fortunately, the only word that came out of her mouth was, "Okay."

Trace laughed. "Your enthusiasm is overwhelming."

She shrugged, determined not to let him see how this playful side of him affected her. "It's a walk on the beach, not a walk down the aisle."

Heat simmered in his gaze. "Want to do that instead?"

She frowned at him. "No, I do not," she said emphatically, proud of herself for not letting her voice betray the fact that she was way too intrigued with the idea.

"Your denial is a little too forceful. A simple *no* would have sufficed."

"Do you have any idea how exasperating you are?" she asked, even as she reached for her jacket.

"No, but I'm sure you'll be happy to fill me in," he said, smoothing the jacket over her shoulders.

The lingering touch made her shiver. It also suggested that going on this walk was a bad idea. Spending any time at all with Trace was probably a bad idea.

Still, she thought as they walked across the expanse of lawn toward the water, it was far from the worst idea she'd ever had. In fact, when he reached for her hand to help her over the rocks and down onto the hard-packed sand, something inside her shifted slightly. Suddenly she couldn't help thinking that perhaps strolling along the beach, hand in hand with this particular man, might very well be the best thing she'd done in years.

10

One of the things Trace had always loved about Abby was that she didn't need to fill every moment of silence with nonsensical chatter. Keeping her hand clasped in his as they picked their way along a stretch of beach that had been narrowed by erosion, he tilted his face up to the sun and breathed in the salty tang in the air. Miles farther inland—in the hills and mountains of Virginia, West Virginia, Maryland and Pennsylvania—most of the tributaries that eventually spilled into the bay began as freshwater streams and creeks, but here the brackish water of the Atlantic was still dominant. Trace had always loved that unmistakable scent, the taste of it on his tongue…or on Abby's skin after they'd been for a swim.

For the first time since he'd come back to Chesapeake Shores, he felt completely and totally at ease. Here at the water's edge, he felt none of the pressure of working for his father, none of the stress of meeting ad deadlines. Nor was he feeling that vaguely uncomfortable, ill-at-ease sensation that hit him sometimes in New York, as if he'd forced himself to adjust to a lifestyle and pace that didn't quite fit.

"You're frowning," Abby noted. "What's that about?"

"Am I? That's odd, because I was just thinking how at ease I feel here."

Now she was frowning. "And you don't feel that way in New York?" She made it sound like an accusation.

Trace saw the trap at once. "Most of the time I love New York. I enjoy what I do there. I don't want to trade it, especially not to work at the bank. But this..." He gestured around at the amazing natural environment with his free hand. "This feels like home. Surely you must feel it, too. Don't you remember how much time we spent on the water back then?" He captured her gaze and held it. "Long, lazy days and sultry nights?"

To his relief, she took the question seriously and didn't jump down his throat for asking it. Nor did she get all jittery over the provocative tone in his voice. She simply looked thoughtful.

"Actually, I think I do know what you mean," she admitted eventually. "I felt it when I first got out of the car the night the girls and I got down here. Seeing Gram, breathing in the air, hearing the sound of the waves, it *is* home. I realized how much I'd missed it." She gave him a defiant look. "Not that I want to live here again."

"Ditto," he said, not bothering to challenge her, even though he wondered if living here on their own terms wouldn't be just fine. Surely she'd achieved what she'd wanted to in the financial world. From everything he'd heard, she was a well-respected portfolio manager with a top-notch brokerage firm. He'd seen her name from time to time in the *New York Times* business pages and in the *Wall Street Journal*. Spotting the articles had filled him with pride in her accomplishments. Surely with her credentials she could work in any of their branches successfully. He'd established plenty of contacts and could write his own ticket when it came to his design work. Why not do that and have this lifestyle, too? From his perspective, it was worth thinking about. But he doubted Abby would agree, not yet, anyway.

"How soon do you think you'll go back to New York?" she asked, proving his point. For her this was obviously a tempo-rary—to say nothing of unwelcome—respite, not a destination.

"The deal I made with my father was that I'd stay six months," he said.

"Are you making any progress in convincing him that Laila is the one who should have the job?"

"First I have to convince him that I'm the wrong person for the job," he said. "I actually think I may have made some progress on that front today."

"Really? How? By being too eager to take him up on his offer to let you play hooky?"

Trace chuckled. "No, he was counting on that. I think right now his desire for me to have a family may outweigh his desire to bring me into the world of banking."

She gave him a puzzled look. "Meaning?"

"You," he said, enjoying the shade of pink that immediately tinted her cheeks. "A hundred years ago, he would have already made an offer to Mick to seal the deal. We'd have had no say in the matter. Be grateful we're living in modern times."

"Why would your father think that you and I have any potential for a future?"

"We have a past," he reminded her. "You're single again. You have two little girls who could use a daddy—"

"They have a father," Abby reminded him.

"Well, of course they do. I'm just trying to explain how things work in Lawrence Riley's mind."

She slanted a look at him. "Well, just in case *you* start getting any ideas, keep in mind that I'm not in the market for a husband. I didn't do so well by the last one. I'm a com-pulsive workaholic. That doesn't make me good marriage material. In fact, I failed miserably in that role."

Trace regarded her with amusement. "I'll be sure to pass

that information along to my father, though something tells me he's not going to be dissuaded from this idea."

"As long as you are, that's all that matters," she said.

She looked so serious, so determined to make her point that Trace couldn't help himself. He bent down and kissed her. He meant it to be just a quick, teasing brush of his lips across hers, but her mouth felt so good, so familiar beneath his, that he went back for more.

By the time he dragged himself away, their breathing was ragged and there was a bemused expression in Abby's eyes.

"Why did you do that?" she asked, rubbing her lips as if to wipe the kiss away. "Especially right after I told you what a bad bet I am?"

He shoved his hands into his pockets to keep from reaching for her again. He shrugged. "Seemed like a good idea at the time."

"Well, it wasn't," she said. Her expression was fierce, but there was a telling hitch in her voice.

Trace took comfort in that hitch. Once in a long while, Abby let her insecurities show in subtle ways that made Trace want to dive in and protect her. That desire usually warred with his longing to ravish her.

His lips curved slowly. "I guess we'll just have to wait and see which one of us is right."

He was pretty sure the wait would have to involve a whole lot more experimental kissing, too.

Abby was still shaken by Trace's kiss when she waved goodbye to him, then walked toward the inn. Even her stupid knees were weak, which was ridiculous.

"Interesting," Jess called out from the porch. "I come home and find two of the world's toughest taskmasters missing. Lo and behold, I discover they've been cavorting on the beach."

"There was no cavorting," Abby said sharply.

She intended to walk right past her sister and avoid any more of her insightful observations, but Jess stood up and followed her inside.

"So, what's going on with you and Trace?" Jess asked, leaning against the counter as Abby tried to pour herself a glass of iced tea with hands that remained unsteady.

"Nothing," Abby said, then took a long gulp of the cold liquid, hoping it would cool her overheated libido. It didn't help. Nor did it buy her much time.

"Didn't look that way to me. The two of you were in quite a lip-lock on the beach. From where I was standing it looked as if steam was rising."

Abby stared at her in shock. "You spied on us?"

"I most certainly did not spy. I went looking for you. When I got to the beach, I saw you and turned right straight around and came back to the porch to wait." She grinned. "I thought it would be fun to see how you tried to explain what happened."

"I'm delighted you find me so amusing."

"Not you," Jess corrected. "The situation. It feels a whole lot like that summer ten years ago when the two of you were sneaking around. You were delusional then, too. You didn't think anyone knew what was going on. Heck, I was barely twelve and I got it. You two were crazy about each other. Still are, from what I've observed." She nudged Abby in the ribs. "I think it's sweet."

"It is *not* sweet. It is just as doomed now as it was back then."

"Why? I mean, I sort of get why you left then. You were following a dream, though why you thought working yourself to death was more important than a man like Trace is beyond me. But that was then. You're successful now. You can call your own shots. If you want Trace in your life, there's nothing to stop you."

Abby sighed and pulled out a chair at the table. Jess made a future with Trace sound so reasonable, so possible, but she knew better. "Come on, Jess, you know it's not that easy. Look how badly I messed up my marriage to Wes, and he's probably the most understanding, undemanding man on the face of the earth. No man is going to put up with the kind of hours I work, the kind of stress I bring home with me at the end of the day."

"Then cut back," Jess said. "Make some adjustments."

"It's not that kind of job. The markets move too quickly. If I'm off my game, I could put someone's life savings in jeopardy."

"And you honestly enjoy working in that kind of pressure cooker?"

Abby nodded. "Most of the time I love it."

"You said most of the time. What about the rest?"

"Then I want what every woman wants—a home, a family, a man to share my life with," she admitted, then added, "I just don't see how I can have that."

"You're an O'Brien," Jess reminded her. "You can have anything you set your mind to. Isn't that what Gram and Mick taught us?"

"They did, but Dad also showed us that it can come with a price. Success cost him his relationship with Mom. Maybe some O'Briens simply aren't meant to have it all."

Jess frowned at her. "What does Mom have to say about your fatalistic attitude? Or is she the one responsible for it?"

Abby regarded her with surprise. "Why would you think Mom's influenced me about relationships?"

"Can you honestly tell me she hasn't? You're the only one of us she has to talk to, so she's probably filled your head with every bitter recrimination she has about Dad."

"No more than you have," Abby said mildly.

Jess winced as the barb hit home. "You're probably right. I do have my issues with Dad." She hesitated, then asked,

"Seriously, has Mom ever opened up to you about what happened back then?"

"Isn't it obvious?" Abby said. "Dad was away too much. She couldn't take it anymore."

"But she didn't just leave him, she abandoned us, too," Jess protested. "We were her kids. We hadn't done anything to deserve that."

Abby frowned, remembering the conversation she'd had with her mother on the day Megan had walked out, her promise to come back for them. "No, and she always meant for us to come to New York to live with her."

"Then what happened?" Jess asked. "Why was it she only came to visit when the mood struck her?"

"I don't know," Abby admitted. The subject was so touchy, she'd left it alone. For her it was enough that Megan was back in her life, but she understood why not having an answer to that question ate away at Jess.

"Oh, well," Jess said. "We all survived. That's what counts, isn't it?"

Her attempt to make light of her pain didn't work. Abby was about to call her on it, but Jess waved her off.

"Forget it. We're getting away from my point. You're talking yourself out of something with Trace that could be really good. You're not even trying for it. It seems to me that's just plain wrong."

Abby couldn't really deny that Jess had pegged her exactly right. She was being fatalistic. Experience had taught her that she wasn't cut out for marriage. Since she didn't enjoy failure, she saw no reason to put herself in that position again, not even with Trace stirring her hormones into a frenzy, reminding her of how good they'd once been together.

She set down her empty glass and stood up. "Let's table this discussion," she said. "I have work to do and so do you."

Jess gave her a disappointed look, then shrugged. "Whatever. It's your life."

"Yes, it is."

But as she went back into the office and dug into the paperwork still piled high on the desk, she couldn't help questioning whether the choices she'd been making all these years, the priorities she'd set, were as good as she'd always believed them to be. Maybe, like her father, she was losing more than she had gained. She wondered if Megan ever felt that way about her decision to walk away from her family.

Carrie and Caitlyn were practically bouncing up and down with excitement on Saturday morning as they awaited their father's arrival.

"How much longer, Mommy?" Carrie demanded. "I thought he'd be here by now."

Abby sighed. "It shouldn't be much longer. He called a few minutes ago and said he was almost to Chesapeake Shores."

"I see him, I see him!" Caitlyn exclaimed, pointing toward a cloud of dust billowing along the distant road.

"I see him, too!" Carrie shouted, racing down the steps and heading for the driveway.

"Wait here," Abby commanded. "You're not to go into the driveway until he's parked the car. Understood?"

"Yes, ma'am," Caitlyn said, though she stayed right at the edge of the grass, Carrie bouncing impatiently beside her.

As soon as Wes's rental car had pulled to a stop, they tore around to the driver's side and yanked open the door. He barely had time to untangle himself from the seat belt before they were both trying to leap into his arms.

Despite the flight and the drive, he looked as if he'd just stepped out of an ad in *Forbes,* featuring clothes for the wealthy businessman at leisure. Even on a weekend, Wesley

Walker Winters looked every inch the executive he was, from his styled brown hair to his designer sports clothes and Italian loafers.

Unlike Abby, he'd inherited his place in the business world, running a conglomerate founded by his grandfather, then handed down to his father. That gave him the luxury and flexibility to make his own schedule. Though he worked hard, he had neither Abby's ambition nor her workaholic tendencies. His priorities, her mother had been quick to point out, were perfectly in order. He was that rarest of men, one who put his wife and children first. He'd told her repeatedly that he understood her drive, respected her for it. He just hadn't been able to live with it.

"Daddy, Daddy, me and Carrie had the measles," Caitlyn announced excitedly.

"I had the most spots," Carrie informed him.

Wes's gaze shot to Abby, suggesting they would have a conversation later about her failure to mention the brief illness. For now, oblivious to his expensive, neatly pressed slacks, he knelt down in the grass and turned their faces from side to side. "No spots now. You must be well again."

"I was well first," Carrie bragged.

He laughed. "I'm just glad you're both well now, so we can do a bunch of fun stuff this weekend."

"Like what?" Caitlyn asked.

"I wanna go for ice cream," Carrie said at once.

Caitlyn immediately scowled at her. "No, that's what we're doing with Mr. Riley, remember?"

"But if Daddy buys us ice cream, we get to have it twice," Carrie countered.

"No!" Caitlyn repeated emphatically. "Mr. Riley said he'd take us, and I'm going with him."

Wes looked bewildered by the argument. Again, he glanced in Abby's direction, seeking an explanation.

"Trace Riley is an old family friend, who happened to stop by when the girls first got sick," she told him. "He made a deal with them that they could have ice cream at Sally's when they were over the measles."

"All we can eat," Carrie said excitedly.

"Well, I don't know about that," Wes said.

For the first time since the argument began, Carrie backed down, clearly sensing that her father might put a damper on that notion. "You can take us for pizza," she said quickly. "We haven't had any since we came here."

"Yes!" Caitlyn said eagerly. "Please, Daddy."

"Pizza it is," he agreed. "Just let me put my things inside and speak to your mother for a minute, and then we'll go into town."

Abby followed him inside, then showed him to a room just down the hall from the girls. When she would have made a hasty exit, he stopped her.

"Why would you allow some man to bribe the girls with all the ice cream they can eat?"

She frowned at the criticism. "It's not as if they're going to stuff themselves until they get sick," she said. "It's the idea that there's no limit that matters. Come on, Wes. You know them. Their eyes are always bigger than their stomachs. They'll order three scoops, eat one like always and that'll be it."

He still didn't look convinced, but he finally nodded. "Okay, I suppose you're right. But you do know this man, don't you? You wouldn't let them go off with him otherwise."

"Of course I wouldn't let them go with a stranger. Besides, I have every intention of going with them. You're getting worked up over nothing."

"Probably so," he admitted. "I'm sure it's because it's been three weeks since I've seen them. So much changes in that amount of time, and I hate missing any of it. Then to have them going on and on about some man I've never heard of— It threw me, I guess. I'm sorry. You know I trust your judgment."

He looked so chagrined that on impulse she gave him a hug. "Well, they're all yours now. Go off and enjoy yourselves. Gram's at church doing flowers for tomorrow's services right now, but she'll be back soon and she'll be around if you need a break."

"Where will you be?"

"I'm helping Jess with something."

He immediately looked suspicious. "What's your sister gotten herself into now? She's the reason you're down here, isn't she? I should have guessed as much."

"Let's not talk about this now. If you really want to know, I'll tell you after the kids are in bed tonight."

For a moment, he looked as if he wanted to pursue it, but he finally backed down. "Okay, then. I'll see you later."

Knowing the kind of discussion that was likely to ensue when she explained what was going on with Jess and the inn, Abby couldn't honestly say she was looking forward to it.

Trace had been working on a design all morning, and by lunchtime he was in need of a break and a meal. Wearing an old pair of jeans and a faded Chesapeake Shores T-shirt that had seen better days, he decided to run to the small, casual pizza shop around the corner and across from the beach to grab a quick lunch. During the summer he'd been a lifeguard, he'd eaten there nearly every day. Sometimes he'd crossed the road on his break to grab a couple slices of pizza. On other days, Abby would pick up subs from the same place and bring them to the beach, where they'd eat lunch together.

He'd just turned the corner onto Shore Road when he

spotted Carrie and Caitlyn coming his way. They saw him
at the same time and jerked free from the man walking with
them, a man he recognized at once as the same one he'd seen
with Abby in New York all those years ago. He'd never forgotten the guy's chiseled good looks and designer attire. He
might be dressed more casually today, but the look still
shouted money and aristocratic breeding.

"Mr. Riley," Carrie shouted, running toward him. "We're
going for pizza. Where are you going?"

"As a matter of fact, I'm going for pizza myself," he said.
He looked up into the wary gray eyes of the man who had
to be their father and Abby's ex-husband. "I'm Trace Riley,
a friend of Abby's," he said, holding out his hand.

"Wes Winters," he said curtly, his handshake solid but
perfunctory. "The girls mentioned you, something about a
promise of ice cream."

Trace nodded. "We made a deal when they were sick."

"And now we're all well," Carrie told him.

"Then I'll have to pay up one day next week."

"You could have pizza with us now," Caitlyn said shyly.

"Not today, kiddo. I don't want to intrude on your time
with your dad. Besides, I need to get back to work."

Caitlyn studied him curiously. "You don't look like you
usually do when you work."

Trace laughed. "Very observant. Today I'm not working
at the bank. I'm doing my other job."

"What would that be?" Wes inquired, studying him as if
he'd just crawled off one of the crabbing boats. There was
a world of disdain in the man's expression. He probably
wore Armani to barbecue steaks, assuming he actually knew
how to do that in the first place.

"I'm a graphic designer," Trace said, which apparently
didn't do a thing to change Wes's obviously low opinion of

him. He couldn't resist adding, "Right now I'm working on something for Astor Pharmaceuticals."

For the first time, Wes's expression shifted slightly. "Good company," he said grudgingly. "I know Steve Astor. We grew up together, in fact."

"Really? He and I were in business school together at Harvard."

The last of Wes's disdain seemed to vanish. "Good school. I went to Yale myself."

"An equally good school," Trace said, barely able to contain a grin. Check and checkmate, apparently. There was nothing like marking turf to energize a man.

"How do you know Abby?" Wes asked, an oddly jealous edge to his voice for a man who'd let her get away.

"We both grew up here," Trace said, then couldn't resist adding, "We used to date."

Wes's expression froze. "I see."

"Well, I'll leave you guys to your lunch," Trace said. "I'm going to pick up a takeout order at the counter."

He was about to walk away when Caitlyn tugged on his hand. He looked down into her upturned face.

"Don't forget next week," she whispered.

"Not a chance," he promised. "Your mom and I will figure out a day."

"Come on, girls. Let's grab that empty table," Wes said firmly.

Trace watched the three of them as they settled down at the table. He could hear them bickering over toppings as he placed his own order. He had to admit that despite his own instinctive dislike of the man Abby had married, Wes seemed like a great dad. He was endlessly patient with them. Nope, he couldn't be faulted on that front.

Still, any man who willingly walked away from Abby clearly didn't have much sense. He counted himself among them, too, so he ought to know. He might not have done the walking, but he sure as heck hadn't done what he should to stop her from going. And in hindsight, he could honestly say now that had been just as stupid.

11

Jess walked into the office at the inn and found Abby staring out the window. She wasn't sure which surprised her more—that her sister was here on a Saturday or that she was apparently wasting time daydreaming.

"I thought you intended to spend Saturdays catching up on all your research for your real job," Jess said. "What are you doing here?"

"Hiding out," Abby admitted with a chagrined expression. "Wes is here."

Jess gave an exaggerated shiver. "Say no more," she said. "If I never see that man again, it will be too soon."

Abby frowned at the comment. "You've never liked him, have you?"

Jess shrugged. It seemed pointless to deny it now that he and Abby were divorced. In her opinion, they never should have married in the first place. Abby's heart, whether she wanted to admit it or not, had always belonged to Trace.

"Sorry, but no," Jess told her. "I tried to, for your sake, but I always thought he was a stuffy, judgmental jerk." She grinned. "Good-looking, of course, but it didn't compensate for the absence of a sense of humor or a personality."

Abby chuckled. "Come on. He's not that bad."

"He is seriously humor challenged," Jess insisted. "It didn't help his case that he made sure I knew he thought I was a total screwup. He's always resented every minute you spent listening to me or bailing me out of jams. He must be apoplectic over this latest turn of events."

"Actually, he doesn't know anything about the inn yet," Abby admitted. "But you're exaggerating about his low opinion of you and his resentment."

Jess regarded her with skepticism. "Please, don't try to spare my feelings. Come on, Abby. You have to know how he feels about me. He always looks at me with that icy expression that says I'm wasting his time and yours. He wants me to feel like I'm lower than pond scum."

The guilty expression on Abby's face proved she had known what Wes was doing. Still, she said, "I never realized he made you feel that way. I'm truly sorry."

"Hey, I'm used to that reaction," Jess said cavalierly. "*Everyone* thinks I'm a screwup. I'm just sorry that he made *you* feel that way about yourself."

Her sister looked shocked by her comment. "But he didn't," Abby protested.

"Of course he did. He'd tell you how proud he was of your success, but the very next second he'd list a dozen things you weren't doing at home or with the girls. He tried to make you feel inadequate and I'm pretty sure he succeeded."

"I most certainly do not feel inadequate," Abby said.

Jess gave her a knowing look. "Not even as a wife and mother?" She leaned forward. "Don't try to deny it, Abby. You know that's why you don't want to get involved with Trace. You said it yourself. *You* messed up your marriage. *You're* a workaholic. Well, who made you see yourself that way? I'll tell you who, Wes Winters. I really hate him for doing that to you. He should have been boasting about all your accomplishments, but he deliberately undermined every one of them with his snippy little remarks. It made you doubt yourself and question your priorities."

Abby seemed surprised by her fierce defense. "You weren't there, Jess."

"No, I wasn't inside your marriage," she admitted. "But I was in New York often enough to see how Wes treated you. What astounded me was that you sat back and took it. I would have kicked his sorry butt to the curb for all that passive-aggressive crap long before he got around to asking me for a divorce."

"It takes two to make a marriage work and two to let it fail," Abby persisted.

Jess seized on the comment. "That's right. It takes *two!* Have you ever once asked yourself how much Wes was at fault for the way things turned out? You need to stop beating yourself up for not meeting his expectations and find yourself a man who appreciates who you are and is interested in being a full partner, which means handling his share of the responsibilities." She gave her sister a knowing look. "Did Wes ever once load the dishwasher after a meal? Did he ever toss a batch of laundry into the machine?"

"No," Abby admitted.

"And yet he expected you to do that and juggle your career and the girls, too, didn't he?"

"Okay, I see your point," Abby conceded reluctantly, then gave Jess a wry look. "You know, everything you're saying about Wes could have applied to Dad at one time. It surprises me you're not more sympathetic to Mom."

"Whole different situation," Jess said. "Dad never belittled Mom. And nothing he did could justify what *she* did." She waved off the subject before they got into a full-fledged fight. "Let's not go there. We're never going to agree about

Mom's decision to walk out on us. You've forgiven her. I haven't. End of story."

Abby started to respond, then shook her head. "You're right. It's better not to go there." She deftly changed the subject. "I assume you've already picked out the perfect man who will never, ever treat me in such a shoddy way."

"Of course. You have to admit that Trace has a lot to recommend him," Jess taunted. "If he weren't so hot for you, I'd give him a tumble myself."

"Why don't you?" Abby said, her tone deliberately nonchalant.

"Really?" Jess said, testing her just to see if she'd own up to the attraction. "You wouldn't mind?"

"Hey, he's a free agent. I certainly have no claim on him. Go for it."

Jess couldn't help it. She laughed. "And have you stick a dagger in my heart the first time you saw me kiss him? I don't think so."

Abby scowled. "I told you to go for it."

"Your lips said the words," Jess agreed. "But the fire in your eyes said something else entirely. I think I'll go with that and stay far, far away from Trace. I don't have time for a man in my life right now, anyway, unless he knows how to run an inn or rip up carpeting."

Alarm flared in Abby's eyes. "What carpeting? Jess, we never talked about putting down new carpeting. There's no room in the budget for that kind of expense."

Jess sighed. "I know, but it would look great, wouldn't it?" she said wistfully. "It would be the finishing touch this place needs to be perfect."

"Well, put that on your wish list for when the inn starts turning a profit," Abby advised. "The carpet we have now will look great once we get the carpet cleaners in here to shampoo it."

"Already at the top of the list." She stood up. "Now, you can sit there brooding for the rest of the afternoon, or you can make yourself useful and help me paint the last guest room."

Abby regarded her with a startled expression. "You're allowing me onto your hallowed turf upstairs?"

"Just this once. You seem in need of a distraction, and I'll be there to supervise. Just try not to drip paint all over the floor the way you did when you helped me paint my bedroom when I was ten."

"That wasn't me," Abby protested indignantly as she followed Jess up the stairs. "It was Kevin. Or maybe Connor. Neither one of them ever had the patience for painting or much of anything else when it came to odd jobs around the house. Mick used to say it was a good thing neither of them wanted to follow in his footsteps, because whatever they built was sure to fall right back down on their heads."

Jess grinned. "You know, I think you're right. It was Kevin."

Abby paused on the steps, her expression sober. "I miss him," she said quietly. "It scares me to death that he's in Iraq."

Jess's good mood evaporated at once. "I know. Me, too. But our brother believes in what he's doing. And last time he sent me an e-mail, he said he'd met a woman, another medic. I think it might be getting serious."

"I hope not," Abby said. "I'm not sure you can trust your emotions when tensions are running high in a situation like they're in. I hope they'll wait till they're back home before they do anything permanent."

"You're probably right," Jess conceded, "but I'm glad he has someone over there. It makes me feel as if there's someone watching his back."

All the talk about Kevin had left both of them in a somber mood. Jess forced herself to shake it off. She prayed every night for her brother's safe return, and that was all she could do, aside from sending him boxes and boxes of Gram's cookies every month. According to Kevin, his unit looked forward to the arrival of those packages as much as he did.

"Come on. Let's go paint," she said, marching up the last of the steps. "I don't want to think about the danger our brother is in or whether he's going to get too serious with a woman he hardly knows." She grinned again. "I'd much rather talk about your love life."

"It's going to be a very boring conversation," Abby retorted.

"Have you taken a good look at Trace? No way is a conversation about that man ever going to be boring."

Judging from the bright pink flags that immediately appeared in her sister's cheeks, Abby didn't disagree. Jess had a feeling that with a few good nudges, those two just might wind up back in each other's arms, precisely where they'd belonged years ago. She might have been only twelve, but she'd seen something probably no one else had—that walking away from Trace had been just as hard on Abby as it had been on him.

Abby had spent a surprisingly pleasant afternoon with her sister. For once Jess hadn't been on the defensive about their forced business relationship. Instead, it had been like old times with all the teasing banter and resulting laughter. She was glad about that. The last thing she wanted was for this situation Trace had created to cause a rift between them. If they could just spend a little more time laughing, maybe they'd come through this rough patch with their bond as sisters intact.

Still hoping to avoid an uncomfortable encounter with Wes, especially in light of Jess's take on her marriage, she'd hung out at the inn until late in the evening, sharing a pizza with Jess and discussing plans for the grand opening just ahead of the Fourth of July holiday, which was only about six weeks away. She'd even mentioned the possibility of hiring Trace to design an ad campaign for them. Naturally Jess had promptly accused her of trying to find ways to spend even more time with him than she already was. Though she'd denied it, she couldn't honestly swear that there wasn't some truth to Jess's analysis of her motivation.

She was still smiling about that discussion when she stepped onto the porch at home and Wes called out to her. Her good spirits promptly fled.

"I've been waiting up for you," he said. "Where were you? It's getting late."

Abby frowned at his tone. It wasn't just possessive. It had a judgmental edge to it, one that was not only uncharacteristic but inappropriate. Still, she fought to keep her response mild. Maybe she was being overly sensitive herself after listening to her sister's low opinion of the way Wes treated her.

"I promised you I was going to stay out of your way, so you could spend this weekend with the girls," she reminded him.

"Were you really being considerate, or were you trying to avoid talking to me about your new boyfriend?"

Abby had been about to sit down, but the question kept her standing, her temper stirring. "First, I don't have a new boyfriend. Second, even if I did, he would be none of your business. Third, I really don't like the tone in your voice, so I'm going to bed."

She was halfway across the porch when he called after her. "Wait, Abby."

She paused but didn't turn around.

"I was out of line," he added.

"Yes, you were," she said. She made no move to go back and join him.

"Can we talk, please?"

"About?"

"Don't blow a gasket, but I do want to know what's going on between you and this guy who's been spending time with my girls."

"They're *our* girls," she reminded him. "And for the last time, there is nothing going on between Trace and me. We're old friends."

"Who used to date," he added.

She frowned. "How do you know that?"

"We ran into him in town. He could hardly wait to tell me that you used to have a relationship. It was also plain to me that he intends to continue it."

"And of course, mindless me, I'll go along with whatever anyone wants. Is that what you're suggesting?" She was beginning to see what Jess had been talking about. Wes really could be a judgmental jerk. How had she never noticed that before? Had she been too busy taking all of his criticisms about her faults to heart?

"Of course you're not mindless," he said, regarding her with what looked like genuine dismay. "I'm just telling you what he said."

"Or what you interpreted based on whatever he actually said," she accused. "I'm not in the mood for this, Wes. We'll talk in the morning, because if we continue this right now we're going to have a really nasty fight."

Even in the porch's shadows, she could see the bewilderment in his expression. "What's happened to you? You never used to take offense so easily."

"Let's just say that I had a conversation today that helped me to take my blinders off where you're concerned."

"With this Trace Riley fellow? What did he say about me?"

She sighed heavily. "Trace didn't say a thing. I haven't seen or spoken to him today."

"Jess, then," he said, sounding resigned. "She knows I've never approved of how she uses you. I'm sure she was eager to retaliate by saying all sorts of unflattering things about me."

Abby could have stood there and debated the point with him. Or she could have simply told him off. Instead, she merely said good-night and walked away. Maybe by morning she wouldn't feel like smacking him silly.

Trace hadn't been able to get Abby out of his mind all day. He'd tried calling her cell phone a couple of times, but either she didn't have it with her or it was turned off or she was ignoring the calls because she didn't want to talk to him.

Taking his phone with him, he walked down to the end of the block and found a bench looking out at the water. The half-moon was sparkling on the waves and the sky was filled with stars. There were quite a few people out for a stroll—couples, groups of teens, families. There were even more people sitting at the various sidewalk cafés across the street. Chesapeake Shores was busy for a May night that still had a slight nip in the air. He saw a few people he knew, but most were tourists who'd come because of the restaurants and quaint shops that stayed open late into the evening on weekends.

He'd thought coming out here would relax him, but it only made him miss Abby more. Flipping open his cell phone, he called her again.

"Yes, hello," she snapped, her tone testier than he'd ever heard it.

"Did I catch you in the middle of something?" he asked, treading carefully.

"Yes, a major-league snit," she said, her tone mellowing slightly.

"Caused by?"

"My ex-husband, if you must know. He was waiting to

ambush me when I got home a little while ago. He was just full of questions about my boyfriend. That would be you, by the way."

She didn't sound overjoyed, though he couldn't tell for sure if it was because of the questions or because of the label her ex had pinned on him.

"Am I supposed to say I'm sorry?"

"For what? You're not responsible for him jumping to all sorts of misguided conclusions. Look, I really don't want to talk about this. Did you call for any particular reason?"

"It's probably not the best time to admit I just wanted to hear your voice, is it?"

Silence greeted the question, though he had a feeling she was fighting a smile. She'd always been quick to anger, but just as quick to let it go.

"Abby, why don't you come meet me for a drink?" he coaxed. "You sound as if you could use one."

"Which is exactly why it's a bad idea."

"What's bad about it? It's still early. I'm down here by the water at the end of Main Street. There are lots of people around. There's no way we could possibly succumb to temptation in this crowd," he teased, even though it was the kind of night that encouraged romance.

"Who says I'd be tempted to succumb to your charms?"

"Maybe it's the other way around," he retorted. "Maybe I'm afraid you'll seduce me."

"You don't sound afraid. You sound eager."

Trace chuckled at her perceptiveness. "Okay, you got me. Come on. It's one drink. Not even a real date."

He could tell she was weighing her options. When she finally said yes, he couldn't be sure if it was his persuasiveness, his challenge or her annoyance with her ex-husband that decided her. Whatever it was, he was relieved. And eager.

"I'll stay put where I am," he said. "You find me when you get here, and we'll pick out a place to go together."

"You're right at the end of Main Street?"

"On a bench facing the bay. The same one where we used to meet."

"I'll be there soon," she said.

Pleased with himself, Trace tucked his phone in his pocket and settled back to wait.

Fifteen minutes later there was a tap on his shoulder, and he turned to find Abby standing behind him. Her hair was windblown, her cheeks rosy.

"You drove Mick's convertible, didn't you?"

She grinned mischievously. "I did."

"What'll he do if he finds out?" he asked, knowing how her father babied the original Mustang and classic Corvette that came out of the garage only for town parades. Abby had ridden in the back of the Mustang the year she'd been Homecoming Queen, but no one in the family other than Mick had ever been allowed to drive either car. "I seem to recall Connor being grounded for a month when he took the Mustang for a ride one night."

"I'm too old to be grounded," she said, and gave him a challenging look. "Besides, Mick's in San Francisco. Who's going to tell him? You?"

"No way, sweetheart. Then I'd have to admit how I found out, because you were sneaking out of the house to meet me. I don't care how old and independent you are, I'm not sure how Mick would feel about that, either."

She came around and dropped down beside him. "I have to admit that creeping out to the garage and taking that car did add an element of excitement to my evening. Took me right back to the times I crawled out of my bedroom window and shimmied down a tree to meet you."

Trace laughed. He'd always loved that reckless side of her, had, in fact, encouraged it. "I've always been a terrible influence on you apparently." He studied her intently and noted that despite her light tone, she didn't look happy. "So did you borrow Mick's car for the thrill of getting away with it, or was there another reason?"

She hesitated, then said, "If I'd taken mine, I was afraid Wes would see me and demand to know where I was going."

Trace bristled. "Why would it be his business?"

"I have no idea. Something tells me that his encounter with you earlier today has something to do with it."

Trace had worried that his casual comment about having a past relationship with Abby would stir up trouble, but for the life of him he couldn't figure out why it should. Their relationship had ended before she and Wes had even met. "Can I ask you a serious question?"

"Only if you buy me that drink," she said.

He stood up at once and held out his hand. "Okay then, let's walk until we find a place that we like. With so many new little cafés along here, there's bound to be something that fits the bill."

Abby took his hand and fell into step beside him. "It really is amazing, isn't it?" she said as they walked past an ethnic smorgasbord of small restaurants. When they were kids, there'd been only the pizza place, which had been a popular teen hangout along with Sally's, a frozen custard and snowball shop that was open only in summer and a gourmet coffee shop that also sold newspapers and magazines.

"Just look at how many new places have opened up since we were living here. I wonder if Dad envisioned this."

"He must have," Trace said. "After all, he designed this row of commercial property along here."

"There was only one block of commercial property originally," Abby reminded him. "Now there are two or three."

"Have you spotted any place that appeals to you?" Trace asked, anxious to get back to that discussion about her ex-husband. Maybe, he admitted to himself, even more anxious to get her alone in the shadows where he could try his luck stealing another kiss.

"They all look fine," she responded. "You choose."

"How about that one?" he asked, gesturing toward one where most of the outdoor tables had emptied. They could have the patio to themselves. "Will you be too cold if we sit outside?"

"No, this feels downright balmy compared to the cold spell we were having when I left New York."

He nodded. "Yeah, that's when I left, too. I got out just ahead of a snowstorm. I don't think the city got much, though."

"If it was the one that fell the night before I came home, it was only a dusting. The roads to the airport were completely clear when the girls and I left to fly down here."

Trace settled her at a table, asked what she wanted to drink, then stuck his head inside to alert a waiter that they were there and needed a glass of wine and a beer.

"Are you hungry?" he asked her when the waiter brought their drinks.

"No, Jess and I had pizza earlier at the inn, but you order something if you're hungry."

"Maybe later," he told the waiter, then turned back to her. "Okay, you have your drink, now I get to ask my question. Which one of you wanted out of the marriage, you or Wes?"

"He did."

"That confirms it," Trace said. "The guy's an idiot."

Abby smiled. "Thanks for the vote of confidence."

"Was he having an affair?"

"Heavens no," she said, sounding genuinely shocked by the question. "Wes lived by a rock-solid set of family values."

"Rock-solid, yet they included divorce?"

"Only after I proved that I couldn't live up to his high standard for being a proper wife. I worked too much. I had too much drive and ambition. I wasn't free for all the social engagements that keep his world spinning."

"Didn't he know that about you when you were dating?"

She nodded. "That's what I've never entirely figured out. I didn't change. I guess he just assumed that once we were married and had kids, I'd forget all about my career and stay home where he thought I belonged. We certainly didn't need my income, but he never figured out that I didn't work because of the money."

"Did you discuss it? Fight about it?"

"Never. One day he just announced that my priorities were all messed up and that he couldn't live like that anymore."

Trace frowned. "Without even giving you a chance to change or compromise? That's not fair."

"You should hear what Jess says about it. She says he was always passive-aggressive, telling me he was proud of me one minute, then taking little digs about my failures as a wife and mother. I honestly never paid that much attention to the digs, maybe because I thought they were fair." She held up a hand. "Look, this is all water under the bridge. We're divorced. Wes is basically a good guy and a great father. I need to get along with him for the sake of the girls."

For some reason, Trace couldn't let it go. "But, Abby, he has no right to come down here and question you about who you're spending time with. Are you sure he's not after something?"

Abby looked bewildered. "Such as?"

"I see two possibilities," he said, treading carefully. He'd picked up on some kind of territorial vibe when he'd met Wes and he couldn't seem to shake it. He didn't want to upset or alarm her, and he had a feeling he was about to do both. On some level, he knew he ought to stay out of this, but he'd started it now, and Abby wasn't likely to let him drop it.

"What possibilities?" she asked, proving his point.

"Either he wants you back and he's jealous of whatever he thinks is going on with us," he began.

Abby shook her head at once. "Believe me, he doesn't want me back."

Trace hesitated.

"Come on," she commanded. "Don't stop now. I'm fascinated by how much thought you've apparently given to me and my ex-husband, a man you've spent, what, five minutes with?"

"You're right. I don't know him, but I've crossed paths with plenty of men just like him. And in those five minutes I spent around him today, I saw something else."

"What?"

"I can't be sure, of course, but maybe he's hunting for ammunition to start a battle for full custody of Carrie and Caitlyn."

As he'd feared, real alarm flared in her eyes. "He wouldn't dare!"

Trace clasped her hand. "Settle down. I'm just saying it's a possibility you need to be prepared for. Don't let your guard down for a minute. Like I said, I've known men like Wes. They almost always act based on some hidden agenda that's in their own interests. They win because they hit when people are least expecting it."

Abby's expression went from indignant to thoughtful. "As much as it kills me to say it, it does make a sick kind of sense. Before he came down here, he threatened to take the girls back to New York with him since I'm going to be here a while longer. I told him to forget about it, but that might have put some crazy idea into his head about trying to take them away from me." She met Trace's gaze, fire in her eyes. "I swear to God, if he tries to pull a stunt like that, I will go after him with every penny I've got."

"Right now you share custody, right?"

"Yes. The girls pretty much divide their time between the two of us. Most of the year they're with me during the week, because I live maybe half a dozen blocks closer to the private school where they go to kindergarten. The nanny walks them to school. They're with Wes every other weekend. Sometimes, especially around holidays, they'll stay with him for the whole week. The nanny just goes with them to wherever they're staying. Neither of us wanted to turn them into pawns in our battle. The whole divorce was totally civilized. We drafted it ourselves and had it approved by the court. He pays generous child support, including their school tuition, but no alimony. I didn't want or need his money for myself."

Trace wondered what Wes Winters might stand to gain by fighting Abby for custody. Maybe he was just a dad who wanted more time with his daughters, especially if he feared they were going to be a few hundred miles away for any length of time, but Trace thought otherwise. Perhaps he'd taken an instant dislike to the man and that was behind his suspicions, but he didn't think so. He was usually a decent judge of character. It was a trait he'd inherited from his father, who claimed that a good banker had to be a good judge of the people he dealt with. His father always said a balance sheet only told half the story about a customer. Instinct filled in the rest.

Since all he had at the moment were suspicions, Trace decided to do a little checking first thing on Monday. In the meantime, he didn't want Abby to get any more worked up than she already was, especially since for the moment he was only speculating based on very little hard information.

"Look, I'm really sorry I stirred this up," he told her sincerely. "He hasn't said anything about the whole custody issue, so it's probably just my imagination."

She could have accepted the easy explanation, but she shook her head, which told him she'd been harboring similar thoughts.

"I'd say you were crazy, if Wes hadn't made that comment when we spoke on the phone before he came down here." She stood up. "I need to get home and talk to him."

"Now? He's probably gone to bed."

She glanced at her watch and sat back down, but she was clearly still agitated. Once again, Trace regretted stirring her up, possibly for no good reason. He had to distract her.

"Look at me," he commanded.

She turned to face him.

"No one will take the girls away from you," he said firmly.

"You don't know how powerful Wes's family is," she said.

"Actually I do," he said. "We have some mutual friends, so I know the circle that puts him in. But powerful people have weaknesses. If it comes to a fight, we'll find theirs." He touched a finger to her lips when she would have responded. "No more speculation. Let's drop this for now."

A flicker of awareness heated her gaze. "What'll we do then?"

"I have an idea, if you're interested," he said, keeping his tone deliberately casual.

Her lips parted. "Tell me," she whispered, sounding faintly breathless.

He knew what she was anticipating, maybe even wanted, and heaven knew he wanted to take her to his place, to his bed, but he knew without a doubt that she'd regret it in the morning. Besides, there was a certain amount of fun to be had in surprising her.

"Let's sneak over to the inn and go for a swim in the pool," he suggested.

She regarded him with undisguised disappointment. "You want to go for a swim?"

He nodded. "I do."

"But we don't have bathing suits," she said.

He winked at her. "I know."

She laughed then. "You really do enjoy leading me astray, don't you?"

"It's my very favorite pastime," he admitted, then grinned. "Next to skinny-dipping, that is."

"If Jess catches us, we'll never hear the end of it."

He sealed his mouth over hers, lingering and savoring before releasing her. "Then we'll have to be really, really quiet, won't we?" He leveled a long, simmering look into her eyes. "What do you think? Are you game? There was a time, you know, when I didn't even have to ask twice."

She hesitated for just a fraction of a second, then nodded. "I'm in."

"You know what, Ms. Abigail?"

"What?"

"I'm glad being married to that stuffy jerk didn't rob you of your daredevil spirit. Did he know about that?"

She looked saddened for a moment, then shook her head. "No. No one's ever seen that side of me except you." Her bright eyes seemed to shimmer with the faint sheen of tears. "You may be the only man I've ever trusted that much."

Her admission nearly shattered him. Trace wiped a tear from her cheek. "Then I'll do my best never to let you down. I promise."

In fact, he'd sell his own soul before he'd hurt her or let anyone else break her heart.

12

Abby had only gone skinny-dipping once in her life, and it was Trace, of course, who'd talked her into it back then, too. He'd said earlier that he was a bad influence on her, but that wasn't how she saw it. Somewhere deep down inside, when she was being totally honest with herself, she knew that the only time in her life when she'd felt as if she were really living was when she'd been with him. As hard as she'd tried, as successful as she'd become, nothing compared to the pulse-racing thrill of being with a man like Trace. Lately, too, she was starting to remember the comfort of being with someone who knew and understood her, who believed in and valued her.

There was a danger to the kind of full-throttle living Trace represented, though. Not only was there the occasional push-it-to-the-limits risk, but it made her vulnerable. Sometimes it was easier to live in a nice, safe cocoon, rather than exposing her heart to the possibility of being broken. That seemed even more critical now that she had two daughters relying on her. If her career took her away from them too much, what would a relationship do to that bond? She was stretched to the limits as it was.

Tonight, though, with the sky clear and star-filled and the

air slightly cool, she felt like taking chances. Borrowing Mick's car proved she was in a reckless mood. Trace was right about that. Her father would flip out if he discovered his precious Mustang had left the garage with her behind the wheel. It was telling that she almost wished he were around to catch her.

As soon as she turned into the driveway at the inn, she cut the car's lights. Behind her, Trace did the same. They parked behind a grove of trees. Then, giggling like a couple of teenagers, they slipped around the side of the inn to where the shimmering turquoise water of the pool beckoned. It had been scrubbed clean, painted and filled just last week, so there was still the faint scent of chlorine in the air. The lights in the pool were on, but the grounds around it were shadowed, which gave the illusion they were secluded from the world.

Abby looked at Trace and caught the wicked glint of anticipation in his eyes. "You go first," she told him.

He studied her, his expression dubious. "You're not going to chicken out, are you?"

"Me? No way. I just want you in the pool, and preferably underwater, when I undress."

"I've seen you naked before," he reminded her.

"Not since I had twins," she countered.

His gaze held hers. "That could only make you more beautiful," he insisted, then added with unmistakable wistfulness, "I wish I'd been there for that."

Seeing the appreciative gleam in his eyes made her wish he'd been with her back then, too. Wes had only made her feel more ungainly, even though he'd loved boasting to their friends about the fact that she was having twins. She realized now that even during her pregnancy, his comments had always been double-edged. As thrilled as he'd been about the twins, he'd always managed to sneak in a dig about her size.

It had all been in good-natured fun, of course, or so he'd pretended. Now she wondered if that had been the case.

"Stop it," she murmured to herself. She'd gone through nearly seven years of marriage with far fewer doubts than her sister and Trace had brought to mind in a single day.

Trace frowned. "Stop what?"

"Not you. Me," she said. "I was thinking about things best left in the past."

"Want to explain that?"

She shook her head and pointed at the pool. "Go, if you're going."

He kicked off his shoes, then stripped off his jeans and T-shirt. His briefs could have served as a swimsuit, but as he got to the edge of the pool, he yanked those off, too, and tossed them aside, giving Abby a wonderfully provocative rear view of broad shoulders, narrow hips and an excellent bare butt. She could have admired the view all night, but he dove in and swam the length of the pool with sure, strong strokes that allowed her to watch the play of well-toned muscles across his back.

While he was swimming, she peeled off her blouse and slacks, but left on her bra and bikini panties, then ran and leaped into the water. She surfaced, sputtering, only to discover that Trace was right there beside her, regarding her with amusement. He tucked a finger under her bra strap and ran it along bare skin, raising goose bumps.

"You cheated," he accused.

"I agreed to the swim. I don't believe I agreed to skinny-dipping."

He surveyed her with a simmering gaze that could have heated the whole pool. "This may be better," he said, his gaze locked on her breasts. The sheer lacy fabric of her bra was clinging to them. "It leaves a little something to the imagination and trust me, mine is in overdrive."

Abby was tempted to stay where she was, enjoying his appreciative glances and the desire swirling in the night air, but she wasn't quite brave enough to risk where it was destined to lead. Not quite yet, anyway. The longer she remained in Chesapeake Shores, the more time she spent with Trace, though, the stronger this pull between them was likely to become.

"I'll race you to the end of the pool and back," she challenged.

"What do I get if I win?" he taunted.

"Satisfaction," she said, then winced at the instant gleam in his eyes. "Not that kind of satisfaction, Trace Riley! Pride. You get to feel proud of yourself."

"My kind is better," he said. "But okay. What do you get if you win?"

She considered the question carefully. What did she really want from this man, aside from the kind of kisses that would make her knees go weak? Suddenly it came to her. "You'll sneak into the inn and steal a couple of towels, so we don't have to drive home soaking wet."

"You want me to go inside, where your sister is probably asleep, and steal towels?" he asked, his expression incredulous. "Isn't that just begging to be caught?"

"Probably, which is why you're doing it instead of me."

"Yeah, but Jess wouldn't shoot you. I'm not so sure whether she'd be as careful if she spots me inside and mistakes me for an intruder who's up to no good."

"She doesn't own a gun," Abby assured him. "You'll be safe enough." She tilted her head. "Of course, your concern about all this tells me you think I'm going to win."

"I'm just trying to use good sense," he countered.

She grinned at him. "Well, that's certainly out of character," she taunted. "That's the deal, though. Take it or leave it."

He met her gaze. "I'll take it. On the count of three, then. One, two…"

Before he ever uttered the *three,* he was gone. "You dirty, rotten scoundrel," she shouted, and took off in pursuit. She was a strong swimmer, though he had the advantage of height. Still, despite his cheating, she'd almost caught him by the time they made the turn at the far end of the pool. She was close enough to get one hand firmly around his ankle. She gave it a hard yank that threw off his nice, even strokes and allowed her to catch up. Her fingertips touched the edge of the pool a fraction of a second before his.

"You cheated," he accused, though his eyes were dancing with laughter.

"Not until after you did," she retorted.

A subtle cough suddenly caught their attention. Abby looked up into her sister's amused gaze and felt her entire, barely concealed body grow hot with embarrassment.

"Hi, sis," Jess said, humor threading through her voice. "Nice to see you, Trace. All of you, that is."

Abby nearly choked at that, but Trace didn't seem even the tiniest bit flustered. He grinned at Abby. "I guess we've been busted."

"I guess you have," Jess agreed.

"A good sister would have gone back inside and never mentioned catching us out here," Abby suggested. "You seem to be taking great pleasure in this."

"I am," Jess admitted. "I figure the two of you are going to owe me big-time if I promise not to spread this little escapade all around town."

"You would tell people about this?" Abby demanded, horrified by the thought, especially with Wes in town.

"You bet," Jess said, grinning. "It's the best gossip I've known in years and years. Mostly this town is pretty boring."

"I'm your sister," Abby reminded her, then pulled out the

biggest guilt card in her arsenal. "The one who's here to save this inn for you."

Jess nodded slowly. "That is a consideration, of course."

"What do you want to keep quiet?" Trace asked, though the spark in his eyes suggested he didn't much care if Jess spread this news far and wide.

Jess's expression turned thoughtful. "I'm not sure just yet. For the moment, I'll settle for the satisfaction of having something to hold over both your heads. Something tells me that will come in handy eventually."

Abby frowned at her. "We'll discuss this later," she said direly. She emerged from the pool and went to pull on her clothes.

"I tossed a couple of towels over there," Jess said, then grinned at Trace. "Maybe you should have Abby bring you one before you get out of the water."

Naturally Trace took that as a challenge. He was about to hitch himself up and over the side of the pool, when Abby rushed over and handed him one of the oversize fluffy towels that Jess had insisted were essential. Right now, Abby was glad she had. It was large enough to wrap securely around Trace's waist.

She whirled on her sister. "Go inside," she commanded as if Jess were a disobedient kid again. "I think you've had enough fun at our expense for one night."

Clearly undaunted, Jess returned her gaze evenly. "I'll go, but if you have an ounce of sense, big sister, your night is just beginning."

After Jess had gone, Abby dared a look at Trace. He didn't seem to be the slightest bit embarrassed about what had just happened.

"She has a point," he said instead.

"Are you crazy? We were just caught cavorting in a pool

where we had no business being. You didn't have a stitch of clothes on, and I barely did. Now you want to do what? Rob the bank?"

He laughed. "I don't think that was what Jess had in mind."

Abby knew it wasn't, but she didn't want to mention what had been in her sister's mind. If she said one single word about sex, it would open up a can of worms that was best locked up and sealed.

Instead, she tugged her clothes on over her soaking-wet bra and panties, then jammed her feet into her sandals. "I'm going home."

"I figured as much," Trace said with an air of resignation. "I don't suppose—"

"No, you are not coming with me. You are not sneaking into my room. We tried that once, and Gram caught us. It would be too humiliating to have that happen again at my age."

"Of course, at your age, we could just walk boldly upstairs and go straight to your room," he suggested.

Abby refused to admit, even to herself, how very tempted she was by that idea. Instead, determined to cut it off without discussion, she said one word: "Wes."

He sighed. "Yes, his presence does put a damper on things, doesn't it? Okay, then, you go home all alone. I'll go home all alone. And neither one of us will get a wink of sleep."

"Speak for yourself. I intend to sleep like a baby."

He stepped closer, tucked a finger under her chin, then covered her mouth with his. It was a splendid kiss. When he ended it, he grinned. "Bet you don't."

She blinked, trying to unravel what he was talking about. It was tricky, since she could barely remember her own name. "Don't what?"

"Sleep like a baby."

Yeah, she was beginning to have her doubts about that, too.

* * *

Abby was sitting in the kitchen on Sunday morning, hoping that a second cup of coffee would kick-start her exhausted brain, when Jess bounced in looking as perky as if she'd had a full eight hours of sleep.

"Gee, sis, you don't look so good," Jess said, her eyes sparkling with laughter. "Late night?"

"Go to hell," Abby muttered. "And don't you dare say one word about anything that went on last night. Wes could wander in here any minute."

Jess immediately frowned. "Sorry. I forgot all about him." She poured herself a cup of coffee and sat at the table. "Where's Gram? She's usually down here making pancakes by this time on a Sunday morning."

"So you came for the pancakes and not to torment me?" Abby queried.

Jess grinned impishly. "Actually I came for both, but I will refrain from all those comments on the tip of my tongue to protect you from the wrath of my former brother-in-law."

"I appreciate that."

"You sure he's here? I didn't see his car outside. Maybe he went into town for an early breakfast."

Abby's head snapped up. "His car is gone?"

"I didn't see it," Jess said, studying her with concern. "What's wrong? Why do you look like you're going to pass out? Every speck of color just washed right out of your face."

Abby didn't waste time answering. She flew up the stairs to the girls' room and threw open the door. They were gone. Her babies were gone!

"Oh my God, he's taken the twins," she shouted at Jess, who was right on her heels. "We need to call the police."

Jess grabbed hold of her. "Calm down. What do you think Wes has done?"

"I think he's taken the girls away with him, back to New York."

"He wouldn't do that, would he?" Jess said, her expression disbelieving. Then she shook her head. "Of course he would, the pig." She stepped past Abby and surveyed the room, then frowned. "Their things are here, though. Are you sure he's taken them?"

Abby didn't know what to think. "Well, not a hundred percent sure, no, but the clothes don't mean anything. They keep a whole wardrobe of stuff at his place."

Just then Gram joined them. "What's going on? Why are you two so upset?"

Jess spoke up. "Abby thinks Wes may have taken off with the girls."

Gram regarded her with dismay. "Why on earth would you leap to such a conclusion? He's just taken them to Sally's for breakfast. He promised them last night that he would."

Abby nearly collapsed with relief. "Are you sure?"

"I was right there when they talked about it. That's why I slept in this morning. I figured no one would be around expecting breakfast before church."

Abby wanted desperately to believe her grandmother was right, but until she saw the girls for herself, she couldn't. "I'm going to town."

"I'll drive," Jess said. "You're liable to run off the road."

"Whatever," Abby said, running downstairs and grabbing her purse in the kitchen on her way out the door. Jess was right on her heels.

"Call me," Gram shouted after them. "Let me know that everything's okay."

"I will," Abby promised. Clutching her purse in her lap until her knuckles turned white, she turned to Jess. "Gram has to be right."

"I'm sure she is," Jess soothed. "When has she ever been wrong?"

"I can't wait till we get there to know for sure," Abby said, reaching for her cell phone. She punched in Trace's number. He sounded groggy when he answered. "Trace, I'm afraid Wes might have left town with the girls. Gram swears they were going to Sally's this morning, but I have to know for sure that they're there. Can you check?"

"I'll call you back in two minutes," he promised. "Sit tight."

"Actually, I'm already on my way into town."

"What the hell are you doing behind the wheel of a car when you're this upset?"

"Jess is driving."

"Okay, then. I'm on my way out the door. Give me another minute and I'll call you back."

She ended the call, but continued to hold the phone in a trembling grip.

"You know we'll be there ourselves in less than five minutes," Jess said.

"Right now every second feels like an eternity," she told her sister, tears welling up and spilling down her cheeks. And if they weren't there, if for any reason her ex-husband had taken off with her daughters, she knew she was going to need Trace with her. She had Jess, of course, and Gram, but she was counting on Trace to find them and bring them back. Maybe he'd even beat a little sense into Wes while he was at it.

Her phone rang. She punched the wrong button, then finally hit the right one. "Yes?"

"They're here, safe and sound," he told her. "I'm standing right outside Sally's. They must have gotten themselves dressed this morning. Carrie looks as if she tried to fix her own hair. Caitlyn's wearing one pink shoe and one red one."

The description, clearly intended to make her smile, only

made her cry harder. She was sobbing and shaking like a leaf when Jess pulled to the curb down the block from Sally's. Trace was there at once to open the door and pull her into his arms. When she was calmer, she hauled off and punched him in the chest.

He blinked and captured her fist when she would have done it again. "Hey, what was that for?"

"You planted that idea in my head, that he might want to take the girls. I would never have thought of it otherwise."

He regarded her evenly. "No, he was the one who planted it in your head. He's the one who mentioned taking them back with him today. You told me that yourself."

"But you thought it might be true. You upped the stakes."

"So what? You're blaming the messenger? All I said was to keep your guard up."

"Well, I feel like an idiot. I got Jess and Gram stirred up for no good reason."

Jess stepped up to join them. "I don't think it was for no good reason," she said quietly. "And don't worry about Gram. I've called her and told her everything is fine."

Abby frowned. "What do you mean about it not being for no good reason?"

"I think Wes deliberately brought those girls into town this morning without leaving a note just so you would be scared to death."

Abby didn't want to believe that. "He probably thought Gram would tell me where they were, which was exactly what happened."

"I don't believe that," Jess said solemnly. "And I don't think you do, either."

"I'm with Jess," Trace said, his expression grim. "If it wouldn't upset the girls, I'd go in there right now and tell him just what I think of him and his stupid games."

Abby tugged on his hand. "Let's just leave. Carrie and Caitlyn are fine. They'll be back home soon."

"I vote we stay right here," Jess said. "There's nothing to prevent Wes from leaving here and heading straight to the airport. Besides, he's seen us. It will look odd if we don't go in there now."

Trace nodded. "I agree. In fact, there's a booth opening up. Let's have breakfast. I'm starving."

"Me, too," Jess said, challenging Abby with a look. "You know you'll feel better if the girls aren't out of your sight."

Jess was right, Abby thought. In fact, Abby was just about certain she'd never willingly let them out of her sight again.

Trace followed Jess and Abby into the café, deliberately keeping one hand on Abby's shoulder as he guided them toward the empty booth. He wanted that weasel ex-husband of hers to know she had backup, in case he was thinking about doing something stupid.

Of course, if Wes also got the idea there was something going on between Trace and Abby, that was okay, too. Trace had no problem with publicly staking his claim. If things had gone the way he'd wanted them to, Abby would have been his years ago.

"Mommy!" Carrie shouted, scrambling from the booth and drawing Wes's attention to the new arrivals. A scowl spread across his face as both of his daughters immediately abandoned him.

Abby knelt down to hug Carrie and then Caitlyn, who'd followed on her heels. "Good morning. Are you having a nice breakfast with your dad?" she asked, giving Wes a pointed look.

"Yes," Caitlyn said. "Daddy said you didn't want breakfast, so how come you're here?"

"I got hungry after all," Abby said.

Trace saw the struggle it took for her not to say more. Just then he felt a tug on his hand and looked down into Carrie's upturned face. "Can we have our ice cream now?" she pleaded.

He glanced toward the plates of half-eaten pancakes and bacon on their table. "Looks to me like you didn't even finish your breakfasts. I think ice cream will have to wait for another day."

"Tomorrow?" Carrie persisted.

He glanced at Abby, who gave him a nod. "Tomorrow it is," he confirmed.

Wes rose up, his face clouded over with barely concealed anger. "Hold on," he said. "Abby, we need to discuss this. I think it would be best—"

"I'm not discussing this with you now," she said tightly. "There are far more important things you and I need to work out. We'll do that when we get back to the house."

Caitlyn and Carrie looked from one parent to another, clearly sensing the sudden tension. Thankfully, Jess stepped in, sliding back out of the booth they'd just claimed.

"Hey, girls, have you seen the cool coloring books down at Ethel's Emporium? They have crabs and seahorses and all sorts of birds that you might see around the bay. Maybe we can find one or two that you'd each like."

Caitlyn's eyes lit up. "Yes, please. Can we go with Aunt Jess, Mommy?"

"Absolutely," Abby said, clearly relieved.

"I'll have them back in a few minutes, Wes, or they can wait and ride home with us, if you don't want to hang around," Jess told him.

"I'll wait," he said tersely. He yanked a chair from a neighboring table and sat at the end of their booth. Ignoring Trace, he asked Abby, "What are you doing here? Did you deliberately follow me just to spoil my morning with the girls?"

"Don't be ridiculous," Abby snapped. "When have I ever deliberately tried to spoil your time with them?"

Wes looked shaken by her heated response. It was evident he didn't know what to make of her mood. "Okay, it doesn't matter, but we do need to discuss them coming back to New York with me today."

"It's not going to happen," she said flatly. "They're staying right here with me. It's the first time they've visited Chesapeake Shores for longer than a weekend, and I want them to take advantage of spending some real quality time with their great-grandmother, Jess and Mick, when he gets back from California."

"How long do you expect this family reunion to last?" he said.

"As long as it takes," she said, leveling a look straight at him.

Trace had to admire her gumption. She wasn't letting Wes bully her. At the same time, though, he felt guilty knowing that he was the one who'd put her in this position in the first place. If he hadn't insisted she stay here to help Jess, she and Wes wouldn't be engaged in this tug-of-war over their daughters.

"Abby, maybe we can work something out," Trace said quietly, his gaze on her.

Wes frowned. "You have no say in this," he said.

"Actually he does," Abby said. "It's okay, Trace. We made a bargain and I intend to keep it."

"What bargain?" Wes demanded.

"That's none of your concern," Trace said. He turned to Abby. "Are you sure?"

She nodded. "A hundred percent."

He leaned back, feeling more optimistic than he had in a very long time. Maybe she was just rebelling against her ex-husband, but it was also possible that in her own way, she was choosing him and the possibilities that had hung in the air the night before. He'd have to wait to find out for sure which it was.

In the meantime, though, he had to admit that he was enjoying watching Abby get under Wes's skin. The woman was no shrinking violet, that's for sure. If he hadn't seen her outside a few minutes earlier, if she hadn't nearly collapsed with relief in his arms, he would have thought her a hundred percent calm and in control. That kind of strength in the face of her own fears was just one more thing to add to the long list of reasons why he was falling in love with her all over again.

13

To Abby's surprise and relief, Jess had insisted on hitching a ride back to Gram's with Wes and the girls. She glanced over at Trace, who was regarding the sour expression on Wes's face with unmistakable amusement. When they were gone, he turned to Abby.

"That must make you feel better."

She didn't pretend not to understand. "It does. He won't even think about taking off with the girls with Jess watching his every move."

"Would you rather be doing that yourself?"

She shook her head. "No, I'm still so furious with him, it's best if we don't spend too much time together until I cool down. With any luck, he'll have left for New York by the time I get back to the house."

"I hope you're not counting on that," Trace said.

Abby sighed. "No, of course not. He wants to talk to me, so he's not going anywhere until that happens." She poked her fork into the scrambled eggs on her plate, eyed them with distaste and then pushed the plate aside. "I'm not hungry."

"How about a waffle instead? With fresh strawberries?" Trace cajoled. "They're in season, and that's the special this morning."

"I don't think so."

"Blueberry pancakes?"

She grinned at his persistence. "Are you trying to fatten me up?"

"No, just trying to make sure you have enough stamina for whatever fight awaits you when you get home."

"Oh, believe me, I can work up a good head of steam without eggs, waffles or pancakes," she said, jabbing her fork into her eggs and envisioning Wes in their place. She met Trace's gaze. "When I thought he'd taken the girls this morning, I really do think I could have strangled him with my bare hands."

"Well, thankfully, it didn't come to that," Trace said, though he seemed to find her display of temper reassuring. "Abby, I am sorry if all my warnings yesterday added to your panic."

She waved off the apology. "No, you were right that I need to be alert. In the past few days I've started to see Wes in a whole new light. It's not that he's not the same man I married or that he's undergone some dramatic change. I must have romanticized him during the years we were together, and now my blinders are finally off. I don't believe he's a truly bad man. And I know he's a good father, but…" Her voice trailed off.

"But what?" Trace prodded.

She tried to put her finger on why she was suddenly so distrustful of a man she'd once loved and respected. It had a lot to do with the things Jess had said about him, forcing her to see his passive-aggressive behavior for what it was. It also had a lot to do with the way he'd been behaving since he'd found out she was in Chesapeake Shores. It would be different if her taking the kids out of state posed a genuine hardship in terms of his visiting rights, but that wasn't actually the case. He reminded her of a spoiled kid who couldn't cope with not getting his own way even for a minute. It wasn't an attractive quality. Had he always been so inflexible and incapable of bending? Or, as Trace suspected, did he have some kind of plan where the girls were concerned, a plan she'd inadvertently given him the perfect excuse to implement?

"He scares me a little," she admitted finally, then shook her head at the absurdity of it. "That sounds ridiculous when I say it aloud."

Trace didn't look as if he thought it was ridiculous, and that scared her even more. "You're not disagreeing with me," she said with a frown.

"Because I can't. Look, I don't even know the man, so I'm probably not being at all fair. I certainly have my own agenda where he's concerned."

"Agenda?"

"In my twisted logic, he took you away from me." He held up a hand before she could speak. "I know that's not precisely what happened, but it feels like that. So, bottom line, I don't like him. Still, I like to think I'm a pretty good judge of people, and that I'm capable of viewing them with an unbiased perspective, even under circumstances like these."

"And?"

"Something feels off to me," he said. "I can't put my finger on it, but first thing tomorrow I'm going to do a little digging. You'd be surprised how much I can discover under the guise of doing a routine credit check on a bank's prospective loan customer."

"You're going to investigate him?" Abby asked incredulously, feeling a little queasy at the thought of it. "I don't know, Trace, that seems extreme." And Wes would be outraged if he ever found out.

"I'm not going to hire a private investigator," he soothed. "I'll just look into a few things. It probably won't turn up anything, and then we can both rest easier."

"I suppose that makes sense," she said reluctantly. It felt a little underhanded and sleazy. Still, this was the father of her girls, a man who wanted to take them away from her, if not for good, then at least for several weeks. She owed it to them, if not herself, to make sure there was nothing going on in Wes's life that might put them in danger. Not that she could imagine him allowing the girls to be in any kind of physical danger, but what if he was about to start legal proceedings to gain full custody? The battle would traumatize them. She had to know if that was even a remote possibility.

She stood up abruptly. "I need to go home."

To her relief, Trace didn't argue. He stood up at once, put money on the table for the bill and tip, then followed her outside.

"You feeling okay to drive? I can take you and have Jess or someone give me a ride back later."

"I'll be fine. The drive will clear my head," she assured him. "Thanks for not making me out to be a nut this morning when I freaked out."

"You could never be a nut," he said, brushing her hair away from her cheeks and tucking it behind her ears. He grinned. "Of course, even if you were a little flaky, I'd still be crazy about you."

He pressed a quick kiss to her lips, then said, "Call me if you need me for anything, okay?"

She couldn't seem to stop herself from testing him. "You'll pick up a bottle of milk and bring it to the house?" she teased, feeling a bit more lighthearted.

He regarded her with amusement. "No problem."

"Feminine hygiene products?"

He blanched. "I can do that," he said firmly.

"A hug?"

A smile spread slowly across his face. "That would be my pleasure."

She reached up and touched his unshaven cheek, liking

the way the sandpapery texture felt against her fingers. It was a testament to the fact that he'd rushed right out the second she'd asked for his help this morning. She felt somehow reassured that he always would.

"Thank you," she said softly.

"For?"

"Being around when I needed you."

"You didn't really need me. You had it all under control. I was just backup."

She stood on tiptoe and kissed him. "It's been a while since I've had backup, Trace." A long time, in fact, since she'd felt the need for it. "It feels good."

"Anytime, darlin'. Anytime."

His words were lightly spoken, but she knew with everything in her that she could trust them. That she could trust him. It made going back to the house to face down Wes a thousand times easier.

When Abby walked around the house, she found Wes sitting alone on the porch. There was no sign of the girls, Jess or Gram. She eyed him warily.

"Where is everyone?"

"They've gone for a walk on the beach," he said.

"You didn't want to go along?"

He shook his head. "No, I wanted to wait for you. We need to talk."

Bracing herself, Abby perched on the edge of an Adirondack chair. "What's on your mind?"

"I want the girls back in New York with me," he said flatly.

She gave him an incredulous look. "Is there some reason you think I might have changed my mind in the past hour? The answer's still no," she said. "This chance to spend time here might have come about unexpectedly, but it's good for them. I won't let you deny them the opportunity to get to know their extended family. Once we're back in New York, they can stay with you longer, if you want them to."

"How am I supposed to see them in the meantime, Abby?" he demanded, trying to stare her down. "You're here for God knows how long. Does that mean I won't even get my regular visits with them? Or am I supposed to turn my life upside down to fly to Maryland every other weekend? You know that's unreasonable."

"Not for you, but never mind, I can be flexible," she said, then made an impulsive decision. "Which is why I'll bring them up to New York in two weeks. They can stay with you for four days, while I deal with a few things at the office, then I'll bring them back here."

"And after that?"

"Hopefully it won't be much longer before we're all back in New York and this will no longer be an issue, but if it comes to that, I'll bring them up again. You'll have your time with them, Wes. I'm never going to try to keep them from you."

He still didn't look satisfied. "What about school? They're missing school now. If they stayed with me, they could finish out the school year."

"They're in kindergarten, not going for an advanced degree in physics," she said impatiently. "Missing the last couple of weeks of school is not that big a deal. I called the school before I came down here to let them know they'd be out for a couple of days, then spoke to their teacher again as soon as I knew we'd be here for an extended visit. Gram and I are reading with them every day. They were already ahead of everyone else with counting and even with some basic math." She met his gaze. "Any other issues?"

His expression remained disgruntled. "I don't like this, Abby. I don't like it at all."

"Yes, I gathered that. What I don't understand is why. You've gone two weeks, sometimes longer, without seeing them when you're off on a business trip or a vacation. Why is it such a big deal that they're down here with me now?"

"At least I don't flaunt my relationships in front of them," he said sourly.

Abby very nearly laughed, but she could see that he was perfectly serious. "I'm not having a relationship with Trace," she said emphatically. "I don't know how many different ways I can say that."

"Don't bother, because I wouldn't believe you, anyway. There's something between you." His gaze narrowed. "I'm guessing there always has been. He was the other man all along, wasn't he, Abby? I always knew there was someone you hadn't gotten out of your system."

"You're being absurd," she snapped.

He regarded her evenly. "Am I?"

She faltered then, wondering if it was possible that somehow she'd held something back from Wes. Was it possible she'd never gotten over Trace after all? Or was this just another of Wes's attempts to make her feel inadequate, as if she were in the wrong yet again?

"Look, Trace and I were young when we were together," she said candidly. "It was over by the time you and I met. I hadn't seen him in years until we both turned up back here a few weeks ago."

"You expect me to believe that? He lives in New York, Abby. Are you trying to tell me you haven't seen him even once up there?"

"That's exactly what I'm saying, because it's the truth. I didn't even know he'd been living in New York until the other day. That's how out of touch we've been." She shook her head. "Why are we even having this conversation?

Whom I date is none of your business. We're divorced. And up until now, I thought we'd been handling that really well for the sake of the girls."

She leveled a look into his eyes. "Don't start stirring up all sorts of ugliness now, Wes. I've never brought up the women in your life since we divorced, but I do know all about them because the twins have mentioned a whole long list of Daddy's *friends*. Don't try telling me you don't flaunt your relationships in front of them, because I know better."

He turned pale at that. "You make it sound as if I'm trotting a whole parade of women in and out of their lives. It's not like that, especially lately. Actually, there's just one woman."

"Really? You're getting serious about her?" She waited for even a tiny twinge of jealousy to strike, but there was nothing.

He nodded, then said, "You should probably know that it's Gabrielle."

Abby knew at once exactly whom he meant. "Gabrielle Mitchell? From the bond department at *my* company?" So much for Wes's supposed objections to Abby's long hours. Gabrielle's career was equally demanding. No, that objection had no doubt been voiced merely to let Wes take the position of aggrieved husband.

He nodded again, a guilty flush in his cheeks. "I've asked her to marry me."

She could have called him on it, asked exactly how long the affair had been going on right under her nose, but she was determined to take the high road. "Congratulations! Does she get along well with Carrie and Caitlyn?"

"She adores them," he said, a smile lighting up his face. "You should see her with them. It's as if they're her own children."

Abby frowned at that. "As long as she remembers that I'm their mother," she warned quietly.

"Well, of course, Gabrielle wouldn't step over that line. I'm just saying that you don't have a thing to worry about when they're with her. I won't be bringing some evil stepmother into their lives."

"Good to know," she said wryly. "And just so you know, Trace wouldn't be any kind of evil stepdad, either. Not that he's going to be in their lives permanently."

"Okay then," he said. "I guess we understand each other."

"I hope so."

"And you'll bring them up in two weeks?"

"I said I would."

He regarded her with satisfaction. "That's good then. I'll go inside and finish packing. As soon as they're back, I'll say goodbye and head for the airport to catch my flight back to New York."

He was almost to the front door when he turned back. "One last bit of advice, Abby. Don't let Jess drag you into her drama, whatever it is. You know in the end it'll backfire on you."

"You have no idea what you're talking about," she said stiffly.

"Actually I do. I've watched your sister take advantage of you time and time again. At some point you have to stop trying to make up for the fact that Megan left. Your mother needs to make that right, not you."

Abby felt the truth of his words, but hearing him point it out grated. Taking care of Jess was an obligation she'd assigned herself the minute their mother had taken off. Bree had been too young herself to care about a devastated younger sister, and Connor and Kevin had been totally self-absorbed teenagers. None of them had noticed that Jess was floundering. Mick was gone, so that left Abby and Gram to deal with all of Jess's struggles in school and her heartache at being left behind by her mother.

"You've made your opinion known more than once," she told Wes. "Your lack of understanding and compassion don't speak well of you, so perhaps you should keep your opinion to yourself from now on, at least around me and my family."

He looked as if he might say more, but then he simply shook his head and went inside. Only when he was gone did Abby realize she'd been holding her breath. She released it slowly.

Wes had been right about one thing—it was past time for her mother and Jess to make peace. Maybe they would never be close, but at least if Jess understood why Megan had left them, perhaps she could forgive her mother and move on.

The opening of the inn might be the perfect occasion, Abby concluded. There would be so much to do that Jess wouldn't be able to fret too much over her mother's presence. And the show of support from Megan might start the healing process. Abby vowed to make a call to New York later on this afternoon.

Of course, there was the very strong possibility that Mick would be furious with her for bringing Megan to town for a family occasion, but he'd just have to get over it. In fact, it was about time those two started communicating again, as well. Heck, if she really started dreaming, she could envision her parents patching things up, too.

Abby knew in her heart that neither of her parents had really wanted the divorce. She'd been old enough to understand exactly what was going on. Her mother had said a few things, expressing her displeasure over the amount of time Mick was away. Her father had reacted heatedly, accusing Megan of not appreciating the importance of his work. The next thing anyone knew Megan had called a lawyer. Once the wheels for the divorce had been set in motion, neither had been willing to stop the process. It was evidence of the O'Brien pride at its very worst.

And she was going to thrust herself into the middle of that, Abby thought wryly. Maybe she was the glutton for punishment that Wes had said she was.

When Trace showed up for Sunday dinner at his parents' house, he found his sister already there, though Laila didn't look especially happy about it. He gave her a questioning look as he went to the bar and poured himself a beer.

"Command performance," she muttered. "Mother got it into her head that we've been neglecting the whole family thing since you got back in town. She thinks if you feel more loved and missed, you'll stick around."

"As if," he replied. "How are we going to get through to Dad that you belong in this job, not me?"

"*We're* not doing anything," she said. "I have my own bookkeeping company. I make enough to live comfortably. I don't need to work for the bank, and I *really* don't need to work for someone who doesn't think I'm qualified for the job."

Trace frowned at her. "Your qualifications have never been an issue, Laila."

She grinned at him. "Oh, that's right. It's my sex."

Their mother walked into the room just in time to overhear Laila's comment, but not its context.

"Young lady, that is not a proper subject for a Sunday afternoon."

Trace grinned. "Laila was referring to her gender, Mother."

Beatrice Riley looked slightly flustered by her mistake. "Oh, sorry. But what does your gender have to do with anything?"

"Ask Dad," Laila said.

"Not that again," Beatrice said impatiently. "Your father offered you a job at the bank."

"About five rungs lower on the ladder than the one he's

given to Trace," Laila reminded her. "Never mind. It's old news. We're here to celebrate the return of the prodigal son, so let's do that." She lifted her glass of wine in a mocking salute.

"Laila, that's enough," Beatrice scolded. "I'm going to check on our meal. I trust you'll be on better behavior when I return."

Trace sat down next to his sister and whispered in her ear, "You're making it very hard for me to turn this around so you wind up with what you want."

She gave him a forced smile. "Didn't you hear me earlier? I have everything I want."

"Then why are you acting as if you're about ten seconds away from imploding?"

"I had a bad night, if you must know."

Trace took a closer look and saw the sadness lurking in her too-bright eyes. "What happened? Did you and Dave have a fight?"

Laila had been dating the same man since college. Dave Fisher was likable enough, but he'd never struck Trace as the kind of man capable of strong passion. He realized it was an odd sort of thing for him to worry about, given that Dave was with his sister, but he thought Laila deserved a guy who could work up some enthusiasm over something. Instead, Dave was solid, nice and about as bland as the oatmeal he ate every morning for breakfast. The only time Trace had ever seen him stirred up was over a three-cent error in his bank statement.

"Dave and I don't fight," she said with an air of resignation. "The man is going to bore me into an early grave."

Hallelujah! Trace thought. "Then end it," he told her. "Find somebody else."

"In Chesapeake Shores? I've known every man in this town since we were toddlers. It's not as if I'm going to wake up one day, take a fresh look at someone and say, 'Oh, my gosh, he's the one!'"

"You won't know that for sure until you break up with Dave. You have no idea who else might be out there. I know for a fact that this place fills up with people on weekends all summer long and that includes professional men from Washington and Baltimore. But you're not going to meet them if you're sitting at home on your sofa watching tapes from the History Channel with Dave."

She sighed heavily. "I suppose you have a point, but it's hard to walk away when you've spent so many years with someone. He's been my safety net. He's a good guy. He really is."

Trace had heard the same thing about another man all too recently. Neither time had it sat well with him.

"Break it off, Laila. You need a fresh start. You'll never be happy if you just keep drifting along in this dead-end relationship."

"It's not dead-end," she said.

He blinked in surprise. "It's not?"

"He's asked me to marry him. Last night, in fact. He wrote it all out on paper, how practical and sensible it would be. The list was quite extensive."

Trace groaned. "Now there's the proposal of any girl's dreams. I'm sure your pulse absolutely raced."

Laila grinned. "It was pretty funny, actually. Or it would have been if it hadn't been so horrifying. I sat there listening to him, and all I could think was that this would be my life until the day I died, looking at lists of pros and cons."

Trace regarded her with alarm. "You're not seriously considering it, are you? I swear if you do, you can forget about the job at the bank. I'll tell Dad to have you committed instead."

"No, I'm not considering it," she said. "I told Dave no. In fact, I broke up with him." Tears filled her eyes. She rubbed them away impatiently. "I hurt him, Trace. He looked so bewildered. It was like kicking a puppy that trusts you. I felt awful."

"Better to feel awful for a few hours or even a few weeks than to be miserable for the rest of your life," he told her. "Dave will get over it. I guarantee you he'll find a replacement in no time, someone who's far better suited to him."

"Maybe I could fix him up," she said, her expression thoughtful.

Trace stared at her incredulously. "Are you crazy? Do you have any friends you dislike that much?"

"Stop it! He's a great guy. He just wasn't right for me."

"Okay, I can leave it at that, but trust me, he won't appreciate you trying to find a replacement for him."

"Why not?"

"Because he's a man. Not only do we not take rejection well, we certainly don't want the woman involved to pop up a few days later offering a fresh alternative like some sort of human sacrifice. If Abby had sent one of her friends to console me after she took off, I would have been furious."

Laila gave him a considering look. "It might have been better if she had."

"Why would you say that?"

"Because it might have proved to you that she was over you. Maybe then you could have moved on, instead of wasting all these years pining for her."

He didn't like the way she'd summed up the past ten years of his life. "They weren't wasted. I built up a very successful career."

She twirled a finger in the air. "Whoopee!"

He scowled at her reaction. "And I dated."

"Name two women you went out with more than twice," his sister challenged. "Oh, wait, there was Rene. She lasted a few months, until you figured out that just because she was the spitting image of Abby didn't mean she bore any resemblance to her otherwise. Anyone else?"

Much to his chagrin, Trace was stymied. "Okay, so I didn't have another lasting relationship, but it wasn't for lack of trying. And Rene didn't look anything like Abby."

"Auburn hair, blue eyes, slender figure," his sister recited. "Sound familiar?"

"Whatever," he said, brushing the comparison aside and ready to drop the subject.

Laila, however, clearly still had points she wanted to make. "Besides, brother dearest, casual sex is not the same as seriously looking," she said, just as their mother returned.

"Don't you try to tell me *this* conversation was about gender," Beatrice said, regarding them both with disapproval. "Dinner's ready, and I don't want to hear one single word about sex at the table."

"Yes, ma'am," Trace said, barely containing a grin. "You won't hear that word come out of my mouth. Of course, I can't speak for Laila. She seems a little obsessed with it today for some reason."

"You are so dead," his sister muttered as she strode past them on her way to the dining room.

His mother paused and frowned at him. "I don't know what gets into you two. Aren't you a little old for squabbling?"

Trace draped an arm over her stiff shoulders. "What else are we supposed to do?" he teased. "You ruled out the one subject we both found interesting."

She rolled her eyes, then regarded him somberly. "What's really going on with Laila? I can tell she's upset about something. She's been in an odd mood ever since she got here."

"Ask her," he suggested. "It's not my news to share."

Worry immediately creased her brow. "She and Dave aren't getting married, are they?"

Trace was relieved he wasn't the only one who'd thought it an unsuitable match. He felt he could reassure his mother that she needn't worry about that. "No."

"Thank goodness!"

"Maybe you shouldn't seem quite so pleased when she tells you," he said wryly.

She scowled. "I know how to be diplomatic when it's called for."

"Speaking of diplomatic, Mother, how are we going to get her the job she wants at the bank?" he asked. "You know she's the one who ought to be there, not me, but she's every bit as stubborn as Dad is."

"I'm very well aware of that. Haven't I lived with your father for nearly forty years? And I made a decision years ago not to get involved in bank business."

She was about to step into the dining room when he stopped her. "Not even if it means your daughter's happiness?"

She looked up at him. "I thought her accounting company was doing well."

"It is. That's not the point."

"You really think working for your father is that important to her?"

"I know it is," he said. "She needs to know he trusts her, that he believes in her."

His mother nodded decisively. "Then I'm quite sure if we put our heads together we can come up with a solution. I'll give it some thought."

"Thank you."

She gave him a sad look. "Just promise me that you won't stay away so long once you do go back to New York."

"I won't," he said. "Being back here this time has given me a new perspective on Chesapeake Shores."

"That has something to do with Abby's presence, I'm sure," she said, studying him closely as she awaited his reply.

"It does."

She hesitated. "Do you think she's feeling the same way? About the town, I mean?"

"If you're asking if we could settle here at some point, I have no idea. First I have to see if she'll consider starting over with me. The logistics of our lives will fall into place after that."

She smiled. "That gives me room for hope, then. Nothing would please me more than to see the two of you together finally and to have you living close by." Her eyes filled with excitement. "Oh, Trace, I know the perfect house for you."

He immediately put the brakes on her enthusiasm. "One thing at a time, Mother."

Unfortunately, she seemed to be on a roll. She ignored his warning. "Perhaps I should run over to the inn tomorrow and invite her to lunch," she said, looking pleased with herself. "Yes, that's exactly what I'll do."

"I don't need you courting Abby for me," he protested.

She gave him a skeptical look that said otherwise. "You lost her before, didn't you, so apparently you can use all the help you can get."

Trace laughed. "You're right. Maybe I can."

His mother was known around town for her persuasiveness. If she could wheedle money out of everyone she knew for a good cause, then surely she could coax Abby into keeping an open mind where he was concerned. And an open mind was all he needed. He was reasonably confident he could take it from there.

14

Abby decided to call in the big guns to persuade her mother that she needed to visit Chesapeake Shores for the opening of Jess's inn.

"Carrie, Caitlyn, come in here. We're going to call Grandma Megan."

The twins came running. They adored her mother, who indulged them with trips to art galleries, plays and regular visits to the Bronx Zoo. Abby doubted they grasped the importance of the art they saw, but being exposed to it was a wonderful thing. And they seemed to love having tea afterward. They were enchanted with the tiny sandwiches and cakes. Back home, they had tea parties with their favorite dolls for at least a week after each excursion. Abby couldn't help wishing Jess had had those same kind of memories with their mother.

Regarding the twins seriously, she said, "Now before I call, I want to explain that I'm going to try to convince her she needs to come down here for the opening of Aunt Jess's inn. You have to help me talk her into it. Tell her you miss her, okay?" she requested, unashamed of her attempt at manipulation. It was, after all, for a good cause.

"We do miss her," Caitlyn said, even as Carrie nodded, then added, "Lots and lots."

Satisfied, Abby dialed Megan's number. When her mother answered, she handed the phone to Carrie.

"Hi, Grandma Megan, it's me, Carrie. Caitlyn's here, too."

Abby hit the button for speakerphone. "I'm also here, Mom."

"Well, my goodness, I was beginning to wonder what happened to my favorite girls," Megan said warmly. "It's been ages since I heard from you."

"We're at the beach," Carrie told her excitedly. "With Gram and Aunt Jess. And Grandpa Mick was here, too."

"I see," Megan said, her voice losing some of its warmth and enthusiasm.

Abby stepped in. "Actually that's why we're calling, Mom. We're hoping you'll join us."

"Absolutely not," she said emphatically, leaving no room for argument.

Fortunately the girls were oblivious to the finality in her response.

"But, Grandma Megan, we really, really miss you and there's going to be a big party, so you should be here," Carrie said.

"Please, Grandma Megan," Caitlyn begged. "It's going to be a really big party. We're going to get new dresses and new shoes. Mommy says we can pick them out ourselves when we come to New York to see Daddy. Maybe you can help us."

Her mother's hesitation told Abby that her scheme was working. Megan had never been able to deny the twins anything, especially not a shopping spree. Their closets were crammed with dresses and outfits from some of the top designers of children's clothes. They had more shoes than Abby did, eighty percent of them courtesy of their indulgent grandmother.

"Okay, so tell me, what's this about a party?" Megan asked, her voice cautious, giving away nothing about her intentions.

It was a tiny opening, but Abby seized it. "Jess has bought

the old inn up the road from our house. That's why I came down here, to help her deal with the remodeling." She saw no point in mentioning the financial difficulties or the role those had played in her continued presence. "The party's on June thirtieth, right before it officially opens. It really should be a family affair, Mom. Please do this for Jess."

"Will your father be there?"

"He's promised to come back from California for it," she said.

"Then you know it's a bad idea, Abby. We can't even be in the same room without having an argument. It's been that way ever since the divorce. There was an unbelievable amount of tension every time I came down there to visit you kids. I doubt your father's suddenly mellowed. If I'm right, we would spoil this for Jess and everyone else. The focus would wind up being on us, when it should be on your sister."

"What makes you think that you and Dad are destined to argue? My wedding was the last time you even saw each other." She winced as she recalled what a stiff and awkward encounter that had been. For most of the day they'd done everything humanly possible to avoid each other. Surely, though, time would have eased the tension. "Don't you think you could at least manage to be civil for Jess's sake? You owe her this, Mom. You know you do. Think about how many other big events in her life you missed."

"Only because she made it plain she didn't want me there," Megan said wearily.

Abby couldn't deny that of all of them, Jess had made it the hardest for her mother to remain in her life. She'd openly rebelled against visiting her in New York, and Mick had never insisted she make the trip. On Megan's visits to Chesapeake Shores, Jess had thrown tantrums when she was young, then pulled convenient vanishing acts as she got older. Abby knew it was because she was hurt and that

Megan should have fought harder to bridge the ever-widening gap between them, but it wasn't too late for her to start doing that.

"Well, I want you here now," Abby said firmly. "And Jess needs you here, whether she admits it or not."

"Please, Grandma Megan," Caitlyn cajoled again.

"I'll think about it," Megan said at last.

"Really think about it?" Abby prodded. "Or will you dismiss it the second I hang up?"

"I'll really think about it," Megan assured her. "Will Bree and your brothers be there?" There was a trace of wistfulness in her voice as she asked.

"I haven't spoken to them yet. I doubt Kevin will be home from Iraq. His tour lasts a few more months. I imagine Bree and Connor will try to make it, though. It will be a real O'Brien family reunion, Mom, and it won't be the same if you're not here."

"I'll give it some thought and get back to you in a day or two," Megan promised.

"If you don't agree, the girls and I will badger you when we get up to New York. You might as well give in now."

"I said I'd think about it. That's the most I can promise."

"Okay, then," Abby said, backing down for the moment.

"Love you, girls," her mother said.

"Love you," the twins shouted back, then scampered from the room to get back outdoors.

"I love you, too," Abby said. "And I'll call you to make plans for that shopping trip with the girls. Bye, Mom."

She hung up and turned to find Gram staring at her with a dismayed expression.

"What have you done?" Gram asked.

"I've invited Mom to the opening party at the inn," she replied with a touch of defiance.

Her grandmother's face filled with dismay. "Oh, Abby, why would you do such a thing? You know it will go badly."

"I don't know that," Abby insisted.

"It's Jess's big night. Did you ask her what she wanted?"

"No, because she would have told me not to do it, even though having Mom here would mean the world to her. She's too angry and scared of rejection to reach out, so I did it for her."

"And your father? How do you think Mick will feel? If he learns about this, he'll stay right where he is, all the way across the country, rather than see Megan under this roof again. It was hard enough on him having her back here to visit you children."

"I think you're wrong," Abby said, though with less confidence than she'd felt a few minutes ago. Gram knew Mick better than any of them. "Maybe they can finally mend fences, or at least find a way to be civil so the family can celebrate holidays and other important occasions together."

Gram shook her head. "You always were an optimist. Well, you didn't ask me what I thought ahead of time, so it's all on you. I hope you don't come to regret it."

Abby sighed at her dire tone. She was already praying that Gram had it wrong and that this wasn't going to blow up in her face. To prepare for the possibility that she'd need some allies, she called Bree next. Her sister, who'd won a grant to write scripts for a regional theater in Chicago, wasn't home, so Abby left her a message. She tried Connor at his apartment in Baltimore and wound up leaving a voice mail for him, as well. Though his final year of law school studies kept him busy, she was sure he'd make time for this.

Now all that was left was to tell Jess what she'd done. And she was pretty sure that it would be best not to do that until she had firm commitments from all of them. At least that would give her a few days to come up with a strategy that wouldn't end with Jess accusing her once again of trying to run—or maybe ruin—her life.

Jess had spent several days back in April interviewing potential chefs for the inn and had finally found the perfect candidate. Gail Chambers had solid credentials, despite only being in her late twenties. She'd been a sous-chef in several excellent restaurants on Maryland's Eastern Shore, but was eager to run her own kitchen. She was also recently married to a man with two children, and they wanted to settle in a small, close-knit community, where the kids would get a solid education but within comparatively easy commuting distance to her husband's job in Annapolis. Chesapeake Shores and the inn were a perfect fit with their needs.

The only issue had been that the inn's kitchen wasn't state-of-the-art. Jess had promised to look into upgrading the appliances, with a professional quality range at the top of Gail's wish list. Now that she had Abby's infusion of cash, Jess decided she could make good on that promise.

"I'm going to meet with the new chef," she told Abby as she headed out at midmorning on Monday.

Abby barely glanced up from the paperwork that she always seemed to be obsessed with. "Have fun," she murmured and went right back to whatever she'd been doing.

Jess was actually relieved for once that Abby hadn't given her full attention. She'd been anticipating an argument about this purchase. She thought she had lots of valid reasons for buying the equipment now, but she had a hunch Abby would find fault with them.

An hour later she and Gail were engrossed with shiny, stainless-steel appliances that could have made any chef weep with envy. One glance at the price tags almost had Jess weeping herself. She'd had no idea that professional commercial-grade equipment could cost this much. She'd looked at their bank balance, though, and knew there was money there for this kind of an investment in the inn's future.

Swallowing her anxiety over Abby's reaction, she turned to Gail. "Okay, we have to be prudent here. If you can only pick one thing, which would it be? A new range? A bigger refrigerator? Something else?"

Gail immediately gravitated to the huge Viking dual fuel range with its convection oven, multiple burners and special cooking surface for grilling. Jess winced at the price.

"It'll last forever," Gail said, clearly sensing her reluctance. "It's the kind of investment you won't regret. If you buy something on the cheap, the repair bills will eat up whatever savings you have in the short run."

"I suppose you're right," Jess said, seeing the logic immediately. Surely, as pragmatic as Abby was, she would get that, too. Still, Jess could envision her sister's reaction. "Is there another model, maybe a smaller version of this one, that would work as well? I mean, we're probably not going to be catering to huge crowds very often."

"But when we do, you'll want something this size. Otherwise there are certain events you simply won't be able to take on. You said something about wanting to do weddings at the inn. Even for a reception of fifty or so, you need the kind of capability this will give you."

Gail had hit on the strongest selling point yet. Jess had big plans for building the inn's private-event business. Obviously they couldn't handle conventions, but small, classy weddings or family reunions would work nicely. Her chef would need the right equipment if they were to pull off that kind of event.

"Okay, we'll get it," she said decisively. "Let's find that salesman and make the arrangements."

She just prayed she'd be alone at the inn when it was delivered. Once it was in place in the kitchen, it would be a whole lot harder for Abby to insist it be sent back. In fact, since her sister seldom went into the kitchen except to grab a soft drink or tea from the refrigerator or to pour herself a cup of coffee, maybe she wouldn't even notice the new purchase. Jess glanced at the monstrous stove and sighed. Hardly likely, she thought. It was much more likely that they were going to have the mother of all fights the instant Abby spotted it.

Jess steeled herself for the argument that would follow. She'd just have to pull rank for once. Her inn. Her decision.

Abby's money, a voice in her head nagged.

No, Jess thought defiantly. It was the inn's money now. Abby had made an investment. She hadn't been given control, except by Trace, but on paper at least, the inn belonged to Jess and Jess alone. She still had the power to write the checks.

Oh, who was she kidding? She'd been spoiling for a fight with her sister over control ever since Trace had put Abby in charge of the finances. It might as well be over a magnificent piece of equipment, instead of all the nickel-and-dime stuff they'd been bickering over up until now.

"You look a little pale," Gail observed. "Are you sure that buying this is okay? It's my dream equipment, but I don't want you to blow your budget to smithereens to get it. I'd like to be able to buy quality produce and meats in a few weeks, not skimp on ingredients."

"It's not a problem," Jess said firmly, reaching for the credit card receipt and scrawling her name across the bottom.

She was able to narrow down the window for the delivery to a couple of hours and carefully made a note of the date and time. Abby had said something earlier about running up to New York for a couple of days, so the timing should be ideal. It was going to be fine, she reassured herself.

Of course, if she was so sure about that, why was she working so hard to make sure the delivery happened when Abby was away? Rather than think about that, she turned to Gail. "Do you have time for lunch? We could start talking about menus."

The chef's eyes lit up. "Fabulous. I already have lots of ideas."

For the next two hours, they sat in a fast-food restaurant jotting down notes about possible main courses, appetizers, breakfasts and, of course, the decadent desserts they both thought were a must. Jess used every piece of paper in her purse, including the one with the delivery information on it. Gail ran out of pages in her notepad, as well. As they left the restaurant, she turned all of her notes over to Gail.

"I'll be in touch in a day or two with some daily menus, as well as a list of possible appetizers for the opening party," Gail promised as they parted.

Jess hugged her, grateful for her enthusiasm and her obvious expertise. "I think we're going to work really, really well together."

"Me, too."

Jess drove home, her head spinning. She was almost as excited as she had been on the day she'd signed the papers to buy the inn. It was all coming together, just the way she'd envisioned it. The opening was only a few weeks away, and after that it would be smooth sailing.

She considered going straight back to the inn to share her excitement with Abby as she'd planned, but decided instead to tell Gram. Somewhere deep inside, she recognized that she was afraid that Abby would find a way to cast a damper over her enthusiasm. Just for today she wanted to bask in what she'd accomplished, rather than listening to another lecture about the mistakes she'd made. There'd be time enough for that when Abby discovered the bill for the new range.

* * *

Abby had dealt with all of the inn's bills by lunchtime and had turned her attention to the job that actually paid *her* bills when she looked up to find Trace studying her.

"You look cute with your brow all furrowed like that," he commented with a grin.

Abby leaned back in her chair. "You have an odd standard for cute."

"Nope. It's just you. I think you're cute all the time."

She gave him an exaggerated scowl. "Just what every woman hopes to hear."

He laughed at her indignation. "How many times have I told you you're beautiful? Didn't that sink in? And sexy. Have I mentioned how sexy you are?"

She caught herself before she smiled. "I don't believe you have. Not the sexy part, anyway."

"I guess I thought that went without saying, since I've been kissing you every chance I get."

There hadn't been that many chances, she thought to herself, but the few there had been were definitely memorable. He clearly didn't need to hear that, though. His ego was massive enough as it was. "What are you doing here, by the way?"

"We have a date. Don't you remember?"

"A date?" she repeated blankly.

"Ice cream with the twins. I figured I'd toss in lunch, too."

"You really want to spend that much time with the twins?"

He frowned at the question. "Why wouldn't I? They're great kids."

"I could change your mind about that by letting you take them to town on your own. I think you'd come away with a different opinion entirely."

He pulled a chair up and sat down beside her. "Abby Winters, are you dissing your own adorable daughters? I'm shocked."

"Just being realistic." She looked over his designer suit, crisp white shirt and silk tie. Great attire for banking, but not for dining with her girls. "What exactly did you have in mind for lunch? You look as if you're dressed for the yacht club."

"I was thinking hot dogs from the vendor at the end of Main Street," he said at once. "The girls can run around outside and work off some energy, while you and I enjoy a little adult conversation."

She shook her head. "You really are a dreamer. And if that's your plan, I suggest you stop at your apartment and change, unless you're experienced at getting mustard, ketchup and ice cream out of your clothes."

"I'm a very neat eater."

"Carrie and Caitlyn aren't."

"Ah, I see. Okay, I'll leave the jacket and tie in the car." He studied her with a wicked glint in his eyes. "Or were you hoping to get a look at my apartment and sneak a peek at me in my underwear?"

"With two five-year-olds present? I don't think so."

"Okay, then, let's go pick them up and get this show on the road."

Abby stood up, but before she could gather up her purse and the sweater she'd worn on her walk over to the inn earlier, Trace snagged her wrist.

"I think I'll have my dessert first," he said, leaning in for a slow, lingering kiss that steamed up the room. "Yep, sexy. No question about it."

Shaken, Abby regarded him with dazed eyes. "That wasn't supposed to be on the menu."

"Really?" he said innocently. "I could have sworn it was today's special."

She gave him a smug look. "Well, since you're so satisfied with that, no ice cream for you later. And no more stolen kisses, either." She didn't think she could take the damage to her nerves. It was getting harder and harder to tell herself that she and Trace were nothing more than old friends, because she was beginning to remember with total, sizzling clarity just how much more they had been.

"Mr. Riley, can we have another ice cream cone?" Carrie begged, even though she already had chocolate pretty much head to toe from the last one. Of course, some of it had ended up on the ground when she'd been running after her sister.

Caitlyn was covered with strawberry ice cream and still had several bites of her cone left, but she bounced up and down beside her sister. "Yes, please," she said, placing her sticky, strawberry-coated hand on his thigh, leaving behind a streak of pale pink ice cream.

Trace glanced at Abby, who was turned away, clearly trying not to laugh. So far he had a streak of mustard down one sleeve, a splash of ketchup on the front of his shirt and now strawberry ice cream. He was pretty sure there was a smudge of chocolate on his face, because Carrie had crawled up onto the bench and patted his cheek earlier while thanking him for the first cone. She'd tilted the cone precariously in the process, and he'd almost wound up with the whole thing in his lap.

He gazed into those earnest little faces and struggled with what to tell them. Logic told him they couldn't possibly still be hungry, not after one and a half hot dogs each, French fries and a double-scoop cone of ice cream. However, he had promised them all they could eat.

Again, he looked toward Abby for guidance, but she pretended to be gazing at the bay, leaving him to handle the situation.

"Okay," he said at last. "But only one scoop and this time

let's get it in a bowl. Then you can sit over there under that tree and eat it with a spoon."

"Okay," Caitlyn said agreeably. "I want vanilla this time."

"Me, too," Carrie said.

"Abby, what about you? Do you want more ice cream?"

"I think one hot-fudge sundae—which you pushed on me, by the way—is more than enough."

He grinned. "I notice you ate every bite, though."

"Well, of course I did! You can't let hot fudge go to waste. That would be a crime."

"Okay, then, two scoops of vanilla ice cream in bowls," he said. "I'll be back in a minute."

He hadn't taken two steps when sticky little hands seized his, one on each side.

"We'll help," Carrie declared.

Something turned over deep inside Trace at the feel of those hands in his. They were so sweet, so trusting. He felt a powerful surge of paternal protectiveness that he'd never anticipated. He knew in that instant that he'd do anything necessary to be sure that nothing or no one ever hurt them.

A few minutes later, with the girls settled in the shade with their bowls of what was rapidly becoming vanilla soup, he turned to Abby.

"They're really amazing, you know. You're clearly a great mom."

To his surprise, she sighed.

"I don't always feel like one," she confessed. "Back home, I work too long. Some days I barely get to spend an hour with them before they go to sleep. I wonder if one day they won't start to resent me for that, the way Jess resents Mick."

"It's not the amount of time you spend with them, it's the quality. They obviously adore you."

"You might think this is crazy, but some days I look at

them and the relationship they have with the nanny, and I actually get jealous. I think she knows them better than I do. She was there for so many of their firsts, and I wasn't."

"Hey, don't beat yourself up for that. You set your priorities, and you did it because it was best for them."

"Did I? Or was it my own ambition that drove me?"

He frowned at the question. "I hear Wes talking now. How many times did he say something like that to you?"

"More than once," she admitted. "Just because he was the one to say it doesn't make it wrong."

"It does if it made you question yourself as a mother. I've seen dysfunctional mothers and, believe me, you don't even reach the bottom rung on the ladder. Remember Delilah Bennett? Now *she* was a bad mother."

Just as he'd hoped, Abby grinned. "You mean because she was basically running a prostitution ring and drug operation out of her house?"

"Exactly. See what I mean? You're not even close."

"I should hope not."

"And Mitzi Gaylord, you remember her? She dressed in tight shorts and sexy tank tops for her boys' Little League games."

"I'll admit that caused quite a stir among the men in town, but I'm not sure it made her an awful mother," Abby said, but she was grinning.

Trace's expression sobered. "Look, being a bad mom is taking off when some of your kids are too little to understand why you're leaving. Being a bad mom is leaving a seventeen-year-old daughter to take over and try to make things right. You lived that with Megan. You know firsthand what it's like to have a mother you can't count on. You will *never* allow your girls to feel that kind of pain." He tucked a finger under her chin. "Don't ever let me hear you question your mothering skills again."

Tears flooded her eyes at his fierce words. "My mom..." Her voice trailed off. She was clearly unable to come up with an adequate defense for what Megan had done to her, to all of them.

"Was flawed," Trace said more gently. "It doesn't make her a terrible person, just human. She made the worst kind of mistake with you, Jess and the others. Trust me, those are the kind of mistakes that damage a kid, not just working hard to earn money to support them."

Lower lip quivering, she whispered, "You're amazing. You always know just what to say, even now, after all these years. It was the same way when we were kids. I'm not sure I could have gotten through any of that without you right there saying exactly what I needed to hear. When Mom didn't come back for us..."

"I was there, Abby. I saw how much it hurt. I'm sure whatever I said back then was pretty trite and superficial, but I wanted so badly to make you feel better."

"The point is you tried. Mick was too lost in his own misery to deal with what we were going through," she corrected. "And Gram was too swamped. As for recently, believe me, Wes never bothered to say anything supportive."

"Yeah, well, he's Wes," he said.

Her lips curved. "That does sum it up, doesn't it?" She glanced over toward the shade, where both girls were sprawled out on the grass, sound asleep, their bowls of melted ice cream forgotten. "I think it's time to go."

"Okay," Trace said. "Just let me say one more thing before we do. From here on out, no matter what happens or doesn't happen between us, you can count on me, understood?"

She held his gaze, then slowly nodded, a smile playing about her lips. "Understood."

There was complete and total conviction in her voice, and for the first time since they'd reconnected a few weeks ago,

Trace actually started to believe there might be real hope for the future. And this time he was going to do everything he could think of to make sure Abby didn't run away from it.

15

On the taxi ride into the city, Abby felt none of the usual excitement she'd always experienced on returning to Manhattan. Stress seemed to kick in on the Triborough Bridge and continue all the way along the FDR Expressway, even though the sky was a brilliant blue and sunlight filtered down in bright shafts between the skyscrapers. It was a perfect early-summer day. It would be a few weeks before stifling heat kicked in and radiated up from the pavement.

Despite her mood, the girls were clearly thrilled about getting to spend a few days with their dad and going shopping with their grandmother. Megan had agreed to meet them this morning for shopping and lunch. Then Wes would pick the twins up at their apartment and take them to his place until Monday evening.

Abby was trying hard not to worry about the plan. A tiny part of her was still fearful that when the time came for her to leave for Chesapeake Shores with Carrie and Caitlyn, Wes would pull some sort of a stunt to keep them with him. She tried to push the concern from her mind, but it continued to nag at her.

As they arrived at their Upper East Side apartment, she spotted her mother walking down the street. At fifty-four,

Megan was still an attractive, vital woman with long legs and an easy, brisk stride. Her short hair, now a shade of honey-blond, was professionally highlighted and accentuated her large, dark blue eyes. Her face was virtually unlined, her figure trim from daily workouts at a gym frequented by a few celebrities. Her taste in clothes was impeccable, which meant she could carry off an outfit from a discount store as easily as she could the designer labels that filled her closet.

When she spotted Abby and her granddaughters emerging from the taxi, her face lit up with unmistakable joy.

As the girls ran straight to her, Abby paid the driver, set their luggage on the curb, then approached more slowly. She still wasn't sure what she was going to say to convince her mother to make the commitment to come for the inn's opening. Thus far, Megan had remained determinedly silent on the subject, her reluctance palpable whenever Abby broached the subject.

"Good timing," Abby said, giving her mother a quick hug. "Come on up while I drop off our bags and then we'll head out."

In the elevator, Abby observed her mother closely, noting a hint of exhaustion in her eyes. "Mom, is everything okay?"

"I've just had a lot on my mind lately. Nothing to worry about, though." She forced a smile. "I'm just so glad you're back home again, even if it is for only a few days. I feel a bit at loose ends when you're gone."

Abby felt a flash of guilt, then dismissed it. "Mom, you have dozens of friends in New York. You have a wonderful job that you love. You've made a good life for yourself."

"That's true, but you're the only family I have here, the only ones who keep in touch."

The hint of nostalgia in her voice made Abby realize what was going on. "Mom, what's really on your mind? Is it my invitation to come to Chesapeake Shores? Has it stirred up a lot of old memories?"

Megan nodded. "That's certainly part of it. Now that you kids, except for Jess, are grown and gone, I've had little reason to visit. The last time was for your wedding."

"But that's not the only thing on your mind, is it?"

Her mother cast a pointed look toward the girls. "Why don't we discuss it later? We have a big day planned."

Abby nodded, but she wasn't willing to put off the conversation for as long as her mom was obviously hoping. The instant they were inside the apartment, she sent Carrie and Caitlyn off to their room to pick out anything special they wanted to take with them to their father's.

"We have time for a cup of tea," she informed her mother, heading into the kitchen without waiting for a response. She took a shortcut that Gram would have abhorred and put two cups of water into the microwave, teabags already immersed in them. Two minutes later, she set the cups of brewed tea on the table, then gestured toward a chair.

"Have a seat, Mom. Our big day can wait a few minutes while we catch up."

Her mother remained standing, her back toward Abby as she gazed out toward the East River. When she finally turned around, her expression was bleak. "We really should go. We don't have a lot of time to fit in shopping and lunch before Wes will be here to pick up the girls."

"We'll manage," Abby said. "Talk to me."

Megan finally sat down with a sigh. "Okay, if you must know, I had a conversation with your father the other night," she admitted.

Abby regarded her with surprise. "You spoke to Dad? Did he call you?"

She shook her head. "No. I wanted to test the waters, see how he'd feel about me coming for Jess's party."

A feeling of dread settled in Abby's stomach. "And?"

"He told me to do whatever I felt like doing," she said wearily.

Abby didn't see the problem, but obviously there was one. "That's good, isn't it? It means he doesn't mind if you're there. He left the door open."

Her mother gave her a rueful look. "We're talking about your father. You have to know there was more. He said that's what I'd do anyway. In other words, he accused me of being selfish."

"How can it be selfish to do something that would mean so much to Jess?"

"Because it would hurt Mick. He won't come if I'm there," she said.

Abby didn't want to believe her father could be so stubborn, but she knew he was certainly more than capable of being pigheaded, especially where Megan was concerned. That's how they'd wound up divorced in the first place. And the truth was that there had been a similar standoff over Abby's wedding, until Gram had put her foot down. Abby knew from her conversation with her grandmother that there would be no similar interference this time.

"Did he actually say that?" she prodded.

"In those words, no. But believe me, I got the message. I could always read him, even when he was being stoically silent."

"Mom, please don't stay away because of this," Abby pleaded. "This is the perfect time for you to make this overture to Jess. The inn opening means so much to her and, even though she probably won't admit it, your support will mean the world. If Dad can't handle you being there, then that's on him."

"Oh, sweetie, you're forgetting that it's his home. I'm the one who walked away. I can't just breeze back in as if nothing happened. He's right. That is selfish. Not only will it hurt Mick, but your sisters and brothers have their issues with me, as well. It has the potential to turn into a big drama, rather than being the happy occasion Jess deserves."

Abby scrambled for some way to persuade her that it could be worked out. "What if I can convince him to say it's okay? Or book you into the inn, rather than having you stay at the house? Will you come then? It may be awkward at first, but the whole point is for this to be a fresh beginning for our family."

Megan regarded her curiously. "Why is this so important to you?"

"Because we should all be together for Jess's big day."

Her mother reached over and squeezed her hand. "You always were a better mother than I was. You fight so hard to keep everyone happy, to make sure that we act like a family, even when things are falling apart. That's not your job, Abby. Mick and I created this family and this mess. It's up to us to fix it."

"Will you do it, then? Will you fix it, so you can be there for your daughter? For all of us? Call Dad back. Really talk to him for once, tell him how important this is."

Megan made a face. "I tried that. I just told you how well it went over." Changing the subject, she asked, "Have you heard from Bree? Is she coming?"

Abby hadn't spoken to her sister, but she had gotten an e-mail that she planned to come. "She says she will."

"And Connor?"

"He may just come for the day, but he'll be there. The only one missing will be Kevin. And you, unless you change your mind."

"I just don't want to make your father any more unhappy than I already have. And the same thing's true where Jess is concerned. I might feel differently if she'd asked me herself. Does she even know we've discussed this?"

"Not exactly," Abby admitted. "I wanted to be sure you'd be there before I said anything. I didn't want to get her hopes up and then disappoint her."

Megan gave her a wry look. "Are you so sure she'd be disappointed? For a very long time after I left, she wouldn't even talk to me on the phone. Every time I visited, she found a way to punish me for leaving. Nothing I tried worked with her." When Abby started to speak, she held up her hand. "Not that I didn't deserve it, but none of you knew the whole story."

"What story is that?" Abby asked, puzzled.

Megan hesitated. "Let's not get into all this now. The point is that Jess isn't going to be happy about me coming."

"Mom, you don't know that," Abby protested again.

"I do know," Megan insisted. "Even though you haven't said it, I know she's balked at seeing me when she's come to visit you in the city. Oh, you've come up with some incredibly creative excuses, but I know it's Jess who's made the choice to turn down lunch or cocktails or shopping, whatever I've suggested the three of us could do."

Abby couldn't deny it. "That doesn't mean you should stop trying."

"I haven't and I won't, but I'm not holding out much hope she'll change her opinion of me," Megan said wearily. "Even right after I left, she flatly refused to come to New York for a visit. I could have forced that, I know, but I knew how badly I'd let all of you down. I guess I kept thinking that I'd work everything out with each of you in time. You and I have done that. I think that's because you were the oldest and maybe had some idea of why I had to leave. But the others are still furious with me and they have every right to be. Regular visits to see them didn't make up for not having their mother around full-time."

There was a question on the tip of Abby's tongue, one she'd never dared to ask before. In some ways she and her mother had achieved a new rapport in recent years, but Abby suspected it was because she'd never asked the really tough questions. She'd let Megan slide, accepting a superficial bond because it was better than nothing. Now, though, it was time to dig beneath the surface. She had to find out why Megan hadn't sent for them as she'd promised on her way out the door.

"Can I ask you something?"

"Of course."

"The day you left you promised me you'd be back for us. Why didn't you come? Why didn't you fight for custody, especially of Jess? She was so young, only seven, and she thought you'd left because she was too much trouble."

Megan reacted to her statement with dismay. "No! How could she have thought that?"

"Mom, come on," Abby said impatiently. "You're not that naive. Kids always think divorce is their fault. It was even worse for Jess because of the ADD. She was a handful. I think all of us were at our wits' end trying to figure out what was going on with her. She needed her mother. Instead, you bailed."

Tears welled up in Megan's eyes. "I know. And I swear to you that I always intended to keep my promise and come back for all of you. I even found a school that would have been ideal for Jess and her special learning needs. I just wanted a little time to get settled, have a place for all of you, get a job so I'd have my own money, instead of relying on Mick for support."

She regarded Abby with an earnest expression. "I honestly did have a plan. At first time simply got away from me. And you were all so hurt and angry. Every time I came back to see you, the chasm between us was wider. It was as if you'd shut me out."

When Abby started to protest that the behavior had been a protective defense mechanism, Megan stopped her.

"I understand why you did it," her mother said. "You were hurt. None of you trusted me. I finally told myself you were better off with Mick, that you were happy in the home you'd always known, that he needed you, too."

Even as she spoke, she waved off the explanation. "That's no excuse. I should have worked it out with him, but when I tried, he told me exactly what I'd seen for myself, that you all were finally getting your feet back under you and that disrupting your lives again would be yet another selfish act. I knew you'd be okay. I knew he was a good father. I let myself believe that would be enough for you. I settled for staying on the periphery of your lives, sending cards and presents, coming to town for those increasingly awkward visits."

"Cards? Presents? Visits?" Abby said incredulously. "What did those matter, when you and Dad were *gone!*"

Clearly shocked by her vehemence, Megan turned pale. "I didn't realize at the time that Mick had taken on even more out-of-town jobs."

"Would you have done anything differently if you had known?"

Megan nodded, though she didn't meet Abby's gaze. "I'd like to think I would have fought harder for custody, as I'd originally intended." When Abby looked skeptical, she added, "I can show you the private-school brochures I pored over. Why did you think that first apartment of mine was so large? I hardly needed all those rooms just for me. Mick paid for it, so we'd all be comfortable."

Abby was startled to realize that the first time she'd visited her mother in New York, there had, in fact, been four bedrooms. Mick must have paid a fortune for such a large apartment. Only years later, after Abby had moved to New York to work and Kevin, Bree and Connor were in high school or college, had Megan moved into something smaller, with only a single guest room. It had apparently taken that long for her to give up on her plan to have her children with her.

"I'm sorry, Mom. I guess it was easy to misjudge your intentions."

"Of course it was. And that's totally my fault. Just asking all of you to come to New York, expecting you to turn your lives upside down because I couldn't be with your father anymore, wasn't enough. I should have fought to make that happen, maybe even moved back to Chesapeake Shores."

"Back with Dad, you mean?"

"No. That would have been impossible. Nothing had changed."

"Did you think he was going to change?" Abby asked. "Dad? He's the most stubborn person I know."

Megan laughed at that. "I suppose, in some insane way, I thought my leaving would force him to stay home, so you would have your dad around. And I knew your grandmother would take up any slack left by me. She adored all five of you. You couldn't have asked for a better mother."

"But you're our mother," Abby reminded her heatedly. "Gram shouldn't have had to fill your shoes."

"No, she shouldn't have," Megan agreed. "Leaving you and your brothers and sisters—I'll regret all that till the day I die. Believe me, I understand how much I lost by handling things the way I did. No matter how often I visited, I missed too many important moments in your lives."

"Do you really have regrets?" Abby asked skeptically. "Does that include Dad? Are you sorry you left him?"

Silence greeted the question, but the patches of pink in her mother's cheeks were answer enough. Abby reached for Megan's hands. They were icy. "Mom, do you still love him?"

To her surprise, her mother blinked back a fresh batch of tears. "I never stopped loving him. I just couldn't live with him—or without him, to be more precise—any longer."

Abby's heart ached for her, for both of them. Because she knew, had always known, that her father was still desperately in love with her mother. Only sheer pride and stubbornness had kept him from going after her years ago.

Thinking of that reminded her of the parallels between her parents' actions and what had happened between her and Trace. Their timing had been off years ago, but the feelings had never completely died. And maybe, if Trace's pride hadn't kicked in when it had, they might have found their way back to each other before she'd gotten involved with Wes.

Of course, that meant that she wouldn't have had Carrie and Caitlyn, and she could never regret having her precious girls. Maybe in the course of a lifetime, things simply happened when they were supposed to.

"Mom, coming home to Chesapeake Shores could open the door to what you really want. Dad's never stopped loving you, either."

"Oh, sweetie, you are such a romantic. Love doesn't always conquer everything. Mick's still Mick. His work is still his priority, which means I'd wind up being all alone and miserable again."

"Not necessarily," Abby insisted. "We're all grown-up now. There'd be nothing to keep you from traveling with him. And, truthfully, I don't think he's nearly as driven now as he used to be. I think he stays away so much because the house is so empty without you there. Come on, Mom, what do you have to lose? Come for the party. I'll talk to Dad myself and make sure he doesn't stay away."

Megan regarded her with a contrite expression. "You've had to step into way too many roles in this family, Abby. I don't want you playing matchmaker, too, especially between Mick and me."

"Fine. Other than making sure you're in the same town, I'll stay out of it. You'll talk or you won't. You'll make peace or you won't. It'll be up to you."

Her mother looked doubtful. "You can really do that? It's your nature to be a mother hen. You're like Gram in that regard."

"Even Gram knows when to stay out of things. So do I."

"And you'll get me a room at the inn, not insist on having me at the house?"

"Absolutely."

Megan drew in a deep breath. "Okay, I'll do it," she said decisively. "What's that your grandmother used to say to all of you? Nothing ventured, nothing gained."

Abby grinned. "The one I remember is nothing beats a try but a failure."

"Then I'll venture and I'll try," Megan declared. She studied Abby worriedly. "But please, sweetie, don't get your hopes up too high. This thing between Mick and me is complicated. It's not going to be fixed in one weekend. The same goes for my relationships with your sisters and Connor."

"But if you stay away, nothing has a chance of being fixed at all." She stood up and leaned down to give her mother a hug. "Now let's get Carrie and Caitlyn and hit Bloomingdale's. The women in this family need some knock-'em-dead party frocks."

Her mother's eyebrows rose. "You, too? Whose eye are you hoping to catch?"

"No one in particular," Abby fibbed.

Megan studied her, her survey thorough, her motherly instincts obviously on high alert. "That color in your cheeks says otherwise. Have you crossed paths with Trace again?"

Abby frowned. "Why would you ask that? I haven't seen him in years."

"Because before I left, you two were inseparable, and you looked exactly the way you do right now. Is he still in town?"

"He is," Abby admitted. "At least for now."

"My, my, this trip could prove even more interesting than I'd already anticipated."

"I'll tell you what you told me, no matchmaking, okay?"

"The way I remember it, you didn't need any coaching from me." Her expression sobered. "Don't let him get away again, Abby."

Abby met her gaze. "I could say the same to you."

It was beginning to look as if Jess's grand opening was going to be a night to remember on several fronts.

Either that or a kickoff for another round of family warfare.

Abby had tried to reach Mick the whole time she was in New York, but either his cell phone was turned off or he was avoiding her calls. Probably the latter, if she knew her father. He didn't intend to discuss Megan with her, and he probably knew that was exactly why she was calling.

That night when she spoke to Gram to fill her in on the flight plans for her return with the girls on Tuesday morning, she said, "When you talk to Dad, please tell him he can't avoid my calls forever. In fact, if I have to, I'll hop on a plane and fly to San Francisco and hunt him down."

Gram chuckled at her fierce tone. "You'd do it, too, wouldn't you?"

"In a heartbeat."

"I told him just that last night."

"He admitted he'd been ignoring my calls?"

"He didn't admit a thing. He said he'd missed a few calls from you. I figured out the rest. I told you he wasn't going to be happy about your inviting Megan back here."

"Well, she's coming, and the next time you hear from

Dad, tell him he'd better call me ASAP. He's behaving like an immature brat."

"Watch your tongue, young lady. Your mother hurt him badly."

"I know that," Abby said. "So does she."

"Then why on earth is she coming here? She's only going to upset everyone. I understood her coming around when your brothers and sisters were younger, but now? If you ask me, it's way too late for her to be coming back to step into her role as your mother."

"She wants to rectify the mistakes she's made."

"She certainly can't do that in one weekend," Gram said irritably. "It's just like her to make herself the center of attention on what should be Jess's big occasion."

Over the years Gram had kept remarkably silent on the subject of Megan. Abby had always assumed it was because she'd understood both sides in the divorce. Now it seemed more apparent that she'd bitten her tongue only out of respect for her grandchildren and their feelings.

"I always thought you loved Mom," Abby said.

"I did. I still do. When she left, it was like losing my own daughter, but that doesn't mean I approve of what she did. Mothers don't walk away from their children. They just don't. I don't care what the circumstances are. Leaving your father, I get that. He was gone more than he was here. Frankly, I always thought she did it in a desperate attempt to get his attention. She didn't count on his pride kicking in the way it did. Then things escalated and we wound up with the mess we're in today."

"I think you're right about that," Abby said.

"Well, be that as it may, she should never have left you, Bree, Jess and the boys behind. I know Mick talked her into giving him custody and settling for visitation rights. He made a strong case that you should be in your own home, surrounded by friends and family, instead of growing up in a strange city. He bears his share of the blame for what happened, but your mother should have fought him tooth and nail to have her share of time with all of you."

"Raising us must have been a huge and unfair burden for you," Abby said.

"Nonsense! You children are my greatest joys. You and your brothers were mostly grown anyway, so you were never any trouble. Bree was always the quiet, studious one, sitting upstairs writing in her journal. I know she took your mother's leaving to heart, but it didn't break her the way it did Jess."

Abby sighed. "It always comes back to Jess, doesn't it? She's the one who really paid."

"And yet she's working hard to put all those difficult years behind her and to pull her life together. Now here you go, stirring up bad memories."

The accusation stung. "That's not my intention," Abby told Gram. "We need Mom back in our lives, even Jess. In fact, especially Jess."

"I hope you're right," Gram said.

"Just make sure Dad calls me, okay?"

"I'll do my best."

"The girls and I will see you tomorrow."

"Now, *that* I'm looking forward to," Gram said, sounding more cheerful. "Have a safe trip home."

"Love you."

Abby disconnected the call, then headed downstairs to catch a taxi to her office. Though she'd made a dent in the piles of reports that had accumulated on her desk in the month she'd been gone, she still had a mountain of work she wanted to get through before Wes brought the twins home that evening.

To her surprise, though she was thrilled to have the distraction, she wasn't nearly as eager to plunge into the stock market whirlwind as she usually was. In fact, to her shock, she was much more excited about the prospect of returning to Chesapeake Shores—and Trace—in the morning.

The ornate gold anniversary clock on the mantel in Abby's apartment—an ostentatious gift from one of Wes's eccentric, wealthy aunts—struck ten. Abby struggled not to freak out as she once again dialed Wes's number, only to have the call go straight to voice mail.

He should have had Carrie and Caitlyn home hours ago. In fact, it was already two hours past their bedtime, and he knew that. He knew she'd be in a panic. This was a deliberate attempt to scare her. She didn't for a second believe that something had happened to them. She wasn't envisioning them in a hospital or careening through the streets in a runaway taxi. She was envisioning them all nice and cozy in Wes's apartment, while he debated with himself just how long to make her sweat.

The stupid clock, which had a gong that could wake the dead, struck the last of its ten notes, shredding Abby's already-frayed nerves. She grabbed it and heaved it across the room, wishing Wes were directly in its path. She watched in satisfaction as it shattered when it hit the floor.

She dialed Wes's home number again and then his cell phone. She got voice mail on both.

"That's it," she muttered, grabbing her purse and yanking open the door. She was going over to his apartment and retrieving her girls. First thing tomorrow, she was going to call her lawyer and do…something. She'd have to figure out what. Maybe Stella Lavery, who thought she'd been way too easy on Wes during the divorce, would have some ideas. In fact, she'd probably be thrilled to have her renowned tactical skills unleashed.

As Abby emerged from the elevator on the first floor, she spotted Wes crossing the lobby, the girls bouncing along beside him, their little suitcases being dragged behind them.

"Mommy!" they shouted eagerly, breaking free of their father and running toward her, the suitcases abandoned in their wake. "We've been to a movie."

"Really? At this hour of the night?" She turned a hard gaze on her ex-husband. "Do you have any idea what time it is?"

Wes gave her a bland look. "I know it's late, but they don't have to get up early tomorrow," he said, all innocence. "I didn't think it would be a problem."

"Actually, they do have to get up early. We have a nine o'clock flight, which means we have to leave for the airport around seven. You knew that, Wes. Don't even try to claim you didn't."

Carrie and Caitlyn were frozen between them, looking scared. Abby and Wes had tried never to fight in front of them, but right this second Abby was so outraged, she hadn't been able to keep the fury out of her voice. She forced a smile for their benefit.

"Come on, sweet peas," she said more cheerfully. "Let's get you upstairs and into bed. We have a big day tomorrow."

"But we have lots to tell you," Carrie protested. "We had the mostest fun ever with Dad and Gabrielle."

"I'm glad, but you can tell me in the morning," she said firmly. She cast one more look at Wes. "I'll call you once I get back to Chesapeake Shores to discuss this. Be sure your phone's on."

"Bye, Daddy," Carrie called out over her shoulder, already skipping ahead toward the elevator.

Caitlyn, who was quick to sense tensions and take them

to heart, lingered beside her mom. Her hand slipped into Abby's. "Bye, Daddy," she said sorrowfully, as if somehow fearing that she might not see him again.

Wes's grim expression faded at once. Though his smile didn't quite reach his eyes, he still tried. "See you soon, angel girl."

Caitlyn's lower lip quivered. "Promise?"

"Always," he said, then turned a warning look on Abby.

"Tomorrow," she said curtly, then walked away.

Inside the elevator, Caitlyn tugged on her hand. "Mommy, are you mad at Daddy?"

"It's nothing for you to worry about," she assured her. "Sometimes Mommy and Daddy just have grown-up things to talk about."

"Daddy says we might get to come stay with him all the time," Caitlyn revealed.

"Caitlyn, you big blabbermouth, be quiet!" Carrie snapped at her. "We weren't supposed to say anything, remember? Gabrielle said so."

Abby felt as if every breath in her body had been sucked right out of her. By the time the elevator opened on her floor, she was shaking so badly she could hardly get her key into the lock.

Inside, she went through the motions of getting the twins ready for bed, tucking them in and kissing them good-night.

Back in the living room, she poured herself a half inch of brandy to quiet her nerves, swallowed half of it, and then dialed Trace's number.

"Hey there," he said. "I was hoping you'd call. Everything set for tomorrow?"

Abby wasted no time on niceties. "Trace, have you done any of that investigating you were talking about?"

"You mean looking into Wes and what's going on in his life?"

"Yes."

His cheerful tone sobered. "Why? What's happened?"

"Caitlin let something slip tonight. She said they might be going to live with him all the time. Carrie shushed her up right away and said Gabrielle—that's Wes's girlfriend—had told them to keep quiet about it."

"It's not going to happen," Trace said fiercely. "I'll get on the computer tonight and see what I can find. If that doesn't turn up anything, then we'll hire somebody to dig around. In the meantime, call your lawyer first thing in the morning to be sure your rights are protected. Don't worry, Abby. There's not a chance in hell he'll get full custody of those girls. You've done absolutely nothing that could justify such a thing."

She sighed with relief at the certainty in his voice. Though she felt the same way, she'd needed reassurance. "God, I wish you were here. I'm so scared, Trace. I'm spitting mad, too, but the fear is winning."

"The second you get back here tomorrow, we'll turn that around," Trace promised. "Nurse the anger, sweetheart. It'll help you to stay strong."

"No, tonight you're the only thing helping me to stay strong. Thank you for that. Just hearing the sound of your voice makes me feel better."

"It's going to be okay, Abby. I'll do everything I can to see that it is. And if I'm not formidable enough, just wait till your father and the rest of your family get wind of this. The O'Briens are a mighty force when they're united."

She smiled at that. "Yes, they are."

And luckily, most of them were going to be in Chesapeake Shores in just a couple of weeks. The thought of them and of Trace was enough to get her through the night. And first thing tomorrow, she'd turn Stella loose. If Wes thought for one single second that he could take her girls, he was in for the fight of his life.

16

The panic and note of defeat Trace had heard in Abby's voice the night before were almost his undoing. If she hadn't been getting on a plane first thing this morning to return to Chesapeake Shores, he would have flown straight to New York last night, if only to hold and comfort her.

Instead, he'd spent the night doing something far more constructive. He'd been digging around in Wes Winters's finances. From what he could discern, they were in a bit of a mess, which might explain why he was so eager to have the girls with him. Not only would he not have to continue paying child support, there was a very good chance a court might rule that Abby should pay *him* for their care.

The rotten bastard! Trace thought, as the picture became clearer. This wasn't about a father's great love for his two daughters. It was all about money. He'd bet everything he owned on that.

Once he'd finished with his credit check, he'd put Wes's name into the search engine to see what else might turn up. That led him to several photos on the New York and Long Island society pages linking Wes with Gabrielle Mitchell, a woman who apparently worked at the same firm as Abby. Trace wondered when and how that had come about, and right under Abby's nose, at that. Yet another despicable action on Wes's part, as far as Trace could tell.

When he did yet another search of Gabrielle's name, he found an interesting item buried in the financial pages of the *Wall Street Journal*. Apparently Wes's new paramour had been questioned recently in connection with some dubious transactions at the brokerage firm. The report was dated just last week, while Abby had been in Maryland, so she wouldn't necessarily have heard any office gossip about the situation. Details were sketchy, according to the brief item, but Gabrielle was among the six people regulators had called in.

Wasn't that interesting? Trace thought. Could it be that Ms. Mitchell had taken a walk on the wild side with investor money? Was it possible that Wes was scrambling for cash to bail her out? Or had *she* engaged in something shady to bail *him* out? Hard to say, but something was definitely fishy here. Trace didn't believe in coincidences.

The minute he thought Abby and the girls would be on the ground in Baltimore, he called her cell phone. It was still set to go to voice mail, so he left a message asking her to call him as soon as she got home or to come by the bank.

He could do more digging, but he had a feeling Abby could fill in some of the missing pieces herself. She certainly knew all the players or could make calls to people at her firm who might have answers that the press hadn't reported.

He finally made it to the bank at midmorning, earning a disapproving scowl from Mariah on his way to his office.

"I know," he said to mollify her. "I should have called."

"Yes, you should have," she said. "I'll let your father know you've deigned to grace us with your presence. He's been looking for you."

A few minutes later, he was pacing impatiently as he awaited Abby's call when his father strode in looking grim.

"You missed a loan-committee meeting this morning," his father said.

"Actually I didn't," Trace replied. "I sent Laila in my place. She was there, wasn't she?"

His father frowned. "Yes, but you can't sneak around behind my back like this, Trace. Having Laila do your job is not going to convince me to give it to her."

"Did she give the reports?"

"Of course she did."

"Were they acceptable?"

"Actually she has a very astute eye," he admitted grudgingly. "Her analyses made a lot of sense."

Trace leveled a look into his father's eyes, which were still blazing with indignation. "Then I don't see the problem. She was on time. She was astute. What more could you ask?"

"That the man I'm paying to do this job be the one actually doing it," he retorted heatedly.

"Actually you haven't been paying me. I haven't cashed any of those checks Raymond's been leaving on my desk. Don't you pay attention to that sort of thing?"

His father's jaw went slack, but before he could speak, Trace added, "Wait, that's not entirely accurate. I am endorsing this week's check over to Laila, since she did the work."

His father dropped down into a chair in front of Trace's desk. "You're paying your sister to do your job?"

"Yes. I'm her front man, since you seem to be more comfortable having a male in this office. Eventually, when you come around, I'll vacate the premises."

"When did the two of you cook up this insane scheme?"

"Actually *we* didn't," Trace told him. "I did. Laila doesn't know what my intentions are. I just asked her to help me out of a jam this week. Told her I was on a tight deadline with a design and begged her to pitch in."

"And you made this plea when?"

"Yesterday, as a matter of fact. Very last-minute."

Despite his bewilderment and annoyance, Lawrence Riley looked impressed. "She did all that work overnight?"

"Pretty much," Trace said. "She's good, isn't she?"

Rather than answering directly, his father grumbled, "That was never the issue. Of course she's good. Rileys understand numbers."

"Laila certainly does," Trace agreed pointedly.

His father sighed heavily. "You really hate the job that much?"

"I don't hate it," Trace said. "I just have another career I love." He met his father's gaze. "But I've promised you a six-month trial and I'll give it to you."

His father's brows climbed. "Don't you mean your sister will, hiding behind your coattails?"

Trace grinned. "If I can pull it off without her figuring out what I'm up to, yes."

His father continued to look unconvinced. "How about this instead? I'll offer her the same position, keep you both on staff for the next few months and we'll see how it goes. She'll have her chance to prove herself."

"No way." Trace shook his head at the absurdity of the suggestion. "Dad, you can't hedge your bets with Laila. It's insulting. Either give her your full support now or resign yourself to the fact that neither one of us will take over the bank."

"When did you get to be so manipulative and sneaky?"

Trace laughed. "Some say I'm a chip off the old block."

His father smiled for the first time since entering the room. "You could be at that. Okay, I'll give this some more thought. Laila did do a damn fine job this morning, especially on short notice. Even Raymond was impressed, and he doesn't think anyone in this building is as capable as he is, me included. He's probably right about that, too."

His father rose to leave, then gave him a hard look. "You got something else on your mind?"

"I'm just worried about Abby. It seems her ex-husband may be about to make her life difficult."

"Anything I can do?"

Trace thought of the financial tangle that might be behind everything that was happening. Abby most likely had the expertise to make sense of it, but another sharp mind might not hurt. "There may be," he said. "I'll let you know after I've spoken to Abby."

He just wished she'd hurry up and get in touch. Sitting around and waiting was starting to get on his nerves.

Abby listened to Trace's message right after she and the girls got into the rental car at the Baltimore airport. As anxious as she was to speak to him, she decided to wait until she got to Chesapeake Shores so she could see him in person. Besides, she didn't want the twins to overhear her talking about their father.

In addition, if she was being totally honest, she wanted more than the sound of Trace's voice. She needed his arms around her. She had no idea when she'd started to feel so strongly that he was important to her again, but there it was. She couldn't deny it. He was the first one she'd thought of when this crisis had come to a head in New York last night. Not Mick or Gram or anyone else in her family. Just Trace. As she turned into the driveway at home, all she could think about was getting the girls settled and heading straight into town to find him.

No sooner had she pulled to a stop than she saw Gram emerge from the house with the portable phone in hand. She beckoned to Abby. "It's your father," she called out.

Abby cut across the lawn, her gaze on the girls to make

sure they weren't heading straight for the beach. Instead, they bolted for Gram.

"Are you surprised to see us? Did you know we were coming?" Carrie asked, bouncing up and down with excitement.

Gram chuckled. "I did indeed."

"Did you bake cookies?" Caitlyn asked.

"Do you even have to ask?" Gram replied, leading them inside and winking at Abby.

When they were gone, Abby spoke to her father. "Hi, Dad."

"Your grandmother said you had something to say to me," he said, sounding distant and irritated.

"I wanted to talk to you about Mom," she said, trying to feel her way through the minefield. She didn't want to make him any angrier. She just wanted him home.

"I'm not discussing your mother with you," he said flatly. "If that's all, I need to be going."

"Don't you dare hang up on me," she said, her determination to remain cool and calm snapping. "Mom is going to be here for the opening of the inn. You need to be here, too. This is about Jess, not the two of you. It was one thing for you to take off every time she came to visit when we were kids, but this is different. It's about our family. You're both our parents and, for better or worse, that makes you part of our lives. I'm sure you can deal with each other for a couple of days. You managed to be civil at my wedding. This opening is as important to Jess as that day was to me."

"Your wedding was one thing. She stayed at the inn for that. We managed to steer clear of each other. Now, though, you're telling me I'm supposed to welcome the woman who walked out on me back under my roof?" he demanded incredulously. "Hell will freeze over first."

"She'll stay at the inn again," Abby said to pacify him. "Any other issues?"

"I don't want her anywhere near my town," he grumbled. "I built the place."

Abby nearly laughed at his possessive tone. "Even Chesapeake Shores, small as it is, is big enough for both of you. No, Dad, you don't want her near you. You're afraid if you see her, you might have a conversation, and who knows where that might lead. You're behaving like a coward, Dad, and that's the last thing I ever expected of you."

"You have a lot of nerve calling me that, young lady."

"Just calling it like I see it." She thought of the one surefire way to get him home without further arguments. "There's something else you should know, another reason you need to be here."

"Oh?" he said suspiciously.

"Caitlyn let something slip last night before we left New York. It seems Wes may be thinking of asking the court for full custody of the girls."

Mick sucked in an audible breath. "Over my dead body! What the hell is he thinking?"

"I've already spoken to Stella this morning. This could amount to nothing, but she's ready to fight him in court if he actually tries anything. Trace is digging into Wes's credit history to see if there's anything going on there that would explain this sudden desire to be a full-time father. But, Dad, I need you here in case anything comes of this. We're going to have to present a united front."

"Don't worry, I'll be there," he said grimly. "I'll take that man apart limb by limb myself if need be."

Abby knew he meant it, too. "Hopefully it won't come to that."

"You need me there now?"

"No, I think Trace and I can handle it on this end, and Stella's on the scene in New York. Maybe Caitlyn got it all wrong, anyway," she said, not mentioning that Carrie had in essence backed her up. "I'm just trying to be prepared."

"Those girls of yours are too smart to make a mistake about something like this," he said, confirming her own opinion. "Either he told them what he planned or someone else did."

He paused, then added, "I'll be back at the end of next week, just in case you need me. If anything comes up and you want me there sooner, call, okay? This takes precedence over anything going on between your mother and me," he said, then continued wryly, "Which, of course, you knew it would before you told me."

"Maybe," she said, smiling. "Thanks, Dad. I'll be in touch if I need you here sooner than next week."

"You sure Trace can do the kind of investigating you need? I can hire somebody in New York."

"I'll let you know if we need that," she assured him. "Just knowing you'll be here soon is all I need for right now."

She was pleased by this evidence that he considered Carrie and Caitlyn his top priority. She thought back to all those years when work would have taken precedence, no matter the crisis at home, including the disintegration of his own marriage. If she could see that he was changing, perhaps her mother would finally start to believe it, too.

Jess had taken off first thing on Tuesday morning to shop for rugs. Abby had said flatly that they couldn't afford to put down new carpeting, but that wasn't the same as saying they couldn't add a few rugs here and there to brighten things up. She'd seen an ad in the weekend paper and started envisioning how beautiful a brightly woven rug would look under the table in the foyer. There were half a dozen other places where new rugs would add a touch of color to the otherwise boring carpeting. Shampooing had made a difference, but nothing could enliven the dull beige color. If there'd been time, she would even have ripped it all up and refinished the wood floors she'd discovered underneath.

She spent the whole morning trying to choose the perfect accents for each of the rooms, then scheduled the delivery for the end of the week. When she realized the time, she raced back to Chesapeake Shores, hoping to be back at the inn before Abby returned from her trip.

Only as she was making the turn into town did Jess recall that this morning was when the range had been scheduled for delivery. She hit the steering wheel in frustration. What was wrong with her? She'd done everything to make sure the stove would be in place before Abby's return, and now she'd blown it. How had she let herself forget about it? It was because she'd started thinking about those rugs, and everything else had been pushed to the back of her mind.

Parking behind the inn, she prayed that she wasn't too late. Maybe the delivery had been delayed.

"Please, please, let them be running late," she murmured as she crossed the lawn. But even before she reached the porch she could see the yellow delivery attempt notice hanging from the knob. She cursed herself every which way for not checking her calendar before she left, then realized she'd never even made a note of the delivery on her calendar. The date had been on one of the slips of paper she'd passed along to Gail with all of their menu ideas. After that, it obviously had slipped her mind completely, just like so many other vital things over the years.

Because of her ADD, she'd learned a whole slew of techniques for staying on task, and they'd served her well, for the most part. But stressed and overwhelmed as she'd been lately, she obviously hadn't employed them as she should have.

She tried not to get down on herself, but when things like

this happened, it filled her with self-derision. She really was a screwup. What had ever made her think she could successfully operate something as complex as an inn?

Jess sank down on the porch step and stared out toward the bay. It wasn't just the stupid delivery. She could reschedule that. It was facing the fact—yet again—that she was in over her head. At moments like this she was swamped with remorse for even trying to handle a project this big. She should have stuck to working at Ethel's Emporium, even if she had been bored to tears. At least there, she wouldn't have had a fortune of her money and Abby's on the line.

Then she glanced around at all the changes she'd made to the inn. Even though a lot of the work had been done inside, there was evidence of her efforts out here, too. The place looked rejuvenated. She'd done work she could be proud of. Even Mick had said that, and he wasn't one to hand out idle compliments.

"Come on, get over yourself," she muttered under her breath. "This is going to be good. It's been your dream forever, and nobody's going to take it away. Not Trace and the bank. Not Abby. And you're certainly not giving up."

The pep talk was enough to get her on her feet. Inside, she called and rescheduled the delivery of the stove, then went on the computer to check for reservations. There were four new ones. See, she told herself. The inn was going to be a huge success. She simply had to stop taking every slip as an omen that bad things lay ahead. For once in her life, she was going to grab her dream and hold on for dear life.

Trace finally gave up on hanging around his office waiting for Abby's call. It was making him stir-crazy, so he walked down to Sally's and ordered a burger and fries. At two in the afternoon, the café was virtually empty, so Sally brought his drink and slid into the booth opposite him. With her ample hips and bosom, it was a tight fit.

"You look like a man with a lot on his mind," she commented. "Want to talk about it?"

"Just because I used to spill all my troubles to you when I was fifteen doesn't mean I intend to do it now," he told her irritably.

"Fifteen, eighteen, twenty-one, the point is I gave you good advice back then, didn't I?"

"As a matter of fact you did," he agreed, thinking specifically of the day she'd told him flat out to chase Abby to New York. Too bad he hadn't taken that advice when she'd first offered it.

"So it doesn't make a lot of sense to start holding out on me now," she told him. "Is this about working for your father?"

"No, I think we're close to coming to terms about that."

She gave a nod of satisfaction. "That's good, then. When's he going to hire Laila?"

Trace grinned at her understanding of the situation. "I'll make sure you're the first to know."

She laughed. "You won't need to. Your sister's not half as tight-lipped as you can be."

He nodded in acknowledgment of the truth in her observation.

"So that means this is about Abby," she concluded. "When you two were in here the other day, it looked to me as if you all were getting pretty tight again."

"We're working on it," he said. "It's not Abby and me I'm worried about. It's her ex-husband."

"That stiff-necked guy who was here with her kids that same day," she said. "He got on my nerves straight off. If I hadn't known those were Abby's little ones with him, I'd have used a few choice words to tell him how I felt about his arrogance."

"Might have been interesting to see how he reacted," Trace said. "In his social circle, I doubt too many people have told him off over the years."

"I wasn't about to upset those sweet girls," she said, then looked past him. A smile broke across her face. "I think the solution to what ails you just walked through the door. I'll be back in a sec with your burger and fries. I'll double the order of fries, while I'm at it."

Trace turned to see Abby hurrying toward him, worry written all over her face. He stood up and pulled her into a tight embrace. It felt so good to hold her that it took him a second to realize that she was shaking. When he looked down, he found tears streaking her cheeks.

"Has something happened? What has Wes done?" he demanded.

Her lips curved slightly. "Calm down. I'm just so relieved to see a friendly face, everything just came pouring out. I had to keep it all bottled up when I saw Gram. I didn't want her worrying, not until we know for sure there's something to worry about."

"Sit. Sally's bringing my lunch. Are you hungry?"

She shook her head.

"Not even for apple pie? It's on the menu today."

A brief flicker of interest brightened her eyes. "Sure. I'll have a piece of pie. And iced tea."

"I'll go tell Sally."

When he returned, he studied her. She did look calmer now.

"What have you found out?" she asked. "There is something, isn't there?"

He described what his research had turned up about Wes's credit problems.

"I want to see that for myself," she said at once. "His family's loaded. How could Wes get himself into credit trouble?"

"No idea," Trace said. "But just because his parents have money doesn't mean he couldn't have squandered his. I thought you might want to see the research for yourself, so I've printed everything out. It's in a folder in my office." He took a breath and considered his next words carefully. "There's more. It's about his girlfriend."

"Fiancée," she corrected.

"That just makes it more relevant," he said, then explained about the item he'd read. "Did you hear anything about the investigation when you were in your office?"

She shook her head. "I was only in over the weekend when no one was around, and then just for a few hours on Monday. I had a lot of business to discuss with my bosses, so there was no time to catch up with anyone else." Her expression turned thoughtful. "I did notice some speculative looks, now that you mention it. And a couple of conversations seemed to be cut short when I got close, but I actually didn't think twice about any of it. I figured people were wondering if I was in hot water for staying away for so long."

"I suspect it was more than that," Trace said grimly. "They were probably wondering how much you knew about whatever's going on between Wes and Gabrielle or at the company. Is there anyone you can ask?"

"A couple of people," she said at once. "Including my boss. If he knows anything, he'll tell me, especially if I tell him what may be happening with Wes and the whole custody thing. He was a real rock when I was going through the divorce. He even helped me find my lawyer."

"Call him," Trace said. "Now."

She blinked at that. "You think it's that urgent?"

Trace nodded. "I think we need to know everything we can find out before Wes takes some kind of legal action to get the girls. To use sports terminology, the best defense is a good offense. If anything comes of what Caitlyn and Carrie heard, we'll be prepared."

Abby nodded. "I'll call now. I'd better go outside, though. The reception is lousy in here. Eat your lunch. I'll be back in a few minutes."

"I'll have Sally warm up your pie and put a scoop of ice cream on it," he promised.

Trace watched her leave, her shoulders squared with determination, her chin up. Seeing her like that made him smile. Her fighting spirit was evidently back.

And unfortunately, something told him she was going to need it. Wes Winters struck him as a desperate man, and men in that position didn't play fair. They played to win.

17

When Abby told Jack's secretary that the call was urgent, she was put right through to her boss.

"What's wrong?" he asked at once. For a man who could be impatient with interruptions, his voice now was filled with nothing but genuine concern. "Did something happen on your trip to Maryland? Was there some kind of accident?"

"No, it's nothing like that. The girls and I are okay." She drew in a deep breath. She'd never liked dragging her personal problems into work, so doing it now made her uncomfortable. "Something's going on with Wes," she said eventually. "You may have the answers I need."

"Oh?" Now his voice held unmistakable wariness.

"Look, I'm really sorry for putting you into the middle of this, but what's happening with Wes may be connected to his relationship with Gabrielle Mitchell. What can you tell me about this investigation she's involved in?"

Jack muttered a curse under his breath. "I'm sorry, Abby. I was hoping you hadn't heard about the two of them, even though they're not bothering to hide it around here anymore. How did you find out they're together?"

"Actually Wes told me himself a couple of weeks ago. I have no idea how long he's been involved with her."

"Too long," Jack said with unmistakable emphasis.

The response gave her pause. "Before the divorce, then?"

"Yes," he admitted.

"Why didn't you tell me? It might have made a difference in the way I handled the divorce and custody arrangement."

Jack hesitated. "You're probably right. But if you remember, you were pretty adamant about keeping it civil, so there would be the least amount of trauma for the twins. When you told me you were getting a divorce, I was relieved you'd come to that decision. I saw no point in telling you something that would only upset you. You didn't deserve that kind of shabby, under-handed treatment by your husband and one of your co-workers. If Gabrielle had worked for me, I'd have sat her down and told her a few hard truths about the kind of game she was playing."

"Maybe I did deserve being made to look like a fool, if I was too blind to catch on to what was obviously happening right under my nose," she said. "Apparently I was stupid about a lot of things where Wes was concerned. Now, though, all I care about is the fact that he might go after full custody of Carrie and Caitlyn."

This time Jack's curse was even more colorful and directed at Wes. "Have you told Stella about that?" he asked. "You have to tell her, Abby. She needs to nip this crazy idea in the bud right away. Surely his own lawyer has told him he doesn't stand a chance."

"To be honest, I don't even know if it's gone that far. I only know what the twins told me, and at five, they're hardly reliable. Still, I'm not taking any chances. I spoke to Stella first thing this morning," she assured him. "Anyway, you can see why it's so important that I know if this sudden interest in full custody is connected to what's going on at the firm. What exactly did Gabrielle do? Anything they can prove? Anything that might be connected to Wes?"

He hesitated so long that she knew she was testing the bonds of their friendship against his loyalty to the company. Evidently he came to the conclusion that protecting her children came first.

"Here it is in a nutshell," he told her. "We were alerted to some trades in the accounts Gabrielle manages that weren't approved by the clients. She claimed she was authorized to make decisions on their behalf, but there's no paperwork on file. The funds she bought went sour or we might not have heard about any of this. Clients don't always question unauthorized trades if they pay off, but they get really testy when money they were counting on starts disappearing. We're talking a lot of money, Abby."

"How much?" she asked grimly.

"Two million, maybe more. We're still going through records of everything Gabrielle has touched in the past couple of years."

Unauthorized trading was one thing. If the trading was in the millions, the fees alone could be a temptation, but she sensed that something more had to be going on.

"How was she profiting from all this? Raking in fees and what else?"

"The SEC is still investigating that, as are our internal oversight people. Right now, it looks as if she was getting kickbacks for bringing the people into some of these high-risk funds."

Abby was struck by a sudden thought. "Was Wes one of those investors who lost money?"

Jack hesitated. "I really shouldn't be getting into the specifics with you like this, but yes. Stella should be able to get those records easily enough with a court order. If she can't…"

"No," Abby said at once. "I won't ask you to violate company policy and get them for me. You're already helping me out. Has Gabrielle been fired?"

"Not yet. The investigation has to play out, but she doesn't have access to any accounts right now. Her future here is uncertain, Abby."

And yet Wes was still with Gabrielle and apparently determined to make her a permanent part of his life and the girls'. If he'd gambled away everything in those risky funds, Trace was probably right that part of his motivation for seeking custody was to put an end to his large child-support payments. And it also seemed increasingly likely that he might try to get money from Abby, especially if Gabrielle's job security was also on the line. He'd never turn to his parents and admit what he'd done to lose his fortune, but Abby was more than willing to fill them in if that's what it took to get them on her side in a custody dispute.

"Thanks, Jack. You've been a big help."

"If you need to use any of this to stop Wes, do it," he said emphatically. "The company might not be happy about extra scrutiny or publicity, but Carrie and Caitlyn are more important."

"You have no idea what it means to me for you to say that, but I promise I'll keep you out of it. I'll stick to using public record as much as I can, then point Stella in the right direction for the rest."

"No need. I'd be happy to get in a few good shots at your ex-husband."

She laughed at the vehemence in his voice. "You say that now, but there's no need for you to get dragged into the middle of this. I figure the company will be unhappy enough with me for taking this public, if Wes forces me to do it."

"Just do what you need to do. I'll back you up," he promised.

She hesitated, struck by something more, something triggered by his solemn promise of backup. "Jack, if this gets ugly, will they fire me for causing bad publicity for the firm?"

"Don't worry about that. I told you, I'll cover your back,

Abby. You're too valuable around here for me to let you go without a fight."

"Even though I've been away for several weeks?"

"You've stayed on top of your work. Not one single thing has slipped through the cracks while you've been away. They have no cause to fire you. Trust me, it will never come to that. I'll see to it."

She breathed a sigh of relief. "Talk to you later, then. And, Jack, I really am grateful."

"Give the girls a hug from me. I'm sorry I missed them while you were up here. How soon will you be back in the office full-time?"

"A few more weeks should do it, and you can reach me down here anytime."

"Take care of yourself, Abby. I mean that."

"I know and I appreciate it." Abby disconnected the call and turned slowly to see Trace studying her worriedly from their favorite booth. She gave him a jaunty wave, then went inside to join him.

"Well?" he asked.

"It's as bad as we thought it was," she said, then summarized everything Jack had told her.

"At least you have Wes where you want him. You need to fill your lawyer in on this."

"I'll give her a call as soon as I get back to the house. This will make her day." She dug into the pie and ice cream that Trace had ordered for her, her appetite much better now. She had a better grasp of what she was up against, and she felt prepared to fight if it came to that.

"Feeling better?" Trace asked, watching her with amusement.

She grinned. "You have no idea," she said as she finished every last bite on the plate. "I do need to get back to the house, though. The girls were down for a nap when I left, something they usually fight. Wes kept them out too late last night and I got them up early to get to the airport, so for once they gave in without an argument. I want to run by the inn, too, and check on things over there."

He studied her with a frown. "Are things okay between you and Jess?"

She shrugged. "We still have the occasional battle over expenses, but she doesn't seem to resent me as much as she did. With the opening getting closer, I think she actually appreciates having someone to help out, and I've tried not to pull rank any more than absolutely necessary to keep the finances on track."

"I'm glad." He picked up a napkin and began to shred it, in a telling gesture that had always been a marker for his nervousness.

Abby studied him, then asked, "Trace, is something on your mind? Other than this mess with Wes, I mean?"

He nodded. "What are your plans, Abby? Will you go back to New York as soon as the inn is open and you find someone reliable to step in and keep an eye on the finances?"

"Of course," she said at once.

Her response seemed to throw him for some reason. He stiffened, then nodded again. "I thought you'd probably say that."

"Then why do you look so surprised?" she asked, then waved off the question. "No, it's not surprise I'm seeing, is it? You're unhappy with my answer."

"Why would it make me unhappy to have you head back to New York? I live there, too, or will once my six-month stint at the bank is over."

"That would be my question," she said. She studied him with a narrowed gaze. "Something's changed these past few weeks, hasn't it? You're actually happy being back here."

He shrugged. "As a matter of fact, I am. I can work anywhere. Why not here?" he asked with a touch of defiance. "Why pay outrageous money for a loft in New York, when I could work just as easily in a place where the air's clean, I can walk to the water, and go boating on the weekend if I feel like it?"

There was a challenge in the question, one she simply didn't have the strength to face right now. She had more than enough going on in her life already without this.

"If Chesapeake Shores is what you want, go for it," she said, but there was no enthusiasm behind her words. Instead, she suddenly felt empty. It was as if, out of the blue, he'd stolen a dream she hadn't even realized she'd been contemplating. In it she'd seen the two of them, together, in New York, spending time with the girls, with her mother. Maybe even becoming a family. In a second, with one casual announcement that he was happy being back here, he'd snatched that future from her.

Just the way he had ten years ago.

Trace left Abby and took out his frustration on the back roads just outside of Chesapeake Shores. Riding his Harley usually calmed him, but today his mood continued to deteriorate. When he finally got back to the bank, he stormed past Mariah without a greeting, tossed his helmet across the room where it shattered an ugly porcelain figurine of an osprey done by someone who clearly didn't appreciate the awe-inspiring beauty of the bird of prey, then slammed his office door for good measure. None of that brought him any satisfaction. It did, however, bring Laila rushing into his office.

"Go away," he muttered. "And close the door behind you."

Ignoring him, she went over and picked up the shards of the figurine and tossed them in the trash. She did it without comment, then sat down and waited.

Trace scowled at his sister. "Why are you still here?"

"Because something's obviously on your mind. Do you want to talk about it or are you planning to break everything else you can lay your hands on?"

"I haven't decided yet," he told her sourly. "At least not about breaking more things. I do know for a fact that I don't want to talk."

"Then I will," she said cheerfully. "I know what you're up to, big brother. By now, I imagine Dad's figured it out, too. How furious is he that you had me do that report today?"

"No idea what you're talking about," he claimed.

"Oh, please, you're not that clever. I can recognize a scam when I see one."

"If I'm so easy to read, why didn't you call me on it when I gave you all the files yesterday?"

"Because I was bored. And I figured it would be fun to throw Dad for a loop this morning. You should have seen his face when he realized you weren't coming to the meeting. And Raymond actually looked a little sick to his stomach when he saw me sitting there."

He stared at her blankly. "Why would your presence upset Raymond?"

Laila rolled her eyes. "You can't be that stupid. He's been Dad's right-hand man since this place opened. I know he thought you'd eventually bail and that Dad would never give me a shot, so he'd be the natural successor."

Trace stared at her incredulously. "Raymond thought he'd be the bank's next president?"

"Of course he did."

"But Dad's never hidden his intention to have one of us in that position."

"No, he's never hidden his determination to put *you* into the job. I wasn't even on his radar, except as a flunky."

"Well, that's changing," Trace told her. "Dad was really impressed with your work this morning, Laila. He said Raymond was, as well."

"Oh, goody. Maybe he'll offer to make me Raymond's assistant since I turned down being a clerk."

Trace met her disgusted gaze. "I think you're going to be surprised by what Dad decides."

"Nothing he does surprises me anymore," his sister claimed. "But enough about me. What did you and Abby fight about?"

"We didn't fight," Trace said, his mood immediately taking another nosedive as he thought of their conversation.

"Well, something obviously happened."

"I'm not discussing Abby with you."

She stood up. "Fine. I'll go ask her."

"Stay out of it, Laila. She has too much going on in her life right now to be bothered with satisfying your curiosity."

She frowned. "Just tell me one thing. You're not about to do something to ruin this again, are you?"

He regarded her with indignation. "I'm not the one who ruined it last time."

"Oh, please, you got all wounded and stubborn, and the next thing I knew you were down here pining away when you should have been in New York fighting for the woman you loved."

"I went to New York," he argued.

She dismissed the reminder. "Too little, too late."

Trace was well aware of that. He didn't need Laila to drag up the memory of just how badly he'd blown it then. "Go away," he ordered. "I have things to do."

"Must not be bank business," she said.

"Why not?"

"Because you'd be trying to hand it off to me. And just

so you know, I am not taking that check that Mariah says you endorsed over to me, either."

"Why not? You earned it."

"It was a week's pay for what amounted to a few hours of work. Actually it was more entertaining than anything I'd done in the evenings with Dave the past few months."

"Which should tell you just how lucky you are that you broke it off with him," Trace told her.

"You have a point," she said blithely, though there was no mistaking the flicker of sadness in her eyes.

Trace pushed his own mood aside and studied his sister. "You are okay with the breakup, aren't you?"

"Of course I am. It was my idea. It's just going to take a little getting used to."

Trace sighed. He could relate to that. In ten years he'd never quite figured out how to live his life without Abby in it. Now it appeared he just might have to do it all over again.

It had been ages since Trace had gone for a run. That evening after leaving the office in a funk, he'd changed clothes and laced up his sneakers, then headed for the shore road. The fact that he took it in the direction of Abby's house was purely coincidental. It wasn't as if he was likely to cross paths with her. The house was a quarter mile back off the road, tucked closer to the bay than the street. Only after it passed the house Mick O'Brien had built for his family did the road cut to the east and start edging along the shoreline and the wide expanse of the Chesapeake.

Running hard, his feet pounding on the pavement, the humid air leaving a sheen of sweat on his skin practically before he hit the curve in the road just past downtown, he kept waiting for the exercise to push Abby out of his head. Unfortunately he couldn't seem to outrun his dark thoughts.

He was a mile up the road, getting closer to her house, when he spotted two little girls walking toward him, bright pink suitcases dragging behind them. Even from a distance he could see the tracks of tears on their cheeks.

He slowed his steps as he approached them, then hunkered down so he could look directly into their eyes. "You girls going somewhere?" he asked.

"We're running away," Caitlyn said sorrowfully.

"We packed our stuff," Carrie added with a touch of belligerence. "Even food."

"Does your mom know you've left home?"

Caitlyn blinked at him. "It wouldn't be running away if we told her."

Even as he tried to assess how long they might have been gone—five minutes, no more than ten, certainly—he scrambled to find a way to get them safely back home that would also salvage their tender pride. He decided on the guilt card, which had always worked with his folks when they'd played it with him and Laila.

"Your mom must be really, really sad and scared," he told them.

"No, she isn't," Carrie told him.

"What makes you think that?"

"Because she's mad at us," Caitlyn said.

"And she doesn't love us anymore," Carrie added.

"I doubt that," Trace said. "She might get upset about something you've done, but your mom loves you more than anything in the whole world."

Carrie regarded him skeptically. "How do you know?"

"Because of the way she talks about you all the time. You two are the very best things in her life." He wanted to tell them how hard Abby was working to make sure her daughters stayed with her, but he wasn't sure how much they knew about any impending custody dispute. It wasn't his place to fill them in.

He looked directly at each of them in turn. "You know, when I was just a little bit older than you, I ran away from home."

Caitlyn's eyes widened. "You did?"

"Yep."

"Were you scared?" she asked, her voice faltering in a way that gave away just how frightened she was herself.

"Not until it got dark," he told her. "Then I got scared." He gave a dramatic shudder. "Too many shadows where monsters could be hiding."

"What did you do?" Carrie asked.

"I decided maybe I wouldn't run away till morning, so I went back home. It's always okay to go where you know you'll be safe. Sometimes that's the smartest, bravest thing to do."

"I guess," Carrie said doubtfully.

"It's true," he assured her. "And do you know what I found when I got back home?"

"What?" Caitlyn asked, edging closer to him as if his mention of the impending shadows of nightfall were already scaring her.

"My mom was crying. She was sure that something really bad had happened, that I'd fallen into the bay maybe."

"But we're not allowed in the bay by ourselves," Caitlyn told him earnestly. "It's a rule."

Trace bit back a grin. "And it's a very good rule."

Just then his cell phone rang. He knew instinctively it would be Abby. He held it out to show the girls. "That's your mom. I'll bet she's calling me to tell me you're missing. Can I tell her you're with me, that we're on our way home?"

The twins exchanged a long, resigned look, then slowly nodded.

"Good decision," he commended them, then answered the phone. "Hey."

Abby immediately started talking, but she was nearly incoherent, her words tangled up with sobs.

"Slow down, darlin', they're with me. They're fine. We're on our way back. I'll explain when we get there. Shouldn't be more than a couple of minutes."

"You're sure they're okay?" she asked, her voice still shaky.

"Here, I'll let you ask 'em yourself." He handed the phone to Carrie.

"Hi, Mommy," she said, her voice small. She listened intently, then said, "I know. Uh-huh. I know. Mr. Riley's bringing us back." She shoved the phone toward Caitlyn.

"Hi," Caitlyn said. "Don't cry, Mommy. We're sorry."

When she handed the phone back to Trace, he asked Abby, "Feel better now that you've heard their voices?"

"I just want to see them."

"Two minutes," he promised. "They were barcly out of the driveway and onto the road."

"They were walking in the road?" She sounded horrified.

"They're okay. Concentrate on that," he said. "We're turning around right now. See you any minute."

He knew better than to expect her to wait for them at the house. They'd barely made the turn into the long driveway when he spotted Abby running toward them. Carrie and Caitlyn abandoned their little pink suitcases and flew into her arms.

The reunion stirred a lump in his throat. He could imagine exactly how Abby had felt for those few frantic minutes when she'd believed her girls had run away from home. She must have been terrified. When he thought of all the ways this adventure could have turned out differently, it made his palms sweat. Because he didn't want to do or say anything to reveal just how much those two little girls with their strawberry-blond curls had come to mean to him, he forced a cheery note into his voice.

"I guess my work here is done," he said. "I should finish my run."

He'd already turned to go when Abby said, "Please don't leave."

He faced her with a quizzical look.

"The girls and I want to thank you, don't we?" she said, looking at each of them.

"Thanks, Mr. Riley," Caitlyn said dutifully.

"We could have found our own way home if we got scared," Carrie insisted, but at a sharp look from her mother, she lifted her gaze to his. "Thank you."

"You're very welcome."

"If you have time to wait, I'd like to talk to you," Abby said.

"About?"

Her eyes held his. "Just stay, please."

Trace didn't have the willpower to resist. "How about this? I'm soaking wet from my run. I'll go take a shower and change, while you get them settled down. Why don't I come back in an hour?"

She nodded. "An hour would be perfect."

Trace wasn't convinced that an hour was nearly long enough for him to do what needed to be done. Oh, he could clean up, put on slacks and a shirt, maybe even shave. But what he really needed to do—steel his heart against the hold this woman, this *family*, had on him—couldn't be done in days or weeks, much less the sixty minutes left to him to accomplish it.

18

Abby had never been more terrified in her life than when she'd gone upstairs to read a bedtime story to Carrie and Caitlyn and realized they were missing. Their suitcases, which had been sitting at the end of their beds earlier, were gone, as well.

Racing downstairs, calling their names, she had drawn Gram out of the kitchen, dish towel in hand.

"What on earth?" Gram asked.

"The girls are gone."

"Gone? What do you mean they're gone?" she asked, an expression of disbelief on her face. "It's only been a couple of minutes since you sent them upstairs, so they can't have gone far. They probably just slipped outside to chase fireflies. You know how they hate going to bed. They're afraid they might miss something."

Abby knew it was more than that, suspected they'd heard her talking to Stella earlier. Though they were much too young to understand the implications of what she'd been discussing with her lawyer, she was sure they'd picked up that it had something to do with their dad.

A search outside the house had turned up nothing. There was no sign of two barefooted little girls chasing fireflies or on the swing set Mick had installed in the yard. Thankfully, though, before she'd gone into a full-blown state of panic, something had told her to call Trace. Hearing his voice had steadied her, even before he'd told her the girls were safe with him.

The whole terrifying incident had lasted no more than twenty minutes, maybe even less, but it had quite likely taken five years off her life.

Now, as she walked upstairs with the twins and went through the motions of making sure they took their baths and brushed their teeth, she debated how to get into any of it with them. They were so unnaturally quiet, she knew they were still upset about whatever had sent them fleeing earlier.

After they'd climbed into their beds, Abby sat on the floor between them.

"Are you going to read to us?" Caitlyn asked, her expression hopeful.

Abby shook her head. "Not tonight. We need to talk."

"It's because you're mad at us, isn't it?" Carrie said.

"I'm not mad," she told them. "But I do need you to tell me why you decided to run away. You know you can tell me anything, right?"

The girls exchanged a telling look. Abby could see that they might as well be exchanging a vow of silence. Even at five, they were as stubborn as all of the O'Briens put together.

"Does this have something to do with your father?" she asked.

Again, that quick, furtive look to bolster their silence.

Abby pressed on, determined to make her own point at least and hoping to reassure them in the process. "You know that running away is never the answer, don't you? It doesn't solve anything and, more important, it can be very dangerous. You could have been hurt tonight if Mr. Riley hadn't come along when he did. You could have gotten lost. Where did you think you were going?"

"To see Daddy," Caitlyn said.

"Caitlyn!" Carrie protested.

Abby closed her eyes against the tide of dismay that washed over her.

"Because you miss him?" she asked carefully. She knew it had to be more than that. They'd just seen Wes and they'd never gotten homesick after leaving him before.

Carrie remained stubbornly silent, but Caitlyn shook her head.

"Why, then?" Abby asked, focusing on Caitlyn.

"Because—" Caitlyn began, only to have Carrie cut her off by accusing her of being a tattletale.

This was one of the drawbacks to having twins. They mostly presented a united front. Unless she separated them and took Caitlyn off alone, it was unlikely she was going to get a straight answer out of them tonight.

Flying blind, she said, "Okay, here's what I think. I think you may have heard me on the phone today talking about some grown-up things going on between your dad and me. I think maybe you got scared that I wasn't going to let you see your dad anymore, so you decided to run away to be with him."

She could tell from the look of surprise on Carrie's face and the relief on Caitlyn's that she was on the right track. She reached up and managed to clasp one small, delicate hand of each girl.

"Listen to me," she said quietly. "No matter what happens between your dad and me, you will always get to spend time with him. You will live with me, but you can see him whenever you want to."

"Really?" Caitlyn asked, her relief evident. "You promise?"

"I promise."

"I told you," she whispered to Carrie. "I told you we could see Daddy."

"But Daddy wants us to live with him," Carrie said defiantly. "And you said on the phone that we have to live with you all the time."

"Your dad and I will work that out," Abby reassured her.

"Why can't we live with him, like he and Gabrielle said?" Carrie asked.

The question cut right through Abby's heart, but she couldn't let them see how upsetting she found it. They were just little girls who adored their dad and feared that something in their relationship with him was about to change. She also knew Wes spoiled them during their time with him, while she tended to be a stricter disciplinarian. In their eyes that made living with him seem like an endless special occasion.

Abby regarded them seriously. "You're just going to have to trust me when I tell you that your dad and I will always do what we think is best for you," she said. With a little impartial help from a court.

"Are you going to punish us for running away?" Caitlyn asked, apparently satisfied for now with Abby's promises.

"Yes," Abby said at once. "What do you think it will take to make sure you never forget that running away is wrong?"

"A time-out?" Caitlyn asked hopefully.

"Carrie, what do you think is fair?" Abby asked.

"No dessert or cookies for a week," she suggested, sounding forlorn.

Abby considered the suggestions. A time-out of some kind would serve no purpose with these two. Even if they were separated—something they hated—they could entertain themselves for hours on end. Sweets, however, would be a real sacrifice.

"Carrie, that's a good one. No desserts, cookies or sweets of any kind for one week." She gave them each a stern look. "And no trying to get Gram or Aunt Jess to break the rules or sneaking into the kitchen when no one's around."

"Yes, ma'am," Caitlyn said.

Carrie looked disappointed by Abby's additional admonishments. Despite having suggested the perfect punishment, she'd clearly had plans for getting around it until Abby had taken away those options.

"Okay, get some sleep," Abby said. "We'll talk some more in the morning." She bent down and kissed them. "I love you girls more than anything. Please don't ever forget that."

Caitlyn sighed. "That's what Mr. Riley said."

Abby smiled. "Well, sometimes Mr. Riley is a very smart man."

And tonight, for whatever reason he'd been in the right place at the right time, he was also her hero.

With the girls tucked in for the night, Abby poured two glasses of wine and went onto the porch to wait for Trace. She must have taken longer inside than she'd realized because she found him already there, his rocker squeaking rhythmically against the floorboards. He was staring off toward the bay, which could be heard, but which was invisible in the inky darkness of the night sky.

Every now and again, a firefly's glow would flicker. The sight of them always took her straight back to childhood, when she, Connor and Kevin and later Bree and Jess would catch as many as they could and put them in old Mason jars with holes punched in the tops, then free them before bedtime.

"Are the girls okay?" he asked when she joined him.

"None the worse for their adventure," she said, handing him a glass. "I, however, am still shaking." She faced him. "Thank God you found them when you did."

"I think they would have turned around soon on their own. It would have been dark in a few more minutes, and Caitlyn was already frightened."

Abby smiled. "Yes, but you're not taking into account that Carrie is determined enough for both of them. She never gives in to fear."

"A scary thought," Trace said.

"You should live with it." She turned as she spoke and saw Trace studying her intently. "What?"

"An interesting idea," he said casually. "Me living with Carrie's daredevil nature. It would imply you and me being together."

Even though her pulse skittered crazily at the intensity in his gaze and the offhand mention of some kind of future, she didn't want to go there. Not after this afternoon when he'd once again dashed her hopes by saying he wanted to stay right here in Chesapeake Shores.

"We can't, Trace. You and me." She shook her head. "It's just not going to happen."

He frowned. "I had a hunch you were going to say that. Your reaction earlier today when I said I like it here was pretty obvious."

"I feel as if we had this same conversation ten years ago," she said wearily.

"No, Abby," he said with surprising heat and more than a little bitterness. "That's just it. We never had any conversation ten years ago. You leaped to some conclusions, made a decision that suited you and took off. I never had a chance to chime in."

"The fact that you didn't come after me spoke volumes," she responded defensively.

"Okay, yes, you're right. And we *have* had this conversation. I waited too long. My bad. I lost." His gaze clashed with hers. "In the end, we both lost."

"Yes, I suppose we did," she admitted. "But I can't regret having Caitlyn and Carrie."

"I wouldn't expect you to." He leaned forward, turned

his chair until he was facing her. "Can we have an honest, straightforward conversation now?"

She trembled under the heat in his gaze. "Okay."

"Something's happening between us again, Abby. All those old feelings, they're still there, at least for me. I don't want to pretend they don't exist. I want to figure out where they can take us."

She was shaking her head before he finished. "I don't think I can handle that kind of complication in my life right now," she whispered. "Everything's such a mess."

"At least let me be there for you. Lean on me. Don't shut any doors."

"And then what? I go back to New York and break your heart all over again?"

"Possibly," he said, then reached for her hand, brought it to his lips. "Or maybe we talk it through like the adults we are now and find a way to make it work. We're not immature kids anymore. Surely we can find a solution that will give us both what we want."

Even as he spoke, Abby realized how desperately she wanted it to turn out that way. She just didn't believe it was possible. So far in her life, love had never once led to a happy ending.

"Trace, I wish I could believe that this won't end badly," she said.

"Look out there," he ordered. "Tell me what you see."

"Where?"

"Up there in the sky."

She gazed up into the sky and saw the scattering of stars. "Stars," she said, taking him literally, but thinking he meant much more.

"Exactly," he said as if she'd just passed an important exam. "You ever see that many stars at once in New York?"

She shook her head. "There are too many lights."

"Which means there must be something special about this place if we can see so many," he told her. "Have a little faith, darlin'. Sometimes those stars up there do align just right, and when they do, anything can happen."

In that moment, with her hand in his and the waves rolling softly along the shoreline in the distance, she could almost let herself believe in happily-ever-after.

Mick walked out of a meeting with the building and zoning officials in San Francisco and turned to his associates. "That's it," he said. "I'm pulling the plug."

Jaime Alvarez, his executive assistant and a talented architect in his own right who'd been working with Mick for months to get this latest development off the ground, stared at him in shock. "You can't do that."

Mick laughed, oddly relieved to have made the decision. He'd never have done it fifteen years ago, or even last year, but today it felt just right.

"I just did," he told his staff. "I'm going home."

The two other men with them were clearly stunned into silence. They turned to Jaime, seeking clarification.

"There will be no development?" Joe Wilson asked. Joe coordinated with all the subcontractors they hired for various jobs. "After all the work we've put in?"

"You were in that meeting," Mick said. "They were going to keep us jumping through hoops, dangling promises in front of us for as long as they could drag it out. In the end, I suspect some of the permits will never be approved. It's time to cut our losses, sell the land and move on."

"And all the subcontractors?" Joe asked, looking shaken. "What about them?"

"They're all excellent local companies and there's plenty of work around for them. We've kept some of them on hold for too long as it is. All the contracts have out clauses. We'll use them, make a few payments if necessary. They're not going to be surprised, any of them. They knew going in, probably better than we did, that getting this development approved was a long shot."

He turned to Jaime. "I'd like you to head up to Portland, take on that project and see it through, unless you have some objection. It was your baby in the first place."

Jaime's expression turned eager. "I'll manage it?"

"Unless you think you need me hanging over your shoulder and getting in the way." He'd made this decision last night in anticipation of having this morning's meeting go exactly as it had—nowhere.

The young architect beamed. "No, I can handle it."

"And I'll just be a phone call away if you have questions," Mick told him. "Joe, what would you like to take on? You interested in going with Jaime to Portland or do you want to get back home to Maryland? Dave, how about you?"

"Let me think about that," Dave said. "We've been in this area for a while now and I like it. I might just stick around, see what work I can find."

Mick nodded. "You know I'd be sorry to lose you, but if you need a reference, you can count on me giving you an excellent one. And if you do decide to come back to Maryland, I'll put you to work back there. Up to you."

"Thanks," Dave said.

Joe looked vaguely envious of the two other men. "Much as I'd like to spend the time up in Portland," he said, "my wife will kill me if she finds out I had a chance to come home and didn't grab it."

"Then you can fly back with me in the morning," Mick said.

Jaime studied him. "I thought you'd be more upset about this. You poured a lot of work into designing this project."

"It won't go to waste," Mick told him. "With modifications, it might suit another location."

"This is the first time in the five years I've worked with you that you seem eager to be heading home," Jaime said.

Mick thought about the observation. "You're right. I am looking forward to it. My daughter and grandkids are there for an extended visit. I'm looking forward to spending time with them. They have some things going on in their lives right now. I'll feel better if I'm close by."

"And Jess's inn will be opening soon, too, right?" Joe said.

"A couple of weeks," Mick confirmed. "I'm real proud of her. She's worked hard to make that happen."

Of course, the opening of the inn meant Megan would be in town, too. He was still trying to figure out how he felt about that. He was every bit as angry about the invitation Abby had extended to his ex-wife as he'd indicated to Abby, but there were other feelings, too. Unexpected feelings.

Megan had been out of his life for fifteen years now. It had been eight since he'd seen her at Abby's wedding. Lord knew, he'd changed a lot in all that time. He wondered if she had. Or if she'd still make his heart race just by walking into a room. Damn, he hoped not. He'd been a fool for love once. At fifty-six, it was too damn late in life to do it again.

Still, he couldn't help thinking about what the next few weeks might hold. And whether he could get through it without adding to the pile of regrets he'd stacked up fifteen years ago.

The sky outside was streaked with the first orange rays of dawn when Abby walked into the kitchen. She'd barely poured herself a cup of coffee when the phone rang. Fearing it would wake Gram at this early hour, she grabbed it.

"What the hell are you up to?" Wes all but shouted in her ear.

"Excuse me?"

"That barracuda of a lawyer you have has been all over my case since yesterday, making threats and demanding paperwork she's not entitled to."

"Not entitled to, or that you don't want to give her?" Abby inquired mildly, refusing to get drawn into the fight. Stella had warned her to stay cool and calm if Wes called and she intended to follow that advice, no matter how hard it was when she wanted desperately to shout right back at him.

"We settled all this when we went to court," Wes said.

"And then you or Gabrielle told our daughters that they were going to come and live with you," she said. "Obviously you've decided that what we agreed to no longer works for you, so I had no choice but to protect my own interests."

Wes sucked in a breath. Clearly he hadn't expected her to find out what he was up to.

"The girls misunderstood," he said, sounding tentative.

"Did they really? They're pretty smart," she commented. "But let's say they did get it wrong. Why would Gabrielle have told them to keep it a secret?"

She could practically hear his mental wheels grinding in an attempt to come up with an explanation she would buy. She let him off the hook. "Never mind. There's nothing you can say to make me believe Gabrielle didn't tell them exactly that or that you didn't put the idea into their heads in the first place."

"Okay, fine," he said testily. "I want to spend more time with them. With you dragging them down to Maryland, I figured I needed to stand up for *my* rights."

"Is it your rights you're worried about or your wallet?" Abby couldn't resist asking. "If they're with you, you'll no longer be responsible for child support. Those payments must be taking a toll now that you've lost a lot of money with a bad investment. Were you hoping the court would make me give *you* child support so you could bail your girlfriend out of her financial mess?"

The silence on the other end of the line was deafening.

"Nothing to say?" she prodded. "I understand. What Gabrielle did is pretty reprehensible. In fact, if I were you, I'd forget about a quick wedding, because I see some jail time in her future. And if you're with her, you can forget about custody of the girls. It will be impossible to convince a court that you can offer a better home when you're preoccupied with your wife's legal defense."

"You can't keep them from me," he protested.

"I don't intend to," she assured him. "You can see them whenever you want. But forget about a change in custody. Frankly, I think you're going to have enough on your plate with Gabrielle's defense without going to court on any other matters."

"She'll never be charged," he said confidently. "You know how this kind of thing gets swept under the rug. It happens all the time."

"Not when there's someone around who's willing to lift up the carpet and show the media where all the dirt is," she said quietly. "I hate resorting to threats, Wes, but you've left me no choice. I have to protect Carrie and Caitlyn."

"When did you turn so vindictive?"

"The minute you decided to go behind my back and try to get full custody of my daughters," she said heatedly, then uttered a sigh. "I'm really sorry it's come to this. It's so unnecessary. I accepted my share of the blame for our divorce and we both did everything we could think of to make sure the girls wouldn't suffer. It was working. You and I had kept everything civil and then you had to go and pull a stunt like this. Maybe Gabrielle was behind it, or this financial disaster she's created. It doesn't really matter."

"Let's just forget this happened, forget we ever said anything to the girls, okay? You don't know what it's like right now, Abby," he said, his tone pleading. "Gabrielle's a wreck. Her career's about to go up in flames unless she can find the money to fix everything. Maybe it will anyway. You can't make it any worse, Abby. If you go public with what you know, or even think you know, consider the fallout for the girls."

"They're five. They don't read newspapers or watch the financial networks." She had to bite back her disgust. "And shame on you for trying to use them to get me to back off."

"What will it take, then?"

She hadn't anticipated his capitulation coming so easily, but she was ready just the same. "Drop your plans to try to change our custody arrangement," she said at once. "I want it in writing that you're foregoing all future rights to even try for full custody, and that neither you nor Gabrielle will ever discuss this with the twins again."

"And if I give you those things, you won't try to make things worse for Gabrielle?"

"Wes, don't you get it? That horse is so far out of the barn, it would take a miracle to corral it. The SEC is all over this. The internal investigators at the firm are looking at every transaction she ever handled. The media's already caught wind of it. They might have had only enough for a very brief item so far, but trust me, they're on top of the story. It's all going to come out, with or without any prodding from me."

"But if you give them another angle, a personal angle, it'll make it worse," he said. "Please, I'm begging you, don't add to the publicity."

She was stunned by the genuine concern in his voice. "You really are in love with her, aren't you? This wasn't just some crazy fling that wound up costing you a fortune."

"Of course I love her. Why do you think I'm so desperate to help her fix this? It's not about the money I lost. I can live with that. I can always make more. I just can't bear the thought of watching Gabrielle being taken down like this. She made a stupid mistake, and she regrets it."

"What about all the other people she hurt, the ones who lost their life savings and unlike you don't have the time or the means to make it back?"

"We'll make restitution to every one of them. I'm already working on it."

Abby was impressed by how hard he was willing to fight for his fiancée. Gabrielle was giving him a chance to be her knight in shining armor, something Abby had never needed him to be.

"Good luck with fixing this," she told him sincerely. "I hope it works out."

"Look, I'll see Stella today. I'll explain there was a misunderstanding and I'll sign whatever you want me to sign."

"I'll let her know everything we've discussed," Abby said. "When..."

She knew what he wanted to ask. She could have let him squirm, but what would be the point? She'd won not only the battle, but the war. "The girls and I should be back in New York right after the Fourth of July. You can see them then. If you'd rather not wait another three weeks, you're welcome to come down here again. I just don't have time right now to bring them up there."

"I'll wait. Tell them I'll be calling every couple of days to check on them."

"They'll love that," she told him. "They miss you as much as you miss them."

"Bye, Abby."

"Goodbye, Wes." She'd been pacing the kitchen as they talked, but now she sank down onto a chair, shaking. Could it really be over? Did he really no longer pose a threat? Tears of relief were streaking down her cheeks when Gram walked into the kitchen.

"What on earth?" she murmured, gathering Abby into her arms. "What's happened? Is it bad news?"

Abby shook her head and managed a wobbly smile. "Good news, actually. I won."

Gram looked confused. "Won what?"

"It's a long story, but the bottom line is that I stood up to Wes and I won."

"Well, good for you. It's about time you stopped letting that man bully you."

She regarded her grandmother with surprise. "You think Wes bullied me?"

"I most certainly do. Oh, he did it with a lot of charm and sweet talk, but there was more than one occasion when I wanted to sit him down and tell him how a real man should treat a woman he loves."

Abby grinned at the thought of such a confrontation. "I'm surprised you didn't do it, and a little sorry."

"Meddling in another person's marriage never leads to anything good," Gram said, then gave her a pointed look. "Which is something you might want to remember when your father and Megan get here."

"Mom's not due for a couple of weeks. Have you heard from Dad? When will he be here?"

"Later today, in fact. He's dropping the San Francisco project, so he'll be underfoot for a while, apparently."

"He dropped it?" Abby repeated, stunned. "Any idea why?"

"He didn't say, but I'm sure he'll be happy to satisfy your curiosity once he gets here."

"Do you think it might have something to do with the fact that Mom is coming home?"

"I'm not going to start speculating about that and did I not suggest to you less than two minutes ago that you should stay out of their relationship?"

Abby smiled sheepishly. "You can't blame me for wondering at least."

Gram chuckled. "No, I suppose I can't. Now let's talk about your love life. How are things with you and Trace?"

"Now who's meddling?" Abby teased.

"Just asking an innocent question," Gram insisted. "He was here late last night. I heard the two of you on the porch talking long after I'd gone to bed."

"We have a lot of things to figure out," Abby told her.

"I just hope you do that together this time," Gram said.

Abby sighed. "Trace said the same thing."

Gram gave a nod of satisfaction. "Good. That gives me hope."

"Hope for what?"

"The future," she said. "And that is all I have to say about that."

Abby laughed. "For today," she retorted.

"Nope. That's it. The rest is up to the two of you." She winked. "See, not meddling. That's how it's done. Take a lesson."

"I'll work on it," Abby promised. "And now I'm going to the inn to check on Jess and the progress she made while I was away. I was so caught up with my own issues yesterday, I never got over there. Do you mind getting the girls up and watching them this morning?"

"Of course not. I think today I'll teach them a bit about gardening. If nothing else, they seem to like playing in the dirt. None of the rest of you were interested, except for Bree." She gave a rueful smile. "Of course, she liked picking the flowers a whole lot better than she liked planting them."

"I remember," Abby said, smiling at the memory. "She'd

yank them from the ground, then bring them in and stick them in a glass, roots and all."

"Hopefully your sister's past that stage now. Otherwise, I'm assigning you to keep her out of my garden when she gets here for the inn's grand opening."

"I can't wait to see her and hear about all her success in Chicago."

Gram's expression sobered. "I'm not sure that last play of hers did that well."

Abby frowned at the comment. "What makes you think that? She was so excited about it."

"She usually sends the reviews, but this time she didn't. And she hasn't brought it up once when we've talked. Those aren't good signs."

"Well, it's a good sign that she's coming home."

"It is indeed," Gram said. "I just wish Kevin were coming home from Iraq, so we'd have everybody here."

Abby gave her a hug. "He'll be home soon, Gram. I know it."

Her grandmother touched her mouth. "From your lips to God's ear."

Amen, Abby thought.

19

It was midmorning on Wednesday, and Abby was paying bills on her first day back at the inn when she heard some kind of heavy truck lumbering up the driveway. Walking to the window, she spotted a delivery van from a high-end appliance company. Instantly, her pulse kicked up a notch. What had Jess done? Since it involved that particular store, it couldn't be good.

She headed for the door, shouting upstairs to her sister as she went. "Jess, get down here, now!"

She was already across the yard and standing behind the van by the time the driver emerged.

"Mind if I take a look at your delivery instructions before you take anything off the truck?" she asked, trying to keep her voice calm. After all, the driver and his helper were just doing their job.

The driver handed over his clipboard and she skimmed through the paperwork. When she saw they were delivering a top-of-the-line range for the kitchen and glanced at the cost, she saw red.

"Sorry," she said flatly. "There's been some mistake. I didn't order this."

Jess came flying out of the inn just then. "I did, Abby. It's okay."

Abby whirled on her and dragged her a few steps until they were out of earshot from the drivers. "It is not okay," she said tightly. "It's going back. It was an unauthorized purchase."

Jess faced her down, hands on hips. "*I* authorized it. It stays."

The driver, who'd easily picked up on the tension, looked from Abby to Jess and back again. "Look, ladies, is it going or staying? We don't have all day while you all settle your turf war. And this is our second delivery attempt. The next one will cost you."

"What do you mean it's the second delivery attempt?" Abby asked.

"No one was around when we came by on Monday."

So, she thought, fuming, Jess had intended for this outrageously expensive range to be delivered and put in place while she was away, making it that much harder to send it back. Obviously, though, she'd gotten distracted by something and missed the delivery. For once, Abby was relieved by her sister's lack of attention to detail. In this instance it had probably saved them from an expense they couldn't afford.

She gave Jess a look that told her she knew exactly what she'd been up to. Jess's determined expression didn't waver. There wasn't so much as a hint of guilt or remorse.

"The range is staying," Jess said stubbornly.

"Take it away," Abby said just as determinedly. "Jess, there is no way the inn can afford a range like this one, not now, anyway. The kitchen appliances we have are just fine. They're all in working order. I've had them checked."

"But I went through the kitchen with Gail to analyze what we'd need to do the kind of events I want to host here," Jess argued. "She says this range is the best for that. She went with me to pick it out. She's the professional. She knows what she's talking about."

"I don't doubt it, but you weren't spending her money.

It's unfortunate you didn't invite me along. I would have told you no on the spot and saved these men a trip."

"Come on, Abby, even you have to see that it's a smart, long-term investment."

"I'm sure it is. And it is a chef's dream range, no question about that, either. Unfortunately, we can't afford it. Period." She turned to the driver. "Take it now, please."

Jess got between her and the truck, her cheeks flaming with color, though whether that was due to fury or embarrassment was hard to say. "If you send it back, I will never speak to you again," Jess declared in a fierce undertone. "I mean it, Abby. We're through. I've kept my mouth shut while you've taken over around here, even though it's my business, but I'm drawing the line now. I know there's enough money in the account for this. I checked before I ordered it."

"And once we write a check of this size, exactly what do you intend to use to pay your staff?" Abby asked quietly. She managed to keep her tone reasonable, even though she was tempted to shake her sister. "Every penny of that cash is committed for the foreseeable future unless you're planning to do all the work around here on your own and for no pay, and that includes covering for your new chef, whom you'll no longer be able to afford."

Jess faltered slightly at that, but she didn't back down. "We'll have cash flow in another couple of weeks."

"Not enough," Abby said flatly. "And I'm not pouring one more dime into this place unless you show some evidence of fiscal responsibility. I'm done. Do you get that? And if I pull out, the bank may pull out right behind me."

Jess's eyes grew round, but her fighting spirit didn't diminish. "You wouldn't do that to me."

"Watch me," Abby said, refusing to relent. This was the last straw. For once she intended to stick to her guns, no matter how upset Jess got with her. Her sister couldn't get a free pass on this. If she did, she'd never understand that there were consequences for acting imprudently.

Jess blinked back tears, but with her chin held high, she turned to the driver. "Take it away," she said quietly. Then she turned to Abby. "And from here on out you stay the hell out of my way. Whatever work you need to do that's related to the inn, you can do at Gram's. I don't care how much of your money you invested, this place is still mine and I don't want you near the inn when I'm here. Since I live here, that means you don't set foot on the premises again, ever. I swear I'll have you arrested for trespassing if you do."

After uttering the mostly empty threat, she took off across the lawn, climbed into her car and tore away from the inn, gravel flying in her wake.

Abby stared after her and sighed, then faced the bewildered deliverymen. "I'm sorry."

"No problem," the driver said. "Looks to me like you got your hands full. You change your mind, just call that number on the invoice and we'll bring it back out here."

"I won't change my mind."

Unfortunately, she knew with absolute certainty that Jess wouldn't, either. It was going to be a tense couple of weeks leading up to the inn's opening. After that, who knew?

Jess was barreling down the shore road when her cell phone rang. She ignored it. She wasn't about to talk to anyone when she was in her current mood. For the first time in her life she actually hated her sister. She hated her for humiliating her the way she had in front of those drivers. She hated her for the position she was now in with Gail, forced to explain that they wouldn't have the new stove. She hated her most of all for being right.

Once again she hadn't thought things through. She'd gotten caught up in the moment, in the dream, and completely ignored reality. She should have realized that money was earmarked for salaries. She should have paid more attention when Abby tried to talk to her about the budget, but frankly all that talk of numbers bored her to tears.

Which was exactly why she needed a business partner, she conceded with a sigh. It couldn't be Abby, though, not for the long haul. She didn't want to be at odds with the one person in her life who'd always been there for her, the person who'd believed in her even when she'd been screwing up. And despite Abby's threat today that she would walk away from Jess and the inn, Jess knew without a doubt that her big sister would never abandon her.

There was a drawback to all that devotion. Jess had never had a success she could really call her own. Abby or one of her other siblings had always been eager to jump in and help her out. They'd fought her battles, coached her through tests. They'd all thought they were doing her a favor, protecting her from humiliation, but they'd kept her from succeeding on her own, too. She loved them for caring so much, but she hated the way she wound up feeling, as if not one single accomplishment was truly her own.

And here it was happening again, she thought with a sigh.

With the top on her car down and the wind blowing through her hair, she was calmer now. By the time she got into town, she could actually see Abby's point of view, as much as it grated. Not that she intended to tell her sister that. Abby needed to understand something, too, that she couldn't snatch every decision out of Jess's hands. They had to work things out together.

Of course, even as that thought came to her, she realized that she was the one who'd carefully avoided just such a conversation about the stove, precisely because she'd anticipated exactly this outcome. Worse, she thought with a wince, the new rugs were yet to come. At least those hadn't cost a fortune, but they had cost more than the budget could probably afford.

"I should probably call and cancel them," she murmured to herself. It would forestall another showdown with Abby.

At the same time, though, she wanted those rugs, needed to have her own way about something. She'd have to think about that.

Pulling into an open space on Main Street, she decided to take a walk along the water, maybe stop in someplace and have lunch, give herself—and Abby—time to cool down before she returned to the inn. Because even though she'd told Abby to get out, she had a hunch she'd find her sister still there and ready to have this out. Unlike her, Abby didn't run from confrontations.

She was thinking about that as she stepped out of the car and bumped straight into her father, of all people. The scowl on Mick's face gave her pause.

"Dad, I had no idea you were back in town." She gave him a peck on the cheek, but his scowl just deepened.

"Where the devil did you think you were going flying down Shore Road like that?" he demanded. "Did you even see there was another car on the road?"

"I didn't hit you, did I?" she retorted defensively. "Of course I was watching for traffic. Have you ever known me to get a ticket for reckless driving?"

"It only takes once to have an accident that could end your life or someone else's." He whipped off his sunglasses and studied her. "You been crying?"

"No. I got something in my eye," she lied. "You know what it's like when you drive a convertible."

"Nice try, but then only one eye would be red and

swollen. Both of yours are red." He tucked a hand under her arm and turned her in the direction of Sally's. "We'll have lunch and you can tell me about whatever's on your mind."

Since he didn't seem likely to release her, she allowed herself to be steered toward the café. She sat down, folded her arms across her chest belligerently until it dawned on her, thanks to Mick's smirk, that she probably looked like a stubborn kid. She tried to make herself relax and drink the diet soda that Sally brought to her along with Mick's coffee as soon as they were seated. Heaven forbid a regular actually wanted to order something different.

"What can I get you?" Sally asked. "The meat loaf's real good today, if I do say so myself. It comes with mashed potatoes and green beans."

"I'll have that," Mick said, his gaze never leaving Jess's face.

"Nothing for me," she said.

Mick rolled his eyes. "She'll have a bacon, lettuce and tomato sandwich on whole wheat toast. Bring her fries, not chips."

Now it was her turn to scowl. "You don't have to order for me like I'm five."

"I do, if that's how old you're acting."

Sally chuckled. "Nice to see some things never change. You two have been squabbling since Jess was a baby. I'll have that order back in a sec." She cast a look at Jess. "Unless you'd like to make any changes to yours?"

"No, a BLT will be fine."

Mick took a slow sip of his coffee, watching her over the rim of his cup and waiting. That was the thing about Mick, as impatient as he was about most things, he'd always been able to outwait one of his stubbornly silent kids. At twelve it had been disconcerting. Now, it was annoying.

Jess finally risked meeting his gaze. "What are you doing home already?"

"I killed the San Francisco project and decided to get back here for a while."

"Really?" She felt a little flicker of delight. "Because of the inn's opening?"

He nodded. "That and the stuff that's going on between Abby and Wes."

Jess frowned. "What's going on between them?"

Her father gave her an odd look, clearly surprised that she didn't know about what was happening in her sister's life. "He wants custody of the girls," Mick said. "It'll be a cold day in hell before he gets it, though. Didn't Abby fill you in when she got back from New York?"

Jess winced. She'd hardly given her a chance. She'd hidden away upstairs when Abby had first arrived at the inn this morning, then they'd had the blowup over the stove. No wonder Abby had been in such an impossible mood, she thought, then corrected herself. No, sending that stove back had nothing to do with whatever was going on between Abby and Wes. She knew her sister well enough to know that.

"We didn't have much time to talk this morning," she told her father.

"But enough time to have an argument, I'm guessing," he said to her. "Is that what sent you flying down the road? You and Abby have a difference of opinion over something at the inn?"

She nodded. "She was right. I was wrong."

Mick looked as if he'd never doubted that much. "You tell her that?"

Jess shook her head. "Of course not. She just made me so darned mad with her high-handed attitude. How could I admit she was right?"

"You'll have to tell her sooner or later."

"I know."

Her father's expression turned uncomfortable. "Look, Jess, I know there have been times, quite a few of them I suspect, when you've thought I favored Abby over you."

"I know you love me, Dad." She meant that, too. She did know that he loved her in his own, distracted way.

"But that's not the same as thinking that I support you or believe in you, is it?"

She sighed. "Not really."

"Well, just in case I didn't make it clear when I was here before, I support what you're doing with the inn and I believe you're going to make it work. That doesn't mean I don't think you also need to listen to outside advice from time to time, whether it comes from Abby or someone else. This is a new venture for you. Like anyone else starting something for the first time, you're not going to know everything right off the bat. I sure as hell didn't when I started my company. I met with every architect who'd see me, tried to work for a few developers to figure out how they did things. I didn't waltz out of college, stick a fancy sign up outside my office and become a success the next day."

"Point taken," Jess conceded, then felt compelled to add, "Abby's never run an inn before, either."

He grinned. "No, but she does have a financial expertise that neither you nor I have. I've got her looking into some investments for me because of that. You should be grateful she's watching your back on the financial side, too."

"I am. I'm the one who begged her to come down here, remember?"

"But then when she gives you advice you don't like, you blow a gasket, am I right?"

"Yes. Okay, Dad, I see what you're saying."

"You'll make peace with her, then?"

She nodded.

His eyes sparkled with knowing amusement at her lack of enthusiasm. "Today?"

"Okay, yes, today," she said, a note of impatience in her voice. "If she's still at the inn when I get back, I'll talk to her and apologize."

He clearly caught the out she'd left for herself. "And if she's gone back to our house, you'll come over there," he said, making it a statement, not a question.

"You're a worse nag than she is," she grumbled.

"Family trait," he said unrepentantly. "Don't think for a minute that you don't have the same gene."

She laughed at that. "Guilty," she admitted just as Sally set her lunch down in front of her. She picked up the sandwich and bit into it. It was the first real tomato of the summer and the flavor burst on her tongue. It reminded her of countless summer picnics on the beach with Abby, Bree, her brothers and Gram. Carefree days spent with the people she loved most in the world. She met her father's gaze and saw that he'd known exactly what he was doing when he ordered it. "Thanks, Dad."

"Anytime, kiddo. Sometimes we all need to be reminded of the memories that make us who we are."

"Okay, an excellent BLT will do it for me. What does that for you?" she asked curiously.

"The scent of lilies of the valley," he said at once. "That was the perfume your mother always wore. Sometimes when I walk outside on a spring day and they're in bloom, I can imagine Megan right there beside me."

Jess blinked back the unexpected sting of tears at the nostalgia in his voice. "You still miss her, don't you?"

"Don't tell another soul," he said, leaning closer. "But I miss her every single day of my life."

Jess reached for his hand. Warm and callused, it wrapped

around hers. "Me, too," she whispered. In fact, she wondered if there would ever come a day when she grew out of being the scared little girl who'd stood inside at the window, Abby holding her hand, as they watched their mother drive out of their lives.

Though Gram had wanted everyone at the house for Mick's first dinner at home, Abby had opted out. She wasn't ready for another run-in with Jess.

Mick gave her a hard look when he heard her plans. "Did you and your sister have a talk this afternoon?"

"No, why?"

He muttered a curse under his breath. "She promised me she'd see you and straighten things out."

Abby gave him a startled look. "You know about the fight we had?"

"I spotted her driving along Shore Road like a bat out of hell. I made a U-turn back toward town and went after her. Sat her down at Sally's and had a little heart-to-heart with her."

"And she actually listened to you?" Abby asked incredulously.

"I thought she had."

"Well, apparently she had a change of heart," Abby replied wearily. "And I'm not up for another discussion about why she can't have the outrageously expensive range she wants. I'm going into town, so you all can enjoy your dinner. I'll take the girls with me."

He looked as if he might argue about her going, but eventually he sighed. "Go, if that's what you need to do, but leave the girls here. I'll see that they get to bed on time."

The thought of an evening out, on her own, was so alluring, she couldn't bring herself to refuse his offer. "Thanks, Dad."

"Enjoy yourself. Maybe you ought to think about calling

Trace and asking him to join you. I can't imagine you two have had much time alone."

"It might be better if we didn't have any," she commented.

His gaze narrowed. "Why is that?"

"A significant difference of opinion about the future," she said, summarizing it.

"Do you want to explain that?"

She shrugged. "Not really."

"Another male perspective might help."

She grinned at the thought of her father giving her relationship advice. "I think maybe you should concentrate on figuring out how you're going to handle Mom being back in town."

He frowned immediately. "Don't start on that."

"Not starting," she said, holding up her hands in surrender. "Not meddling." To prove it, she leaned down and gave him a kiss on his cheek. "Night, Dad. Thanks again for looking after the girls tonight and for trying to talk to Jess."

"Night, angel girl. Enjoy yourself."

Her eyes misted at the endearment. It had been years since Mick had called her that. He'd had special nicknames for all of them, but they'd fallen by the wayside as they'd become adolescents and then adults. Hearing it again reminded her of just how close they'd once been, how she'd flown into his arms when he'd come home at the end of the day. She walked back across the room and gave him a fierce hug.

"I love you," she whispered, her voice hitching.

"Love you, too," Mick said, his voice thick.

As she left the house, she reminded herself that there had always been a handful of men who, unlike Wes, had loved her unconditionally. Her dad was one of them. Her brothers were on that list. And as she drove, she picked up her cell phone and called the fourth. Trace answered on the second ring.

"Hey, there. I wasn't expecting to hear from you tonight.

I heard Mick was back in town, so I figured you all would be having some big O'Brien family dinner."

"Everyone else is at the house," Abby told him. "But I'm footloose and looking for company. You available?"

"I can be. I'm finishing up a design right now. I can shower and shave and be ready in a half hour. You want to meet somewhere?"

Abby thought about that, then thought about the sparks that had been dancing between them ever since she'd returned to Chesapeake Shores. It might be idiotic to want to see where they led, given what she knew about his intentions for the future, but she couldn't seem to stop herself from saying, "Why don't I just come by your place? I'd like to see what you're working on."

There was a long hesitation, as if he knew that there was more on her mind than peeking at a couple of designs. "You sure about that? You and me alone could be dangerous."

"And I'm in a reckless mood," she told him. "Shower fast. I'll be there in ten minutes."

He laughed then. "Should I bother with clothes?"

"Well, of course," she said, amusement threading through her voice at the eagerness she heard in his. "Let's at least preserve the illusion that this is an innocent visit."

"Abby, Abby," he murmured. "What's gotten into you tonight?"

"I think Gram would say the devil, but I prefer to think that for once in a long time I'm just going after what I want."

"And what you want is me?"

"Tonight, yes," she said, her tone sobering. "Can you accept that?"

"I can as long as you swear to me there'll be no regrets."

She thought about that, thought about what it had been like years ago being with him. As difficult and sad as it'd been when she'd walked away after discovering what it was like to make love with Trace, she had never regretted sharing that experience with him.

"No regrets," she promised him now. "Can you say the same?"

"If there are any, I'll find a way to live with them," he said. "I want you, Abby O'Brien Winters. Always have. Always will."

She smiled. That was all she needed to hear.

20

Trace opened the door to his apartment wearing jeans undone at the waist and nothing else. No shirt. No shoes. His hair was still damp and tousled and he smelled of soap and maybe a faint hint of refreshing aftershave. Abby swallowed hard at the sight of him and had to restrain herself from jumping into his arms before the door closed.

"You look good," she murmured, her gaze locked on his chest and a sculpted set of six-pack abs. How did a man who worked at a drafting table and computer—or in a bank—all day stay so fit? However he did it, someone should pay him a fortune to go on billboards to advertise his regimen. She was pretty sure he could deliver a ton of profits to some company in the fitness industry.

Heat in his eyes, Trace closed the door behind her, then backed her against it. "You look pretty amazing yourself," he murmured, brushing her hair aside to kiss her neck. "Smell good, too." His tongue flicked across her skin. Her temperature shot so high, she was surprised she didn't singe him.

"Taste even better," he said in a low voice that sent shivers dancing through her.

Abby was having difficulty standing. She placed her hands on his shoulders, then jerked them away. His skin was too warm, too smooth, and way too tempting. All of this was moving way too fast…yet not nearly fast enough. After the day she'd had, after being basically accused of being stuffy and rigid, she wanted nothing more than to mindlessly go with the flow, to be ruled by passion for once.

She caught the immediate glint of amusement in Trace's eyes as she pulled back. Of course, with the door at her back, she didn't have a lot of wiggle room. With his eyes locked with hers, he reached for one of her hands and lifted it back to rest on his shoulder, then placed the other one on his chest.

"Stay," he whispered. "I like having you touch me. It stirs up all sorts of indecent thoughts."

Abby frowned at him. "We're pretty much tossing out the whole innocent-visit thing, aren't we?"

He held himself perfectly still, his gaze steady on hers. "Up to you."

With his heat flowing through her, and his faintly masculine aroma surrounding her, Abby knew she couldn't walk away, knew there was no point at all in pretense. As a girl she might have been awkward and undecided in a situation like this, but she was a woman now, a woman who knew her own mind, at least when it came to this. At least for tonight.

Instead of answering, she stood on tiptoe and sealed her mouth over his. With her hands linked behind his neck, her body was pressed into his. She could feel every hard plane, every rippling muscle, to say nothing of the very dramatic evidence of his arousal.

The kiss ended eventually with both of them breathless, their eyes glazed over with desire. At least his were, and she knew hers had to be the same.

"Where's the bedroom in this place?" she asked boldly. "Or do you have some macho thing about ripping our clothes off right here in the foyer?"

He grinned. "It is an intriguing thought, but I think this occasion calls for a little more romance and finesse. Wine?"

She shook her head, her gaze on his steady.

"Something to eat?"

She declined again.

"Candlelight?" he offered.

"Just you," she told him, giving him a gentle shove.

"Well, you can't turn me down if I do this," he said, scooping her into his arms and cradling her against his chest.

Abby immediately snuggled into all that amazing heat and relished the comfort of knowing that same strength would always be used to protect her.

In his bedroom, which had little in the way of decoration, the king-size bed stood out in sensual invitation. He set her down in the middle of it, then followed her.

For what seemed like an eternity they simply lay there, face-to-face, gazing into each other's eyes, absorbing the moment that had been inevitable, but forever in coming…ten impossibly long years, in fact.

It was Trace who finally broke the spellbinding moment. "I've missed you, Abby. For all these years, I've felt as if a part of myself was missing."

She started to speak, but he touched a finger to her lips. "Don't," he said. "I know you had another life during that time. I don't expect you to feel the same way."

"But I do," she protested. "I don't think I realized how much I missed this, missed *us* until right this second. Now I can't imagine how I went so long without you."

A slow, soft smile of satisfaction spread across his lips. "Let's see if I can remember what you like," he said, his gaze intense.

His mouth found the spot at the base of her neck that made her head fall back. Pushing aside her blouse and un-hooking her bra, he nuzzled each breast, his tongue flicking over the nipples until they hardened. With sure, tantalizing strokes, he caressed her stomach, his fingers dipping low until they found her moist, hot core. Abby would have moved away to shed her slacks, but he kept her in place, tormenting her until she was gasping for air and for the finish he was carefully, deliberately denying her.

"You're a tease," she accused when she could find sufficient breath to speak.

He grinned. "And you love it."

"I could turn the tables on you," she said. "I've learned a few moves over the years."

He stilled at that and she thought at first she'd made a terrible mistake, inadvertently dragging Wes into bed with them without even mentioning his name. Then Trace regarded her with an intrigued expression and flopped over onto his back.

"Show me your stuff," he teased, whatever emotion he'd felt before nowhere in sight now.

Responding to his good-natured taunt, she rose on her knees and bent over him, peppering his face, his bare chest and even lower with kisses, all the while slowly sliding down the zipper of his jeans. When she reached inside, his sharp, indrawn breath told her he hadn't expected that, hadn't anticipated the bold touch and clever, wicked way her fingers were dancing over his hard shaft.

His eyes alight with amusement and barely banked desire, he flipped her on her back and went to work stripping her of her clothes. Then with a few clever, wicked touches of his own, he brought her right to the peak of satisfaction, but wouldn't let her tumble off that beckoning cliff.

"Not without me," he said quietly, his gaze locked with hers as he knelt over her. He slowly slid deep within her, never once looking away, as if to be sure she knew it was him, experienced this moment with him.

No, she realized, it was more than that. It was as if he needed to, was determined to see right into her heart.

Their bodies fell at once into a natural rhythm. Like waves on the shore, the sensations rose and fell, gathering intensity, stealing breath, demanding…everything. Passion peaked with an explosion of fireworks brighter than anything she'd seen in ten years of New York's most spectacular Fourth of July celebrations.

As the sparks died down and the colors faded, she snuggled into Trace's embrace. At home. Again.

Trace awoke slowly to moonlight streaming in his windows and the sound of distant thunder rumbling in the air. Waves were crashing on the shore as an early-summer storm approached. He relished the wildness of it, a wildness that could only be lackluster in comparison to having Abby back in his bed. In astonishment, he realized this was the first time she'd actually been in his bed and not wherever they'd been able to steal a few hours alone, most often a blanket on the beach.

He rolled toward her, then realized she was gone. For a moment, he felt an almost incomparable letdown, but then he heard her stirring around in his kitchen.

Pulling his jeans back on, he went in search of the woman he would never again deny loving.

He found her setting his table with the mismatched plates and silverware that had come with the apartment, items culled from Mrs. Finch's attic. She'd lit two candles, maybe for the ambience, maybe in anticipation of a likely power outage if the storm hit hard. She was wearing one of his T-shirts, which came to midthigh and outlined the shape of her breasts and hips in a provocative way he doubted she'd realized.

For the moment, she was oblivious to his arrival, so he stood perfectly still, watching her work. She was cutting and dicing with surprisingly sure strokes given that the knife probably hadn't seen a sharpener in fifteen years. There was a little mound of onion and another of green pepper on the cutting board. To that, she added some tomato when she'd finished.

She tossed a dollop of butter into a large skillet, then waited until it started to sizzle before adding all the vegetables. After giving them a chance to cook for just a moment, she poured in a bowlful of eggs she'd whipped into a froth.

Every movement, each time she stretched, hitched the T-shirt a bit to give him a brief and intriguing glimpse of her bare bottom. As starved as he was, it was a toss-up whether he wanted the meal she was making or her the most. To his delight, he realized he could have both.

He walked up behind her, lifted her hair and kissed the back of her neck.

"You're bothering the cook," she said, though it sounded as if that pleased rather than annoyed her.

"I'd be interested in bothering her a lot more, if she's willing."

She faced him with a grin. "Before we eat?" she asked in disbelief.

He drew in the aroma of the frittata she was apparently creating. "Maybe after."

"Nice to know what your priorities are," she commented, as she sprinkled grated cheddar cheese over the top of her creation, then slid it into the oven to set the eggs and melt the cheese.

"What time is it?" he asked, trying to focus on the mundane since looking at Abby was getting him hot and bothered all over again.

"Not quite ten," she said. "There's a storm brewing. Is that what woke you?"

He shook his head. "I think I woke up because I knew instinctively that you'd left my bed."

She slid an arm around him and tucked her hand just inside the waistband of his jeans at the small of his back. The comfortable intimacy of that touch suddenly made him think about having nights like this for the rest of their lives. That's what he wanted. He was pretty sure she did, too. Coming here tonight was an admission of that, in its own way. She wouldn't have come, if on some level she wasn't ready for a shared future with him. How long, though, would it take for her to admit that to herself? And when the time came could they find a compromise about their living arrangements?

A few minutes later they were seated at the table just inside his balcony doors where they could feel the cooling air as the storm got closer. At first they both ate as if they were starving, but then Trace leaned back and studied her. Despite the rumpled sensuality of her appearance, the slightly swollen lips and rosy cheeks, there was an unmistakable hint of sadness in her eyes.

"Okay, spill it," he said to her.

"Spill what?"

"I know you came over here tonight for my body," he began, drawing an annoyed look from her. "But what drove you to my doorstep, when all the other O'Briens are at your place? You usually love those family occasions."

"Not tonight. I didn't want to spend the evening with them," she said stiffly.

He studied her with a narrowed gaze. "You and your grandmother have a fight?"

"Don't be ridiculous."

"You and Mick?"

"Mick and I are fine."

"Then unless those little girls of yours have found a new way to get under your skin, the problem has to be Jess."

Her instantaneous frown told him he'd nailed it. "What'd she do now?"

"Do you really want to spoil this evening by talking about my sister?"

"I don't want to spoil anything and I could care less about Jess. I do care about anything that upsets you."

She set her glass down on the table with a thump, her eyes flashing with fire. "We had an argument," she said tightly. "We'll both get over it. Now drop it, okay?"

He persisted. "About something at the inn, I assume," he said, assailed by guilt once again. "Dammit, I never should have used my position at the bank to put you in this position. What was I thinking?"

"You were thinking that somebody has to make Jess understand reality," she countered, then added with an air of resignation, "It might as well be me."

"No," he said forcefully. "It shouldn't be you. You're sisters and I've driven a wedge between you. That's insane. Tomorrow I'll talk to Laila about taking over. You'll be free to head back to New York, if you want to."

She stared at him in astonishment. "You want me to go home now? After this?" She waved her hand in an all-encompassing gesture that he assumed was meant to include him and what had happened here tonight.

"I never said I wanted you to go. I said you'd be free to go if that was what you wanted."

"No," she said at once, her chin jutting defiantly. "I'm seeing this through."

Despite his willingness to let her go, relief flooded through him at her refusal. He could only hope that her determination to stay was not only about Jess, but maybe about him and their future, as well.

Abby got home before dawn, after spending most of the night in Trace's bed. She slipped inside, doing her best not to wake anyone, but to her dismay she encountered Mick on the stairs. He was on his way down, fully dressed and ready to start his day. He eyed her with a look she couldn't entirely interpret. It was somewhere between protective fatherly concern and amusement.

"Long night," he commented. "You must have found a way to occupy your evening."

Abby regarded him with defiance. "I am not discussing my evening with you."

He held up his hands. "Believe me, I do not want to hear details." Still, he gave her a hard, assessing look. "You know what you're doing?"

She sighed at that, thinking of all the possible complications there would likely be. "I hope so." Hoping to force a change of subject, she asked, "The girls okay?"

"They're still sound asleep. I checked on 'em just now."

"Okay, then, I'm going to take a quick shower and get ready to go to work."

He frowned at that. "Come with me," he ordered. "You can spare time for a cup of coffee before you take that shower."

Abby followed reluctantly. She knew that tone, though. Ignoring his command would only delay whatever he had to say.

When they were in the kitchen and he'd filled the coffee-pot and turned it on, Mick sat down at the table opposite her. "Did I miss something? Did Jess apologize?"

"No."

"Didn't she order you off her property?"

Abby gave him an incredulous look. "Do you honestly

think I'll pay any attention to that? I have a job to do, whether she's happy about it or not."

"Why does it have to be you? You know the bank could give someone else oversight of the inn's finances."

"Trace already offered to do that," she admitted. "I turned him down."

Mick looked dismayed. "Why would you do a darn fool thing like that? Do you want to ruin your relationship with Jess forever?"

"I'm not going to ruin anything," Abby said, leaving the table to pour the coffee. She handed Mick his in his favorite mug, one Connor had gotten for him years ago that said World's Best Dad. She sat back down and tried to make him see her point of view. "Dad, if someone else takes over they're not going to be half as understanding of all Jess's issues."

Even though she said it, she knew that wasn't entirely true. Laila would certainly understand. She'd been around the O'Brien house during all those difficult years after Megan first left. She knew about Jess's tendency to lose focus. She'd cut her some slack.

But not as much as Abby would. And she certainly wouldn't insist, as Abby intended to, that Jess find some manageable way to organize what needed to be done and started to follow through. So far, none of the techniques she'd learned to stay on task seemed to be working.

Mick shook his head, his disapproval plain. "You can't spend your entire life bailing your sister out of jams. She has to grow up sometime."

"She will, Dad. She's accomplished so much. We'll figure out the best way to make sure she handles all the rest. First, we just have to get the inn open."

"How's that coming? I know what Jess has told me, but I want your assessment."

"We're actually in very good shape. All of the redecorating and renovations are finished. Jess hired a chef." She made a face as she said that.

"The one who wanted the fancy range?" he asked.

Abby nodded. "I honestly don't think she made a big issue of it, though. I think Jess just got it into her head that we had to have it."

"You sure this isn't a necessity? If it is, I could..."

"No, absolutely not," Abby said at once. "The equipment we have is perfectly fine for now. And if you go out and buy it, it will undermine the lesson I'm trying to instill in Jess about fiscal responsibility."

He nodded. "You're right, of course. I just thought maybe I could make some kind of contribution, something to commemorate the start of the business."

Abby saw that he really did want to do something to show his support of Jess. "Dad, it's a really expensive range. Wouldn't a bouquet of flowers be enough?"

He laughed. "Not my style. Your mama's the only one who ever got flowers from me and that was only after I discovered the kind of reward I could get for my thoughtfulness."

Abby held up a hand. "Too much information," she said, but then turned thoughtful. "You could send Mom flowers for her room at the inn, you know. It would be a really nice gesture of welcome."

Mick scowled at her. "Don't go getting any ideas about your mother and me. That ship has sailed."

Abby thought it might be about to return to port, but she kept her opinion to herself. "Dad, do you really want to make a gift of the stove to Jess? It would be an amazing gesture, and I shouldn't be the one to stand in the way of your making it."

"I'd like to do it," he confirmed.

"For Jess? Not because you think it'll make peace between us?"

"It's for your sister, so she knows she has my support. If it eases things between the two of you, so much the better."

Abby studied him and saw the real yearning in his expression to make this grand gesture. How could she stop him from reaching out to Jess? She stood up and hugged him. "Do it, Dad. I'll bring the paperwork back with me later today and you can call and make the arrangements."

He nodded. "Consider it done."

"Then I'm going upstairs to take that shower." She kissed his cheek. "You're a great guy, you know that, don't you?"

He shrugged. "I may be a great guy, but I haven't always been the best father. I'm going to do my best to fix that before it's too late."

Abby heard the determination in his voice, saw the commitment in his eyes. It was a far cry from the sad, defeated man he'd been in the months and years after Megan had left.

"If I know one thing about you, Dad, it's that you can do anything you set your mind to. You planned and built an entire town, for heaven's sake. Anything else you decide to tackle should be a piece of cake."

He shook his head. "I understand bricks and mortar and infrastructure, and maybe even a little bit about what it takes to turn a bunch of houses into a real community," he said. "You kids…you're a whole other kettle of fish."

"Well, I have faith that you'll figure it out," she told him.

To her surprise, she wasn't just saying the words he wanted—or needed—to hear. She meant every one of them. Her dad, the man she'd idolized as a little girl, was really trying to find his way back to his family.

* * *

On Monday Trace once again cajoled Laila into coming into his office to pick up the folders scheduled for review by the loan committee on Tuesday. To his relief, though not his surprise, she didn't put up much of a fight.

"Have you looked at these?" she asked, tucking the folders into her briefcase.

"Nah," he said. "I can't be at tomorrow's meeting. You'll have to do the report again."

His sister frowned at him. "You're not even trying to be sneaky about this anymore, are you?"

"What's the point? You know what I'm up to. Dad knows it. So does Raymond, for that matter. Since everything's out in the open anyway, why should I bother with pretense?"

Laila sat down in the chair opposite him. "Do you really think this is going to work?"

He shrugged. "Eventually. Dad's stubborn. He's not stupid. You're the future of this bank, not me."

"And you have absolutely no regrets or second thoughts about that?" she asked.

"None. This spot is rightfully yours, Laila. I have a career."

"One that will allow you to go back to New York to be with Abby," she guessed.

"That's one possibility," he admitted.

Laila frowned. "Trace, she doesn't want to live here. You know that."

"Things change," he said, hoping he was right about that. If it came down to it, he would return to New York, but he hoped Abby could be convinced that their future was right here in the town her father had built, where her family had roots going back a couple of generations. To him that meant something. He hoped it did to her, too.

In fact, he was suddenly hit by exactly the thing that

might convince her. "I've got to go somewhere," he said, jumping up and snatching his jacket off the back of the chair. "Hold the fort. Look over those folders here, if you want to." He grinned. "Get the feel of what's going to be your office one of these days."

Laila shook her head and followed him out the door. "I think I'll hold off on getting too far ahead of myself. Dad has to be the one to tell me that office is mine."

Outside, Trace gave his sister a quick kiss on the cheek. "He'll come around," he promised. "Just do the job the way I know you can. He won't be able to deny what's right in front of his face."

Laila didn't look convinced. "We're talking about Dad. He wasn't entirely willing to believe I'd graduated with honors from the master's program at the Wharton School of Business until he held the diploma in his hand."

"Like I said, he's stubborn as a mule, but all he really wants is for the bank to be in good hands once he retires. Those are your hands, sis. No question about it."

She blinked back tears. "Do you have any idea how much your faith in me means?"

He winked at her. "Some." They'd spent a lifetime being there for each other. He'd gotten his share of support and motivation from her, especially after Abby had taken off. "Go, get to work. Prove Dad wrong and me right." He grinned. "For once."

"And where are you going?"

"Secret mission," he told her.

And, if he handled this just right, it would ensure the future he wanted for himself.

21

With Gram teaching the girls the basics of gardening, Abby arrived at the inn just in time to see another delivery truck pulling out of the driveway, this one from a carpet company. Her temper shot into the stratosphere.

She and Jess had had a discussion about new carpet. It, like the stove, was an expense they couldn't handle right now. She thought she'd made that clear. That meant that Jess was deliberately defying her, probably in retaliation for not being allowed to keep the stove.

As tempted as she was to bolt straight inside and have yet another knock-down, drag-out fight with Jess, she simply couldn't do it. She couldn't face her right now when she was so furious she wanted to shake some sense into her. She turned on her heel and headed to the beach. Maybe a brisk walk would be enough to calm her down so they could have a rational discussion about this latest unauthorized purchase.

Or not.

The day had dawned sunny and clear with the June temperature already hovering in the midseventies. It was heading for the high eighties by afternoon. The air was already thick with humidity, as well, but there was a breeze along the shore.

With the wind blowing in her face and the smell of salt and seaweed in the air, Abby felt her sense of peace returning. When she came to a sun-kissed boulder that had been smoothed over by the waves at high tide, she climbed up and sat down, drawing her knees up to her chest in the position she'd always favored for thinking when she was a girl. She rubbed her fingers over the boulder, letting its warmth seep into her.

One of the things the sea had always done for her—whether river, ocean or her beloved Chesapeake Bay—was to put things in perspective. The reminder that this huge rock, the beach, the waters of the bay had all been here for far longer than she or anyone she knew had been alive gave her a sense of the continuity of this place. It would be here, just like this, long after she was gone, assuming careless or greedy people didn't plunder it with treatment that killed the sea life, destroyed the habitat of so many birds and shifted the delicate ecological balance beyond repair. Just the thought of that made her feel physically ill. It was one reason she was so grateful to her uncle for the fight he waged on a daily basis to preserve it.

Since there was only so much she could do herself about the unwitting destruction of such a unique setting, she focused on the other problem that was paramount in her life: Jess. How could she make her sister see with total clarity that she was creating a precarious financial mess for herself? She'd seen it in black and white. She was on notice from the bank. Abby had told her the situation she was facing.

And yet Jess continued to make these impetuous purchases, blindly determined to have what she wanted when she wanted it. Was Abby really doing her any favors by fighting her on any of it? Would it be better to let her flounder, destroying the inn's chances of succeeding, ruining her dream?

No, she thought at once. She simply couldn't let that

happen. It was out of the question. Tough love might make sense in some situations, but not this one. The stakes were too high. Which meant somehow getting through to Jess. She sighed. Was that even possible anymore? Jess was beyond listening to anything she said. Maybe it would be smarter to let Trace put Laila or almost anyone else in charge.

Abby let that thought simmer as she absorbed the sun's heat and let the soft splash of the waves soothe her. In the end, though, she knew she couldn't let anyone else step in, not without making one more attempt to get this right herself. She owed that not to the grown-up Jess, but to the little girl who'd spent way too many years blaming herself because their mother was gone.

Maybe it wasn't Abby's obligation to make that up to her, but she'd taken it on years ago. She had to follow through now, acting on those same maternal instincts that were a thousand times stronger now that she had Carrie and Caitlyn in her life. It had been pure instinct years ago with Jess, but now it was a way of life.

Rising slowly, her mind made up, she brushed the sand from the top of the boulder off her legs, then started back toward the inn. Despite the heat, the sand at the edge of the water was still cool between her toes, the water cooler still. She felt refreshed and at ease with her decision by the time she made her way back to the inn across the wide expanse of lawn.

And maybe it would have stayed that way if she hadn't walked in and practically stumbled over a half dozen or so rolls of carpet still sitting in the foyer. With that reminder of Jess's latest folly, most of her good intentions shot right out the window.

Jess had seen Abby walking toward the inn earlier, then making the sharp turn toward the beach. She'd known without question in that moment that her sister had seen the carpet delivery van leaving. Despite her conviction that the purchase had been a good one, her stomach had knotted as she tried to view it from Abby's perspective. She knew with absolute certainty that Abby would see the new rugs as yet another betrayal of what should have been their mutual goal: to get the inn open and make it profitable.

"I am such a screwup," she muttered, taking a seat on one of the steps leading upstairs to wait for her sister's return. All of her stubborn determination to insist on this one victory faded. She took her cell phone from her pocket, removed the carpet invoice from her other pocket and reluctantly dialed the carpet company's number.

Sucking in a deep breath of resolve, she said, "I just had six rugs delivered to The Inn at Eagle Point. I need them to be picked up, today if possible."

"Are they defective?" the woman on the other end of the line asked.

"I haven't even looked," she admitted.

"Then I don't understand."

"The purchase was a mistake. I need to return them and have the amount of the sale credited to my account."

It took her fifteen minutes of cajoling and a conversation with a supervisor to get the commitment that the carpets would be picked up later in the afternoon. There would be a restocking fee, but it was minor compared to what she was saving by returning the rugs.

"Thank you so much," she said. "I really appreciate it. And I'm very sorry for the inconvenience."

She clicked off the phone with a sigh. It had been the right thing to do, but she couldn't pretend to be happy about it.

That was the precise moment Abby picked to return, almost stumbling over the largest of the rolled-up rugs that blocked the door. Jess watched the color flame in her cheeks, saw that there was more than likely an expletive on the tip of her sister's tongue. She held up a hand to forestall it.

"They're going back," she said before Abby could say a word. "I've already called. They'll be picked up later this afternoon."

She could tell she'd caught Abby by surprise. She'd probably been spoiling for a fight and now Jess had stolen her thunder. She forced a faint smile. "Sometimes I am capable of recognizing and doing the right thing."

Abby picked her way over the rolls and sat down on the steps beside her, shoulder to shoulder as they'd done so often through the years. "What made you decide to send these back?"

"It finally sank in that you and I are on the same team here. I'd turned us into adversaries."

Abby nodded, not denying it. She slanted a look toward Jess. "Don't you understand that saying no to you just about kills me?"

"When I'm being rational, I do," Jess told her. "Other times, not so much."

Abby nodded in understanding. "I know how badly you want everything in here to be perfect from day one, but the place is already amazing with all the changes you've made. It's warm and cozy and inviting." Nudging Jess in the side, she grinned. "And what fun would it be if you had absolutely nothing left to fix or change or decorate after the opening?"

At the suggestion that she might be easily bored by the inn so quickly if there weren't more projects to do, Jess bristled, then let it go. She knew Abby hadn't intended the comment to be a dig. Relaxing finally, Jess grinned back at her. "I never looked at it that way. As soon as we're in the black, I can think about ordering these rugs again." At Abby's dismayed look, she added, "I swear they weren't that expensive." She gave Abby a sly look. "Want to peek at them?"

"I don't think you should unwrap them," Abby cautioned.

"But you do want to see them, don't you?" Jess taunted. "I know your curiosity must be killing you to see what I thought was so special about them that I was willing to risk your wrath. How about just one? We can roll it right back up again."

"Okay, yes, I'm curious," Abby admitted. "But just unroll one."

Jess already knew from the size and invoice number which one had been intended for right here in the foyer. She carefully slit the paper with the utility knife she kept in her pocket for a dozen different uses that came up during the day. When she unrolled it, she heard Abby's gasp.

"Oh, my, it's beautiful," her sister said. "The colors are so rich, the design is amazing with the flowers in the middle and the border of seashells. It's perfect for right here under this table. It really brightens up the area and the beige carpet actually provides a nice backdrop for it. It'll look even more spectacular when there's money to rip out the carpet and refinish the wood floors."

Jess chuckled at her enthusiasm. It was the same reaction she'd had when she'd first seen it. "I know," she said, experiencing a moment of triumph.

"Are the others the same?"

"No, I chose each one to go with the color scheme in the room it was intended for. The biggest one is for the sitting room. Some are mostly flowers, like this one. Others are very beachy. All of them are bright. I wanted the vibrancy they'd add to the decor. I figured they would make up for not pulling up the carpet and getting the floors refinished." She regarded Abby with an earnest expression. "I swear I only bought them for the rooms where the carpet seemed particularly boring."

Abby couldn't seem to tear her gaze away from the one they'd unrolled. "Open another one," she said unexpectedly.

"But—"

"Just do it before I change my mind."

Jess slit the paper on a second rug, this one with a vivid teal background and larger seashells that added cream and hints of pink and coral to the design.

"For the room at the end of the hall on the left," Abby guessed at once, nodding her approval. "It's perfect." She pointed to the largest. "That's for the sitting room?"

Jess nodded.

Abby sighed, then said, "Go ahead, open it."

There was barely room to spread this one out, so they carried it into the sitting room with its deep green walls, furniture upholstered in a lighter shade of celadon green edged with the same dark shade as the walls. Large pots of artificial flowers that she hoped to replace with real ones during the summer season gave the room its additional color. The new rug, also a deep green, had a single huge bouquet of splashy summer flowers in the middle, bordered by a thin band of light green. It couldn't have been more perfect if they'd had it woven themselves.

Abby knelt down at once, her fingers sinking into the deep pile, her eyes alight just as Jess's had been when she'd spotted it in the store. She leaned back on her heels and looked up.

"I know I'm going to hate myself for doing this, but call them back. We're keeping the rugs."

Jess stared at her in astonishment, hardly daring to believe her ears. "Really?"

"They're too perfect. How can we let them go, knowing they might not be available when the budget frees up some cash? Let me see the invoice."

Jess handed it over, still not quite believing that her sister was giving in. "Look, it really is okay if we can't afford them," she said, trying not to let hope seep into her voice.

Abby smiled at her. "The fact that you'd already made the call to have them picked up means a lot. It's true that the inn can't afford them right now, but I can. They're my gift to you."

"No," Jess protested. "You've already invested in the inn, to say nothing of coming down here to help me. I can't accept this, too. It's too much."

This time it was Abby who dug in her heels. "They're staying, Jess. They're the perfect finishing touches and I want to do this for you. I want you to see how much I believe in you and in the inn."

Jess wanted the carpets to stay so badly, but she still didn't feel right accepting them. "You shouldn't make it easy on me. I screwed up."

"But with all the right instincts," Abby said, standing up and giving her a fierce hug. "Just look at how this rug sets off everything in this room. It pulls everything together."

Jess frowned at the comment. "Is that why you gave in, because you like my taste?"

"Partly, maybe. Would that be so bad? But the real reason is because you actually got the point about why they should go back. It gives me high hopes that what I've been telling you really is starting to sink in. I'm not rewarding the bad behavior, I'm rewarding what you did before I got here." She shrugged. "Besides, they're just too gorgeous to send back."

"I felt the same way about the stove," Jess blurted, ruining the moment. Abby immediately scowled.

"That's in a whole other league, Jess," she said tightly. "And you know it. That stove cost a fortune. It was an extravagance, especially when the one we have works just fine. These rugs cost less than half as much and they're part of the decor. They'll add to the ambience for the guests."

Jess winced. "I get what you're saying. I'm sorry I

spoiled this rare moment of total rapport between us. No more whining about the stove. I promise."

Abby nodded, but Jess thought she caught a little glimmer of something in her eyes. At first she thought maybe it was approval, but then she decided it was something else entirely, as if she knew something that Jess didn't. It was there and gone so quickly, though, that she couldn't be sure she hadn't imagined it.

"I'll call the carpet company right now," she said, wanting to get away from Abby before she did something to make her sister change her mind about keeping them. Before she left the room, she embraced Abby. "I know I haven't said this nearly enough, especially lately, but thank you. And I'm not talking about giving me the rugs. I mean for everything. My whole life you've been the one person, other than Gram, I knew I could count on."

"You can always count on Mick, Bree, Connor and Kevin, too," Abby reminded her.

"Not like you," Jess insisted, teary-eyed and embarrassed by it. "So, just thanks, okay?"

Abby's eyes were filled with unshed tears, as well. "I'm sorry for being so hard on you about some of this, but you do know I love you, don't you? That will never change."

"Right back at you."

And from this moment on, she was going to do everything in her power never to let her big sister down again.

Trace stood on the beach looking up toward the house that sat on a precipice above it. It wasn't a mansion by any means—just four bedrooms and three baths—but it had a sunlit den that could be turned into a studio, a smaller room off the kitchen that had been intended for a live-in house-keeper, but which could make an ideal office for someone working from home. There was also a sprawling flagstone patio edged with flowers and a chef's dream of a kitchen with stainless-steel appliances, granite countertops and cherry cabinets. A thriving herb garden was just outside the kitchen door.

"What do you think?" Susie O'Brien asked, her expression eager. "It's pretty amazing, isn't it? Houses like this don't come on the market all that often. It's the only one we have right now and several people looked at it last weekend. If you ask me, Uncle Mick outdid himself on the design for this one."

"He did," Trace agreed, wanting this house for himself and Abby and the girls with a ferocity that shocked him.

When he'd been struck by the idea of buying the perfect house, he'd envisioned something exactly like this in the back of his mind. When he'd gone by Susie's office, though, he'd not been overly optimistic that he'd find one. He'd known, just as she said, that they rarely came on the market. Water views were in high demand, especially those that Mick himself had designed and built in the early stages of Chesapeake Shores. His national reputation made anything he'd designed especially desirable.

Impulsively he pulled out his checkbook, knowing the risk he was taking by not asking Abby how she might feel about him buying a house for the two of them. The grand gesture could prove to be an unwelcome surprise. Hopefully, though, he could persuade her that this would be the perfect home for their family or, if not a year-round home, at least a summer house which would maintain their roots in Chesapeake Shores.

"What'll it take to guarantee I get this?" he asked Susie.

Susie gave him a startled look. "The asking price would lock it up, I'm sure. And if you do it quickly, hopefully you'll avoid getting into a bidding war. That happened on the last house like this that came up for sale."

Though it went against Trace's nature not to bargain, he nodded. "Then that's the offer I'm making. Take it to the owners and keep in mind that I do not intend to lose this place," he said, trusting her not to use that bit of knowledge to the owners' advantage.

"Let's go back to my office and do the paperwork," she said. She gave him a grin. "I don't suppose you'll have any trouble getting your loan approved."

Trace chuckled. "No, I don't suppose I will."

In fact, the biggest obstacle he faced would be getting Abby to say yes when he asked her to stay here and share this house with him. He figured, though, if he bided his time, lured her back into his bed a few more times, she might be willing to concede that living with him was an excellent idea. Moreover, she might even consider building their future right here.

When Trace turned up at the house just in time to help Abby put the girls to bed, his arrival drew a knowing glance from Gram and a more suspicious one from Mick.

"You're spending a lot of time with my daughter lately," Mick commented.

"I am," Trace agreed.

"Any particular reason for that?" Mick pressed.

Abby's grandmother didn't do a very good job of hiding a chuckle at the question. Trace winked at her.

"The usual reasons, sir," he told Mick. "I enjoy her company."

Mick tried to stare him down, evidently aware that Trace had been enjoying a whole lot more than Abby's company. That hard, knowing look gave Trace pause. He didn't buckle under it, but he decided damage control might be called for.

"If you're asking me if my intentions are honorable, sir, they are," he assured Mick. "I want to marry her. I'd prefer it, though, if you didn't say anything. I don't think Abby's quite ready to make that kind of commitment yet."

Mick's expression eased. "Well, it's certainly not the kind of thing she should be hearing from me before she hears it from you." His gaze narrowed a bit. "You sure you have the situation under control, though? Do you need any advice?"

This time Gram didn't even attempt to hide her guffaw. "Mick O'Brien, stay out of this. You're the last person on the planet who ought to be giving anyone relationship advice."

To Trace's surprise, Mick just grinned. "You might be surprised by what I know about handling the opposite sex, Ma."

"Not likely," Gram muttered. "Trace, why don't you go on upstairs? I know the girls would love it if you were there to help tuck them in. They've been asking about you."

He nodded. "I'll see you later, then."

Inside, he took the stairs two at a time, then slowed as he neared the girls' room. He had to be careful not to let Abby see his excitement about the house and start asking questions he wasn't ready to answer. He'd gotten word that his offer had been accepted just before coming over here, but as much as he wanted to share that, he knew he had to keep it to himself a while longer. Hearing that he'd bought a house would only spook her right now.

"I hear a couple of rowdy little girls who sound much too wide-awake," he announced as he entered their room.

Abby's head snapped around. Her eyes lit with surprise and pleasure. A slow smile spread across her face. "I wasn't expecting to see you tonight."

"I was at loose ends and I missed you," he said, shoving his hands into his pockets to keep from reaching for her.

She looked amazing with her hair tousled, probably from being outdoors, and her skin glowing. She was wearing short shorts, a tank top that clung to her curves and no shoes. Her

toenails had been painted a soft shade of coral that comple-
mented her lightly tanned legs and feet. She didn't look a
day older than she had the last night they'd spent together
before she took off for New York all those years ago. If
they'd been alone in the house, he would have dragged her
straight down the hall and into her bed. As it was he settled
for dropping a chaste kiss on her forehead. To his amusement, she seemed as disappointed by that as he was.

He lowered himself to the floor beside her. "So, what's
tonight's story?"

"Mommy's reading to us about Alice," Carrie told him,
her excitement evident in her sparkling eyes.

"Alice in Wonderland," Abby confirmed. "Right now,
we're at the Mad Hatter's tea party."

Trace leaned back against the edge of Caitlyn's bed and
felt her creep closer. "Sounds exciting. Carry on."

"You want to hear the story, too?" Carrie asked, sounding amazed.

"Absolutely. Mostly I've avoided tea parties, but one
thrown by a Mad Hatter? Now, who wouldn't want to be
invited to that?"

Above him, Caitlyn giggled. Next thing he knew, she'd
slipped off the bed and snuggled against him. Before he
could adjust to that, Carrie, not to be outdone, was on his
other side. Abby stared at the three of them with an expression he couldn't read. A faint smile played about her lips,
but then she looked down and began to read.

Trace couldn't focus on the story at all. He was too caught
up in the realization that this was what it was like to be a
dad, to have a family, to be with people he wanted to spend
his life protecting and loving. Lost in a sea of unfamiliar
emotions, he didn't notice when the girls fell asleep or when
Abby's voice faded.

At Abby's touch, he blinked and met her gaze.

"They're asleep," she whispered. "We have to get them into bed without waking them."

"I'll do it," he said, rising, then gently lifting first Carrie, then Caitlyn back into their beds. Impulsively he bent down and pressed a light kiss to their cheeks. "Night, angels."

He waited at the doorway while Abby did the same, then tucked their covers up around them. When she emerged from the room, he spun her around and backed her into a wall.

"I've been wanting to do this ever since I got here," he murmured, tucking a finger beneath her chin and claiming her mouth. He raked his fingers through her already-mussed hair and held her still, while his tongue plundered.

With his blood humming through his veins, he could have stayed right here, lost in the taste and sensation of her kisses, but common sense had him drawing away. He couldn't take a chance on the girls waking and catching them, not until he and Abby had settled things between them.

He did take her hand, though, as they walked downstairs. "Your father asked me my intentions toward you," he informed her as they headed for the kitchen, rather than the porch where Mick and Gram were waiting.

Abby's gaze shot up. "So sorry," she said. "What did you tell him?"

"That they're entirely honorable."

She regarded him with amusement. "He caught me coming in the other night, so I doubt he believed that."

"I embellished a bit. He seemed content with what I had to say."

She paused as she was about to pour two glasses of tea. Her eyes filled with suspicion. "Meaning?"

"Nothing you need to worry about. Just trying to soothe

him before he decided to break my jaw. You might have warned me that he was onto us, by the way."

"I could have," she admitted. "Maybe I just wanted to see how you'd handle yourself if he gave you a rough time."

Trace chuckled. "Then I'm sorry you missed the showdown."

She handed him one of the glasses, then took a sip from her own. "This is getting complicated, isn't it? You and me, I mean. If it were just the two of us, it might not, but there are all these other people to take into account."

"No," he said at once. "It's between us, Abby. We're the only ones who can decide if we can make each other happy."

She shook her head. "You know it's not that simple. The girls—"

"Will be happy as long as you are."

"You can't replace Wes in their lives," she said, though without much vehemence.

"I'd never even try. For better or worse and despite my own low opinion of him, he's their dad and that bond is unbreakable. I recognize that. I respect it. My place in their lives will be whatever we decide makes sense."

"I saw you with them just now," she said. "They already adore you."

"Is that a bad thing?"

"Of course not. It just adds to the complications. When we go our separate ways—"

"We're not going our separate ways, Abby," he said heatedly. "Not this time."

She blinked at the intensity of his response. "You sound so sure."

"I am sure and before too long, you'll be just as certain."

She seemed amused and vaguely troubled by his confidence. "You have a plan to accomplish that?"

He nodded, grinning at her. "I do."

"Maybe you should give me a couple of hints now."

"So you can get all your defenses into place? I don't think so. You'll just have to take my word for it for now." His gaze locked with hers. "Can you do that? Can you give this a little more time, so it can play out?"

She sighed and moved toward him. "When you look at me like that, I think I could give you just about anything you ask for."

"Then how about one more kiss before we go outside and face another likely inquisition?" he said, tilting her chin up so he could claim her mouth.

There was more than a little trust in that soul-searing kiss. There was hope and maybe even the first fragile hint of the commitment he wanted more than anything.

22

Three days before the opening party for the inn, Abby was in town when she spotted her sister Bree climbing out of a rental car in front of Sally's. She was wearing a loose-fitting dress that hung on her slender frame, sandals and none of the usual bangles that decorated her wrists. Her lush auburn hair had been caught up in a careless knot on top of her head. She looked beautiful, as always, but there was something else, something Abby couldn't quite put her finger on at first. Then she got it. Bree looked sad, almost lifeless. Even her eyes, usually sparkling with intelligence, wit and excitement, looked dull.

Abby hurried down the block and called out. The instant Bree saw her, her expression became more animated, her smile as bright as ever. After catching that first uncensored look, though, Abby didn't buy the transformation.

She wrapped Bree in a hug, aware that her sister's embrace was a little too tight, as if she needed to hold on to something familiar.

When they stepped apart, Abby caught her hand. "Let's have lunch and catch up."

Even though it had been evident that Bree had been heading to Sally's herself, she looked hesitant. "Maybe we should go straight to the house. I called Gram from the road. She'll be watching for me. I was just going to grab a quick cup of coffee first."

"Then we'll call her and let her know I found you and claimed first dibs," Abby said, determined not to let this chance to spend some alone time with Bree slip away.

Though it was obvious she wanted to, Bree didn't argue. She went inside and settled into a booth, dutifully smiling at Sally's greeting, but seeming to shrink away from all the other greetings that were called out by locals who recognized her. Many of them had read in the weekly newspaper about her success as a budding young playwright-in-residence at a Chicago regional theater. Those who brought that up received little more than a polite nod of acknowledgment from her sister.

As she placed the call to Gram and explained Bree's delay, Abby studied her sister. She didn't like what she saw any better now than she had when she'd first spotted her on the street. "I'll have her there in an hour," she promised. "We need a little bit of girl time."

As soon as she'd disconnected the call, she faced Bree. "You look good. A little too thin, maybe, but otherwise as gorgeous as ever."

"I look like hell," Bree contradicted.

There was an edge in her voice that told Abby she believed what she was saying. "You could never look like hell," Abby told her impatiently. "Why would you say that?"

Bree shrugged. "I've stopped deluding myself about everything."

Abby frowned at her defeated tone. "Meaning what?"

"Nothing. I shouldn't have said that." Bree forced another smile. "So how are those sweet girls of yours?"

Reluctantly, Abby accepted the change of topic. Once

Bree clammed up, no amount of prodding was going to get her to talk. "The girls are amazing, as always. And a real handful. I had no idea how much of a handful they could be until the past few weeks down here without the nanny around for backup. I've been paying her, just so we don't lose her, so I've actually considered having her come down here if we're here much longer. I probably should have done that right away, but Gram claims she enjoys spending all this time with Carrie and Caitlyn."

"Tell me about this extended stay of yours. How did that happen? I was surprised when you said you'd been here for almost two months."

"Jess needed some help getting the inn ready, so I decided to stick around for a while." It was shading the truth a bit, but she knew Bree would jump all over her if she knew the whole story. Her sister fell into the camp that thought they all babied Jess way too much instead of forcing her to rely on herself. To emphasize that this had been as much about her as Jess, she added, "It's been wonderful for me to spend so much time with the girls. They love it here. And Gram and Mick are spoiling them rotten. It's going to be impossible to get them back into their regular routines once we're home again."

"Yeah, what's the scoop on Dad? He gave up the project in San Francisco? Has he ever done that before, just walked away?"

"Not that I'm aware of," Abby admitted. "I want to believe it's because he's trying to make up for years of never being here for us." She leaned across the table to add in a whisper, "And because Mom's coming for the opening."

Bree's jaw dropped. "Mom's coming here?" There was shock and maybe even a touch of dismay in her voice.

Abby scowled at her tone. "You're not going to make a

big deal out of that, are you? Things could be tense enough as it is. I haven't even had the nerve to tell Jess yet. It'll be hard enough to make her see that this is a good thing without having to do battle with you, too."

"I'm just surprised," Bree claimed. "How'd you talk her into it?"

"Laid on a ton of guilt," Abby admitted.

"And Dad? How did he take it?"

Abby made a face. "He wasn't overjoyed at first, but he's not going to make a fuss," she said. "I hope."

"Skip hoping and go straight to prayer. This could blow up in your face, big sis."

Abby beamed at her. "Which is one reason I'm so glad you decided to come home. You're going to be my backup and help me keep everyone on their best behavior."

"I doubt all the diplomats at the United Nations could pull that off," Bree said dryly. "O'Briens aren't known for their reticence, much less their tact. Witness the last Christmas dinner when Gram insisted on inviting Uncle Tom and Uncle Jeff and their families. Dad was barely civil to his own brothers."

Abby very much feared she was right. "Okay, enough about all the drama around here, what's going on in your life?"

"Same old thing," Bree said, dodging the question. "We really should get out to the house. I'm anxious to see Gram."

Abby was struck by her omission. "But not so eager to see Dad?"

"Mick's never known quite what to make of me," Bree admitted. "I spent too much time in my room, reading and writing in my journal. The rest of you are all so outgoing, just the way he is, but I hang around in the background, observing life instead of living it, according to some theories I've heard recently."

Abby picked up on the hurt in her voice. "Who said that?"

she demanded sharply. Whoever it was definitely had a cruel streak and she didn't like that, not where her sensitive sister was concerned.

Bree waved her off. "It doesn't matter. We're talking about Dad. Mostly, I don't think he even noticed me, especially after Mom left."

Abby sighed, knowing that Bree was at least partly right. "He barely noticed any of us then." She reached across the table and gave her sister's ice-cold hand a squeeze. "He's changing, Bree. I think you'll see it right off. He's really trying to reach out."

Bree gave her an amused look. "Same old Abby, always wanting everything tied up in a nice, neat bundle, everyone getting along. Haven't you learned that life's not like that?"

There was a bitter undertone to her voice that startled Abby. It was true that Bree had always been the quiet one, a bit of an outsider in her way, but she'd been totally focused on her goals and content in her own skin. It wasn't like her to take potshots at anyone else.

Abby forced herself not to take offense and to keep her tone even. "Trust me, after dealing with Wes, I know just how badly life can suck. I prefer to focus on the positive. Sue me."

Bree winced at her response. "Sorry. That was uncalled for. I know you've had a tough time. I'm just exhausted. Once I've settled down and had some rest, I promise not to be so bitchy."

Abby accepted the apology. Even though she desperately wanted to dig deeper and find out what was behind Bree's mood, she let it go. There'd be time enough to find out, though that would only happen if Bree wanted it to. There wasn't a woman in the world who could keep her own counsel as well as she could.

Trace had accepted his mother's invitation to a family dinner with an ulterior motive. Tonight was the night he intended to force his father into making a decision to give the job at the bank to Laila. She'd been doing excellent work the past few weeks under the guise of helping him out of the jams he manufactured, but the pretense was starting to wear thin on all of them. Besides, he had several important design jobs with deadlines rapidly approaching. He wouldn't have to manufacture the crises in a couple of weeks. They'd be real enough.

Because he didn't want Laila to have to sit through his exchange with his father, he decided to have it out on the ride home from work. He'd hitch a ride back into town with his sister after the evening ended, assuming she was still speaking to him by then. She still had reservations about his attempts to manipulate things in her favor.

"Tell me why you're not driving yourself over for dinner," his father said, regarding him with suspicion.

"This suit's hardly the right thing to wear on my Harley and Mother would flip out if I showed up in jeans," he said, then added, "And I thought we could have a little time alone to talk without Raymond hovering over us at the bank or Mom hovering over us at the house."

Understanding dawned on his father's face. "This is about your sister, then."

Trace nodded. "She's been excelling at every single thing she's done, hasn't she?"

For a moment, he thought his father might not acknowledge Laila's accomplishments out of pure stubbornness, but eventually he sighed and said, "She's proved herself to be more than competent."

Trace slanted a look at him. "You're not surprised by that, are you?"

"No, of course not. She didn't get that master's degree in business by not knowing a thing or two," he admitted.

"Does that mean you're ready to give her a shot at the job?" Trace pressed.

His father pulled off to the side of the road and turned to him. "Are you really that sure that a career at the bank is something you'll never want? You're determined to walk away?"

His father didn't even try to hide his disappointment, but at least he seemed to recognize that the battle was all but over to keep Trace working with him.

Trace nodded. "I love the design work, Dad. More than that, I'm successful at it. I set my own pace, take jobs that will challenge me." He grinned as he loosened his tie and opened the collar of his shirt. He'd stripped off his jacket even before getting in the car. "Best of all, I don't have to wear a suit and tie, except for the occasional meeting with a prospective new client." That last alone was a huge plus in his book.

Trace saw the dismay in his father's eyes, but Lawrence Riley had always been a man who knew when to cut his losses. "Okay, then, I'll speak to Laila tonight. Make her an offer."

"The same one you made me," Trace warned. "You can't offer her less, not in terms of money or in the scope of her responsibilities. In fact, you ought to be offering her more, just to prove you have faith in her, to show that her hard work has won you over."

His father frowned at the suggestion. "Now you're telling me how to run the bank?"

"No, I'm telling you how to make sure Laila takes this job and how to mend fences with her in the process."

"You think I haven't learned my lesson on both counts? She's already told me once what I could do with what she described as a 'handout.'"

"Well, she's a Riley. She has her pride, too."

His father pulled back onto the road. They rode in silence

for a few minutes and then he asked, "Does that mean you'll be heading back to New York right away?"

Trace hadn't meant to get into this tonight, but his father had just given him the perfect opening. "The truth is I'm hoping to stay right here in town."

"In that tiny little apartment?"

"Actually I've made an offer on a house. I think you've probably been there. It's owned by the Marshalls, up on the north end of Shore Road, past the inn."

His father whistled. "That's one that Mick O'Brien built, isn't it?"

"It is and it's amazing, Dad. It'll be perfect for a family."

His father gave him a quick, sharp look. "You have one of those?"

"I'm hoping to," he admitted.

A smile tugged at his father's lips. "Abby, I assume."

"If she'll have me, but this is not for public discussion, Dad. I haven't proposed yet. I haven't even told her about the house. I'm afraid it will make her skittish."

"You filed your loan application at the bank yet?"

"I've filled out the paperwork and pulled all the credit reports, but obviously someone else will need to go over everything."

"Leave the file on my desk first thing tomorrow. I'll handle it myself. I know what they were asking for that place. You have enough for a down payment? If you need help, I can—"

"Thanks, Dad, but I've got it covered."

His father gave him an approving look. "That's good, then. Your mother's going to be thrilled about this."

"Please don't mention it just yet."

"If you insist, but my marriage hasn't lasted all these years with me keeping things from her."

"I know and you won't be in that position for long, I

promise. I want Abby to have this opening at the inn behind her so she can think straight about the two of us. If I push it when she's feeling overwhelmed, I think she'll turn me down flat."

"You've loved this woman for a long time, haven't you?"

"Seems like most of my life," he agreed.

"I'm glad it's finally working out, then."

Trace studied his smug expression and thought, not for the first time, that his father had been hoping for just this outcome when he'd dragged Trace home. He chuckled.

"You happy with yourself?" he inquired.

"Me? I didn't have anything to do with this," his father claimed.

"You weren't hoping that Abby would ride in on her white horse to save Jess, when you brought me here to work at the bank and deal with that financial mess at the inn?"

"I knew it was a possibility Abby would come," he admitted, "but no more than that."

"Dad, you always loved playing the long-shot horses at Pimlico and Laurel. Something tells me you weren't above doing the same thing with my love life."

His father responded with a deep-throated chuckle. "You'll never gather enough evidence to prove that."

"Well, just in case that *was* your intention, thanks," Trace said.

Coming back to Chesapeake Shores, whatever his father's motives had been in getting him here, couldn't have been timed any more perfectly. It seemed he was within stretching distance of grabbing everything he'd ever hoped for.

Abby and Bree were drowning in last-minute party preparations, while Jess was at the front desk reviewing both the party guest list and the first week's reservations. The inn's first visitors would arrive the morning after the party and bookings were solid for the rest of the summer. Even though Abby had thought everything was under control, glitches kept popping up—some of them, she discovered, because Jess had failed to make follow-up phone calls. After discovering that had happened with both the caterer who would be working with their chef and the florist, she was about to throw in the towel, when she caught Bree studying her.

"What's Jess done now?" her sister asked quietly.

Protective as always, Abby immediately tried to minimize it. "She forgot to confirm a couple of things. No big deal. It's handled now."

Bree shook her head. "How on earth is she going to keep this place running without you?"

"She'll be fine," Abby insisted, not wanting to reveal her own doubts about that very thing. "I've already started interviewing bookkeepers. The new chef has a good head on her shoulders, and she understands that her responsibilities include more than cooking. She has to manage the restaurant operation."

"But what Jess really needs is a business partner," Bree said. "You know she's not going to listen to anyone else."

"She will," Abby insisted. "She has to, and I think she understands that. This is her dream, after all. She'll fight for it."

"Until something more important or more interesting comes along," Bree said.

Abby frowned. "Why are you so down on her today?"

Bree's cheeks flamed. "I'm not. I want her to succeed. It's just hard for me to see you working your butt off for *her* dream, while she keeps letting critical stuff fall through the cracks."

"It's all handled," Abby repeated. "This party's going to be amazing, and the actual opening will be a huge success. You'll see."

"If you say so," her sister said, though her demeanor radiated doubt.

"I do."

Just then Trace wandered in. Abby felt the color rise in her cheeks as he headed right for her and claimed her mouth with a heated kiss.

"My, my," Bree said, her eyes wide. "This is something no one told me about."

Trace whirled around, his expression startled, then grinned when he spotted her. "Hey, Bree. Welcome home."

"Too bad nobody welcomed me like that," she said, getting to her feet. "I think I'll head back to the house. It's a little steamy in here all of a sudden."

"Don't leave on my account," Trace said. "I was hoping to steal Abby for an hour or two for lunch. You're welcome to come with us."

"Do come, Bree," Abby pleaded. "You haven't had crabs since you got here." She turned to Trace for confirmation. "We can go to Brady's, can't we?"

"Absolutely. Nothing I like better than watching a couple of women get down and dirty with a pot of butter, a mallet and a couple of dozen crabs."

Bree laughed. "You have a very odd sense of what's sexy, but I'll pass, thanks. Gram's ordered crabs to have at the house tonight."

"That's right," Abby said. "I forgot. We could go someplace else."

Bree shook her head. "Being a third wheel to you two got old years ago. Have fun." She stared pointedly at Abby. "I think you and I need to talk later. I'm just putting you on notice."

Abby could imagine how that conversation was likely to go. The only person in their family more adept at interrogation than Mick was her sister. She might not be forthcoming herself, but she had a reporter's hard-hitting, uncompromising interview skills. Oh well, she and Trace had handled her father okay. Now that she'd had a fair warning, she could have her answers all worked out and completely unrevealing for her nosy sister.

"Bree looks good," Trace said when he and Abby were seated at one of the new little cafés along the waterfront with their thick, grilled sandwiches and glasses of iced tea. Panini Bistro had only three or four tables inside, but they made up for that with plenty of outdoor seating with bright blue-and-white-striped umbrellas to offer shade on these increasingly warm late-June afternoons. Every table was occupied, mostly with people in swimsuits who'd walked over from the beach.

Abby shook her head at Trace's observation about Bree. "There's something off with her," Abby said. "She seems brittle, like she's about to break into a million pieces, but she won't open up."

Trace studied her expression. "You're really worried about her."

Abby nodded.

"Do you suppose you could think about something else for a minute? Or do you want to talk about your sister?"

She shook her head. "There's nothing I can do about Bree until she decides to talk." She met his gaze. "What's on your mind?"

"Look, I really hate to bring this up right now. You have more than enough on your plate, but I need to know how you want me to handle something."

She stared at him with alarm. "You sound serious. What's wrong? Nothing's messed up with the inn's finances again, is it? I've been watching every penny."

He held up a hand. "Slow down. It has nothing to do with the inn. It's Wes. I heard from him earlier today."

Her eyes widened in shock. "You heard from Wes? Why? Did he call you? What did he want?"

Trace reached in his pocket and withdrew the papers that had arrived at the bank bright and early this morning. He'd been seeing red ever since a process server had barged into his office with an indignant Mariah right on his heels. He'd managed to get his temper under control before coming to see Abby.

"He sent this," he said, handing over the legal documents.

Abby gave him a questioning look, then took the papers and started to read. "You have to be kidding me!" she exploded. "He's taken out a restraining order to keep you away from the girls? He can't do that. You'd have to pose some kind of threat."

"That would usually be the standard," Trace agreed. "He has to have some judge in his pocket to pull this off. Or maybe they're fake, though they look authentic to me, and they've been notarized."

Abby flipped through the rest of the pages, her expression increasingly incredulous. As soon as she'd turned the last page, she reached for her cell phone.

Trace put his hand over hers. "No. I'm not asking you to deal with this. I'll handle Wes. I just need to know how you want me to proceed. Can I beat him to a pulp, or would you prefer that I go through nice, tidy legal channels?"

"You shouldn't have to deal with him at all," she said furiously. "This is outrageous."

"Of course it is. He's just blowing smoke because he's scared to death he's going to lose his close relationship with his daughters, especially if you decide to stay down here."

"But I'm not—"

"You might," he corrected. "But that's a topic for another day."

She sat back, looking stunned. "I thought Wes and I had

settled things. Why would he do something this crazy now? Do you think he's having some kind of breakdown? His behavior's certainly erratic, that's for sure. Or else he's retaliating for my forcing him to give up the custody suit."

Trace squeezed her hand. "His reasoning hardly matters. Let's just assume it's as simple as wanting to keep me away from his girls and, by extension, you."

"But why?" she asked, looking perplexed. "We've been divorced for years."

"But I'm the first real threat to the status quo who's come along."

"I suppose."

"Here's what I'm going to do. I've already booked a flight to New York for this evening and scheduled a meeting with my attorney for first thing in the morning. I promise you this will be handled by the end of the day tomorrow." He met her gaze. "It does mean, though, that I won't be here for the party tonight. I'm sorry. I know how important tonight is for you and for Jess."

"Don't worry about that, just take care of this. I could fly up with you."

"No, you have way too much to do right here, and Jess would never forgive you if you miss this party."

"I swear, I could kill Wes if he did something like this purely out of spite."

"I'm more inclined to think it's desperation. Bottom line, though, is that we'll work it out between us. He knows that order's not worth the paper it's written on. There's absolutely no legal justification for it. And with everything we know about him and Gabrielle, I think I can make him see reason. We're holding all the cards, Abby."

Abby still looked shaken when they got back to the inn. Trace kissed her long and hard to put some color back into her cheeks. "Stop worrying," he commanded.

"How can I?"

"Focus on the party and think about what I have planned for you the next time we're alone."

She studied him with sudden interest. "Really? You have a plan?"

"Sweetheart, when it comes to you, I've had plans for years."

He kissed her again, then left while that bemused smile was still on her lips and her eyes were sparkling with real anticipation.

23

When Abby walked back into the office at the inn, she was still seething over that idiotic restraining order that Wes had somehow manipulated a judge into signing. That had to be how he'd managed it, by asking for a favor from some golf buddy or client of the family conglomerate, because there was certainly no way he could have gotten it otherwise.

Muttering under her breath, she tossed her purse on her desk, then noticed Jess sitting in the shadows.

"Hey, is everything okay?" Abby asked.

"That's what I'm wondering about," Jess said, her expression surprisingly grim for a woman who was about to see her dream come true in just a few hours.

Already in a lousy mood, Abby lost patience. "I don't have time for riddles. If something's wrong, just tell me."

"Why is number ten, our best room, showing up on the computer as reserved when I can't find the name of the guest or a credit card number on file?"

Abby sucked in a deep breath. She'd counted on Jess not noticing that. Naturally, for once, her sister had paid attention to details. She should have had this conversation with her days ago, but she'd kept putting it off.

"I did that," she said eventually.

"I guessed that much, since you're the only other person who knows the reservation system, but why?"

Abby met her sister's gaze. "I'll explain but you have to promise to let me finish before you get upset."

Jess's gaze narrowed. "You're not comping a room to Wes, are you?"

Abby was shocked she would even think such a thing, but of course Jess didn't know about his latest stunt. "Absolutely not," she told her sister. "Actually the room is for Mom. She'll be here this afternoon."

For a moment her sister sat there in apparently stunned silence. Then she was on her feet. "*No!*" she said emphatically, her fist hitting the desk. "Not in my inn. Why is she even coming back to town? Nobody wants her here."

"I do," Abby said quietly. "And if you'll look past all these years of pent-up anger and hurt, I think you do, too."

"No, I don't," Jess said fiercely. "When has she ever been here for me?"

"She tried, Jess. You know she did. You shut her out. How many times did she beg you to move to New York? She wanted you with her, Jess. She wanted all of us."

"Oh, please," Jess mocked. "If she'd wanted us there badly, she would have made it happen."

"Not if she could see how painful it would be for us to be uprooted from our home here," Abby said quietly.

"She *abandoned* us," Jess repeated stubbornly. "I've never understood how you've been able to forget all that."

"I haven't forgotten anything," Abby said quietly. "And Dad should have insisted you go, at least for a visit, because she's your mother. He was as much at fault as she was. I think it gave him some kind of perverse satisfaction to force her to come back here time after time if she wanted to spend any time at all with us."

"Look, I know she was your mother until you were seventeen. She was mine until I was seven, and then she left. I don't think she gets enough points to be called a mother after that."

Abby had known this was going to be hard, but she hadn't realized just how difficult Jess would make it. Her bitterness ran even deeper than Abby had realized. Not that she could blame her, but there had to be some way to use this occasion for these two people she loved to make peace.

"Sweetie, she's coming here to support you. She's reaching out. No one's asking you to forgive her the second she walks in the door, but please just give her a chance."

"Why should I?" Jess demanded. "This is my big night, and I don't want her here."

There was a gasp behind Abby and she whirled around to see Megan standing in the doorway, her expression filled with shock and dismay. Abby was on her feet at once. "Mom, she didn't really mean that."

"Yes, I did," Jess said, though there was a faint hint of regret in her eyes. Despite her anger, she was too softhearted to deliberately hurt someone the way she'd just hurt Megan.

Abby scowled at her and turned back to Megan. "It's going to be okay. We just need to spend some time together, all of us. We need to remember how to be a family."

Megan shook her head, her gaze never leaving Jess's face. It was as if she couldn't get over the sight of this young woman whom she'd seen so rarely through the years. "No," she said softly, her voice shaky. "I should go. Jess is right. I don't belong here."

Jess cast a hard look at Abby. "What were you thinking?" she muttered, then brushed past Megan and left the room.

Abby winced, but used her sister's departure to draw Megan inside and lead her to a chair. "Don't listen to her, Mom. I just sprang this on her. She needs time to calm down."

Her mother gave her a rueful look. "I doubt I can stay till Christmas."

Abby couldn't manage to muster the grin her mother had obviously been hoping would break the tension. "It won't take that long, I promise. I'll have another talk with her. Please, stay."

Megan looked torn. "I knew this was a bad idea when you first suggested it, but I wanted so badly to see everyone, I said yes anyway. Tell me, is Mick's reaction going to be any better? Has he mellowed at all since I spoke to him?"

"He's had time to digest the news," Abby assured her. "I think he'll be on good behavior."

Megan sighed. "Well, that's something, I suppose."

"Then you'll stay?"

"I really want to," she said, her expression wistful.

"Then do it. I'll show you to your room." Abby grabbed her mother's suitcase and carried it upstairs. There was no sign of Jess as they went, for which Abby was grateful. She had a hunch that one more scene would send Megan fleeing right back to New York.

Abby used the key to open the guest room door, then gave it to her mother. "This is the largest room we have. I think you'll be comfortable in here. I've booked it for a week, in case you decide you want to stick around."

Megan's eyes widened with appreciation. "It's really lovely. The decorator has excellent taste."

"That's all Jess," Abby said. "You should tell her that when you see her."

"I doubt she cares about my opinion."

"Of course she does. She just doesn't dare admit it, even to herself. Keep reaching out, Mom. If she rejects you a few times, well—"

"Maybe it's what I deserve," Megan said, completing the thought.

Abby started to argue, then opted for honest. "Yes, maybe it's what you deserve." She hugged her mother. "I think everything you need is in here. Nobody's staffing the front desk till tomorrow, so call me on my cell if you discover something's missing. The party's at seven."

Megan nodded, her expression somber. "I'm looking forward to it." She said it with all the conviction of someone heading to death row.

Mick had been restless all day. He would have attributed it to worry about Jess and wanting to be sure nothing would go wrong on this night that meant so much to her, but he knew better. It was all about Megan. He hadn't been able to get her out of his mind for days.

Normally he would have gone out to a job site to distract himself, but he'd made a vow to himself to stick close until after tonight's party and tomorrow's grand opening, just in case Jess or Abby needed his help with anything. Not that either of them were in the habit of turning to him, he thought with regret. He'd taught them years ago not to count on him.

When the silence started to get to him—or rather when his obvious agitation started to drive Gram crazy—she was the one who suggested he go for a walk on the beach. "You used to enjoy that," she reminded him. "Back before you got so driven that you didn't have time for the things that really matter."

He grinned at her. "Leave it to you to turn a simple suggestion into a lecture on past sins."

She laughed. "I have to sneak my points in when I can. Now, go. It's making me nervous watching you pace up and down in my kitchen. I have to finish baking for the crowd who'll still be here tomorrow morning. I expect Connor and

Bree are going to want my cinnamon rolls for breakfast." Her expression turned nostalgic. "It'll be nice to have a full house again, won't it, Mick?"

He nodded. "I wish Kevin were going to be here."

Gram squeezed his shoulder. "He'll be home soon. Let's focus on that."

"Getting him out of Iraq won't happen soon enough for me."

"Nor me."

He bent down and kissed the top of his mother's head. "I'll get out from underfoot. You're right. A walk on the beach sounds like the perfect way to clear my head."

She studied him knowingly. "It's filled with thoughts of Megan, isn't it?"

He nodded, seeing no reason to deny it.

"That's natural enough. I hope Abby knew what she was doing inviting her back here."

Mick sighed. "I doubt she had any idea, but there's no question her heart was in the right place. Abby's always wanted this family to be at peace. I'm just not convinced we can pull that off in a couple of days."

"Well, nothing beats a try—"

"But a failure," Mick said, completing the familiar refrain. "I think Abby got her determination and optimism from you."

"Maybe," his mother said. "But she got her big heart from you."

Mick wasn't so sure about that. As he walked to the beach, he tried to remember the last time he'd let anyone get close, opened his heart to another person, even his kids. Megan's departure had robbed him of his ability to trust or to love. Worse, he'd never been able to blame her for going. After all, in essence he'd gone first, taking job after job in places that required him to be gone for weeks, even months at a time. What sort of arrogance had made him think any woman would put up with that, even a wife as devoted as Megan had been?

He remembered with vivid clarity the way she'd looked on the day she'd told him she'd had enough. It had been on this very beach with the wind in her hair, color high in her cheeks and a de͏̲͏̲ ͏̲f sorrow in her eyes that had almost brought him to his kn͏̲ He'd been about to beg her to change her mind when she'd touched a finger to his lips and shaken her head.

"It's too late," she'd said, her lapis-blue eyes welling with tears of regret. "You are who you are and I can't ask or expect you to change." Her hand slid to his cheek. "I'm so very proud of the work you've done. This town is a real community, just the way you envisioned it. I just wish you'd spent half as much time building our family. I love you, Mick, but I can't stay here any longer. Bearing all the responsibility is smothering me."

Back straight, chin high, she'd walked away from him then. Only because he knew her so well, loved her so much had he known that she walked away crying.

He'd shed plenty of tears of his own that night, alone in their bed because she'd already moved into a guest room after they'd argued yet again. He wasn't too proud to admit it. He was, however, too proud or too stupid to go crawling after her the way he should have done. He hadn't tried to stop her from getting into that taxi, either. That was the regret he'd live with till eternity.

He looked up then and, as if his thoughts had conjured her, he saw Megan a hundred yards ahead, walking toward him. The shock of seeing her again stopped him in his tracks and because she was looking down, watching the froth of waves against the sand, he had time to drink in the sight of her.

Her hair was much shorter than he'd ever seen her wear it, but it suited her face. The color in her cheeks was from the sun, not makeup, and her lips were coated with some kind of pale peach gloss that made them look ripe and tempting. Desire that had no business being part of their relationship now slammed into him. It was a shock to realize the attraction hadn't died despite all the effort he'd put into killing all the good memories between them.

He dragged his gaze away from her face, noted the way her flowing pants and shirt molded themselves to her trim body courtesy of the wind. He was about to check to see if she still wore that kick-ass red polish on her toes when she glanced up and caught him staring.

Her tentative smile started, then faded. "Hello, Mick."

He nodded, almost tongue-tied, which was the most ridiculous, unexpected thing that had ever happened to him. He'd won her heart by talking his fool head off.

There was a flash of hurt in her eyes at his silence, but her gaze held steady. "You knew I'd be here?"

Again, he nodded. "I'm…I'm glad you came."

She lifted a disbelieving brow at that. "Really? You didn't sound overjoyed when I called you to discuss it."

He shrugged. "I've been persuaded it's past time for you to be with your family on a special occasion."

She laughed then, the light, merry sound washing over him, cheering him as did Gram's glass windchime when it stirred in the breeze.

"Obviously Abby's been busy talking both of us into something that may or may not be for the best," she said. "Jess has already made her position clear. She'd like me to leave."

Rather than relief, unexpected alarm flared. "But you're not going, are you? She needs you here, Meggie."

At the use of his old nickname for her, her expression faltered. "It's been a long time since you've called me that."

"I know. It seemed wrong, as if it belonged with happier times." Uneasy with veering off onto personal terrain, he asked, "What did you think of the inn?"

"It's absolutely stunning," she said with enthusiasm. "Jess has excellent taste."

"Expensive, too," Mick said wryly, thinking of the range he'd had delivered that morning as an inn-warming present. Somehow Abby had kept Jess away from the kitchen during the delivery and that new chef of hers had promised to bar her from the premises until all the food had been prepared for tonight and the party was under way. At some point in the evening he planned to duck into the kitchen and show it to her.

"Nice to see she inherited one of my traits," Megan joked. "Though there are others that might have been more useful."

Mick shoved his hands into his pockets. "You look good, Meggie. Not a day older than when you left."

She laughed at that. "And you're still full of blarney, Mick O'Brien."

He stood there, uncertain what to do or say next. Fortunately, Megan hadn't lost her ability to navigate uncharted emotional waters or her knack for ending an awkward moment.

"I should get back," she told him. "I'm glad we ran into each other here, Mick. It'll make tonight easier."

She touched his hand, a caress so light and fleeting, it was almost as if he'd imagined it. And then she was gone, striding along the hard-packed sand and away from him. Again.

Trace decided not to wait for his meeting in the morning with his attorney before settling things with Wes. Instead, he took a cab straight to Wes's apartment, which was only blocks from where Abby lived with the girls. Trace wasn't crazy about the proximity, but it made sense for them to be close by for the sake of the twins.

He was wondering how he was going to make it past the somber doorman when opportunity presented itself in the form of two couples heading inside for a party. He made himself part of the group the second they'd been waved in and headed with them to the elevator, glad that he'd found the apartment number before leaving Maryland.

Upstairs, he rang the bell, then waited for Wes to appear. Instead, it was Gabrielle who answered the door. She was as beautiful as she'd appeared in the society-page pictures he'd seen, even without makeup and with her hair yanked back in a ponytail that made her look younger than thirty-two, the age given in the article accompanying one of the photos.

"Who are you and how did you get up here?" she demanded heatedly. "If you're another reporter, I have no comment."

She was about to slam the door in his face when Wes wandered into the living room.

"I'm here to see your fiancé," Trace told her, pushing his way into the room.

Wes regarded him with alarm. "Call security, Gabrielle."

Trace leveled a look at her. "That won't be necessary."

She stood where she was, her expression uneasy. "Wes, what's this about?"

Wes shot a defiant look toward Trace. "I imagine he's here about the restraining order I got against him."

Gabrielle's eyes widened at that. "A restraining order? Why?"

"I don't want him anywhere near Carrie and Caitlyn," Wes said.

His girlfriend blinked at that. "You think he's a danger to the twins?"

Trace answered for him. "No, he thinks I'm a danger to him. What he really wants is to remove me from Abby's life, isn't that right, Wes? You figure if you can make it impossible for me to be anywhere near the girls, Abby will cut me out of her life, too."

"No, it's just about the twins," he insisted. "You pose a threat to them."

"You're going to have to explain that one to me," Trace said.

"I don't have to explain anything to you," Wes said belligerently. "I made my case to a judge and he agreed."

"You made your *so-called* case to a man who's just made thousands of dollars on a deal you recommended, thanks to a bit of inside information passed along by Gabrielle. Isn't that what really happened?" Trace asked.

Wes looked stunned that he'd put those pieces together.

Trace regarded him with amusement. "I told you I had contacts in the city. Our mutual friend Steve was happy to make a few calls for me." Trace turned to Gabrielle. "Aren't you in enough of a mess without adding insider trading to the mix?"

She sat down hard on the edge of a dining room chair, looking shaken. "Wes? Is he telling the truth? You used information I mentioned to you?"

Wes nodded. "I had to. I needed this favor. It was the only way to be sure that Abby would bring the girls back to New York."

"I think maybe you can forget about that," Trace said. "She's not very happy with you at the moment. As for me, I expect you to clear this matter up first thing in the morning or I'll slap you with a defamation of character suit that'll make every paper in the city."

Wes tried to stare him down, but Trace didn't so much as blink. Finally the other man sighed. "I just want to keep on seeing my girls."

"You will," Trace promised. "As long as you never pull something this stupid again. Abby would never keep your daughters from you. She knows they adore you. How many times does she have to tell you that before you believe her?"

"But you—"

"I know you're their father, Wes," he said solemnly. "I swear to you that I will always respect that unless you give me cause to think you're the one who's a bad influence on them. Please don't ever give me the ammunition to believe that."

"You say that now, but I know you'll try to make them hate me," Wes said, still not convinced by Trace's pledge.

Trace tried again. "I won't say a negative word about you to Caitlyn or Carrie. Neither will Abby. You may not know me, but surely you know her well enough to know she would never do that. She'd never let me do it, either. Your daughters are amazing and if things work out with Abby and me, I'll be as good to them as if they were my own, but I won't ever try to keep you out of their lives."

Wes's relief was obvious. "I just had to be sure, you know. They're the most important people in my life, next to Gabrielle. I don't know what I'd do if I lost them."

"You're not going to lose them," Trace said again. "At least not because of me."

Wes hesitated, his gaze locked with Trace's. Eventually he reached for the phone. "I'll call my attorney now. He'll have that order lifted by morning."

"Thank you," Trace said. "And we understand each other?"

Abby's ex-husband nodded.

"Okay, then," Trace said, satisfied. "I'd better get going. There's a party at the inn tonight and I'd like to get there before it's over." Despite his earlier anger, Trace felt some sympathy for Wes and his fears about losing his girls. "Just so you know, I'm pretty sure Abby plans to bring Caitlyn and Carrie up to spend some time with you next week."

Gabrielle's eyes lit up as much as Wes's did. "Oh, I can't wait," she said eagerly, slipping her hand into her fiancé's. At a warning glance from Wes, her expression faltered. "I know Abby despises me, but maybe if she knew how much I love the girls, she'd change her mind."

"Maybe so," Trace said. He'd heard the sincerity in her

voice and knew without a doubt that whatever else he thought of Wes or, for that matter, Gabrielle, they truly did love the twins. He'd have to remember that the next time he wanted to throttle the man.

Jess was in her element, Abby thought as she watched her sister weaving through the throng of people who'd come for the party. She gave every single guest—except for Megan—enough of her attention to make them feel special, then moved on to someone else. She even spent a few minutes with the twins telling them how beautiful they looked in their new party dresses.

Everywhere she turned, Abby heard compliments about the inn's fresh decor. Even the mayor, accompanied by Mrs. Finch wearing an enamel broach of a spray of her beloved lilacs, paused to tell her how delighted he was to have the town's most luxurious tourist hotel open for business again.

"The inn may be small, but it always stood for quality," Bobby Clark told Abby. "I suspect Jess will be doing a booming business in no time."

Mrs. Finch's eyes turned misty, her expression nostalgic. "It reminds me of the way it looked when Mick first built it and my David and I used to come here for Sunday dinner every week."

"I'll bring you this Sunday," the mayor promised. "We'll give the new menu a test run. Something tells me it will surpass the old one, if tonight's appetizers are any indication."

Lawrence Riley approached just in time to hear the comments from Mrs. Finch and the mayor. He beamed at Abby. "Now that's the kind of thing I like to hear," he said, giving her a kiss on the cheek even as he shook the mayor's hand. "I have to admit, Abby, you and Jess surprised me."

"All I did was pay the bills," Abby insisted. "Everything else is Jess's doing. She had a vision for what she wanted the inn to be and I think she's accomplished it."

"Darn straight she has," Mick said with pride, circling an arm around Abby's waist. "Can I steal this beautiful woman for just one minute?"

He led Abby to a secluded corner.

"What's up, Dad?" Abby asked, noticing his worried expression.

"It's your mother. Have you seen her standing over there all by herself? You brought her here, Abby. You have to do something."

Abby stared at him incredulously. "Me? You're an adult. You're more than capable of carrying on a conversation with her. Has it occurred to you that everyone else may be waiting for some signal from you about whether she's to be welcomed or shunned?"

Mick was too much of a Southern gentleman to ignore Abby's claim. "You think so?"

"Dad, everyone in Chesapeake Shores knows she walked out on all of us. Their loyalty is to you. She certainly understood that. When she came to visit us, she barely left the house. Most of the time she was here and gone before anyone in town knew about it."

Mick looked startled by that.

"Come on, Dad, take her around a bit. She has old friends here who I'm sure are just dying to catch up with her. In the meantime, I'll round up Bree and Connor and make sure they spend some time with her, even if neither one of them is wildly enthusiastic about it."

"I notice you didn't mention Jess."

"She's going to be an even harder sell than I anticipated. I'm not going to push it tonight. It could spoil this whole evening for her. It's enough that she hasn't tossed Mom out on her backside, which I know she wants to do."

He hesitated. "I think I know a way to help with that," he said. "How?"

"Just leave it to me." He took off across the room, his expression grim. When he reached Megan's side, he bent down and whispered something in her ear. Abby saw her mother shake her head, but Mick was adamant about whatever he was saying. Then the two of them headed for Jess, her mother with obvious reluctance.

"Oh, no," Abby whispered. This wouldn't be good. She hurried through the crowd to try to stop them, but she was stopped by too many people en route. By the time she reached the other side of the room, Mick had a firm grip on Jess's hand and was dragging her toward the kitchen. That's when Abby got an inkling about what he was up to and relaxed.

She arrived just in time to hear Jess protest that she didn't have time to spare right now.

"You'll be glad you made time for this," Mick told her, not loosening his grip. He opened the kitchen door and held it until Jess finally stepped through.

Even from where she was waiting, Abby could see her shocked expression as she saw the Viking range she'd wanted so desperately. She looked up at Mick, her mouth agape. "You bought this?"

"Your mother and I did," he said. "We both wanted you to know how proud we are of you."

Megan looked uncomfortable, but she went along gamely. "It was your father's idea."

"But your mother was on board the second I told her about it," he insisted.

Abby smiled at his determination to include Megan in his generous gesture, his magnanimous attempt to help mend fences between her and their daughter. She also had a feeling that Megan would write him a check for her share before the night was over. She'd long since stopped taking any kind of alimony from Mick, and she wouldn't accept this expensive gesture, either.

"But how did you know how much I wanted this?" Jess asked. Her gaze shifted and she spotted Abby. "You told them, I suppose."

Abby shrugged. "I might have mentioned how disappointed you were when it had to go back."

Jess laughed. "Disappointed? I was an absolute shrew to you." She crossed the room and hugged her, then went back to face their parents. "Thank you so much, Dad." She swallowed hard, then added, "You, too, Mom."

Abby saw Megan blink back tears, saw Mick give her waist a squeeze, and knew that everything she'd hoped might happen tonight would come about eventually. It might take time. It might not be easy, but her family would be whole again.

24

As Abby watched while the party wound down, Bree and Connor were slowly drawn back into Megan's orbit. It wasn't so much a thawing as a mix of determination on Megan's part and longing on theirs. It seemed that every time Abby glanced their way, her brother and sister were laughing and her mother was looking more and more relaxed. Relieved, she reached for a flute of champagne, then turned to find her cousin Susie standing beside her.

"Did your dad come tonight?" she asked Susie. "I haven't seen him."

Susie shook her head. "Jess invited him, but Dad didn't want to risk getting into some kind of argument with Mick and spoiling the evening. Those two are still like oil and water. It's ridiculous, if you ask me, but you know how stubborn they are." She glanced pointedly toward Megan. "It's probably a good thing Dad stayed away tonight, though. One family reunion is probably about all this occasion could stand. How did you pull that off?"

"Gentle persuasion," Abby claimed. "And a whole lot of prayer."

"Uncle Mick keeps circling back to her," Susie said. "Do

you think there's any chance they'll get back together after all this time?"

"I'm really, really trying not to think that far ahead," Abby claimed. "Now tell me about you. How's the real-estate business around here?"

"Surprisingly good. In fact, just last week I made a huge sale."

"Really?"

"One of Mick's original houses, in fact, just up the road from here."

Abby's eyes lit up. "The Marshalls' house? I saw the For Sale sign when I first got back to town."

Susie nodded, though her expression had grown oddly wary.

"I used to love that house," Abby exclaimed. "I always thought the glassed-in sunporch was amazing. Who bought it?"

Now there was real worry in Susie's eyes. "You don't know?" she asked cautiously.

Abby frowned at the question. "Why would I know?"

"I just thought… Oh, well, never mind."

Abby's suspicions went on full alert. Trace? Surely not. He wouldn't do something like that without mentioning it to her, would he?

"Was it Trace?" she demanded.

Susie flinched at the direct question or perhaps it was because of her sharp tone. "I should never have said anything," Susie said, obviously dismayed. "I'm sure he meant it to be a surprise."

"Yes, I'm sure he did," Abby said tightly, then regarded her cousin apologetically. "Susie, don't worry about spilling the beans. You didn't do anything wrong."

"I just opened my big, fat mouth when I shouldn't have," Susie grumbled. "Great job of protecting my client's confidentiality."

"It's not as if you blabbed to the universe," Abby soothed her. "You told me only because you assumed I already knew."

"I hope Trace understands that."

"Believe me, he'll have more important things to worry about," Abby said grimly. Like trying to explain why he'd bought a house in Chesapeake Shores without saying a single word to her. Either, like Susie, he'd made a whole lot of assumptions about his powers of persuasion or he was making his own intentions clear and leaving it to her to stay or go.

She fingered the cell phone in her pocket and was about to go outside and call the louse, when she turned and saw him walking toward her. Susie spotted him, as well, and immediately gave Abby a quick kiss on the cheek. "I think I see my cue to leave heading this way."

"Chicken," Abby called after her, then turned to wait for Trace.

"You look amazing," he said. He leaned down to kiss her, but Abby dodged the gesture. The flare of heat in his eyes died at once, replaced by wariness. "Something wrong?"

"When were you going to tell me?" she demanded. "The day I left for the airport to go back to New York?"

Trace cast a glance toward Susie's retreating back and sighed. "You know about the house."

"I do."

"You always loved that house," he reminded her.

"I did, but it doesn't mean you should go out and make a purchase like that without even talking to me. I thought we were trying to work things out, taking one day at a time."

"We are."

"So you bought a house here to shift the odds that I'd agree to stay in Chesapeake Shores?"

"I bought a house because I knew you loved it," he corrected. "If, when all is said and done, you want to go to New York, we'll go, but at least we'd always have our own place here for weekends or vacations."

She didn't entirely believe that's what he wanted. "But you want to live here." She knew it sounded like an accusation, rather than a question.

He shrugged, then nodded. "I do, but I meant every word I said. I'm going where you go. I love you, and I'm not about to lose you again over something as ridiculous as which city you like. I can work anywhere. New York even has some benefits for me. Most of my contacts are there." He looked deep into her eyes. "Want to get down off that high horse now and kiss me like you mean it? I've just been to war with your ex-husband. I think I deserve a warmer welcome than the one I just got."

Abby wasn't quite ready to let the issue go, but she did kiss him. As heat swirled through her, it seemed less and less important to insist on getting her own way. Compromise was good. She'd have to think about that.

Meantime, though, she met his gaze. "You're back sooner than you expected to be. What happened with Wes?"

"I decided not to wait for morning. I had a little chat with Wes and Gabrielle tonight. Bottom line, he's going to see that the order is withdrawn."

Abby could envision her ex saying whatever Trace wanted to hear just to get rid of him. "You believe him?"

"I do. All he really wanted was to be sure I wouldn't convince you and the girls to stay here and keep them from him."

"He wasn't far off the mark about your plan to keep me here, was he?"

"No, but those girls are his daughters. No matter how we settle things between us about where to live, he'll be in their lives. I'll repeat that as many times as I have to, though he's not going to believe it until he's tested me a few hundred times, more than likely."

"What made you realize that's what he wanted to be sure about?"

"I knew how I'd feel in his shoes," he said simply. "I may not be their dad, but I love those little girls with all my heart already."

Abby smiled at the sincerity in his voice. She looked up and studied his expression. "Do you really, really think we can make it work this time?"

"I know I love you more than anything. I'll do whatever it takes to keep you happy."

Abby drew in a steadying breath. "I love you, too." It was the first time she'd risked saying the words aloud, even though she'd known in her heart for weeks now.

Trace grinned. "That wasn't so hard, was it?"

"What?"

"Putting your heart on the line."

"If you must know, it was scary as hell."

Trace frowned at that. "Not with me, Abby. It should never be scary with me."

But it was. Not because she didn't trust his love for her. It was just that he held the power to turn her whole life— the life she'd fought so hard to claim in the heart of the business world—upside down.

The whole family was sitting around the kitchen table at the house, even Megan. Though she looked a bit ill at ease being there, Mick had insisted she join them for the early-morning breakfast. It was just 7:00 a.m., planned for the early hour because Connor had to get on the road back to Baltimore for work at the law office where he was clerking for the summer. Abby and Jess had a thousand things to do before the first guests started arriving at the inn that afternoon. It was the start of the long Fourth of July holiday, and they were booked solid. In fact, they'd had to turn away several people.

"I should leave and go back to New York," Megan said at once when she heard that. "I'm in your biggest room."

"Mom, I reserved that for you," Abby assured her. "I'm paying. We're not losing money on it."

Jess's gaze darted up at that. "You're planning to pay for the room?"

Abby nodded. "Of course."

Jess shook her head. "No, you're not. We're talking about family. Family is not paying to stay at my inn."

Though it wasn't entirely clear whether she was more concerned about Abby's checkbook or her mother's feelings, her remarks brought tears to Megan's eyes. She reached for Jess's hand, but Jess withdrew it from the table before her mother could clasp it. The fragile moment died.

Mick stepped in to save the tenuous peace. "I think you should put your mother and me to work today. Let us help out."

Jess gave him a quizzical look. "Doing what? Carrying bags?"

"I can do that, if it's what you need. And your mother could help Gail in the kitchen. She's quite a cook."

Jess looked thoroughly bewildered by the offer. "Why would either of you do that?"

Mick leveled a look into her eyes. "We're talking about family," he said, tossing her words right back at her. "Family does whatever it can to help out on a big day for any one of our own. For one reason or another, your mother and I have missed out on way too many big moments in your lives." He included Abby, Bree and Connor in the comment. "Let us start trying to make up for that."

"I've already offered to help Gail with some baking today," Gram chimed in.

"You have?" Jess said, astounded. "I had no idea."

"You can tell her I'll be bringing a batch of my carrot-cake cupcakes over around three o'clock, so they'll be there if the guests want tea and a snack after they check in."

Abby listened to the exchange with a sense of satisfaction. Surely now Jess would have no doubts about her place in this family. Only Connor, who was leaving in an hour, and Bree, who'd been unusually quiet even for her, hadn't chimed in with an offer to pitch in today. It was Bree who worried her, but she couldn't sit her sister down and try yet again to figure out what was going on until after the inn was operating smoothly. Maybe by tonight she'd have a few minutes to spare to see why Bree looked so lost.

They were all about to leave the table and head off to handle their respective assignments when Abby's cell phone rang. Glancing at the caller ID, she saw it was her boss. She realized it had been days since she'd spoken to Jack, even though she'd sent in daily e-mails to update him on her accounts and on the situation with Wes that he'd helped her to resolve.

She excused herself and walked outside to take the call.

"How was the party?" he asked at once.

"A huge success. Today the first guests arrive."

"And then you'll be back with us full-time?"

"Very soon," she said. "Why? Are people up there rumbling about my being away so long?"

"No, the opposite, in fact. Something's come up out of town and they're wondering if you might not be the perfect person to handle it."

Abby waited for the familiar stirring of excitement at the prospect of a brand-new challenge, but it didn't come. The out-of-town part was worrisome. She was actually hesitant as she asked him to explain.

"I know you love working here in the city," he began. "But recently I've started getting the feeling that maybe you're conflicted about your responsibilities here and your family down there."

Abby's heart seemed to stall in her chest. "Are you firing me?"

"Heavens, no," he said at once. "Far from it. The Baltimore office needs fresh leadership. It can't be much more than an hour or so away from Chesapeake Shores, right?"

"On a good day," Abby said wryly, thinking of the traffic jams she'd encountered on that route on recent trips.

"Well, we think you'd be perfect for the job. You have the organizational skills and the portfolio skills to turn that office into one of the most profitable in the company. It's been lagging behind in terms of the client portfolios down there. We've been losing clients, who see their friends making better profits with other brokerages. You could change that and be close to your family. We'd still want you to be in New York on a regular basis, at least once a month to consult with us, but this whole operation would be yours, Abby."

She heard the enthusiasm in his voice, but she couldn't get past her fear that the company wanted her out of the way. "Why do I feel as if I'm being put out to pasture? Is this a punishment because of that whole situation with Gabrielle?"

"Absolutely not. It's an amazing opportunity for you and, to be honest, for the company to turn around a bad situation."

Abby tried to see it from his perspective, but she couldn't deny the sense that he was painting a rosy picture to make it easier for her to swallow what amounted to a bitter pill. In her business, New York was the place to be, the heart of the financial world. Baltimore was…nowhere.

She swallowed hard. "Do I have a choice about this?"

"Of course."

"You sure about that?"

"You work for me. It's my call, so, yes, I'm sure. You say the word and you stay right here."

That made it easier, she thought with relief. "Can I think it over?"

"Call me the first of the week," he suggested. "How's that?"

"First thing Monday morning," she promised. Maybe by then she could wrap her mind around the implications of this so-called "opportunity" for herself and maybe even for her future with Trace.

By Monday, though, Abby was no closer to a decision than she had been when Jack had first called. She needed to go to Baltimore, to get a firsthand look at the situation she'd be walking into. It was the only way to decide if it was a challenge she'd enjoy or if she'd come to resent being trapped in a dead-end position.

With Bree promising to keep an eye on the girls and Jess proving herself to be more than capable of handling the day-to-day operation at the inn, Abby got into her rental car and drove to Baltimore. When she reached the firm's offices, she sat across the street staring at the building. Instead of the skyscraper she was used to, the offices here were in a four-story, historical building with some charm, but little to distinguish it from other similar buildings around it. That alone gave her pause. Something about walking into the marble-floored lobby of a soaring building had always made her think big, made her feel as if she were part of something magnificent.

Inside the building, which also housed a law firm, an insurance agency and doctors' offices, she made her way to the fourth floor. The elevator opened onto plush, navy-blue carpeting and a massive reception desk. The immediate impression was of wealth and class. She was somewhat re-assured by that.

The receptionist looked up at once. "You must be Mrs.

Winters. Go right in. Mr. Wallace is waiting for you. It's the big office in the corner on the left." She grinned. "Best view in the place. You can see the harbor."

The impression created by the lobby extended to the back, where offices were private and decorated simply but elegantly. When she tapped on Mitch Wallace's door, she almost missed seeing him because of the stunning view behind him. Working boats and yachts dotted the blue water. He grinned at her apparently awestruck expression.

"Worth the price of admission, isn't it?" he said, shaking her hand, then gesturing toward a chair. "I swear it's the only reason I took this job thirty years ago. I'm going to hate saying goodbye to this view."

"You're retiring?"

"End of the month," he confirmed. "You going to take my place?"

"I'm still undecided," she admitted. "Tell me about the office. I hear it's been underperforming."

He nodded, clearly not offended by the characterization. "It has been. I came in here as a proven manager, not an analyst. I've got a lot of young men and women working for me who are eager and ambitious, but they all want to be in New York. Most of them can't see that the best way to get there is by proving themselves here with what they refer to as nickel-and-dime trades. From everything I hear about you from the folks in New York, you could take their skills to the next level."

"You're saying what this job needs is a teacher," she said, frowning. Did she really want to train a bunch of younger people so they could head for New York and replace her? The thought made her even more unsure whether this was the right place for her.

Just then a man who looked to be no more than twenty-five or twenty-six poked his head in. "Sorry to interrupt," he said, acknowledging Abby with a nod. "Mitch, I have Harry Fleming on the line. He's determined to make a trade that doesn't make any sense to me. Can you speak to him?"

Mitch glanced toward Abby. "Want to take a shot at it?"

"Sure," she said, then gestured toward the broker. "Get on the line with us, okay?"

Looking surprised, he nodded, then picked up the second phone in the office as Abby spoke to the client. "Mr. Fleming, I'm Abby Winters. I'm here from the New York office. Maybe I can help you. Why don't you tell me what you want to trade and why? The broker here seems to have some reservations about it."

"Fool kid's still wet behind the ears," he muttered.

Abby noticed that said ears had just turned bright red. "I don't know about that, sir. Most of our brokers have solid credentials. Perhaps, though, he's not understanding what your specific goals are with this trade."

He mentioned the name of the company he wanted to sell. Abby winced. It was a blue-chip stock, one on which she knew they still had an enthusiastic buy recommendation. Then he told her the stock he was hoping to purchase with that money.

"That one still has a lot of upside," he told her confidently. "The other one's a dinosaur."

Abby glanced across the room at the young broker and winked. "You certainly have a point, Mr. Fleming, but I was the corporate analyst who studied that particular stock just last week. I looked at their future prospects, their cash flow, their price-earnings ratio and I have to tell you, it's very likely you'd be making a huge mistake. You might have some gains in the short term, because there's a lot of attention being paid to the stock right now, but unless you keep a close eye on it and get out fast, you'll lose as much as you make. Maybe more."

Her comments were greeted by silence. "You sure about that?" he asked.

"I put a high-risk label on it myself," she told him. "I'm sure the broker's concern stemmed from that. We're not recommending it right now. The decision is yours, of course, but I think your broker was just trying to prevent you from taking a loss. Now if you have some cash in your account and want to speculate with a few shares, that's something else entirely, but I wouldn't trade the other stock for this one."

He sighed. "Let me speak to Dave again," he said. "And thank you for setting me straight. Don't know why he didn't do it in the first place."

"I think he was trying to, sir. He's just not as blunt as I am," Abby suggested. "Here's Dave now."

She sat back down and met Mitch Wallace's gaze. There'd been something about that phone call that had reminded her that there were real people affected by some of the decisions she made. She'd always understood that, of course. But engrossed in her analysis of reports from dozens of different companies, sometimes she lost sight of what that human contact felt like.

Before she could say any of that, though, Dave hung up and looked at her with real respect. "Thank you. I think he was about two minutes from pulling his whole account because I couldn't make him see my point. It's a good thing you were around."

He left the room, then, and Abby saw Mitch studying her intently.

"See what I mean? You could make a real difference here."

Abby nodded slowly. Maybe she could. A part of her wanted to call New York and suggest that she take over on a trial basis, but she immediately dismissed the idea. She needed to make a commitment, to this job and these people, to Chesapeake Shores and to Trace. It was time.

Trace had never intended to fall in love with Abby all over again. He certainly hadn't expected to be crazy about two pint-size imps with tempers that matched their strawberry-blond hair. Well, Carrie's did, anyway. Caitlyn was a bit more even-tempered. She must have gotten that from her father, because Abby had more fire than any woman he'd ever known.

It was time, past time probably, to make his intentions clear. He thought they already had an understanding of sorts, but he wanted it all this time—marriage, a family, happily-ever-after—and he wanted it now. He'd intended the purchase of the house to make his point, but that had pretty much clouded the issue. He'd have to remember that surprises might be fine, but *big* surprises could backfire.

He left the bank, walked over to his place and took a look at the Harley he'd owned ever since high school. He shook his head. It wasn't exactly a family vehicle. Pulling out his cell phone, he called his sister. "I need a ride. Can you pick me up at my place?"

Still grateful to him for interceding with their father, Laila didn't waste time on questions. "Give me five minutes."

Once he'd told her where they were going, she kept shooting speculative glances his way. Finally she lost patience. "Are you going to tell me or not?"

"Not," he said at once, chuckling at the look of annoyance on her face.

She turned into the car dealership, parked, then followed him as he walked straight over to a minivan. "What do you think?" he asked.

Sudden understanding dawned on her face. "You're going to ask Abby to marry you, aren't you? You're buying a family car."

"Did I say that?"

She elbowed him in the ribs. "You didn't have to. There's nothing else on earth that could persuade you to give up your Harley."

"Okay, you got me. Now tell me what you think of this one?" He pointed inside, staring in amazement. "It even has a DVD player for the backseat. Can you imagine that?"

She gave him a wry look. "Cars have a lot of accessories these days that don't come with a bike. It's about time you grew up and discovered them."

He frowned at her taunt. "It has nothing to do with growing up, Laila. I just never had to think about owning a car in the city."

She tucked her arm through his. "Fair enough. Are you sure you want to buy the first one you've looked at?"

He shrugged. "It's a car. It functions. It looks safe enough for the kids."

Laila rolled her eyes. "You are hopeless. Okay, if this is the one you want, let's go inside and you can sign the papers. I have to tell you, though, it's going to kill some poor sales guy that he can't use all his bargaining skills on you."

When they were halfway across the showroom floor, a salesman started heading their way. Laila jerked him to a stop. "Do not pay sticker price," she warned him. "It's a rip-off. Let me handle this."

Trace regarded her with amusement. "Be my guest."

To his amazement, she managed to bring the price down significantly and an hour later, Trace was crossing the lot with the keys in his hand.

"You going to see Abby now?" she asked.

He nodded. In fact, he had the ring tucked in his pocket, though something told him she might be more impressed with the car.

Rather than going straight to the inn, Trace parked the new car in the driveway at the house he'd bought, then walked down the road to the inn. He found Abby in the office, juggling several phone calls. She barely glanced up at his arrival.

When she finally hung up on the last call, she gave him a weary smile. Trace stood up and held out his hand.

"You need a break. Come for a walk with me."

To his surprise, she stood up immediately, took his hand and followed him through the French doors and across the lawn toward the beach.

"I can't be gone long," she said as they walked along the sand. "The phones have been ringing off the hook today with locals wanting to make reservations for out-of-town guests."

"Jess's inn. Jess's problem," he told her as he led the way along the beach for the half mile it took to reach his new house. She seemed oblivious to where he was taking her.

A frown knit her brow. "But I'm just—"

"Trying to help. I know. So does she, but that doesn't mean it's not grating. The inn's taking off. Bring in the bookkeeper and let Jess run the place from here on out."

"Do you really think she can do it on her own?"

He met her worried gaze. "Do you?"

She hesitated for a heartbeat, then nodded. "I really think she's ready."

"Good. Then my mission is accomplished and you and I can move on to other things, like what's next for the two of us."

She studied him with a narrowed gaze. "You're basically admitting you deliberately kept me here for your own nefarious reasons?"

"Nefarious?" he protested, not liking the way it sounded. "I wanted another chance with you."

"You wanted revenge," she corrected, then grinned slowly and wound her arms around his neck. "Funny how things can backfire, isn't it?"

He lowered his lips to hers. "Indeed it is, but you'll never hear me complaining."

He broke off the kiss. "Come with me."

She glanced around and seemed to realize where they were. "The house you bought."

He met her gaze. "Our house, I hope."

He led the way up the steps to the yard, then around the house, where the car was sitting in the driveway. "Our car."

Her mouth dropped open. "You bought a minivan?"

"I can hardly ride the girls around on the back of the Harley." He winked. "I still hope to get you on there from time to time, though. The car's just to prove how responsible a stepfather I'll be."

A soft smile played on her lips. "Never a doubt about that," she told him.

He took a deep breath, then launched into the speech he'd rehearsed. "Look, I know you're not sure you want to stay here and if you don't, that'll work, but this house is right for us. Your dad built it, so it seems to me an O'Brien ought to live in it. If we only use it for vacations or on weekends, that's okay. All I care about is the two of us being together."

"Me, too," she said. "Before you get too carried away with all the sacrifices you're prepared to make to win me over, you should know that I took a new job today."

Trace stared at her blankly. "A new job?"

"Running the Baltimore office. The traffic back and forth, by the way, is a total pain, so we might want to consider an apartment nearby, but this is home, Trace. This house, right here, with you. I think it's just been waiting for us to come home."

Trace couldn't stop the grin that was spreading across his face. "You didn't even wait to see the ring or hear the proposal. I was planning to wow you. I intended to tell you that I've been in love with you for longer than I can remember. I want to marry you and be a dad to your girls, and maybe even have a couple of kids of our own. And just in case you're worried about it, Carrie and Caitlyn approve. I've already asked their permission, though I'm not entirely sure they knew what was at stake. Your grandmother and Mick have given this a thumbs-up, as well. I haven't gotten to your brothers yet and given the way we used to get along, that may be just as well, but I'll win them over, because I know that's important to you."

There were tears in her eyes when he finished, happy tears, he hoped.

"Okay, now you've wowed me," she whispered. "The answer's yes."

"And the ring? Do you want to see it?"

"Oh, I want it," she said. "But only because it's a sign that we belong to each other."

Still not quite able to believe it had all come together the way he'd dreamed it would so many years ago, he slid the diamond solitaire onto her finger.

"Have you thought about when you want to get married?" he asked, drawing her down beside him on the steps of what would be their first and only home together.

"Soon."

"And where?"

"At the inn, of course. Nefarious designs by a stuffy old banker aside, it brought us back together. Besides, I wouldn't want to risk Jess's wrath by having it anywhere else."

Trace laughed. "I love you, Abby O'Brien Winters."

"And I love you, Trace Riley. I think I'm beginning to see what Mick saw when he planned this town. It's the perfect place to fall in love and raise a family. I think there might be something in the air."

Trace took a deep breath, but the only aroma he could detect was lilacs. Funny thing, too, since they'd been out of season for months. Maybe there really was a bit of magic in the air.

* * * * *

Turn the page for an exciting preview of
FLOWERS ON MAIN by Sherryl Woods.
You won't want to miss this next story in her
CHESAPEAKE SHORES *series,*
on sale from MIRA Books in May 2009.

"I've just discovered that there is one major flower wholesaler close enough to supply the store," Bree reported to her sister, not even trying to mask her dismay. This was an unexpected and very unwelcome wrinkle.

"So what?" Jess asked. "As long as they're good, you'll be fine. Are you worried that the prices will be higher because it's virtually a monopoly or something?"

"I'm worried because that wholesaler is Jake Collins," she snapped. "Why didn't you tell me he now owns Shores Nursery and Landscaping?"

Jess blinked at her tone. "Hey, don't jump on me. I thought you knew. He's worked there forever, even when you were going out."

"There's a huge difference between him working there and owning the place. And as I recall, they didn't operate as a wholesaler back then. Now he's apparently one of the biggest growers around here, too. What's he doing, taking over the flower world, acre by acre?"

Jess shrugged. "I don't see why any of that matters. It's been years since you two split up. You're both adults. This is business. Surely you can be civilized."

Bree wasn't so sure of that. Their last encounter had been

anything but civilized. She'd expected a little anger, but not the heat radiating off Jake in waves that could have roasted marshmallows.

"It will be awkward," she said finally in what was the most massive understatement she'd ever uttered.

"Then don't deal with him," Jess suggested, still unconcerned. "As big as the business is now, he probably has plenty of people working for him. He's usually out on jobs, anyway. I see him all over the place." She grinned. "He looks really, really fine, by the way."

Bree knew, though she had no intention of acknowledging just how fine she thought he looked. This situation was disastrous enough as it was. If Jess or anyone else in the family thought there was so much as an ember of that relationship that wasn't stone-cold, they might try to fan it back to life.

"I can't avoid him. It seems I have to deal directly with *Mr. Collins* if I want to open an account. *Mr. Collins* makes those arrangements. *Mr. Collins* decides if Shores Nursery can accommodate another wholesale customer. If not, she's sure *Mr. Collins* would be happy to recommend an alternative, although there's no other grower or supplier half as good within a fifty-mile radius. I wanted to reach through the phone and strangle her perky little neck."

Jess stared at her. "Okay, Bree, what's really going on here? Is this just about some kind of old news between you and Jake?"

"Of course. What else could it be?"

"I'm not sure, but to tell you the truth, for a second there, you sounded a little jealous."

"Jealous? That's ridiculous." She frowned. "It's just that this woman sounded so, I don't know, adoring. It made me a little crazy."

"I'll say," Jess confirmed. "What I don't get is why. I thought you were the one who dumped him."

"It wasn't exactly like that," Bree said.

Interest sparked in Jess's eyes. "Then what was it like?"

Bree sighed. "Never mind. You said it. It's old news. I'll figure out some way to deal with him to get the flowers I need."

Of course, that assumed that if she ever succeeded in getting past his obviously protective gatekeeper, *Mr. Collins* would even give her the time of day.

Jake crumpled up the fifth message he'd had from Bree in two days and tossed it in the trash can. He scowled when he realized that Connie had caught him doing it. She marched into his office, a lecture clearly on the tip of her tongue.

"Don't start with me," he warned.

"You need to call her back," she told him in her oh-so-patient mother-hen voice.

"I don't have to do anything," he said grimly.

"Now there's the mature reaction I'd expect from someone your age," she commented. "Let me rephrase. You need to call her back if you expect me keep working here, brother dear. I'm getting tired of trying to fend Bree off, much less pretending that I don't know perfectly well who she is and why you're avoiding her. If she ever recognizes my voice, she's going to start asking a whole bunch of questions I don't want to answer. You don't pay me enough to run interference between you and Bree."

"I'm paying you enough to get your daughter through college, which is more than anyone else would," he retorted. "She starts next year, if I recall correctly. How's that tuition money adding up? Can you afford to be fired?"

She gave him a sour look. "Sometimes it is very hard for me to understand why Mom always liked you best. You are not a nice man."

"But I am a very good brother," he teased. Because of that, she knew he would never, ever fire her, despite his constant threats. Connie's ex-husband paid decent alimony and child support, but Jake considered it his responsibility to see that she and Jenny Louise had whatever else they needed.

"You're an annoyance," she retorted.

"But you love me anyway," he said. His expression sobered. "Please, keep Bree away from me. Consider it your personal mission."

"Assistants aren't allowed personal missions," she retorted.

"But sisters are."

"Jake, you're the one who made the rule about not taking on any new wholesale customers unless you personally approve it. You said we only have so much stock available, and you don't want to get overextended and wind up disappointing a good customer. Do I not have that right?"

His expression brightened. "That's it. Call her back and tell her we've talked. You can explain that, unfortunately, due to huge demand, we're not taking on anyone else right now."

"But the florist in Myrtle Creek just closed," she reminded him. "Jensen's was one of our bigger accounts. If Bree's done her homework, she's going to know that."

"What makes you think she's done her homework?" he asked wearily. "Last time I checked, she was writing plays, not running any kind of business."

"And last time I checked, she was the smartest woman you've ever known. She's certainly smart enough to ask around about the best suppliers in the region. I'll bet that's exactly how she got our name. Ted Jensen probably recommended us when he decided to retire after his heart attack."

Okay, that was possible, but not insurmountable. "If she brings that up, tell her we'd only kept supplying Ted because he'd been a customer for years."

Connie rolled her eyes. "That ought to go over well. How on earth will it look if we refuse to supply a new business right here in Chesapeake Shores, a business owned by an O'Brien, no less? You'll never hear the end of it. The chamber of commerce will be all over you. And if you think there was talk when you and Bree broke up, it'll be nothing compared to the speculation *that* would stir up."

They were still debating the point when the door to the outer office snapped open and Bree strode through and straight into his office. She was wearing shorts that made her legs look endless and a halter top that made his mouth water. Strands of curly auburn hair had sprung free of the knot on her head, and with the sunlight behind her, it looked as if she were on fire. The color was high in her cheeks, as well. She was not a happy woman. Jake braced himself to deal with all that heat and sexiness and walk away unscathed.

"If the mountain won't come…" Her voice trailed off as she spotted his sister.

"Connie, hi," she said. Unmistakable relief spread across her face as something else apparently registered. "Oh my gosh, you're the one I've been talking to on the phone all this time. I'm so sorry. I should have recognized your voice."

Connie grinned. "Frankly, I was just as glad you didn't. I really didn't want to get caught between you and this hardhead over here. Now you two can battle this out between yourselves. I'm going home to cook dinner." She gave her brother a smug look. "Shall I make a plate of humble pie for you? Or will you be making other plans for dinner?" She glanced pointedly at Bree when she said it.

"I already have dinner plans," he retorted. As of two minutes ago, he planned to drink it.

"You've been avoiding me," Bree accused, sitting across from Jake, her shorts hiking up. She hadn't worn such a revealing outfit deliberately, but judging from the rapt gaze on Jake's face, she was glad she had. At this point she was willing to take advantage of any edge she might have. Maybe that didn't speak well of her as a woman, but she was desperate. After a week it had become clear that Jake was even less anxious to deal with her than she was with him. Both of them had to find a way to suck it up and figure out a way to conduct business.

"Have not," he muttered. "I've been busy."

"Well, you don't appear to be busy right this second," she said cheerfully. "So let's make this deal now and I'll get out of your hair. Unless you drive the delivery truck, you'll never have to deal directly with me again."

His jaw hardened. "There's not going to be any deal, Bree. Not between us."

She leveled a look directly into his eyes. "This is business, Jake. I'm not asking you to go out with me or to trust me or to have any kind of personal contact beyond whatever it takes to get this agreement on paper. It's simple. I'm opening a flower shop. You sell flowers. It's pretty cut-and-dried."

"Nothing with us was ever simple or cut-and-dried," he said, walking slowly around his desk to perch on the edge. Their knees were almost touching, hers bare, his clad in faded denim. "It's bound to get complicated faster than the ink will dry on our agreement."

She swallowed hard, but managed to keep her voice steady. "How so?"

He leaned forward, oh-so-slowly, until her pulse fluttered wildly at the nearness of his mouth. It hovered over hers. Their breath intermingled. Suddenly she wanted his lips on hers with an urgency that took her by surprise. Memories of a hundred other kisses—deep, tantalizing, soul-stirring kisses—swarmed in her head and left her dizzy.

As if he sensed her turmoil, he drew back, his expression smug. "See what I mean?"

Oh, yeah, this definitely had complication written all over it. But she couldn't let that stand in her way. She wouldn't. Flowers on Main was going to be her fresh start. She'd do whatever it took to make it a success.

"I need these flowers, Jake."

"Get them from someone else. There are other growers."

"Everyone says you're the best. And you're the closest."

"I'm also unavailable."

"Are you speaking personally now or professionally?"

He frowned at her flip attempt at humor. "Both, just to keep the record straight."

"That kiss that almost happened said otherwise."

"It didn't happen, did it?"

"All that proves is that you've got great willpower. I'm duly impressed. In fact, a man with that much willpower surely won't be tempted to ravish me just because I get a few posies from him every few days, so there's really no reason not to deal with me, is there?"

"How about I don't want to? Do you have an argument for that?"

"Because you're scared," she accused.

"Of you? Don't be ridiculous."

"Prove it."

His eyes widened. "You're making this a challenge?"

"Why not?" she asked with a careless shrug. "Let's see if you've got what it takes to stay away from me, Jake. Make this deal. Deliver the flowers personally. And keep your hands to yourself. That will suit me just fine."

She saw him struggle with himself. He clearly wanted to

show her that she no longer meant anything to him, that he was well and truly done with her. But he also knew he didn't stand a chance of making good on it. Whatever there'd once been between them, it was still there.

$1.00 OFF

New York Times bestselling author

SHERRYL WOODS

draws you into a world of friendships,
families and heartfelt emotions in
her new Chesapeake Shores series.

On sale March 31   On sale April 28   On sale May 26

$1.00 OFF the purchase price of one book
in the 2009 Chesapeake Shores
trilogy by Sherryl Woods

Offer valid from March 31, 2009 to June 30, 2009. Redeemable at participating retail
outlets. Limit one coupon per purchase. Valid in the U.S.A. and Canada only.

52608605

5 65373 00076 2   (8100)0 11593

® and TM are trademarks owned and used by the trademark owner and/or its licensee.
© 2009 Harlequin Enterprises Limited

MSWTRI09CPN

Look for the Sweet Magnolias series
from *New York Times* bestselling author

SHERRYL WOODS

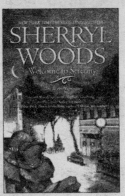

All available now!

New York Times bestselling author

SHERRYL WOODS

brings you three beloved stories about
friendship, family and love in the town of
Trinity Harbor.

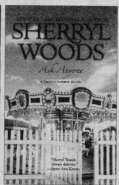
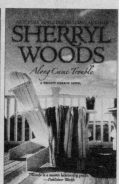

MSWBLTRI09R

REQUEST YOUR
FREE BOOKS!

2 FREE NOVELS
FROM THE ROMANCE/SUSPENSE
COLLECTION PLUS 2 FREE GIFTS!

YES! Please send me 2 FREE novels from the Romance/Suspense Collection and my 2 FREE gifts (gifts are worth about $10). After receiving them, if I don't wish to receive any more books, I can return the shipping statement marked "cancel." If I don't cancel, I will receive 4 brand-new novels every month and be billed just $5.49 per book in the U.S. or $5.99 per book in Canada, plus 25¢ shipping and handling per book plus applicable taxes, if any*. That's a savings of at least 20% off the cover price! I understand that accepting the 2 free books and gifts places me under no obligation to buy anything. I can always return a shipment and cancel at any time. Even if I never buy another book from the Reader Service, the two free books and gifts are mine to keep forever.

185 MDN EF5Y 385 MDN EF6C

Name _____ (PLEASE PRINT)

Address _____ Apt. # _____

City _____ State/Prov. _____ Zip/Postal Code _____

Signature (if under 18, a parent or guardian must sign)

Mail to **The Reader Service:**
IN U.S.A.: P.O. Box 1867, Buffalo, NY 14240-1867
IN CANADA: P.O. Box 609, Fort Erie, Ontario L2A 5X3

Not valid to current subscribers to the Romance Collection,
the Suspense Collection or the Romance/Suspense Collection.

Want to try two free books from another line?
Call 1-800-873-8635 or visit www.morefreebooks.com.

* Terms and prices subject to change without notice. N.Y. residents add applicable sales tax. Canadian residents will be charged applicable provincial taxes and GST. Offer not valid in Quebec. This offer is limited to one order per household. All orders subject to approval. Credit or debit balances in a customer's account(s) may be offset by any other outstanding balance owed by or to the customer. Please allow 4 to 6 weeks for delivery. Offer available while quantities last.

Your Privacy: Harlequin is committed to protecting your privacy. Our Privacy Policy is available online at www.eHarlequin.com or upon request from the Reader Service. From time to time we make our lists of customers available to reputable third parties who may have a product or service of interest to you. If you would prefer we not share your name and address, please check here. ☐

BOB08R

SHERRYL WOODS

32529 SEAVIEW INN	___ $6.99 U.S.	___ $8.50 CAN.
32457 MENDING FENCES	___ $6.99 U.S.	___ $8.50 CAN.
32436 FEELS LIKE FAMILY	___ $6.99 U.S.	___ $8.50 CAN.
32415 A SLICE OF HEAVEN	___ $6.99 U.S.	___ $8.50 CAN.
32363 STEALING HOME	___ $6.99 U.S.	___ $8.50 CAN.
32336 WAKING UP IN CHARLESTON	___ $6.99 U.S.	___ $8.50 CAN.

(limited quantities available)

TOTAL AMOUNT	$ _____
POSTAGE & HANDLING	$ _____
($1.00 FOR 1 BOOK, 50¢ for each additional)	
APPLICABLE TAXES*	$ _____
TOTAL PAYABLE	$ _____

(check or money order—please do not send cash)

To order, complete this form and send it, along with a check or money order for the total above, payable to MIRA Books, to: **In the U.S.:** 3010 Walden Avenue, P.O. Box 9077, Buffalo, NY 14269-9077; **In Canada:** P.O. Box 636, Fort Erie, Ontario, L2A 5X3.

Name: _____
Address: _____ City: _____
State/Prov.: _____ Zip/Postal Code: _____
Account Number (if applicable): _____

075 CSAS

*New York residents remit applicable sales taxes.
*Canadian residents remit applicable GST and provincial taxes.

MIRA®

www.MIRABooks.com

MSW1208BL